Chad Fury and the Stone of Destiny

Doug Gorden

DEDICATION

In Memory Of
Cas William Walters, Jr.
1929 - 2015

CONTENTS

ACKNOWLEDGMENTS

This book is a work of fiction.
Any resemblance to any person or persons living or dead is purely coincidental.

There are several people that I wish to thank.

To my wife. Thank you for your creative input into the story and for your help editing. The book would not exist without you.

To Cindy. Thank you for editing. One set of eyes is never enough, especially the way I type.

Ginger, thank you for your assistance with the final edit. Your help was greatly appreciated.

To Corey, my friend. Your creative talents with a camera and your help with the cover photo were priceless.

To Dwayne. Thank you for lending your arm for the cover photo. If your arm becomes famous, remember who it is you have to thank…

FOREWORD

If you haven't read the first book, I suggest reading "Chad Fury and the Dragon Song" before starting this one. But if you're like me, you probably won't. You'll dive right in, all the while telling yourself that you can pick up enough of the story that it won't be a problem.

For those of you that want to forge ahead with book two and skip book one, here are a few things that you might want to know.

Chad was a fairly average young man. He was about to graduate from college with a pre-med degree. He also had a girlfriend who he was planning on turning into a fiancé. But, as with all good stories, that wasn't going to happen.

Chad decided to get a tattoo as a graduation present to himself. That's how he met Lisa and the women known as the Sisterhood. The members of the Sisterhood are aliens from another universe and a planet they call El-yana.

The people of El-yana, the El-yanin, are dying. They tried to remove all of the undesirable genes from their population. That left them with too little genetic diversity for their species to survive. The El-yanin have been scouring planets in different universes looking for enough compatible DNA to save their species.

The El-yanin look like us, but they have two main differences. They have a second set of fully formed vocal cords, and can use them to control people (humans will do whatever they say). And they have the ability to read people's thoughts and memories, but it requires that they touch the blood of the other person.

I could tell you more, but I'd just end up rewriting the first book. Instead, I just ask that you sit back and enjoy the tale.

CHAPTER ONE

John's right fist landed firmly on my jaw. My head snapped back. I put up my right arm to block the blow I knew would be coming next. I easily deflected the blow from his left hand, turned slightly, leaning on my left leg to brace for the kick that would follow.

I spit out my mouth guard. I wasn't going to need it. I wasn't going to let a second blow land on my face. I grinned at John, "Come on. Is that all you got? My grandma hits harder than that!"

I looked in John's eyes. I could see his frustration and anger rising. I heard Mike Spencer, John Shannon's coach, laughing in the background. This is what I was being paid for: to turn sparring matches into real fights, both physically and mentally.

I was the most sought after sparring partner here at Frank's Octagon. Frank's was a decent little gym on the outskirts of the Vegas suburbs, full of aspiring young fighters hoping for a break.

This was the way I had found to supplement my university salary. All I had to do was fight just a little better than these wannabe fighters and let them wear themselves out trying to take me down.

A voice I recognized rang out from behind me, "Drake!" The voice belonged to Frank Campbell, the gym's owner.

I deflected John's kick, ignored Frank, and continued sparring.

"Manning! You need to get out now. There's somebody with a badge here to see you."

I nodded at John, "We're done."

I relaxed my shoulders and dropped my arms. John didn't stop. He saw this as an opportunity and went for the cheap shot.

John sent a sweeping kick with his right leg straight for my knees. Instinctively, I spun a hundred and eighty degrees and placed my back toward John. I bent my knees. When John's right leg came close I caught it and locked his leg with my right arm.

With a firm grip on John's leg, I jumped backwards. He landed on his back and I was on top of him. I pulled John's leg across my body and let the pressure build in his knee. It didn't take long; John's hand thumped the floor signaling me to stop.

I rolled off of him and stood to my feet.

"A fight's over when I say it's over! Pull a stunt like that again and I'll mop the floor with you…I won't *let* you tap out next time."

John looked up at me, "Drake, dude, you gotta teach me that move."

"I just did, *dude*."

I turned and headed to the edge of the ring, removing my gloves as I went. An unfamiliar voice started talking. The voice was distinctly female.

"Drake Manning?"

My eyes found the face belonging to the voice and I smiled, "That's me, what can I do for you?"

From inside the ring I towered over the five foot, seven

inch brunette. She looked up at me with blue eyes. They were a little too blue. I was sure she had to be wearing colored contacts.

"Mr. Manning, I'm Deputy Marshal, Lyman with the U.S. Marshals' Service. There's somebody back at the office who needs to talk with you."

"Do I have time to change?"

"Sure, make it quick."

In less than twelve minutes I was outside the gym and standing next to the very attractive Deputy Marshal, Lyman.

"Excuse me, Deputy." I smiled. I smiled because I had noticed the absence of a ring on the Deputy's hand. I thought I'd casually test the waters and see how willing she might be to spend a little more time with me.

"I didn't bring a car, Deputy. Mind if I hitch a ride, Miss Lyman?"

"Sure. Follow me."

There was nothing casual in her voice; it was all business. I followed her to a black sedan in the gym's parking lot and got into the passenger's seat.

"Well, Deputy, what's this all about?"

"I don't know, and I don't care."

That pretty well killed any conversation we might have. I was left with no option but to let my mind wander. I probed my memories during the drive to Las Vegas Boulevard, near what had come to be known as the Old Vegas Strip.

My memories took me back to Oklahoma City and the time before I had entered WITSEC, the Federal Witness Protection Program. Back then, my legal name was Chad Fury.

Chad was responsible for some very dangerous people being behind bars. Was it time for me to testify? No, surely not. It had been almost a full year since Sirhan Jadiddian was arrested in that warehouse. Still, the Marshals wouldn't drag me out of a gym just to tell me that I needed to get ready to testify. That would simply be a phone call.

Maybe it was mom, or Uncle Allan? Maybe one of them was here to see me? If they were here, that could only mean a death or illness in the family. But, no, that couldn't be it either; I'd know already. Uncle Allan and I were secretly keeping in touch through the TOR network. The Marshals would have a fit if they knew I had contact with anyone from Chad's past.

Deputy Marshal Lyman parked the car in the garage across from the turquoise building housing both the US Courthouse and the Marshal's office. She unbuckled her seatbelt and opened the door. "We're here. Follow me."

CHAPTER TWO

Deputy Marshal Jim Clayton was seated behind his desk just inside the Marshals' office. He was working on something on his computer. He didn't acknowledge me for several seconds.

I liked Jim. He seemed like an honest, hard-working, family man. If you ever saw him on the street, you'd probably underestimate him. His red hair, blue eyes, and pale skin made him look a little juvenile. But talk to him a few minutes, and somehow his five foot nine inch frame seemed more like seven feet tall.

"Hello, Drake. I'm glad you could make it."

"I didn't have much choice. At least you sent a pretty escort for me."

Deputy Marshal Clayton laughed, "This is Vegas, you might not want to use the word '*escort*' around here. It's not always a compliment."

I chuckled, "OK, you have a point. But, what's this all about anyway?"

"You missed five counseling sessions in the last three months. Counseling is provided to help you adjust to your new life. Your sessions are Mondays at four P.M.; don't miss."

"Seriously? You dragged me all the way down here on a Friday afternoon just to tell me that?"

"No, Drake. I didn't, but I'm going to ride your case every time you're not following the program. That's my job.

Another thing: a lot of time and effort was spent getting you a job at the University. Teaching Biology and Chemistry is a respectable job, around respectable people. Letting yourself get beat-up at a gym isn't."

"An instructor's salary is barely enough to cover rent. I like to eat too. But if it will make you feel better, I promise I won't miss any more counseling sessions. Now what's this all about?"

"To begin with Drake, I don't believe you. You'll keep missing your counseling sessions and I'll keep riding you about it. But aside from that, you've got a visitor from Oklahoma City. Follow me."

Deputy Clayton stood up from behind his desk, crossed behind me and went to a wooden door in the middle of the adjacent pale-green wall. He grasped the doorknob with his right hand, turned his head and looked at me.

I crossed the wood floor to the door. Deputy Clayton turned the knob and gently eased the door open. I took a deep breath. I felt the palm of Jim Clayton's hand rest against my shoulder blade and I heard him say, "It will be alright, Drake. She just has some questions for you."

After crossing the threshold I saw Agent Saysha Givens of the FBI seated at the end of an old rectangular table. There were five empty, well-worn blonde oak chairs spaced evenly around the well-worn table in the center of the room. Agent Givens gestured toward the chair nearest her. The door closed behind me.

"Have a seat, Chad. We need to talk."

As I went to the chair and seated myself I noted how much Agent Givens looked the same as the day I had gone into Witness Protection. She was wearing what could have been the same navy suit and white blouse as the last time I saw her. Her hair was pulled back tightly behind her head, which made her chin and nose seem sharp and imposing. She was an attractive African American woman, but she successfully overcame her attractiveness with her choice of clothes and her demeanor.

"It's a surprise and a pleasure to see you, Agent Givens."

"I wish it was a pleasure, Chad. But, the Department of Justice is not going to use their dime to send me on a pleasure trip. I may as well get to the point. Eric Schwartz is dead."

"That's far too fast for Oklahoma justice, what happened?"

"When Eric was arraigned for the murder of Emily Smith he plead guilty, was sentenced to death and sent to the McAlester State Penitentiary.

Two weeks ago, last Monday morning, he was found dead in his cell."

"If it was suicide I don't think you'd be telling me about it in person."

"No, it wasn't suicide."

Agent Givens picked up the briefcase sitting on the floor next to her and placed it on the table. She opened the case and pulled out a yellow envelope.

She hesitated, "Chad, this is very...unsettling. Eric was... skinned alive."

Agent Givens placed the envelope on the table in front of me and returned the briefcase to the floor. She nodded at me.

I opened the envelope and pulled out the pictures carefully. The sight of the first picture made me sick. I ran to the trashcan near the door, dropped to my knees and vomited.

When I had finished, Agent Givens was standing next to me. She handed me a tissue to wipe my mouth. She opened the door and called for Deputy Clayton who arrived promptly.

"Officer Clayton, would you please show our friend to the restroom? And when you return, could I trouble you for a couple of bottles of water?"

Deputy Clayton was silent. He picked up the trashcan with one hand and took my elbow with the other. He walked with me out of the Marshals' office and placed the trashcan in the hallway. He continued walking with me to the restroom and gave me some privacy as I attempted to regain my composure.

Inside the men's room there were five porcelain sinks. I took a position behind the center one. My right hand was shaking as I turned the knob and started the cold water flowing.

I saw my reflection in the mirror. I was white as a sheet. I splashed water on my face and rubbed it in an effort to scrub away the memory of what I had just seen.

I knew I would never be able to erase the picture now burned in my mind; Eric's skinless corpse lying in the center of a concrete floor. To his right, a neat pile of skin. It looked as though his skin had been pulled off in strips, folded, and carefully stacked in neat little piles. And then there was the blood…lots and lots of blood everywhere.

I applied more cold water, and rubbed my face.

CHAPTER THREE

After I had regained some of my dignity, Deputy Clayton walked me back to the room where Agent Givens was waiting. Along the way we stopped at a vending machine and he gave the machine five dollars in exchange for two large bottles of water.

Back inside the room, Agent Givens and I each drank our water in silence. She was watching me, I suppose, to make sure I was through being sick.

"Are you feeling better now, Chad?"

"Yes, I believe so. Thank you."

"Don't feel bad about getting sick. I almost did the same thing the first time I saw the picture."

"So, just why did you show that to me?"

"Remember the last time we saw each other, Mr. Fury?"

"I do."

"I told you that keeping secrets has a price. Your secret is killing people."

"Killing people? You seriously think I had anything to do with this?"

"I don't know for sure, but you're the only connection

I have to seven recent murders.

After Sirhan Jadiddian was arrested and that warehouse was shut down, people started talking. Some of those people were talking about a group called the 'Company'. Every single one of those people who talked about The Company is now dead. Six people all had their throats cut.

And then there's Eric. Two of the people who talked claimed he was part of The Company.

Before all this happened, no one in the FBI had ever heard of The Company, but I have the distinct impression that you know something about The Company."

"I'm sorry, but nothing I could have said would have stopped any of that. It might have made things worse."

"Mr. Fury, Chad. I don't see how things could get much worse. Let me tell you the rest of the story. I have some more pictures to show you."

"Please, no. I'd rather not…"

"Don't worry. They're nothing like the first one."

Agent Givens took the yellow envelope from the table and pulled out three black and white photographs.

"When Eric was processed and booked at the State penitentiary, the guards noticed scars all over his body. There were so many scars that they sent him to be examined by the prison doctor."

Agent Givens handed me the pictures. The pictures were of Eric, and yes, he was covered in scars.

"Chad. The doctor stopped counting at two-hundred fifty. There were over two-dozen cuts that appeared to be fairly recent.

What is it that you can tell me about what happened to Eric? How much do you know about his scars?"

"I'm sorry, but there's nothing I can tell you. I…"

"Mr. Fury, you're a horrible liar. You know something and I *intend* to find out what it is."

"I wish I could help you. I really do."

"The entire McAlester State Penitentiary is in an uproar right now. Do you know why?"

"Uh…no."

"When the guards found Eric, no one in the entire prison claimed to have heard or seen anything. None of the inmates on Death Row will admit to hearing anything.

The coroner told me that there were no drugs in Eric's system. He would have been screaming, and he didn't die quickly.

We found bloody prints from five different people in that cell. One set of those prints matches prints found in two cold cases. Those two cold cases are just like fifteen other cold cases we have, stretching back to nineteen-fifty-four. In each of those seventeen cases, the victim was female. Each victim either died while clutching a little crystal cube, or a crystal cube was found next to the victim.

While you were in the Cleveland County Jail you were shown pictures of Emily Smith's murder. There was a little crystal cube in one picture. You recognized that cube. We have a recording of you giving a name to that cube. You called it a transresinator."

I was starting to get very uncomfortable. My mind took me back to that moment in the County jail, in Oklahoma, back when all of this was just starting. I broke out in a cold sweat then, and I was doing it again.

"Agent Givens. I just can't tell you anything. No one would have believed me then, and no one will believe me now."

"Cut the crap, Fury! You're in WITSEC, the Federal Witness Security Program. You couldn't *be* more safe. But there are people out there dying and I'm *going* to know why!"

Agent Givens thumped the table once and stared coldly at me to make her point.

I shook my head, "Right. Safe. The only safe people are the ones that don't know anything about The Company. Didn't you just tell me five people walked into a State penitentiary, took their time torturing and murdering a man, and left without so much as a single witness? Do you honestly think *anybody* could be safe?"

Agent Givens was silent. She sat there with both palms flat on the table, leaning forward, and frowning. After a few seconds she leaned back in her chair and placed her hands in her lap.

"The prison guards claim they didn't see anything. The guards that monitor the video feeds were all found staring at blank screens. When they were questioned they all said the same thing, that the cameras were working just fine; that there was nothing wrong. We never were able to convince them otherwise. It was just like what happened with Sirhan Jadiddian."

"Are you telling me Sirhan was murdered too?"

"No. He's missing. He was transferred to a Federal facility in Texas. Five days ago the guards found his cell empty. The men and women in the guard room were all staring at blank monitors…Just like McAlister Prison."

I exhaled loudly. I closed my eyes and covered my mouth with my hand. I stayed like that for several seconds before I let my hand slide off of my face and drop into my lap. I opened my eyes.

"Tell me about that recording you have of me in the warehouse…do you still have it?"

There was a long pause. Agent Givens shifted in her chair before speaking.

"Yes. It's safe."

She lied. I knew she lied…I smelled onions.

"Oh my God! What happened to it? How did you lose it?"

"I told you, it is safe."

I smelled the onion-like odor again, only stronger.

"Now who's a bad liar? Tell me what happened."

Agent Givens paused. She looked genuinely frightened. She reached into the pocket of her navy suit jacket and pulled out a digital recorder. She shut it off. She cleared her throat loudly.

"OK, Fury. Nothing's being recorded. I suggest we tell

each other everything. I'll go first."

Agent Givens held out her right arm in front of me and turned it over. On the inside of her forearm was a four inch long cut.

"The day after Eric was murdered, one man, maybe more, I can't be sure, broke into my house. A tall thin man told me to sit still and put out my arm. I did. I tried not to, but I did. I couldn't do anything else."

The man cut my arm. He grabbed my arm over the cut and asked me questions about Sirhan and then about you. I didn't tell him anything, but he kept asking questions, more and more questions.

I reported the break-in. They stole a few things, a little jewelry and a gun I kept in my nightstand by my bed. I never told anyone what I just told you about the cut and the questions."

"And the recording of me? What about it?"

"I kept it in a safe deposit box, at my bank. I checked on it a couple of days later. It's gone. Now it's your turn."

I pushed my chair back and turned it sideways so I could fully face Agent Givens. I rested my right arm on the table top. I took a deep breath, let it out slowly, and began.

I told her about getting the dragon tattoo on my arm and about meeting Lisa. I told her how I was abducted by the Sisterhood and how they tried and failed to change me into a half-human, half-animal monster.

Agent Givens interrupted, "Mr. Fury, I want the truth, not some cockamamie story about magic and monsters! You're going to give me the truth, and you're going to give it to me *now*!"

"First, it's not magic. It's science and aliens. But, remember that recording of me?"

"Yes."

I curled the fingers of my right hand. I raised my hand above my head and brought it quickly down on the table top. Immediately my hand changed.

Agent Givens jumped up, throwing her chair

backwards. The chair hit the floor with a thud and Saysha Givens let out a brief little scream which she stifled quickly. She stood and there stared at my hand.

My first and second fingers had fused into a single digit. The same was true of my other two fingers. The two new fingers were covered in shiny red scales. Both new fingers ended in a single, golden-yellow claw. The thumb was a perfect mate for the two fingers.

I heard footsteps outside our door. I put my hand under the table as the door opened. Deputy Jim Clayton peered inside.

"Is everything OK? I thought I heard something."

I turned toward the door. "Everything's fine. Agent Givens saw something…It could have been a mouse."

Agent Givens gave me a dirty look, and then looked at Deputy Clayton.

"We're fine Deputy. I thought I saw something, I was just startled."

Deputy Clayton looked around the room.

"If you're sure you're OK…I'll be right outside the door."

When the door closed and we were alone again, Agent Givens righted her chair and sat down. I looked her in the eyes and spoke softly, "Agent Saysha Givens, welcome to the Twilight Zone."

CHAPTER FOUR

It had taken some time to tell Agent Givens my story. To save time I only hit the high points. I told her about the Abomination and the Sisterhood and their ability to capture memories by touching blood. I could tell that she was having trouble believing everything, still it was the only story she had and it appeared that she was willing to go along with it until a better explanation came along.

Agent Givens stood up from the table. "Well, Mr. Fury, I guess we're done for now. There wasn't a thing you said that I'm able to use."

I stood to my feet. "I know. That's why I never bothered in the first place."

Agent Givens took her briefcase and left the room. I followed. She passed by Deputy Clayton seated at his desk and exited the office without saying a single word.

Jim stood up from his desk and spoke to me, "It looks like neither one of you are very happy, Drake. I hope things work out."

"I hope so too."

Jim offered to drive me home and I accepted. We made the trip from the courthouse to my apartment in Spring

Valley in just over forty minutes of almost total silence. I guess neither of us felt much like talking. What little was said, was almost meaningless.

Jim let me out of the car in front of my building at exactly ten p.m. We exchanged our goodbyes, and he added a few words about me needing to make my next counseling session. I pretended to ignore it.

As I approached the metal stairs on the outside of the apartment unit I considered getting a burn phone and calling Uncle Allan. He could check on mom and make sure she was safe. I climbed the stairs wondering what I should be doing, if anything.

The Abomination had asked Saysha Givens questions about *me*. There was little doubt in my mind that someone would be coming for me. The Company had stolen the recording of me chasing and catching Sirhan, and then using my claws to cut through Lisa's ropes. Why take that?

I knew I had to contact Lisa. She was still my contact with the Sisterhood. I would have to let her and the Sisterhood know about this.

I stood at the door to my apartment: number two-eighteen. I shook my head and fumbled for my keys in my pocket. I found the apartment key and slid it into the deadbolt lock; it turned a little too easily to the right. I didn't hear the sound of the bolt scraping against the strike plate. My heart skipped a beat and I froze.

I tried to reassure myself, "Stop it! It's nothing. You probably just forgot to lock the door." Hearing the words come out of my mouth didn't help.

I turned the knob slowly. I carefully opened the door and a faint odor of burnt cinnamon crossed my nose. I knew that smell. It was the same smell I had noticed with all three of the Abomination I had met. I decided against going in.

I closed the door slowly and quietly. I backed away and stood at the top of the stairs. I never took my eyes off of the door.

I waited for a couple of minutes. I started to call Jim Clayton, but put my phone back in my pocket. After all, what would I tell him? I decided it was best to take care of this myself.

I walked quietly back to the door. I put my back against the wall to one side of the door. I listened. I strained to hear. I heard a few noises from the adjoining apartments, but nothing from inside my apartment. I reached across the door and turned the knob. I gently pushed the door open and waited. I still heard nothing.

I hurried through the door and backed up against the wall. I left the lights off. I didn't need them. In the dark I would have a definite advantage over anyone inside.

I stood there and listened. Still, there was no sound. I sniffed the air. The burnt cinnamon smell was fainter than when I had opened the door the first time. I relaxed a little.

Whoever broke in was probably gone by now. Still, I left the lights off while I entered every room, checked behind every door, and inspected the shower in the bathroom.

I returned to the front door, closed and locked it. I turned on a light. I hadn't noticed before, because I was looking for people and not looking at the room. But now I clearly saw that someone had been there. The cushions on the sofa had been removed and were stacked in the floor. The chair cushions were standing up in the chairs. The drawers of the end tables were open.

My bedroom was the same; every drawer had been opened and furniture had been moved. I couldn't tell if anything was missing. If anything was, it might take a while to figure out what was gone.

All of the obvious things were still in their proper places. The television, my computer, even the jar on the dresser where I threw my loose change. It was all still there.

I went to the kitchen last. Once again, each drawer and

each cabinet door was standing open. But there, on the refrigerator door, hanging by a piece of gray duct tape was a large manila envelope. The envelope was hand-addressed to me by someone who had used a black, felt-tipped marker.

"Chad Fury
AKA Drake Manning"

I swallowed hard. I took the envelope off of the refrigerator. I opened it carefully. Inside the envelope were four photographs. They were the same four pictures Agent Givens had shown me earlier.

I needed to contact the Sisterhood. I couldn't wait until I saw Lisa again. Lisa would check in on me every couple of weeks or so, by just showing up somewhere at the University where I was teaching. That was usually on a Wednesday. If I actually needed something I was supposed to leave a message on the message boards on the TOR network.

I went to the bedroom and opened the lid of the laptop sitting on the small desk in the corner. I had been using the blue mug sitting next to my computer to hold ink pens and thumb drives.

I dumped the contents of the mug out on the desktop. All of my thumb drives were gone. There should have been a blue one and a red one there. The blue one had the Tails operating system and the red one had my encryption software and the message board addresses I needed.

I pulled my cell phone out of my pocket and dialed Jim Clayton. He answered on the sixth ring.

"Jim Clayton, how can I help you?"

"Jim, it's Drake. I need you to get ahold of Agent Givens. She's got to come over here right away."

"Hold on Drake. I can't do that. She's not supposed to know where you live; she doesn't even know your new name."

"I don't think her knowing my new name or where I live is going to matter much. Somebody broke into my apartment. They've gone through all my things, and they left an envelope addressed to me. They put both names on the envelope; my new name and my real name."

"You're kidding me, right?"

"No, I'm serious."

"I'll be right over. Just lock the door, sit tight, and don't touch anything else."

After hanging up, I put the cushions back on the sofa, sat down, and waited. I didn't have to wait long. There was a knock on my door just before midnight. Before I could open the door, a voice called to me, "Drake, it's Jim."

I had known it was Jim before he spoke. I was on edge and all of my senses were in high gear. I had recognized Jim by the sound of his footsteps outside my apartment.

I opened the door and let Jim inside. In typical Jim-fashion, he looked me in the eyes, put his right hand on my shoulder and said, "Drake, are you OK?"

"I'm good. Just rattled…and concerned."

Jim let his hand fall back to his side.

"Drake, let me have a look around."

I followed Jim through my apartment, answering his questions as he went.

"Drake, what did they take?"

"I haven't gone through everything yet, but they…" I almost mentioned the thumb drives, but I caught myself. "They only left something, as far as I can tell."

"Show me."

I took Jim into the kitchen, picked up the envelope from the counter by the sink, and handed it to him. "Here. This was taped to the refrigerator door."

Jim examined the outside of the envelope. "So that's your real name, Chad Fury? I never knew it."

"I thought you knew everything about me?"

"No, I only knew what I was told, and I was only told what I needed to know."

Jim opened the envelope and pulled out the pictures. He thumbed through them quickly.

"Oh my God. What is this?"

"Those are the same pictures Agent Givens showed me earlier. That first one is why I threw up. I had probably better not say much more about them."

Jim put the pictures back in the envelope and laid the envelope on the kitchen counter.

"Drake, pack your bags like you're never coming back. While you're doing that, I've got to wake some people up."

CHAPTER FIVE

I woke up at eight a.m., Saturday morning in a very uncomfortable motel bed. But then, I wouldn't have slept all that well anyway, there were too many questions running through my mind. There were too many problems that needed to be solved.

I got up and crossed over to the window. I pulled the curtain slightly to one side and looked out through the dirty glass. There were two uniformed men standing guard in the parking lot. They were making no effort to hide the fact that I was being watched.

I left the window and headed for the bathroom where there was one of those little hotel coffee pots sitting by the sink. I plugged it in and filled it with water. I picked up a little filter pack of ground coffee, dropped it in the holder and closed the lid. In about ninety seconds I was sipping a fresh, and somehow unsatisfying, cup of coffee.

I went to the edge of the bed and sat there drinking my coffee. My mind was consumed with the events that had transpired just hours ago.

Someone from the Abomination, The Company, had been in my apartment. That person had looked through everything I owned. They took the flash drives I was using to connect to the TOR network. Now I couldn't leave messages for Lisa and the Sisterhood, or email Uncle Allan.

Whoever took the drives also left that envelope. Why do both? Why take the drives and leave the envelope? There had to be a reason.

My mind went back to the beginning; when I first encountered the Abomination's hunters. I had run into a man in a ball cap in the hallway outside Lisa's hotel room. The man used his vocal abilities to try and force me to abandon Lisa. It was a deliberate effort to separate me from their intended target.

Was that what this was? Was I the target and the Abomination was once again trying to isolate me from Lisa and the Sisterhood? Perhaps they were and maybe they even wanted to drive me away from Las Vegas too?

But if they wanted me out of the way, they could have simply killed me. There had to be something else. Was there something they wanted from me?

I knew the cold and calculating Abomination didn't do anything rashly. The Abomination are cunning. They play the long game; they watch, wait, evaluate, and control events like a chess master moving pieces around a board. I had to assume that the situation I found myself in was exactly the situation they wanted.

I finished my coffee, went to my big blue rolling duffle bag and placed it on the bed. I opened the bag and pulled out clothes for the day. I went to the bathroom to perform my morning rituals. The entire time I was shaving, brushing my teeth, etcetera, I was thinking about my next move.

The real turning point for me last year was when I let Uncle Allan help me. He introduced me to game theory and helped me understand what was happening and what I should be doing. I learned from him that I always had to keep my opponent's goal in mind. But what was their goal this time?

I saw two possibilities. Perhaps the Abomination wanted me separated from Lisa, the Sisterhood, and far away from Las Vegas. The last time I saw the Matron she told me they were responsible for my being relocated to Las Vegas. Lisa had even chosen my new name for me.

There was also another possibility. It was very possible the Abomination wanted me to get in contact with the Sisterhood. Perhaps instead of separating me from the Sisterhood they were trying to use me to lead them to the Sisterhood. I had only one way left to contact the Sisterhood; that was the transresinator the Matron had given me.

Before I was relocated to Las Vegas the Matron came to see me at the Federal Transfer Facility in Oklahoma City. She gave me a transresinator, the small glass cube with the silver and gold edges. She had shown me how to use it to send an emergency message; an SOS of sorts. That was my only way left to contact the Sisterhood and Lisa. Is that what the Abomination wanted?

"No," I said aloud, "There's no way they could know the Matron gave me a transresinator. I never told anyone about it."

The day before I left for Las Vegas I was allowed to see my mother and Uncle Allan one last time and say goodbye. That day I gave Uncle Allan a package and told him not to open it, but to mail it to me once I had an address. The package contained the transresinator and some other things Lisa and the Sisterhood had given me, such as the lock pick set and the two watt laser.

A few months later I used the TOR network to send Uncle Allan my mailing address at the University of Nevada in Las Vegas where I was teaching Biology and Chemistry. Uncle Allan sent the package and I carefully hid the transresinator.

I now needed to get to the campus, retrieve the little glass cube, and contact the Sisterhood. But how? How could I get away? Just how much flexibility was I being given in my new situation? I had to find out if the guards were supposed to keep me here, or if they would simply accompany me wherever I went.

I finished dressing, filled my pockets with my usual things, billfold, credit cards, cell phone, and keys. I took the room key from the dresser and put it in my pocket. I exited the motel room and closed the door behind me.

The sun was bright, the sky was blue, and it felt like it was already well on its way to ninety degrees. That meant it was going to be a hot day, especially since it was only nine-thirty a.m.

A uniformed officer walked up quickly, "Excuse me, sir, you can't be outside. You need to remain in your room."

The officer put the palm of his right hand flat against the middle of my chest. I almost knocked it away. I stopped and looked him in the eyes. "What am I supposed to do for food? There's no room service here, and there's a restaurant across the street."

"I'm sorry sir. You have to go back into your room."

"I'm not a prisoner. If I were, I'd have breakfast being brought to me by now."

"Sir, I have my instructions. You need to go back inside."

The officer was just doing his job, and arguing with him was useless; he had no authority to make decisions of any kind.

I returned to my room. After going inside, I locked the door behind me. At least I had part of my answer, I was expected to stay in my room. I pulled my cell phone from my pocket. I dialed Jim Clayton. Jim answered on the fourth ring.

"Hello, Deputy Marshal, Jim Clayton speaking."

"Jim, it's Drake. I'm really sorry to bother you, but there's a problem."

"What's wrong, Drake?"

"This isn't going to work."

"What?"

I thought Jim sounded a little irritated.

"I'm not being allowed to leave the motel room. There's no room service, I can't go across the street for food, and I just drank the only cup of coffee in the room. Plus, I need to get ready for my classes on Monday. I've got a lab to prep and tests to give."

"I'll be over in forty-five minutes. What would you like?"

"Steak and eggs would be great…and coffee."

"Got it. Coffee and a donut."

"I said…"

"I heard you. I'll bring you coffee, and *something*. I'm also taking you back to the Courthouse to talk with Agent Givens."

Jim hung up the phone and I returned to the edge of my bed to sit and think. As I sat, I measured time by the growling of my stomach. My stomach measured the passing minutes at a much different rate then my watch.

At long last there was a knock at the door. I went and opened it. On the other side was Jim Clayton. There was a noticeable absence of breakfast in his hands.

"Jim, I thought you were bringing me something."

"I did. It's in the car. You can eat on the way.

I followed Jim to his car. He drove and I ate. It wasn't long until I had finished my last swallow of coffee and Jim parked the car at the courthouse. Before I got out of the car, I asked, "Jim, what's going on in there?"

"Some very upset people are discussing *you*. When you called, I was listening to them sit there and blame each other for what's happening. This is Vegas, I'll give you fifty-fifty odds that not much has changed."

CHAPTER SIX

Jim Clayton introduced the people in the room. It was the same room I had been in at the Marshal's office the previous day. Agent Saysha Givens, I knew. There were two other faces: U.S. Marshal Clint Oliver whom I had met only once, and Special Agent Frank Gerald whom I had never seen before.

Clint Oliver was a tall, thin man with dark hair. He looked less like a member of law enforcement and more like, well just about anything else. But by the way he was sitting he was letting everyone know he believed he was in charge.

Special Agent Gerald was from the local FBI office. He looked exceptionally average with his sandy-blonde hair, blue jeans and knit shirt. He also looked a little too young to be doing this kind of job.

Jim Clayton and I took our seats; the conversation appeared to pick up wherever it had left off when I entered the room. Agent Givens was full of fire, and it was obvious she was not about to give away any ground.

"Mr. Oliver. I *understand* it is the duty of the Marshals Service to *protect* the witness. It is also *my duty* to make certain there *is* a case to prosecute. And, of course, we can't do that if there's *no* witness.

There's one group about which we are lacking real, actionable information: The Company. Anyone who seems to know anything about The Company ends up murdered. Mr. Fury knows something about The Company, but evidently not enough for us to act upon."

Marshal Oliver looked thoroughly irritated and locked his gaze on Agent Givens.

"Agent Givens. We do not use people as bait! That's the stuff of movies. It's not how the U.S. Marshals Service operates!"

"I'm not talking about using *anyone* as bait! I'm simply saying that moving him is useless. Someone obtained copies of the crime scene pictures and put them in Mr. Fury's apartment. That was not only a breach of information proprietary to the FBI, but it was also a breach of information held by the Marshals Service. Namely, details of Mr. Fury's new identity, including his new residence.

Both agencies would be best served to find this leak and put a stop to it *before* relocating Mr. Fury to another city under a new identity."

The U.S. Marshal leaned back in his chair, tilted his head toward the ceiling and closed his eyes. He stayed that way for several seconds, after which he lowered his head and addressed me.

"Mr. Fury, tell us about The Company and your involvement with them."

I looked at Agent Givens. She nodded and added a word of caution.

"Mr. Fury, Chad. Go ahead, but refrain from speculation about motives and…other things. Stick to *verifiable* facts."

I understood her meaning; any talk of aliens would only make me look crazy.

"I met a woman, Lisa Smith. Her friend, Emily Brown,

had been murdered. I was a suspect because Emily Brown's finger prints were in my car. She had driven me back to my dorm room because I was in no shape to drive. Just a couple of hours later, she was murdered in her apartment.

Emily Brown was murdered by three men. Eric Schwartz, Samuel Smith, and Kane. I don't know Kane's full name. Those three men were part of The Company. They called themselves 'hunters'.

Lisa and Emily were part of a women's group; sort of a secret sorority, if you will. The Company wants those women; why, I don't fully understand.

In an effort to clear my name, I tried to capture these men. I was able to capture Eric and turn him over to the FBI. I killed Samuel in self-defense. And, Kane is gone."

Marshal Oliver interrupted, "What do you mean, he's gone?"

I thought, but found no easy way to say I had turned him over to the Sisterhood; I remained vague.

"I have no idea where Kane is. But, you asked earlier what I know about The Company. I know The Company is responsible for a series of unsolved murders stretching back for years.

I also know that they have their hands in all kinds of crimes including human trafficking and drugs."

Marshal Oliver massaged the back of his neck with his left hand.

"Well, Mr. Fury. I can understand why The Company isn't too happy with you."

He turned to face Agent Givens, "Tell me again what you're thinking."

"Marshal, we have two goals. We need to keep Chad safe, and we need to find the leaks in our own organizations. I believe the best way to do that is to watch Mr. Fury very closely, here, in Vegas. Yes, find him another apartment, but here, not in some other city."

"I still don't like it."

"Mr. Oliver, between the resources of the FBI and the Marshals Service, we can cover Mr. Fury."

"Alright. I'll agree to not relocating him to another city, right now. However if there is another incident, or there is any indication that his life is in danger, he *will* be relocated."

The conversations continued for a while, but the result was that I would be taken to an FBI safe house until a suitable apartment could be found. The Marshals would continue to guard and watch the existing apartment for a little while, just in case someone came back. The FBI, on the other hand, would provide protection as I went to work and conducted my so-called normal life.

CHAPTER SEVEN

Jim Clayton drove me back from the meeting. We had left the Marshal and Agent Givens in the room still discussing my future. It appeared that somehow they felt my future didn't involve me.

Jim's phone rang as we pulled up to the motel. The safe house was ready. I was to be taken there immediately.

Jim parked his blue sedan close to the motel room. We both got out of the car. Jim went behind the car and opened the trunk.

I went into the motel room to gather my things. I put my dirty laundry in a plastic bag provided by the motel, and put the bag in my rolling blue duffel.

I put my laptop bag over my shoulder and scanned the room to see if I was leaving anything behind. I patted the outside of my pants pockets as a quick sanity check; I felt my billfold, cell phone and keys.

As I exited the room dragging the large bag behind me, I saw Jim leaning up against the car casually waiting in the hot parking lot. He was rolling up his shirt sleeves. Jim called my name. "Drake. I need the room key."

I stopped, let go of the duffle bag and dug the key out

of my front pocket. I tossed it to Jim. He snatched it out of the air with his right hand, looked at it briefly and put it in his pocket. I continued pulling my bag and went to the rear of the blue sedan. Jim met me there.

"Here. Let me get that for you."

I took a step away from the bag.

"Thank you."

I saw the inside of Jim's left arm when he reached for the bag, my heart stopped momentarily. There was a four-inch long cut. It looked fresh.

As Jim placed the bag in the trunk I asked, "Jim, how did you get that?"

Jim gave me a funny look. "I grabbed the straps and lifted it up."

"No. Not the bag, the cut on your arm?"

Jim looked at his right arm, and then his left.

"What are you talking about?"

I swallowed.

"Jim, the inside of your left arm, it's cut."

Jim looked again at his arm and then gave me a puzzled look.

"My arm's fine. What are you talking about?"

I exhaled, "Never mind. It must have been a trick of the light. I thought I saw something."

I dropped my laptop bag in the trunk next to my duffle bag. Jim closed the trunk lid. We both got into the car. Jim started driving and I kept trying to keep my eyes away from the cut on his arm.

I couldn't help but wonder if seeing the cut on Jim's arm was planned, or if it was an accident. Was I being sent a message? Was I being told that I was being watched?

One thing was obvious. The Abomination knew everything that both the Marshals and the FBI knew about me. The only things they could not know were the things I had never told anyone else.

"Jim, has anything unusual happened in the last couple of days?"

He glanced at me and then fixed his gaze back on the road and the traffic.

"That's an odd question, considering…Nothing '*usual*' has happened since Agent Givens arrived from Oklahoma City."

"I just have a feeling that the people who are after me are closer than anyone knows."

"Don't worry. That's why we're headed to the FBI safe house. Only a few people know where it is, and nobody's talking. Hell, you couldn't even bleed it out of me."

That was an odd thing for Jim to say. I wondered, if it was possible that a part of his mind knew what had happened to him; that he was he about to remember something.

CHAPTER EIGHT

The FBI safe house looked very ordinary from the outside. Of course, I'm sure that's how it was supposed to look. The two story tan-colored house with its terra cotta roof was very much like any other house in Summerlin, Nevada or almost any other U.S. city for that matter.

Jim pulled his blue sedan into the driveway and waited with the car running. After about fifteen seconds the garage door began to open. Jim pulled the car inside and turned off the engine.

I started to get out, but Jim grabbed my arm.

"Not so fast. You don't get out until the garage door is completely down."

I waited and we both exited the car at the same time. Jim hit a button on his key fob and the trunk lid popped open. I went to the rear of the car, retrieved my things and closed the trunk.

Jim was standing at the front of the garage holding open the door to the house. I went inside and found myself standing in an alcove next to a washer and dryer. In front of me, just through the alcove was the kitchen. Special Agent Frank Gerald and a woman I had never seen before were standing in the kitchen.

I followed Jim through the alcove and sat my things on the floor. Special Agent Gerald spoke first.

"It's good to see you Mr. Fury…Oh, I should be calling you Drake Manning."

Special Agent Gerald looked at Jim and thrust out his hand.

"Thank you for bringing Drake here. I'd like for you to meet Special Agent Brenda James."

The usual pleasantries and plastic smiles were exchanged and then Jim Clayton quickly made his farewell saying that he knew I was in good hands. He exited the way we had entered.

I heard the car start, then Frank Gerald picked up a garage door remote and pressed the large button with his thumb. I heard the garage door open. When I could no longer hear the sound of the car engine, Frank hit the button again and closed the door.

Special Agent Brenda James took a step toward me. Her long brown hair flowed gracefully with a slight bounce. At five feet six inches she had to tilt her head up slightly for her hazel eyes to lock onto my face. I matched her gaze.

Special Agent James reached out her hand with her palm up, "Mr. Manning. May I see your cell phone, please?"

I retrieved my phone from my pocket and placed it in her hand.

Special Agent James never looked at the phone but casually placed the phone on the counter out of my reach. She turned back to me and began speaking in very unemotional tones, and I began to see her as much less attractive.

"It's time for you to learn the house rules. Number one, no phone calls. You will not make or receive any unscreened calls while you are here. There are no land lines; no phones of any kind installed in this house. If you need to make a call you will do so at the discretion of, and with the assistance of, one of the two agents in the house. Do you understand?"

She had done it; she had shattered her own feminine mystique and I was now taking pleasure in finding flaws in her features. There were little wrinkles starting to form around the corners of her eyes. I smiled.

"Yes, I understand. No phone calls."

She continued, "There is no internet in the house. There is cable television in the downstairs den, but nowhere else."

I noticed a small blemish on her forehead just above her left eyebrow.

"Alright, what else?"

"The windows are to remain closed, and the curtains drawn at all times. You *will* stay away from the windows."

I couldn't help but notice that the little finger on her right hand was crooked, and the nail on that finger was chipped.

I nodded to indicate I would comply.

"Furthermore, you *will not* go outside of the house. The kitchen and bathrooms are fully stocked. If you need something, tell one of the agents and someone will get it for you."

I looked at her hair and was disappointed that I could not find a single flake of dandruff. I nodded again and she had the audacity to continue.

"You *will not* leave the house unaccompanied. We have your schedule. You *will* be driven to your work and returned here. Outside the house an agent *will* be with you at all times."

I sniffed the air, I frowned because she did not have any offensive odors.

"I understand. Is there anything else I can't do?"

"Not at all. Please make yourself at home; I'll show you to your room. Your room is at the top of the stairs, on the right. The bathroom is across the hall."

I picked up my bags and followed Special Agent James through the kitchen, past the dining room, into the foyer and up the stairs to the first room at the top.

I entered the room and Special Agent James did not; she turned and descended the stairs without a word.

The room was definitely more comfortable than the motel I had come from, but to be honest, it was nothing special. There was a queen size bed centered against the wall to my left taking up the majority of the room. The bedspread was some sort of patchwork quilt that had too many colors. The light brown carpet looked new and the beige walls looked freshly painted.

As for furniture, the room had a single nightstand with a small lamp on the right-hand side of the bed. There was a chest of drawers against the wall opposite the foot of the bed, a chair on one side, and a closet on the other.

I lifted my blue rolling duffle bag onto the bed, unzipped it, and started unpacking. At some point while I was putting my clothes into the chest of drawers, I realized this whole situation was no good.

The Abomination had compromised the FBI and the U.S. Marshals Service. There was no telling what commands they had been given. Anyone could be acting as an unwilling pawn. I had to leave.

I stopped unpacking and put my clothes back in the oversized rolling duffel bag. There was room for my laptop bag; I put that in there too. I placed the bag in the closet and closed the closet door.

I returned to my previous goals. I needed to get a message to the Sisterhood and to Lisa. I needed to talk to Uncle Allan and make certain he and mom were safe. And, I had to be somewhere that the Abomination didn't know about and where they couldn't track me.

Last year I had escaped from the Cleveland County Jail because I took the first opportunity that arose, and I didn't hesitate. This time wasn't that much different, except this prison was a little more comfortable and the guards assumed I wanted to be here.

If I was going to escape I needed to understand my cage and how I was being watched. I went exploring. I started with the upstairs. There were three other rooms. Two of the rooms were furnished with two twin beds each. The third room was nearly empty, except for shelves with children's games and a small table with three child-sized chairs.

At the end of the hall was a door. A quick look behind the door revealed a dusty attic and a lot of empty space. I stepped inside. For anyone else, it would have been pitch black. But my eyes adjusted easily to dim light.

Looking around I saw cables running across the ceiling joists. I took a moment to make a mental inventory of the cables. There were several heavy, flat Romex electrical wires, a round cable that was probably for the cable television, and one other wire that looked like some kind of computer data cable.

I squatted down and reached out my hand to touch the cable. A small scorpion crawled onto the back of my hand; I shook it off. I looked at the cable and wondered what would happen if the cable somehow broke? I would have to keep that as an option. I didn't want the FBI to have any more videos that would be difficult to explain.

I got up, left the attic and headed downstairs. I wandered through the rooms trying to look a little restless and not be too obvious that I was looking for cameras.

I started with the den. The walls were covered with dark wood paneling, and the room was filled with brown furniture. There was a flat screen television on the far wall. A DVD player, a TV cable box, and a couple of remote controls were on a shelf beneath the television. A bookcase to one side had a collection of DVDs, mostly family oriented stuff.

I left the den and headed back to the entryway where the staircase landed. Behind the staircase was a closet. The door was locked. I supposed that might be where the controller for the video equip.m.ent was hidden. I listened and I heard an electrical hum.

I continued to the back of the house where there was one more room. I stuck my head through the open door. Inside I saw Special Agent Frank Gerald sitting on the edge of a twin bed with his shoes off. Against the wall to my immediate left was a desk with a computer and four monitors showing scenes from the interior and exterior of the house.

"May I help you, Drake?"

"Sorry to interrupt. I was just looking around the house."

"Well, feel free. But please close the door when you leave. I'll be here all night, and I need to catch a little sleep. Agent James will be somewhere downstairs if you need anything."

I nodded, turned, and closed the door. I headed back to the den to turn on the television, pretended to watch, and think.

As I sat on the sofa with the television remote in hand, I saw a glimmer of hope on the glowing TV screen. The local news was on, and the attractive blonde newscaster was reporting that a storm was headed to Vegas. It was being called a hundred year storm.

Las Vegas is, as everyone knows, a city in the desert. Deserts are not totally without water. It does rain some, and the rain is usually short lived. But on rare occasions there are big storms with lots of wind and lots of rain. There's a one in one-hundred chance of a storm like that in any given year. From the sounds of it, that kind of storm would be coming tonight, sometime around eleven P.M..

I leaned back and grinned. The Abomination could manipulate a lot of events, but I doubted they could control the weather. This storm was an opportunity for me to act in a way that neither the FBI nor the Abomination would predict.

I sat the remote control on the sofa cushion next to me, closed my eyes and thought. I was going to need some rest too. Special Agent Gerald wasn't the only one who would be up all night.

CHAPTER NINE

The rain came. I sat on the bed and listened as the first drops of rain pecked softly at the bedroom window. It was about ten minutes past eleven. I was ready. I had changed into my darkest clothes, a pair of black jeans and a plain black tee-shirt.

I got up from the bed, crossed to the door and flipped the switch on the wall turning out the light. I opened the door quietly, exited softly, and carefully closed the door behind me. I padded gently down the hallway in my bare feet, heading for the attic door.

As I opened the attic door there was a crack of thunder. I'm sure it made me smile. I proceeded quickly to the bundle of wires and cables I had spotted earlier. I pulled out my pocket knife and two paperclips before squatting down on the edge of a ceiling joist. I clenched the paperclips in my teeth so I wouldn't lose them.

At the point where the data cable was crossing over the electrical cable. I lifted the data cable and carefully stripped away about half an inch of insulation, exposing the delicate copper wires inside.

I turned my attention to the electrical wire. I made a

small hole in the outside edges of the flat electrical wire where I knew the positive and negative wires ran.

I unbent my paperclips and shoved the end of a paperclip into the hole on one edge. I did the same with the second paperclip. There were now two bare silver wires protruding from the outside edges of the electrical wire. I bent the wires across the top of the electrical cable, each wire was parallel to the other with just about a half-inch gap.

I exhaled and listened to the storm. The thunder was close and the rain was pouring down. The rain beating on the roof caused the attic to roar. I held the exposed wires of the data cable against the bare paperclip wires. There was a blue electrical arc and smoke as the data cable smoldered.

I used my knife to pick out the hot paperclips. I wrapped the paperclips in a handkerchief and took them with me.

I left the attic as quickly as possible and made my way downstairs to see what effect, if any, my work had on the surveillance system.

At the bottom of the stairs Agent Gerald was opening the closet door underneath the staircase.

"Do you need something, Drake?"

"Yeah, the power's out upstairs."

"I'm not surprised. It looks like we had a lightning strike."

"Really? What's in there, the circuit breaker box?"

"No. That's in the garage. I'll check it in a minute. I need to look at this."

"Let me see. I'm pretty handy with electricity and stuff."

"Back off Drake. I'll have to call in tech support for this."

Frank closed the closet door and locked it. He turned his back toward me and went into the back room. I moved a little closer to the room and listened. He was on his cell phone.

"Hello, this is Special Agent Frank Gerald. I need tech support."

There was a long pause before he spoke again.

"Hey Mike, it's Frank. I'm at the safe house. I think there was a lightning strike. The cameras are out all over the house…"

That was all I needed to hear. I moved quickly up the stairs to the bedroom. I took out my oversized duffel and put it by the window.

When I opened the window the wind drove the rain inside. I pushed my bag through the window and dropped it. I just hoped my laptop would be OK. I crawled out of the window and hit my fingertips on the stucco wall. My claws appeared.

I pulled the window closed and scaled down the wall to the ground below. The ground was mostly sand. A few homes in Vegas have grass in their yards, but keeping grass in the desert is difficult.

I stood on the ground in the pouring rain. A crack of lightning lit up the area like day. I grabbed my duffel bag and trotted over to the privacy fence. I lifted the bag up and pushed it over. I followed quickly.

I picked up the bag and used the shoulder straps to hang it from my back. I went to the sidewalk and began running east. I didn't put on my shoes; I didn't want them. The pounding of my feet as I ran caused them to transform, and my claws gave me more traction on the wet surfaces than the best running shoes.

Since coming to Vegas I had taken to running in the desert. I had timed myself and found my top speed to be forty-five miles per hour.

I was headed to my office at the University of Nevada, I guessed about twelve miles away. In Vegas, because of the traffic and the crush of people, nothing is very close. It could take longer to go a mile in Vegas than anywhere else in the world.

Tonight was different. The storm had driven people off of the streets and I could make the trip easily. I figured I could be at the university in less than twenty minutes. That was actually faster than I could drive it. Driving would take at least twice that long.

I reached the intersection and tried to get my bearings. I was on Sahara Avenue. I had no GPS, and I didn't know the Summerlin area very well. I had to depend on recognizing the landmarks as I went.

When I arrived at Buffalo Drive, I knew where I was. I headed due east. I soon came to Highway 15, headed south to Flamingo Drive, and continued east to what the locals call the New Vegas Strip. Along the strip the pouring rain had driven the tourists off of the sidewalks, but cars were still crawling along, bumper to bumper.

The lights from the hotels and casinos revealed just how much water was pouring down the street and into the storm drains. There had to be at least eight or ten inches of water racing down the street, flowing around the cars slowly crawling through the downpour.

I slowed and trotted through the water in the street. I saw a few faces in the cars looking in awe at the crazy man running in the rain.

When I'd crossed the street, I was on the south side of Caesar's Palace. I started running again and was soon at the university campus. I went to the science building and stood beneath the overhang at the side door.

I removed my duffle bag and I pulled out a bathroom towel I had packed. I dried off as best I could. The towel, to be honest, didn't do that much good. I pulled out my shoes and put them on.

I looked through the glass door and pulled on the handle. It was locked. I took out the key from my wet jeans, slid it into the lock and turned it. I pulled open the door and let myself inside.

I had gotten used to the temperature of the rain, but now standing in the air-conditioned hallway I was suddenly not only wet, but very cold.

I dragged my wet, oversized rolling duffle bag behind me and proceeded to the stairs. My shoes squeaked on the linoleum and I left a trail of water as I went.

On the second floor I went to my office, the fifth door on my right. I put my key in the door, stepped inside, turned on the light and closed the door.

I looked at my office suspiciously. Had the Abomination been here? I sniffed the air. There was no burnt cinnamon odor. I looked at my things. The desk and the bookshelf looked undisturbed.

The Abomination had gone through my apartment. They also knew where I worked. Had they left this place alone? Was my office some sort of trap? Were they wanting me to be here? There was no way to know right now, but one thing they could not have predicted is that I would be here at just after midnight on a Sunday morning, during a rare desert storm.

I sat down my wet bag and pulled out some dry clothes to wear. Just getting out of the wet clothes made me feel several degrees warmer. As I dressed, I continued to wonder if the Abomination had been here.

I went to my desk and sat down in my chair. I pulled open the center desk drawer and stared. Inside was something dried and hard, about eight inches long and three inches wide. I picked it up. There was a yellow sticky note on it. All the note said was "From Eric, for Chad." I dropped it and heard my own voice, "My God, Eric's skin."

So the Abomination had been here. They wouldn't have found much in my office. I had done a very careful job of hiding the transresinator and the original thumb drives Lisa had given me.

I closed the drawer, went to the bookshelf and pulled a box from the bottom shelf. Inside the box were several things Lisa and the Sisterhood had given me when this whole mess started. There were the two hats Lisa had given me, the fedora and the ball cap with the infrared LED lights. There was the two watt laser, the lock pick set, and the hard drive with the forensic software.

I took out the ball cap and tested the power. It still worked. I put it on. I picked up the laser. I tested it. It was dead. I put the laser and the charging cord in my duffel bag. I reached back in the box and retrieved the lock pick set. I put that in my back pocket; I was going to need it in a few minutes.

I went to the door. I turned out the lights, exited and locked the door behind me. I thought about that piece of skin in my drawer. I wondered if I should show it to the FBI. What could they do? What would they do? Why leave the skin? What exactly was the Abomination after? Whatever it was that the Abomination wanted, I wasn't going to let them have it.

I headed down the hallway to the stairs and then down to the basement. In the basement was the geology department lab and storage room. I soon found myself facing the two double doors to the geology storage room. I pulled out my lock pick set and went to work.

I inserted the tension bar into the lock. I pulled out the small tool called a rake and inserted it into the key hole. I gently probed. I counted seven pins. I teased the pins up and down until finally the lock turned under the pressure of the tension bar.

I pushed the door open. It was pitch dark inside, even for my eyes. I found a light switch and flipped it on. A bank of fluorescent lights flickered and hummed. Ahead of me were rows and rows of dusty old shelves with labeled boxes. I grabbed a stool from a nearby table and carried it to the far corner of the room.

Several months earlier Uncle Allan had sent my package with the transresinator and other things. I tried to hide the transresinator someplace no one ever looks. I searched the campus and decided upon this room.

This room had the dustiest and greatest number of

unused boxes I had ever seen. I chose an old cardboard box on the top shelf at the back of the room. Inside the box was a collection of geodes from Missouri. According to the label on the front, it was collected in nineteen-eighty. From the amount of dust on the lid it appeared it had not been disturbed since.

I placed the stool at the end of the row of shelves. I climbed onto the stool and pulled the box from the top shelf. I descended, placed the box on the stool and opened the lid. Inside was my little red cloth bag with the transresinator and the two thumb drives.

I wasted no time. I opened the bag and took out the transresinator. I put the cloth bag and the drives in my pocket. I held up the two inch glass cube and admired it. It was beautiful with the delicate silver and gold edges. I turned the cube over in my fingers until I found the side with four silver edges.

I placed the cube in the palm of my right hand, with the silver edges facing up. I placed the index finger of my left hand on the top of the cube. The cube glowed orange and began to pulse in unison with my beating heart.

The Matron had set the pass code to be ten vocal tones I could easily remember and reproduce. I sang the first ten notes of the "Happy Birthday" song. The cube glowed green.

I took a deep breath and tried to remember the tones the Matron had taught me that would initiate the emergency call. It was five tones. From the starting tone, I went up one step, down three, back to the starting tone, and up one step. It took me three tries to get it right.

At the end of the third try I felt a small tingle in my hand, and the cube glowed red. I closed my eyes and focused my mind on the recent events. I thought about Eric's death, Sirhan missing from prison, and all of the rest.

When I finished, I opened my eyes and looked at the cube resting in my palm. It was not glowing and it was cold against my hand. I had no way of knowing if my message had gotten through.

CHAPTER TEN

Lying on my office sofa was uncomfortable, and I was thinking about moving to the floor when I realized the storm had ended. I looked at my watch; it was five a.m..

After retrieving the cube and sending the message I returned to my office and fired up the TOR network on my office computer. Since I was booting from the original thumb drive Lisa had given me, I had no fear that any malware was monitoring what I was doing.

I sent an email to Uncle Allan using the TOR email service. I told him everything and asked him to keep mom safe.

I then posted encrypted messages on the message boards used by the Sisterhood, just in case the message I sent using the transresinator had failed.

It was now all down to waiting. Waiting was one of the most difficult things I did last year; not knowing what to do and just having to wait. But, I always found waiting to be easier with a hot cup of coffee.

I sat up, looked over at my desk, and eyed the coffee cup sitting on the edge. I went to the desk. I picked up the white mug with the golden dragon design and held it gently in my hand.

Katy Hargrove, a history professor here at the university had given me the mug. She had seen a glimpse of my dragon tattoo once, and assumed I liked dragons. The mug was a Christmas gift.

Katy always seemed to blush and be a little tongue-tied around me. I had considered going out with her, and the one time we had gone out to a local pub, it was with a group of faculty. Nothing came of it. I wasn't ready to make commitments. After all, at what point when you're dating someone is it the right time to ask, "By the way, would you like to know my real name?"

Relationships and commitments are something I don't need. No, wait. I'm going to be honest with you. I do need relationships, but it's asking far too much to bring a total stranger into all of this drama.

I carried my coffee cup down the hall to the faculty lounge. I rinsed out the glass coffee pot, put it under the brewer, added a filter pack to the basket, and pushed the brew button. I waited a good seven or eight minutes for the coffee to finally finish brewing. Afterward, I filled my cup.

I then went on a search for a vending machine. The vending machines were on the first floor near the main elevators. I fed the machine a dollar and fifty cents in exchange for a little package of chocolate covered doughnuts. They were the kind where the dark, waxy coating clings to your teeth for several minutes after the donuts are gone.

I walked back to the office, sipping my coffee and regretting my choice from the machine. As I approached my office, I noticed the door standing ajar. I knew I hadn't locked it, but I was certain I had closed it. I pushed the door open cautiously with the back of my right hand.

As the door began to open I heard a familiar voice that made my heart beat just a little faster.

"Hello, Dragon Boy!"

"Lisa! It's you!"

Lisa was sitting on the couch with her legs crossed. Her hair was red this time. She was wearing a blue, loose fitting paisley top that looked like it belonged in the sixties, blue jeans and bright blue tennis shoes.

"Well of course it's me, silly."

I moved to the desk to put down the coffee and doughnuts. Lisa stood and came toward me. When my hands were free I turned. I was a little stunned to find her standing in my personal space.

Lisa threw her arms around my neck and kissed me. In a couple of seconds the shock left and I realized I was kissing her at the same time she was kissing me.

Our lips slid past each other and after a moment more I removed my arms from around her and pushed gently on her shoulders. Our faces moved away from each other just a few inches.

"Lisa, what's all this?"

"I got your message, silly. I'm flattered and I feel, well, you understand."

"Uh, no I don't. What message?"

"The transresinator…"

Lisa put her palms on my chest and pushed gently as she backed up a step. Her face looked puzzled.

"Chad, didn't the Matron explain the transresinator to you?"

"Uh, well, she showed me how to send an emergency message. That's all."

"Oh, I feel like such a…"

"Lisa, what? What should I know about the transresinator?"

"Chad, the transresinator is the *ultimate* communication device. It is to the telephone what the phone is to pen and paper.

It's like this…Your cell phone carries your voice…"

"OK."

"Your voice carries inflections, changes in tone. You

can pick up on someone's mood and emotions based on the voice. And you could never pick up the same thing from a letter, right?"

"Sure."

"The transresinator can transmit words, but words are sloppy. It also transmits your thoughts *and* emotions.

I must say, your mind's a mess, unfocused. You should rely more on words, but your emotions were unmistakable. I know how you feel about me. And I have...*feelings*...for you."

"Whoa, hold on. I wasn't trying to tell you how I feel. I'm sorry if I made you think I have feelings for you...I mean...I do have feelings, but I'm not sure just what..."

"Oh, shut up! You're such a typical man! Men don't even know how they feel most of the time. I swear, when a man loves a woman, the man's the *last* one to know about it!"

"I...uhm...I mean."

Lisa sighed, "Don't even try. I forgive you because I know how you feel, even if you don't. That's enough for now.

We need to go somewhere and talk about everything else that's going on. How about buying me some breakfast?"

I was thankful for the change of subject. I backed up half a step and sat on the edge of the desk.

"Breakfast sounds good, Lisa. What would you like?"

"Do you like scones? I know a place, and I can guarantee that we won't be followed."

I shrugged my shoulders, "Ladies choice."

"Before we go, Chad, we need to take care of something. Do you have your transresinator?"

"Sure, but it doesn't work. Sending the message must have burned it out, or drained the battery, or something."

I stood and went past Lisa, around my desk and opened the third drawer on the right. I retrieved the small red cloth bag. I pulled the cube from the bag and handed it to her.

Lisa proceeded to give me instructions, "Put it flat in your palm, silver edges up."

I positioned the cube in my palm and Lisa pulled a similar cube from her purse. She placed her cube on top of mine, with the silver edges of both cubes touching. She placed her index finger on top of the cubes.

Lisa looked at me.

"You ready?"

"I guess."

Lisa sang, it was more of a chant, than a song. A second later, an electric shock went through my arm and my cube glowed orange again. A moment more and the orange light from my cube was pulsing in unison with my heartbeat.

Lisa removed her cube and placed it in her purse.

"OK, Chad, you're good to go now."

"What just happened?"

"The emergency message is more of a *panic* message. After the message is sent the transresinator is locked and requires what you might call a reboot of the operating system. It's a safety feature."

"What do I do now?"

"Keep your transresinator with you at all times. I'll explain over breakfast."

"About breakfast; where are we going?"

"Follow me."

I forced the transresinator into my pocket and followed Lisa out of the building to the nearest parking lot. She walked gracefully over to a red motorcycle and picked up two helmets. She tossed one to me, and we put them on.

Lisa drove; I held on behind with my arms around her waist. It felt really nice, even comfortable to have my arms around her. When I realized just how natural it felt, I think I may have blushed. I wondered if it could be true; was there some part of me that actually *loved* Lisa?

Before I had the opportunity to think much more

about my feelings, Lisa began slowing to a stop. We were at the edge of the highway sitting on an embankment. At the bottom of the slope was a spillway. A small stream of water from the previous storm was flowing out of a dark tunnel that looked like it led deep underground.

"Lisa, why did we stop here?"

"That's part of the flood control system. There are miles and miles of tunnels under the Vegas Valley. Most of the tunnels are interconnected. It's a great way to get around unnoticed. But you have to be careful down there. More than a thousand people live in the tunnel system."

"You're yanking my chain. Nobody lives there."

"That's not true, Chad. Have you never wondered why you don't see many homeless people on the streets? This is where they are. It's protection from the heat and most people don't go into the flood control drains."

"I take it we're going down there?"

"We are."

Lisa started the bike moving and worked it carefully down the slope. She drove slowly in the stream of water and into the gaping hole under the road.

The light on the motorcycle cut through the darkness and showed the graffiti on the walls. There was some debris, wet cardboard and other assorted trash presumably washed along by the recent storm.

After a little while Lisa announced very loudly, "We're directly under the strip."

I looked around and all I saw was a set of rungs in the concrete wall leading up to a manhole cover.

Lisa drove on and made a right turn down a connecting tunnel. We passed several other connecting tunnels before she stopped and turned off the motorcycle. She took off her helmet and her long red hair flowed out like a waterfall.

Above us and to the left was a rectangular hole leading to the street. I could hear the sound of people and traffic. The hole let in enough light to display our surroundings.

"OK Chad. We're here."

"Not much of a breakfast place. What I'm smelling doesn't remind me much of scones."

"We'll walk the rest of the way, it's not far. Take out your transresinator, I need to show you something."

I pulled the cube from my pocket. There was a red arrow on the top surface of the cube. The arrow was pointing toward the wall opposite the storm drain. No matter how I turned or rotated the cube, the arrow stayed on top and kept pointing toward the wall, like a compass needle.

I looked at Lisa and asked, "What exactly am I seeing?"

"You're within two hundred fifty feet of a portal. The transresinator is pointing in the direction of the portal."

"So, there's some kind of portal on the other side of the wall?"

"No. It's right there, where the wall is."

Lisa reached out her hand and gently touched the wall with her palm. The wall shimmered and waves went out from her hand like she had dropped a stone in a pool of water. The waves stopped suddenly about four feet on her left and right, but continued to the ceiling and the floor.

"Lisa, what is that?"

"That, is a portal. On the other side is London, England. Give me your transresinator."

I handed the cube to Lisa.

"OK, Chad, now touch the wall."

I stepped up to the wall and touched it, just like Lisa had done. Nothing happened. I felt the cool concrete. I slid my hand over the surface in several directions. It was just a wall.

"What gives? I don't understand."

"Chad, here's your transresinator. Either hold it, or put it in your pocket, or something. You can't access the portal unless you have the transresinator."

I took the cube from Lisa and held it in my left hand. I touched the wall gently with my right palm. The wall shimmered and waves went out from where I touched it. The surface felt cold, and gave easily like pressing on a thin film of plastic floating on water.

Lisa started speaking while I was staring at the waves I was making with my hand.

"Chad, let's go. Just step through."

"No. Explain first. I'm not going in until you explain it. What is it, really?"

"It's a portal. When you step through you will immediately be in London."

"So, this is some kind of a worm hole? A tunnel that will transport me through space?"

"No. It's a portal, a doorway. Does any door you've ever used actually *transport* you anywhere?"

I shook my head in disbelief at Lisa, "Doorways let a person walk into the adjacent space. You said London's on the other side of that thing. I know for a fact that London's thousands of miles away from here. There's nothing but dirt and rock on the other side of that wall."

"Chad, the way you're used to traveling, it's over five thousand miles away. But it's also just a couple of feet from you right now."

"No. That's not possible. I can believe a lot of stuff, but I can't buy that."

Lisa looked around the tunnel like she was looking for something, and then looked at me.

"Chad, take off your belt."

"What?"

"Just do it. Maybe a visual aid will help."

I put the glass cube into my pocket and took off my belt. I handed the belt to Lisa. Lisa took the belt with both hands.

"Chad. Let's say the belt buckle is Las Vegas. And, over here, at the other end of the belt is London. That's pretty far away, right?"

"Sure."

Lisa brought her two hands together so that the buckle

and the end of the belt were touching.

"What about now?"

"Wow! So, Lisa, you're telling me that you've folded space?"

Lisa faked sobbing, "Oh, *Chad*, no!"

"Well, what then?"

"You've taken physics. You're even teaching science classes. Think about it, and you tell me. What would it take to fold space? What is the one force in the universe that bends and warps space?"

I answered her reluctantly, "Gravity?"

Lisa nodded, "And it's not possible to localize gravity to a controlled shape like a rectangular doorway. More than that, what would be happening if there were enough gravity to bring Las Vegas and London next to each other?"

"That would be, kind of like a mini black hole. We, and everything around us would be sucked into it."

"Good. So what's happening here?"

"I don't know, Lisa. Please just tell me and don't make me guess."

Lisa handed my belt back to me and I put it on while she talked.

"Chad, can you put a cube into a two dimensional space, like a flat piece of paper?"

"No. A three dimensional object cannot be contained in a two dimensional space, part of it will always stick out."

Lisa stared at me silently, like she had given me some great clue and I should be picking it up and running with it. But I had no idea where this was leading.

"Chad. Every object you're used to dealing with is three dimensional. Right?"

"Of course, it all has height, width, and depth."

"Everything you know in your entire universe is three dimensional. So, what does that tell you about your universe?"

"The universe is sitting in a really big three dimensional

box."

Lisa exhaled in what sounded like exasperation. "Chad, my dear…the universe is sitting in a really big three dimensional box, or…"

I looked at her questioningly and presented my answer in the form of a question. "It might mean that the universe is sitting in space that has more than three dimensions?"

Lisa threw up her hands and raised her head toward the ceiling.

"Hallelujah! He understands!"

"I do? What is it that I understand?"

Lisa dropped her hands, lowered her head, and exhaled.

"Chad. The space that contains this universe has more than three dimensions. If we could perceive this multi-dimensional space, all of our three dimensional objects would look like points sitting on top of each other.

It's like this. Think of standing in a room with countless doors. Each door is near you and every time you look in a different direction, you see a different door. Each door is actually a different place.

There are an infinite number of doors, and by moving just a little bit you would fall through a door and land somewhere else."

That doorway, in that wall, is simply a doorway that already exists. A little bit of multi-dimensional reality has been exposed to our three-dimensional space. And for that little piece of the multi-verse, Las Vegas and London are right next to each other."

"My head hurts. How is this even possible? You mean to tell me that you can open a portal to anywhere, at will?"

"It's possible by using what you would call a quantum computer. A quantum computer interacts with the world on a quantum level. And, we can't open and close portals at will.

The calculations are immense, they take a long time, and exposing other dimensions takes a lot of energy. The transresinator points you to an existing, nearby portal and allows you to interact with it.

Chad, I'm tired of playing this game. I'm hungry and I want out of this stinky hole. Let's go. We can talk more about this later."

Lisa took my left hand with her right, squeezed it tight, and started walking into the wall. She disappeared through the shimmering puddle, and I was pulled along.

CHAPTER ELEVEN

My head was spinning, and everything was out of focus. All I could see was a blur of shapes and colors. It was a little like being very, very drunk.

"Chad. Chad. Are you OK?"

I recognized Lisa's voice, and I felt a hand on my arm. Slowly the room began to settle down and my vision cleared. I was standing in a room with a stone floor and old wooden beams in the ceiling. Old glass windows were divided into small squares letting the light filter into the room. The smells were new; I had definitely never been in this place before. I heard a second female voice laughing.

"You'll be OK. It's just a bit of sensory overload. You get used to it after a while."

I almost recognized the voice. It was familiar, and yet somehow not. I just couldn't quite place it. I looked over toward the voice and saw an attractive young blonde woman with steel blue eyes. The woman appeared to be in her mid-twenties. I couldn't quite place the face, but the eyes were very familiar.

"Excuse me," I said, as I tried to make sense of the face. "Do I know you?"

The woman laughed again, "I must look very different to you now. The first time I saw you, I asked you, 'Did you dream?' And you replied, 'Go to hell.' I also cut you, right there."

The blonde woman drug her right index finger across the top of my left pec.

"Matron? But…that's not…I mean you're too young."

"I still think you're impudent."

I looked at Lisa.

"Lisa, what's going on here? Where am I, and is this really the Matron?"

"Chad, you're in the Tower of London, the Byward Tower to be precise, on the first floor. And, yes, this is the Matron, sort of."

"There's no such thing as 'sort of'. Either she is or isn't."

The young woman spoke up.

"Chad. I am, in every way that matters, the Matron you knew. Only…you knew my pre-self."

I shook my head.

"Pre-self? What the hell is a *pre-self*?"

"The Matron you knew was old, and dying. You would call me a clone. Before the Matron you knew died, I was awakened and given her memories.

Chad, there's a lot we need to talk about, and I'm in a mood to answer questions. But, not here. Let's get something to eat."

The young blonde woman claiming to be the Matron led the way out of the room. We were soon outdoors, and based on the position of the sun, it looked like it was the middle of the afternoon.

We walked a few blocks and were soon sitting at a small table inside a pastry shop, drinking coffee and eating scones.

I wasn't in a mood for sightseeing or just sitting around wasting time. There were a million questions burning in me and now seemed like the time to ask some of them.

"Excuse me, Matron, but you mentioned earlier that you were in the mood to answer questions. If you are still in that mood, I'd like to ask."

The Matron swallowed a bite of her cinnamon scone and took a sip of hot tea. She put down her cup and looked at me.

"I am, but I reserve the right to not answer any question that I don't like."

"Understood. Let's start with you. You said something about a pre-self and cloning. Please explain what's going on with that."

"I believe Lisa once told you that our group came here almost fourteen-hundred years ago."

I nodded and she continued.

"When we came, there were two hundred female volunteers for the program. There was also a group of scientists, technicians and workers: forty-two men and women.

This was a long-term project because of the difficulty of locating suitable subjects. The rarity of the genetic traits we are looking for in your population, plus finding a mate that is compatible, means that only about one in seventy-five million men is a suitable subject.

We needed to sustain our original group of scientists and volunteers for the duration of the project. We also needed to take back as many suitable offspring as possible. We couldn't afford to have children indiscriminately; the results are disastrous.

There was only one option. Every member of the project was cloned. First, this provides as many subjects as possible for the genetic re-seeding of El-yana. Secondly it eliminates the need for our group to procreate. Cloning gives us all the time we need to complete our project."

I thought for a moment before speaking.

"Matron, if the traits are so rare, why keep groups of yourselves here on Earth? Why not just open a portal every few years and take the DNA back through?"

"Doorways like you came through are difficult to create. It can take a quantum computer months to complete the calculations to locate a doorway. It also takes significant energy to then expose that doorway to our dimension. Once exposed, we leave it in place. Leaving it in place requires no energy.

Doorways between universes are different. The calculations take much longer, and the energies required are much higher. Once we create a door like that, we can't leave it open for long. It's not like the smaller doors. The energy requirements are just too great.

Our best option was to come, wait, clone ourselves, and collect what we needed as we found it. We will return when we have all of the genes we need."

"Matron, why are you answering my questions? Every time we've spoken before, you told me very little. Why tell me now? What's changed?"

"That's very perceptive of you Mr. Fury. Things have changed. The Abomination is watching you. They've let you know they are watching. Why?"

"Matron, I honestly don't know."

"Mr. Fury, There are only a few possibilities."

The Matron lifted her right hand and held up a finger. "They want to know what you know." She raised a second finger, "they want to take something you have." She extended a third finger, "They want to make you do something for them." She extended her fourth finger, "They want to kill you."

The Matron lowered her hand and wiped it on a napkin as she continued. "Mr. Fury, I'm telling you this because you need to understand what it is we're asking you to protect. What's at risk is not only our lives, but our cloned selves, our cloned offspring, and our ability to return home with the DNA that can save our planet."

I leaned forward to ask my next question. "About that, the length of time needed for your project and the rarity of the traits you're after. The fact that two different species, from two different universes just happen to be genetically similar enough to crossbreed...something doesn't add up. What is it you're not telling me?"

The Matron leaned back in her chair with her hands folded in her lap.

"Mr. Fury, my mood has changed. I'm done answering questions. We need to deal with the current problem. Tell me about the events of the last few days. I need to know everything."

I thought about withholding my answers until the Matron answered all of my questions, but I gave in and related everything from when I was taken to the U.S. Marshal's office to when I left the FBI safe house.

After hearing the story, the Matron leaned forward. She bit her lower lip. She looked as though she had something to say but couldn't quite get it out.

Lisa jumped into the conversation. "Matron, Chad, if I may. We can't know what the Abomination wants unless they tell us. And there's only one person here they *might* tell. Chad, you've got to let the Abomination find you. Find out what they want."

"No, I don't *have* to. I could run away from this entire mess. Just a little over an hour ago I was in Las Vegas. You have the ability to send me and anyone else you choose to any place on this planet. Why not just send me, my mother, and my uncle to here, or someplace out of the way? You can go back to your private little feud and I'll live out a peaceful and quiet life."

I sat back in my chair and waited for the Matron's answer.

"Chad." The Matron leaned forward. She looked at Lisa, then at me. "Chad, you can't be serious. I'm worried about Earth and El-yana!"

I smelled something. There was a hint of onion-like odor. I couldn't be sure if the smell was part of normal bakery odors, or if she'd just told a lie. I watched her carefully trying to discern signs of deception.

The Matron continued, "If the Abomination get our books and our technology then think of what that would mean to you and your planet.

They naturally have the ability to control people with their voices, but add to that the ability to open portals and travel instantaneously to anywhere on the globe…they would be unstoppable. You've met three of them. There is nothing redeemable in any of them!"

I knew she was right. They were dangerous to the Sisterhood and to humanity. I had to do something. At the very least I had to find out what they were up to.

I looked the Matron in the eyes. "Tell me, how do I find out what they want?"

The Matron reached over and touched my hand across the table. "Chad, you let them find you. When they find you, they will tell you. Then, you tell us."

"Sure, I'll tell you, *if* I'm still alive."

Lisa chimed in, "Chad, they want you alive. At least for now."

I pulled my hand away from the Matron's. "OK, ladies, I'm in. What do I do?"

Lisa put her hand on my shoulder. "Chad, go back to your apartment, and keep the life that we created for you."

"What do you mean by, *life we* created?"

Lisa squeezed my shoulder. "Chad, I picked your new name, Drake Edward Manning. The Matron and I influenced the Marshals to relocate you to Las Vegas. And didn't you think it's odd that a university would let you teach with only an undergraduate degree?"

Lisa's hand dropped from my shoulder and I stared at her. "Lisa, the university is letting me teach as long as I am working on a Master's degree."

"Exactly, Chad. Trust me; that is highly unusual. You have us to thank for that."

I sighed. "Well, what do I do now? Are you going to fix it for me so that I'm back in witness protection?"

The Matron spoke up quickly. "No. You will call Jim

Clayton and tell him you are out of the program. You're keeping your job and your identity as Drake Manning. But, you are not looking to them for any protection; you're out.

Then you'll call Agent Givens of the FBI. You will tell her the same thing, except that you will keep in touch and you will testify whenever asked.

After that, you'll wait. The Abomination will find you soon."

The Matron reached into her purse and pulled out a man's billfold. "Here. Take this. The arrangement is just like before. Inside the billfold you'll find a bank card and credit cards. The bank card and the credit cards have the name Drake Manning on them. We will maintain a balance of three hundred-thousand dollars in the bank account to use as needed while working for us.

Lisa, take him back, and keep us updated."

CHAPTER TWELVE

The world was on its side, spinning. That, plus the odors from the storm drain were enough to make me return the orange scone I had eaten. Lisa held my elbow. I wondered how anyone ever got used to the portals.

"Chad, we're going to have to get you acclimated to the portals. After all, you may need to use them to escape, and it would be best if you didn't require an hour to recover after each trip."

I nodded.

"Chad, do you think you can ride?"

I nodded again.

Lisa got onto the waiting motorcycle and I stumbled toward her. I got on behind her and held on, just hoping I was sitting upright. She started the bike and she drove us slowly down the tunnel continuing on in the direction we had started. After a few minutes the dizziness was gone and I was seeing light ahead of us piercing the dark tunnel.

We exited onto a flood channel; a concrete-lined gully that would guide flood waters out of the storm drains and into a reservoir somewhere in the distance. The motorcycle easily climbed the embankment and I saw familiar landscape. We were near Highway 95, not far from Fremont Street, the old Las Vegas Strip. The sun was high in the sky, it was almost noon. Lisa stopped the motorcycle.

"Chad, I'm taking you back to your apartment. Get a new cell phone, and call me when you get a chance. Here's the number you should use."

Lisa reached into her hip pocket and pulled out a little slip of paper and handed it to me. I put the paper in my hip pocket without looking at it.

Lisa continued driving us along the surface roads back to my apartment. It was about a forty minute drive before we were there. We both got off the bike.

"Lisa, would you like to come inside?"

"No, not this time. I have a lot to do for us to be ready. But watch yourself."

I nodded. I bent my neck slightly, tilted my head, and kissed her goodbye.

Lisa pulled away in surprise.

"Chad, I thought you didn't know how you feel about me?"

"I don't, entirely. But I know that I felt like doing that."

Lisa closed the distance between us. We kissed. She pulled her lips away from mine and leaned in close to my ear. She whispered, "Watch yourself, Dragon Boy, and call me."

"I will," I said in my most reassuring voice. "And you...don't be a stranger."

Lisa got on her motorcycle and I watched her drive away. I turned and took the stairs to my apartment, two steps at a time. At the top I walked to my door and inserted the key. The bolt turned and I entered.

Everything inside the apartment was just as I left it, except messier. It seems the FBI, or the Marshals, or some other arm of law enforcement had done a thorough job of rummaging through my things after I left. There was black powder on every solid surface. Displayed in the powdery residue were fingerprints; lots and lots of fingerprints.

I ran my forefinger through the black powder on my dining table. The powder stuck to my skin. I tried wiping my finger on my jeans. I now had a black streak across my leg and black powder still on my finger.

I went to the kitchen to wash my hands and plan out the rest of my day. I noticed my watch before I stuck my hand under the running water. It was twelve forty-five in the afternoon. I would have a full day of cleaning and straightening ahead of me, plus I needed to replace my cell phone and get my bag from my office at the university.

After washing my hands I pulled my car keys from my pocket and headed out of my apartment. I locked the door behind me and ran down the stairs. I trotted over to my black Ford Interceptor and opened the door. I let the door stand open for a minute to let the heat escape.

I sat on the hot leather seats, started the engine and closed the door. I drove toward the shopping mall and along the way I found a store with the name of my phone company. I pulled into the lot, parked and went inside.

I wasted no time selecting a new phone; I simply asked for the best they had and put it on the Sisterhood's credit card.

As soon as the phone was activated I retreated to a quiet corner of the store to make my first call. I dialed a number that I did not need to look up. The phone was answered on the fourth ring, "This is Deputy Jim Clayton."

"Jim, it's Drake."

A string of profanity came through the phone. I pulled it away from my ear, held it out in front of my face and just stared. I was awestruck that the device wasn't melting as Jim's colorful language poured into the atmosphere.

When the profanity stopped, I put the phone back to my ear and spoke. "Listen, Jim. I can't do this…the whole witness protection thing."

"Damn it, Manning! What *the hell* do you think you're

doing? People who leave WITSEC *die*, and it usually doesn't take them long to do it!"

"Jim, I'm not safe anywhere. Anyone trying to protect me is at risk. I'm better off doing this alone."

"Drake! You're out of your mind! If you go back to being Chad, you're done."

"Jim, I'm going to keep being Drake Manning. I'm going to keep my job and my apartment. I'm just not relying on the Marshals or the FBI to keep me safe."

We argued on for a while, but in the end Jim Clayton gave up. He said he would call the local FBI office and let them know what I had decided.

I made a call to Uncle Allan and told him everything that had been happening. He didn't like me working with the Sisterhood. It had always been his opinion that the Sisterhood shouldn't be trusted. I couldn't disagree, but I also didn't see any options. His only real observation was that I had developed a knack for getting in over my head. He also volunteered to keep an eye on my mother.

I chose not to call mom. Talking to her was difficult. I had never told her about the Sisterhood or what they had done to me. She didn't know anything about what had happened other than I had met a girl named Lisa, and her friend had been brutally murdered. She also knew that I had been a suspect because Lisa's friend had been driving my car the night she was murdered.

There were a lot of other details Mom didn't know, like exactly how I had made contacts with human traffickers and an arms dealer. But she did know that I had been part of a sting against those people, and as a result, a deal had been made to clear my name.

But, there were just too many awkward details I would have to fill in if I were to call mom, so I didn't. Instead, I left the phone store and headed to the university to collect my things and return to my apartment.

The rest of the day was uneventful. I unpacked my bag, cleaned and straightened my apartment, and spent a lot of time thinking. I had nothing but questions that seemed to have no answer.

CHAPTER THIRTEEN

More than a week had passed since I left the FBI safe house. It was eight days earlier that I had eaten scones in London with a younger version of the Matron. Since then, absolutely nothing important had happened.

I finished buttoning my shirt and then filled my pockets with the essentials I kept on my dresser. That included my keys, billfold, some loose change, nail clippers and a Swiss Army-style pocket knife.

There was a new essential I had: my transresinator. I opened my sock drawer and pulled it out from behind a small pile of socks at the back of the drawer.

I placed the transresinator in the backpack which I kept on the floor, at the end of my dresser. I threw the backpack over my shoulder and headed for the apartment door. I stepped outside, pulled the door to, and turned the key in the lock. It was then I thought I heard someone running down the stairs.

By the time I got to the stairs, there was no one in sight. I sniffed the air. I caught the scent of perspiration, but not burnt cinnamon. Whoever had been there was human, all human.

I surveyed my surroundings before descending the steps. I had the feeling I was being watched, and shook it off. I told myself aloud, "It's just your imagination, Chad. You can't help but be edgy. A full week's passed and nothing's happened." That only made the paranoia worse.

It was Monday, and I normally take the bus to work on Mondays. I only drive my car only Fridays because traffic is lighter and I can get a decent parking spot. I hesitated and considered breaking my routine.

If I was being watched, then being predictable would only make me an easier target. Then again, if I wanted answers I didn't want to make it too difficult for The Company to get to me. I chose to stick to my routine.

The bus ride was totally normal, but somehow I couldn't shake the feeling something bad was about to happen. I had that feeling all day, in each of my classes. And, I wish I could say that my day was normal and it was all in my head, but I couldn't.

My first class was General Chemistry. And for some reason the text book had chosen to put discussions of electron orbital hybridizations and electron spins in the last few chapters of the book.

I began the class the same way I always did. "Alright, ladies and gentlemen. Everyone was supposed to have read chapter twenty-seven, so let's start with your questions about the reading. What questions do you have?"

I didn't even have to look her direction to know young little Stacey Adams would be the first one to throw out a question. She was smart, there was no debating that, but I was never quite sure why she asked so many questions. I rarely felt like it was because she wanted answers. I was never sure if she was flirting or she just liked to hear herself talk.

"Doctor Manning…"

"Please, Stacey, I've told you before. I don't have my Ph.D. It's Mister Manning."

Stacey shifted in her seat. She blinked her big brown

eyes in the middle of her brown face.

"Mr. Manning, then, just how does a quantum computer work?"

I froze. I think even my heart stopped beating. I sniffed the air, checking for signs of burnt cinnamon. I wondered, was the Abomination using my students? I was definitely going to find out.

I walked over to Stacey and looked as closely at her arms as possible without being too obvious. There were no cuts. That was a slight relief, but only slight. That didn't mean they weren't controlling her.

I walked past Stacey and around the perimeter of the room.

"Class, how many of you have the same question from the reading?"

Not a soul raised a hand.

"Miss Adams, no one else has the same question. So, let's keep the discussion to this week's chapter."

"But Mister Manning, it is in the chapter, page five hundred thirty-seven."

I returned to the front of the room, took the text book, and turned to page five hundred thirty-seven. There in the middle of the page was a section on quantum computers.

"My apologies Miss Adams, I had forgotten that this was in this chapter. But I can see how it ties in with discussions of electron spin and orbital hybridization.

Who in here is also taking computer classes?"

About one-third of the hands went up. I pointed to Barry Scranton, a bright young man who is usually very silent in my classes.

"Barry, tell us how a normal computer works. How does it store information in memory?"

Barry cleared his throat and stuttered more than a little.

"Uhm…well, the cohm, computer uses transistors. E…each wa..one or zero ih, ih, is an elec trical charge."

I felt sorry for Barry, so I took over.

"Exactly. The presence or absence of an electrical

charge represents a one or a zero.

In a quantum computer the information is represented by the quantum states of subatomic particles."

I looked across the room and saw twenty-five blank faces. I continued on, hoping that something I was saying would start making sense.

"What subatomic particle do you think might be used for a quantum computer?"

I saw nothing but blank faces.

"Come on people…what's this chapter of the book about?"

A timid voice sounded from the back of the room, "electrons?"

"Exactly. Electrons are unique. A single electron is both a particle and a wave. It is not a particle that behaves like a wave, and it is not a wave that behaves like a particle. It is both a particle and a wave at the same time.

As a particle, it has a spin. We can refer to the spin as being clockwise or counter clockwise. An electron can change the direction of its spin simply by flipping over. But, much like it is both a particle and a wave at the same time, its spin can be clockwise and counterclockwise at the same time. This is a fundamental concept in quantum mechanics."

I looked across the class and saw that I had lost all of them. There wasn't a single face that looked like there was any understanding of what I was saying. Rather than fight a futile battle of making them understand what I said was right, I forged on.

"A quantum computer makes use of the spin of the electron. By measuring the spin, there are three possible states that can be represented, a clockwise spin we will call a spin up, a counterclockwise spin we will call a spin down, and a state where the spin is both up and down at the same time.

Anyway, this is all verging on physics that is beyond the scope of this class. If you want to know more, research it on your own.

I think we need something to refocus our thoughts therefore, consider this. A proton walks into a bar. The proton says to the bartender, I want sixteen beers. The bartender says, that's a lot...are you sure you want sixteen beers. The proton says of course I'm sure, I'm positive."

My effort at humor was met with thunderous silence and blank stares. I gave up and moved on with my lecture.

CHAPTER FOURTEEN

Teaching my classes that entire Monday had been a waste of time and effort. I was either talking over everyone's head, or I was just so distracted and paranoid that I couldn't connect with any of my students. I was a mess. If something was going to happen, I wished it would go ahead and happen quickly. But then again, what is it people often say? Be careful what you wish for?

I walked out of my office at four thirty-five that afternoon and headed for the bus stop with my backpack hanging from my shoulders. It wasn't a bad walk, only about half a mile to the east of the campus.

As I approached the bus stop I noticed a young man in a black tee-shirt and blue jeans. The man seemed to be looking around nervously. As I got closer I saw that his arms were covered in tattoos down to his wrists, and there were a number of metal piercings in his ears and eyebrows. He looked like he was not much more than eighteen and he was somehow out of place in this part of Vegas.

The breeze was blowing the man's scent my direction. I sniffed the air for signs of burnt cinnamon, but what I caught instead was the same perspiration that I had smelled that morning outside my apartment. I braced myself for whatever might be coming.

I took a few more steps and positioned myself in the shade under the bus stop shelter. The young man looked furtively a couple of times to his left and right, and then spoke to me.

"Is your name Chad Fury?"

"That depends. Who's asking?"

I shifted my weight to my right leg which was closest to him.

The young man looked at me with menacing brown eyes, "I want your backpack and everything in your pockets."

"Just keep wanting, fella. What you don't want is the trouble it's going to take to get it."

I took my eyes off of his eyes just long enough to see motion in his right hand. He gave his wrist a flick and the handle of a butterfly knife swung open to reveal a double-edged blade. With a second smooth motion the knife turned in his palm and his fist closed around the handle. The blade was pointed toward the ground leaving his thumb near the base of the handle.

The way the young man held the knife spoke volumes; he had no intention of threatening me, his goal was to hurt me. People who hold a knife with the point out are sometimes trying to threaten and scare their opponent. But anyone who holds a knife in a fist, with the blade pointed down means to do real damage. From this position he could throw punches at me and let the blade slice and hack along the way.

I kept my eyes on the man's hands. People will tell you not to take your eyes off of your opponent's eyes in a fight, but that's for ring fighting. On the street it's different; keeping your eyes on your assailant's weapon can give you an advantage. It makes you look untrained, weak, and afraid; that's something you can use.

I raised my palms up to my shoulders and said, "Easy

now, fella. Let's talk this through."

The young man remained silent and took a step with his left foot. I knew what was coming next and gave him one last warning.

"Put the knife away and go back home…you don't want to do this."

To my surprise he froze and started speaking in flat, almost robotic tones. "I have to. Ladon told me to kill Chad Fury, and now I have to."

As soon as he stopped speaking, he moved again. He took a step with his right foot and threw his punch. I turned to my left to avoid his fist and blade.

I grabbed his wrist with my left hand and his forearm with my right. I pulled his arm close to my chest. My right shoulder was closest to his body. I kept a tight grip on his wrist with my left hand and I released my right hand. I raised my right elbow even with his face and pulled my arms apart hard. My right elbow struck the man's nose. The pull of my left arm, plus a rotation, sent the man to the ground.

The young man laid on the sidewalk, on his back, with his nose bleeding. He continued gripping the knife in his fist. I stepped hard on his wrist. His hand opened and I kicked the blade into the street.

I backed up three or four steps giving him the opportunity to change his mind and leave. I hadn't noticed that he wasn't alone. I backed up to something cold and hard against the back of my skull. A male voice spoke from behind me.

"Yo, tough guy. You gonna die."

I hoped I could buy myself a few seconds by playing the coward. I put my hands up next to my ears and tried to sound scared as I said, "Please don't hurt me!"

I made a quick turn to my right. As I turned, my right hand pushed the gun away from my head. As I completed the turn, the palm of my right hand was over the slide of the pistol. I gripped it tight.

My left hand found the man's wrist and locked on. I pulled his wrist toward my chest with my left hand, and pushed away with my right. The pistol broke free from his grip and I sent my fist and the gun directly into his dark brown face. Blood spurted from his lips and a look of shock registered in his eyes.

My left arm pushed the man's wrist up over his shoulder, and I continued the motion downward behind his back. His knees bent and he went down hard, on his back.

I stepped back three steps, tapped the bottom of the gun's magazine, pulled the slide to ensure a bullet was chambered and pointed the gun at the man. I yelled out, "Stay on the ground!"

At that same moment a black car pulled up with a siren sounding and lights flashing. A blonde woman in plain clothes got out, pulled a pistol and started speaking in a very authoritative voice, "Put the gun down! You're all under arrest!"

I bent my knees and using just two fingers I carefully placed the pistol on the ground. I stood up again, slowly.

The blonde woman walked around the front of the car with her pistol pointed in the general direction of the three of us. She didn't ask any questions, she just said, "Don't anybody move. You move, and I shoot."

She stood silently there at the front of her car, pointing her weapon at us for about three or four minutes until a blue and white cruiser showed up and came to a stop behind the black car.

Two of Las Vegas' uniformed finest stepped out of the cruiser and headed our direction. They pulled out their handcuffs and cuffed the two men on the ground. The woman lowered her pistol and spoke. "I'll follow you two to the station. I'll take Drake Manning with me."

She looked me in the eyes, "Get in the front seat."

I went to the car, put my backpack on the floor of the front seat, and sat down in the passenger side. I left the door open because of the heat.

As I sat in the car and waited. I watched the woman talking with the uniformed officers. Her features had softened and her posture relaxed.

"Thank you for getting here so quickly," she said to the men.

The taller of the two answered, "No problem, ma'am. We were close by. Is there anything you can tell us for our report?"

"Not much, I'll fill you in at the station. Just make sure you send a copy of your report over to the Bureau. I'll need to add your report to my paperwork."

Both men nodded and started putting my two new acquaintances in the back of their cruiser. That's when I noticed details about the men. Both of them looked to be between 18 and 22 years old. Both were dressed the same; blue jeans and black tee-shirts. Both had their arms covered in tattoos, both had a black, ace of spades tattooed on their right forearm. Both had three silver rings piercing their right eyebrow.

The woman sat down in the driver's seat, and I closed my door. She closed her door, started the car and fastened her seatbelt. She turned her head my direction before speaking. "Drake Manning, I'm Special Agent Sandra Ellis with the FBI."

"You got here very quickly."

"You've been under surveillance."

"I see." I leaned back in the seat, "Well, I suppose that you'll want to know…"

Special Agent Ellis cut me off in mid-sentence, "Please don't. Don't say anything. I don't want the paperwork to be any more complicated. If you say anything, I'll just have to write it up in my report."

"OK, then." I nodded my head at her. I sat there, she sat staring at me, and the car just sat there.

"Well?" she asked.

"Well what?"

"Well?"

"Uh…Thank you?"

"You're welcome. And?"

I screwed up my face as I answered back, "And what?"

"Your seat belt. I'm not going anywhere 'til you put it on."

"Oh. I'm sorry." I reached with my left arm, took hold of the buckle, pulled it across my body and fastened it. As soon as the buckle clicked, we were on our way.

It was only a short fifteen minute drive down Highway 15 to the police station. Special Agent Ellis pulled the car around to the back of the building and parked the car in a handicapped space near the door. She shut off the engine and I just sat and stared at her.

"What?" she said.

I continued to stare with my mouth open.

"It's OK, Manning. Nobody's going to give *me* a ticket. Besides, I'm not planning on being here very long."

Agent Ellis unfastened her seatbelt and opened the car door. I did the same. I followed her through the glass doors into a waiting area.

There was a rectangular piece of glass in the wall directly ahead of us. Behind the glass was a uniformed officer sitting at a desk. He appeared to be typing something into a computer.

My escort walked to the glass and rapped on it with her knuckles. The man looked up briefly and then back down to his computer monitor.

"What can I do for you." The man spoke in a flat, emotionless tone, it was not a question.

Agent Ellis reached into the hip pocket of her grey slacks and pulled out a thin black wallet. She opened the wallet and pressed it against the glass.

"I'm Special Agent Sandra Ellis. FBI. A couple of officers brought in two men just a few minutes ago. I've got Drake Manning with me. You should be expecting us."

The man behind the glass never took his eyes off of the

computer monitor. He seemed to be speaking to the computer screen and not us.

"Agent, Ellis, is it?"

"Yes."

"Go through the door on your right, straight down the hall to room seven. You can leave your prisoner there."

I didn't like the word prisoner and I let him know it. "Hey, I'm not the one under arrest, I…"

Agent Ellis waved me off, "Let it go, Manning. You'll be OK. Nobody's arresting you."

The door to our right buzzed. Agent Ellis pulled the door open and we stepped through. As we passed the man at the desk on our left, he spoke up loudly.

"Agent Ellis. Stop back here on your way out. I'll need your signature on the paperwork."

"Sure thing," she said without breaking her stride.

We walked almost all the way to the end of the hall before seeing a door with the number seven painted on it. Agent Ellis opened the door and held it open. I went inside.

The room was an interrogation room, similar to one I had occupied last year in Oklahoma. There was a table with four chairs, and one wall was a mirror starting from four feet off of the floor, reaching to the ceiling.

I walked over to a chair facing the mirror, dropped my backpack on the floor, and took a seat. Agent Ellis stood in the doorway.

"Manning, you're on your own now. I'm headed back to the Bureau. Someone will be in to talk with you later."

Agent Ellis closed the door and left me there alone. I was sure my being left alone was unusual, but then again, why would I expect anything to be usual?

I looked at my watch, frequently. I sat there for a little less than fifteen minutes, but it seemed four times as long.

At last the door opened. Deputy Marshal, Jim Clayton stepped though the doorway and came to my side of the table. I sat there, looked up into his face and said, "Well, this is unexpected."

Officer Clayton pinched the material on his trouser leg and tugged it slightly as he took a seat on the table top. I wondered if he was just being casual, or if this was so that he could look down on me.

"Drake, I told you that it wasn't smart to be out on your own. You could have been killed!"

"Look, I'm OK." I spread my arms for effect.

Officer Clayton shook his head. "Right. Sure you are. And next time it will be more men after you, or a drive by shooting, or who knows what? But what I want to know right now is, what do you have to do with the G. B.s?"

"Aren't they a music group from the seventies?"

Officer Clayton screwed up his face and stared at me for a couple of seconds.

"Same letters, wrong order. G. B.s, not Bee Gees. G. B. is short for Gangland Boys. What do you know about them, Drake?"

"Absolutely nothing. I've never heard of them before in my life. And, I've never seen those two guys before today. So, what's a B. G.?"

Officer Clayton put his left hand on the table and leaned for support.

"That's G. B. Like I just told you, it's short for Gangland Boys. They're a hybrid gang."

"Hybrid gang? You're just making that up."

"No. Hybrid gangs started showing up in the eighties. They're a cross between the gangs of the thirties and forties and the street gangs of today. Street gangs have geographical boundaries. They stick to their neighborhoods. By default they're made up of members with the same ethnic and social backgrounds.

Hybrid gangs have mixed ethnic and social backgrounds, and they don't have territories and hoods. They consist of men and some women from all ethnic groups and social backgrounds. They're usually between eighteen and thirty years old, and they all have special skills the gang finds useful.

Some members of the hybrid gangs are enforcers, they're skilled fighters and good with guns and knives. They also have thieves, con artists, hackers, and couriers they call runners.

The hybrid gangs do what they do for money. They run cons, they extort businesses for protection money, they sell drugs, and they dabble in the sex trade. They also hire out their runners to organized crime."

"What's all this got to do with me?"

"That's what I want to know, Drake. What *do* they have to do with you? What did they say to you? Did they say why they were after you?"

"The guy with the knife said Ladon told him to kill me, and now he had to."

"Who is Ladon? What do you know about him?"

"I've never heard the name before."

"OK, Drake. I'm strongly suggesting that you let the FBI put you in a safe house until we get you out of Vegas with a new identity."

"No. I'm not going. It won't change anything."

Officer Clayton's mouth opened slightly, and his eyes widened.

"Drake Manning. You get that idea out of your head right now!"

"What?"

"I've seen that kind of look before. I can tell by the look on your face that you think you're going after the G. B.s to take care of this yourself!"

"So what if I am? You can't protect me. Nobody can. And, I either wait for somebody to do me in, or I go after them myself. You tell me, which is better?"

"Damn it, Manning! You're not using the brains God gave a crowbar!"

"Am I free to go, or are you going to lock me up?"

"I should lock you up for your own safety, but I can't. Go home. Think about it for a while. Call me when you're ready to leave Vegas. In the meantime, we're still going to watch you."

CHAPTER FIFTEEN

I had taken the bus home from the police station. During the bus ride I called Lisa. Since I was being watched by the Marshals, the FBI, and whomever the Abomination had following me, Lisa suggested I meet her for breakfast. That's why I found myself at six a.m. on Tuesday morning, sitting in a well-worn booth at The Dollar Diner, about four miles east of the university.

I had passed by the place a couple of times but never gone inside. As I sipped a very bad cup of coffee and looked at my surroundings, I congratulated myself on my good taste for never having come in here up to this moment.

The diner was old and so were the wait staff and the clientele. There was grease in the crevices of the yellowing linoleum tiles that was probably older than me.

I waited impatiently and looked at my watch wondering when Lisa would show. My waitress came by twice to take my order, and twice I had told her I was waiting for someone.

It had now been a full fifty minutes since I sat down, and still no Lisa. Bee, my waitress, came by a third time to warm my coffee and check on me. She made a little conversation as she poured the black liquid from a pot.

"Listen, handsome, you should go ahead and order now. I think you've been stood up. Although I can't imagine why any young thing would stand you up. If I was just two years younger, there's not another woman around who would stand a chance."

I smiled and chuckled, "Really, two years younger? Why two?"

"Because," she leaned a little closer, "two years ago I would have been called a cougar for chasing after a gorgeous thing like you. Now they'd just call me a crazy old woman."

I laughed at her joke.

"Well, maybe if I was just two years older, then…"

"Listen, are you going to sit there flapping your jaw, or are you going to order? You sit there much longer and I'll have to seat you with the Romeo Club."

"The what?"

"The Romeo Club. It's that group of shriveled old men near the front door. They call themselves the Romeo Club. It stands for Real Old Men Eating Out."

"Oh, I see. Well, I don't want that. I'll have the biscuits and gravy, and two eggs over medium."

"Coming up."

Bee turned, wiggled her behind once for effect, looked over her shoulder and winked. Somewhere between the bad coffee and that display, I lost my appetite.

A few minutes later Bee was bringing my order. As she sat the plate in front of me Lisa came sliding into the booth. Bee looked at Lisa, then at me and said "Well, that's disappointing."

"What?" I replied.

"From the looks of her," Bee nodded toward Lisa, "I don't stand a chance. Well, at least I can dream."

Lisa screwed up her face at me, "What's that all about, Chad?"

"Oh nothing. Just maybe early onset dementia. Anyway, where were you? What took you so long?"

"I was making sure we were safe. There's a black car outside with two FBI agents watching the front door. I snooped around. I couldn't tell if there's anyone else watching you. So, fill me in, Chad. Tell me about yesterday."

I told Lisa every detail. I stopped part way through the story when Bee came back to the table and Lisa ordered a cinnamon roll and coffee.

I finally finished the story and waited for Lisa to put in her two cents worth. Her face was gim, "Chad, what do you think?"

"Me? I was waiting for you to have some big plan, just like last year. Remember? You always seemed to know what to do about everything, and the plan always started with a shopping trip."

"Well, this is different. Last year I was trying to help you hide. This time you're…well…you're bait. It sounds to me like the fish are nibbling and you're finding the hook uncomfortable."

"You're dammed right I'm uncomfortable!"

I had unintentionally raised my voice, and heads around us turned. I sank back into my seat and went silent.

Bee walked up carrying a pot of coffee. She poured a little into our cups while she sang, "Love on the rocks, ain't no big surprise, pour me a drink and I'll tell you some lies…"

When Bee left, I continued, "Lisa, I've *been* fishing. I can't tell you the number of times the fish got away. And come to think of it, it never mattered whether I caught the fish or not, the bait *always* died."

"What are you trying to tell me, Chad? You want out? You want to take your chances on the run?"

"No. Running's no good. Neither is sitting and waiting for only God-knows-what to happen. I want to change the rules of the game, and I'd like a little help."

"What does that mean?"

"It means, Lisa, I want to track down the G. B.s and find the person who told them to kill me."

"I don't know, Chad. If you can be patient, they *will* come to you."

"Oh, they'll come alright. And when they do, they'll have their trap set. I'll be like a caged animal and everything will be happening on *their* terms. I won't have a snowball's chance of getting out alive and telling anyone what they're up to."

Lisa leaned back in silence. She sat there a moment. She opened her mouth like she was going to speak, and then closed it. She leaned forward.

"You want to find the Gangland Boys. You said you need help. What do you need from me?"

"I don't know enough about the gang to be able to find them. The only people that know something are the police. The police are not going to answer any of my questions. You, on the other hand, could walk into the police station, ask your questions, and they would tell you. I need you to find out where to start looking."

Lisa frowned at me, "I don't know, Chad. That's not the way the Sisterhood usually does things."

"That's right, they don't. They let themselves be bait, and then they send out a monster to hunt down the hunters. People die. And just where has that gotten the Sisterhood?"

"OK, Chad. I'll look into it. I'll see you at your office later today, say four-thirty?"

"That's fine."

"Chad. You leave and I'll pay the check. I need to stay behind to make sure nobody in here remembers us."

As I walked out the front door I heard the high-pitched whistle of the El-yanin. I paused a moment and walked on.

In the parking lot, I noticed a familiar looking black car. I was feeling a little mischievous, so I walked over to the black sedan where a man and a woman were sitting in the front seat. I tapped on the driver's side window until it rolled down.

I bent down to view a man I had never seen before sitting behind the wheel. Across from him was Special Agent Sandra Ellis.

"Special Agent Ellis, what a pleasant surprise."

Agent Ellis glared at me, "Manning! What the *hell* are you doing?"

"I just had breakfast. You should try the biscuits and gravy. And make sure you're at one of Bee's tables. She's one really hot cougar. I'm into that sort of thing, if you didn't know."

The car window rolled up as I continued talking, so I figured I had overstayed my welcome. I headed off to my car, got in, and made my way toward the university.

CHAPTER SIXTEEN

Tuesday's classes were normal, except for my own distractions and anxieties. Fortunately, finals were approaching, and this was the last week of actual classes. That meant I needed very little preparation of new material and I was spending most of my class time reviewing what would be on the final exams.

Four-thirty came and went, and there was a distinct absence of Lisa. Another five minutes passed and my desk phone rang. I answered it.

"Hello, this is Drake Manning. How can I help you?"

There was a pause.

"Chad, it's Lisa. I've got information, but I can't meet you right now."

"Why, what's up? Is everything OK?"

"I'm not sure, Chad. Something's going on at your office building. One of the FBI agents from this morning is watching the building. I've spotted three of the Gangland Boys prowling around campus, and there are some other people who just look out of place."

"Are you safe, Lisa?"

"I am, but you need to watch yourself."

"OK. I will. We'll meet up when you feel it's safe."

I had no sooner hung up my phone when there was a knock on my door. As I looked up from my desk I saw a face I had seen all semester, carefully peering through the doorway.

Stacey Adams bit her bottom lip and stood silently in the doorway. She had a cell phone in her right hand, and a single earbud in her right ear. The left earbud dangled freely in front of her.

"Come in, Miss Adams. What can I do for you?"

"Mr. Manning, I need to talk to you. Do you have a few minutes?"

"I think I can spare a little time. Please sit down."

I remained seated as Stacey Adams crossed the threshold and closed the door behind her. She quickly took a seat in front of my desk, facing me.

Having a female student in my office with the door closed was something I tried to avoid. I got up from my desk and crossed to the door. As I reached for the handle Stacey said, "Mr. Fury, leave the door closed."

I turned and stared in shock at the sound of my real name coming from one of my students. I stood by the door a moment before I spoke again.

"What's this about? And, why did you call me 'Mr. Fury'?"

"Don't be naïve. My name is Ladon. I'm speaking to Stacey Adams through her cell phone, and she's repeating what I have to say. The phone's camera is showing me your every move. Now please take a seat. We need to talk."

I returned to my desk and seated myself uncomfortably.

I sat across from Stacey as she held the phone's camera toward me and spoke. "Mr. Fury. I'm the one who's been poking you with a sharp, pointy stick."

"I don't understand."

"Don't play games, Chad. You understand more than

you're letting on. You understand at least a few things. You're just acting cautious because you're in an unfamiliar situation."

"I take it you're the Ladon who sent the Gangland Boys after me?"

"I'm also the man who put the pictures in your apartment, and who has created the situation you're in right now."

"Just what exactly is the situation I'm in right now?"

"That's what we need to talk about. You don't fully comprehend the magnitude of what's taking place. You have a lot to learn about the El-yanin, The Company, and humanity."

"So, fill me in; enlighten me."

"Not here, not now. I've been leaving you clues to follow, but I get bored easily. I've decided not to drag this out any longer. Come to my place, tonight, at eight."

"And just where is your place, Ladon?"

"I assume you're familiar with the Old Strip on Fremont Street."

"I am."

"The last decent place on the east end of the strip is the Old Chicago Hotel and Casino. Go there. Go to the casino entrance facing Fremont. My men will greet you."

"And if I decide not to go?"

Stacey Adams stood up from her chair and crossed around my desk to the window behind me. I stood up and moved away to give her access.

Stacey faced the window, dropped her phone, and placed her palms flat against the glass with her arms above her head.

A second later three shots rang out. There were sounds of breaking glass and Stacey's knees buckled. She crumpled toward the floor.

I lunged toward her, and my hand caught her in the middle of her back. I lowered her gently to the carpet. I could feel warm wet liquid on my hand beneath her. The front of her blouse was being soaked with dark red blood.

"I'm calling for help!" I looked at Stacey, there was no sign in her eyes that she comprehended anything. Her eyes were nothing more than dark orbs focused on something far away.

I pulled my hand from beneath her, reached to my desk phone and dialed 911, and placed the phone on speaker.

A dispassionate voice came through the speaker, "911, what is your emergency?"

"I'm at Las Vegas University; a student's been shot!"

I gave my name and all of the particulars to the operator as I knelt over Stacey and put pressure on her wounds. The blood flowed freely around my hands, and there was nothing I could do to stop what was happening.

I was still talking to the 911 operator, and kneeling over Stacey when I heard a voice commanding me, "Get back."

The voice had come from the man who had been in the car with Agent Ellis earlier that morning. He came toward me while pulling out a pair of surgical gloves from a pocket. As I backed up, he took a position over Stacey and began applying pressure on her wounds.

My eyes caught the man's eyes, and he shook his head slowly from side to side. I backed up a couple of steps and just stared at the scene.

From that point forward, my little office began filling up with people. First came two campus police officers, followed closely by four paramedics with a gurney.

I stepped out of my office and into the hallway to give everyone room to work. I took a position near the door and let my shoulders fall back against the wall; my head hit the wall with a thud. I closed my eyes and just stood there.

I don't know how long I was there, but my solitude was broken by a gentle baritone voice and light pressure on my right shoulder.

"Drake, can you tell me what happened here?"

I opened my eyes to see Jim Clayton staring into my face.

"Officer Clayton, Jim. I…don't know, exactly…"

"Drake, that young lady in there was shot. I'm assuming they were gunning for you and got her instead."

"No. That's not it. She was shot to send me a message."

"Chad you need to tell me everything that happened. But first, where's the restroom?"

I gestured, "Down the hall, on your right."

Officer Clayton just stood there until I spoke up, "Well?"

"I don't need the restroom, you do. Look at your hands, Drake."

I looked down at my hands. They were covered with Stacey's blood. I turned silently and headed toward the men's room. Jim Clayton followed.

Inside the men's room I took a position behind a sink and began working on removing the blood from my hands. I became light-headed and swallowed hard as I watched the water in the sink turn red and swirl gently down the drain.

Jim leaned against the sink to my left and started pumping me for information. "OK, Drake. Who is that girl, and what was she doing in your office?"

"Her name is Stacey Adams. She's one of my students. She showed up at my door. I wasn't expecting her. She had her phone in her hand and only one earbud in her ear. Ladon was on the other end of the phone."

I continued scrubbing my hands.

"Drake. Are you telling me this, Ladon person, was talking to Stacey over the cell phone and she was relaying to you what he was saying?"

"Yes. That's right." I started scraping the red beneath my nails under the stream of water.

"What did Ladon want?"

"He wants me to meet him somewhere. Tonight. At eight."

"So, she delivered the message and then?"

I stopped scrubbing. I turned off the water and pulled a paper towel from the dispenser.

"Oh my God, Jim! I asked what would happen if I refused to meet him. Stacey got up from her chair, stood in front of the window with her palms against the glass, and was shot!"

I wiped my hands and threw the paper towel in the trash can next to me.

"Drake, you need to come back to WITSEC. Let us move you to a new city. You need a new identity."

"No." I shook my head, "That won't help. This will just start all over again, only somewhere else."

"Drake, just what do you think you're going to do? What options do you have, really?"

I looked at Jim. His mouth opened slightly and his eyes widened.

"Drake! No! You can't consider meeting this, Ladon. You'll end up dead."

"And just what *are* my choices? He'll keep sending people after me. Who knows what he'll do next?"

Jim and I argued for a while, and I finally just left. As I exited then men's room I saw a gurney being wheeled out of my office. The body on the gurney was completely covered with a sheet. I turned my back to the scene and went down the stairs at the other end of the hall.

As I descended the stairs, I looked at my watch. I couldn't believe the time. If I was going to meet Ladon, I had to leave now.

CHAPTER SEVENTEEN

Fremont Street is always full of people in the evenings, and this Tuesday night was no different. I moved slowly through the crush of people and street performers until I was standing outside the entrance of the Old Chicago Hotel and Casino.

Three people sailed overhead on the zip lines beneath the giant video canopy covering the street. Part of me wanted to run away, but I knew the only way to end this was to go through it.

My legs were heavy, like lead. But, I forced my knees to bend and my legs to move me toward the Casino entrance. As soon as I crossed the threshold, two men in pinstripe suits and matching fedoras came up to me. The smell of burnt cinnamon reeked from them. One of the men said, "Mr. Fury, follow us."

The men turned and I followed. I hadn't taken more than four steps when two more men in pinstripe suits took up positions behind me. A few more steps later and two more men came. Each one took a place on either side of me.

Six men, all in pinstripe suits and fedoras, reeking of

burnt cinnamon, formed a tight circle around me. We moved as a single unit, winding our way through the casino, around the crap tables and past rows of slot machines. We worked our way through the crush of people drinking and gambling; winning and losing their hard earned cash.

It wasn't long before the red carpet beneath my feet gave way to pale, nearly white marble. My surroundings had changed; gone were the massive chandeliers, the brass fixtures, the dark-wooden gaming tables, and the casino noises. Surrounding me now were marble floors and walls forming a broad walkway leading to the hotel, restaurants, and shops.

What had not changed was the number of people. We had left the mass of people in the casino only to find ourselves swimming in a stream of humanity flowing in opposing currents. The people around us seemed to instinctively move aside and let us pass wherever we wanted to go.

We passed an alcove of elevators decorated with a sign reading, "Capone Tower". There was a picture of Al Capone at the back of the alcove and some kind of verbiage that I didn't have time to read.

A little further along we passed a glassed-in patio featuring a central swimming pool with marble statues around the edge. It was dark outside and the patio was filled with swirling colored lights and people drinking and dancing to very loud music.

We passed the hotel lobby filled with lines of people, most with baggage, waiting to talk to someone behind the counter. The décor was similar to the casino, with all of the brass, red carpet, and dark-wood furniture. The hotel staff were dressed in pinstripe suits and fedoras.

We passed another alcove of elevators, this one was marked as the "Dillinger Tower." The hallway took us past the gift shops and high-end clothing stores. Soon we were at the entrance of "Valentine's Steakhouse." The young girl at the front stepped aside as our group entered without so much as slowing our pace by a single step.

We pushed on toward the back of the restaurant and into a banquet room. As we entered the room, two of my escorts dropped off and closed the doors behind us. The two men remained at the doors and stood a silent guard on the interior of the room. The remaining four men propelled me forward, past empty tables, and up to a solitary table in the center of the room.

A solitary man sat at the table. I took in the sight of the lone man seated behind the white tablecloth with a centerpiece of rosebuds and a single white candle.

The man at the table appeared to be in his late fifties or early sixties. His mostly gray hair was cut short and parted on one side. His eyebrows were in the latter stages of transitioning from dark brown to gray.

The man's face was long and thin. His eyes were blue-gray, sitting above dark shadows. His nose was sharp and pointed, making a statement of its own above thin, narrow lips.

His right hand was grasping a glass of blood-red wine. Long, thin fingers curled around the bulb of the glass. The man didn't smile, his face was nearly expressionless. He didn't make a single sound. He merely gave a slight nod and the remainder of my entourage separated, backing away and taking positions several feet from the table.

I stood there, looking at the man, just waiting. He looked me up and down a moment before breaking the silence with a mature baritone voice.

The words came out slowly, in an odd cadence. "Mr. Fury. I...am Ladon. Please be...seated."

The man used his wine glass to gesture toward the chair closest to me. I seated myself and Ladon continued speaking.

"I'm pleased to see that you arrived on time. I'm also pleased to see that there are blood stains on your shirt. That means you took me seriously. You didn't waste any time getting here. What I can conclude from these facts is that my conditioning of you is working. I have you *almost* exactly where I want you. After this evening you will comply with whatever I say."

"Cut the theatrics, Ladon. I'm here. What do you want?"

"What, indeed? I want a great many things, some of which I will reveal tonight, and some I will tell you later."

"Why not tell me everything now?"

"Because, Mr. Fury, my boy, I've spent a great deal of time poking you with a very sharp stick. I've been learning how you react to different stimuli. I have just a little more poking to do tonight, before you are ready to hear everything.

But there's something else you need to know. I don't only deal in punishments, I deal in rewards. You are to be rewarded for arriving on time. I've taken the liberty of ordering your meal for you."

Ladon sat the wine glass down, raised his right hand, and snapped his fingers. Before he could lower his arm, one of the six men who had escorted me was standing at his side. The man put his hand on Ladon's shoulder and bent slightly to look into his face. Ladon looked back into the man's face as he crossed his left arm over his chest and patted the man's hand.

"Adolf, be a dear. We're ready for our meals."

The man replied, "Yes, Ladon," and backed away.

As Adolf left I cleared my throat, "Well, that was…well…creepy."

Ladon looked at me and frowned, "You're far too quick to pass judgment. Adolf is my son. What you saw was fatherly affection and nurturing."

"Uh, no. What I saw was creepy; I don't care who you are."

Ladon leaned forward, "After tonight, my dear boy, you *will* reserve your tongue. Very soon you will acknowledge *me* as your master, and *you* will be my very willing and humble servant."

As Ladon leaned back in his chair, a woman in black slacks and a white shirt came to the table with a bottle of wine and a glass. She sat the glass in front of me, uncorked the bottle, filled my glass, and sat the bottle on the table. She backed away from the table without a sound.

"Drink up Mr. Fury."

I pushed the glass away from me and sat back in my chair. "I prefer to drink with friends."

"Don't be that way. For the moment, you are in no danger. You've not eaten anything for several hours. It's been a stressful day for you. You may as well take a moment and relax."

I exhaled a puff of air in disgust, "Normal people don't just turn off the stress and relax at will. You're damned right I'm stressed. And I don't want anything from you except information. I want to know why I'm here."

"In due time, Mr. Fury. You may not want to eat, but I do."

With that, two women in black slacks and white shirts appeared with our plates. One of the women placed one of the plates in front of me. On the plate was a large, delicious looking portion of prime rib. The juices from the meat were running across the plate and touching several stalks of asparagus topped with a white sauce. The remaining space on the plate was taken up by a huge baked potato.

"I hope you enjoy your meal, Chad. This is, quite frankly, one of the best steaks in all of Nevada."

I pushed the plate away from me, leaned back in my chair, and folded my hands in my lap. Ladon looked at me, took his knife and fork, and cut into his steak. He put a bite in his mouth and chewed. I watched him eat in silence.

After he had consumed half of his plate, Ladon refilled his wine glass. He held it with the stem between his fingers. He took a sip of wine, swallowed, and said, "Mr. Fury, Chad. What do you know of the group you call the

'Sisterhood'?"

"I know what I've been told."

"And what pray tell is that? That they came here about fourteen-hundred years ago? I'm assuming you know they are after DNA; traits that they claim will save their race and their planet."

"That's pretty much it."

Ladon looked into his wine glass, and then looked at me, "Chad. Have you never wondered about the probabilities, the odds? The odds that a species, not only from another planet, but an entirely different universe could stumble across a different race, and the two races could mate; interbreed?"

"I have, recently."

"Good. I was beginning to think you were a complete dullard. So, what are the odds?"

"I don't know the numbers, but it has to be astronomical; nearly impossible."

"Let me tell you about the El-yanin. I expect you to sniff the air as I talk; I know you can quite literally smell a lie. Stop me if you smell anything that indicates I'm lying."

"Alright. Go ahead."

"Well, Chad, the women you know as the Sisterhood came to Earth fourteen-hundred years ago, but other El-yanin came here in Earth's pre-history."

"I don't understand. If their planet is dying, how can they carry out a plan that lasts tens of thousands of years?"

"Time, Chad. That's the key."

"You're telling me that they're time travelers?"

"No. Not in the sense that they can pop around though time and space like popular science fiction.

Time is a river flowing through the entire universe. You can swim against the current, but ultimately you are swept along with it. The river of time carries you forward, always forward."

"Ladon, what are you telling me?"

"If you want to travel through time, you must leave the

river. If time were a river, you could go to the shore, walk along the bank, and enter the river at any point.

But, there is no riverbank. There are only entire universes sitting side by side, each with its own river of time flowing at its own unique rate. If you could leave this universe, you could enter another at any point in its timeline."

"OK, so what's this got to do with anything? Why are you telling me this?"

"Chad. The El-yanin project is only a few years long from the perspective of their universe."

"Cut to the chase, Ladon. Why is any of this important? Why did you have me come here? What does any of this have to do with me?"

"Alright, Chad, here it is. The El-yanin realized they were dying and needed new genes introduced into their race to survive. It's just like the cheetah. Here on Earth, it's endangered because there's not enough genetic diversity in its population."

"I understand that. Go on."

"The El-yanin came here in Earth's ancient pre-history. They found a planet they could exploit. They modified the environment to favor the mammals. They introduced their DNA into the apes and created the species of man. They killed off the Cro-Magnons to favor the rise of the Homo sapiens. I'm saying that there's been nothing natural about human evolution. Earth's evolutionary history has been one giant, carefully controlled experiment. And now, we're approaching the end of that experiment."

I sat there, considering what Ladon was telling me. He was asking me to believe a lot. One thing was obvious; he believed it. But just because he believed it, that didn't make it true.

Ladon looked at me with what might have been a little bewilderment. "Chad, do you not understand what I'm telling you?"

"Sure. I understand, we're here because of them. But

where's the big crisis? Why is this so upsetting to you?"

"Let me tell you why. What is it that you do when you end an experiment? You clean up the mess and put everything away. Their plans are to clean up the Earth and not leave any trace of their activity behind."

"Ladon, now you have my attention. Why would they cleanse the Earth, and how would they do it?"

"In order for the traits they needed to appear naturally, they had to re-create their own species, or at least something very close to it. That's why we are so much alike. They made man in their image. They also gave humans an intellect; an ability for science and scientific advancement. Eventually humans will create quantum computers and gain technology equal to the El-yanin. The El-yanin want humans gone before they become a threat.

This is how they will cleanse the Earth. They will destroy the Higgs boson. I'm sure you've heard of the Higgs boson.

Some of your scientists have called the Higgs boson 'the God particle.' It's the quantum particle that holds all matter together. Destroy it, and the atom it is in becomes a tiny nuclear bomb. Just imagine if every molecule of water on the planet went nuclear."

I was having a difficult time comprehending what he was saying. All I could do was ask, "Ladon, you're telling me that when they leave they are going to do what?"

"Chad. Here is what will happen. Before they leave they need the books we have. The books are songs. The songs are the interface to their quantum computers. Just like you would type into a keyboard, they sing to control their computers.

To find the books, they are going to unleash the monsters they have created. They call the monsters, 'protectors'. That's what they tried to do with you; to make you into a half-man, half-animal monster. But, of course, you know that.

After they make a creature, they send it after us. Then

they put the creature in stasis. They freeze it.

When they are ready, they will thaw out their creatures and let them loose on every continent to hunt us down. They will follow after those creatures and look for the books.

I'm not entirely certain they need the books. It may be that all they need is for us to be out of the way so that we can't stop what's next. In either case, they will unleash *hundreds* of monsters on this planet.

After they take us out of the picture, they will open portals back to El-yana. The quantum computers will remain behind with a program running. The program will destabilize the Higgs boson in the Earth's oceans. The planet will burn as every molecule of water becomes a tiny nuclear bomb."

"Ladon, last year two of the Sisterhood came to my uncle's house to take Kane and deliver Eric. One of them, Carlee, told me that they had helped me because my interests and theirs ran in concert. She said that one day they would not and we would be enemies. Is this what she was talking about?"

"It probably was, Chad."

"What you're telling me is that you, the Abomination, The Company, or whatever you call yourselves are the only hope for humanity?"

Ladon leaned forward and his eyes narrowed.

"Chad, we offer humanity a chance to live."

"Ladon, what are *your* plans? How do you stop this, and what happens after you do?"

"We will take their technology from them. We will use it as we see fit. We will keep the women around as breeding stock. And we will step onto the stage of this world as its gods."

"I see, nothing *too* ambitious."

"We are, and will be, gods to all humanity. We will open portals to other planets and rule over those worlds as well."

"And where do I fit into all of this?"

"You my young friend are a mistake, a happy accident if you will."

Ladon swirled the wine in his glass as he continued, "Chad, you killed one of their creatures with your bare hands. We want you, or more precisely, your abilities. We want to understand how you came to be. When we understand it, and duplicate it; we will add those abilities to ourselves. We will be stronger, faster, and able to kill their creatures with our bare hands."

I gave Ladon my best look of contempt as I lowered my voice to answer. "Do you really expect me to willingly let you experiment on me?"

Ladon leaned forward and smiled, "I expect that and *much* more. You will join our stables. We will breed you with the El-yanin women. And, when you're not doing that, you will work for us, running our errands and killing whatever needs to be killed."

I couldn't believe what I was hearing. It took a moment for my mouth to close and words to come back to my mind. I leaned forward and shook my head, "Ladon, you are seriously messed-up if you think I'll go along with any of that."

"You will, and much, much more. But first, it's time to introduce you to another pointy stick."

Ladon raised his right hand and snapped his fingers. Adolf retuned and looked Ladon in the eyes.

"Adolf, be a good son. It's time for the laptop."

Adolf backed away several feet before turning and leaving the room.

"You see, Chad, that's respect. That's what I expect out of all of my children and my servants. When you leave the presence of a god, you back away. You never show disrespect by turning your back toward your god. Soon you will do the same."

I just sat there. I had no words to throw out to a man who honestly expected to be treated like a god.

Ladon sat there too, alternately swirling the wine in his glass and taking another small sip. Soon Adolf returned following two women in white shirts and black slacks. The ladies cleared the table and Adolf sat a laptop computer on the table in front of Ladon. Ladon nodded and Adolf backed away.

Ladon opened the lid of the computer and typed a few times on the keyboard before turning the machine where I could view it. "Here, Chad, take a look."

I looked at the screen. There was my name at the top and a familiar series of numbers after it. Filling the screen were columns of numbers.

"That Mr. Fury, is your bank account. Your account number, your balance, and all of your transactions."

Ladon reached out and touched the keyboard.

"Next we have your credit card statement."

Ladon typed another key.

"This is you standing in front of your apartment."

Ladon continued hitting keys and changing the image. He showed me pictures of myself teaching my classes, sparring at the gym, and other images of me doing all of the things I do in an average day.

"What's the point, Ladon?"

"The point is, that I know everything you do. I've been watching you for a long time. I have control of your life. I can get to you at any time I wish. And, it's not just *your* life I'm holding in the palm of my hand."

Ladon reached up and hit the keyboard again.

"This is your mother, standing in front of her house. She's watering her flowers."

My blood boiled when I saw the picture. Anger filled my voice and I didn't want to hide it. "Leave my mother out of this!"

Ladon smiled. He touched another key, "And this is your uncle."

The next several pictures alternated between Uncle Allan and my mother. Like the pictures of me, they were doing very normal things.

Ladon closed the laptop and stood up. The six men, including Adolf, returned and surrounded the table. Ladon handed the laptop to Adolf and spoke to him. "Adolf, is the demonstration ready?"

"Yes, father. She is."

"Good. Please lead the way to the penthouse."

Ladon looked at me, turned his palm up, and flicked his fingers indicating that I was to get up from my chair. I complied.

We walked across the room as a group and exited through the swinging doors to the kitchen. We passed through the kitchen to a service hallway. From there we walked down a cinderblock hall and past gray metal doors until we came to a service elevator. We all stepped inside.

Adolf pushed the top button on the panel and the car groaned as it began to move. It was about a fifteen second ride to the top. The car stopped and the doors opened to an alcove.

Our party exited as a single unit, passed out of the alcove and turned right. We walked down a red carpeted hallway to a black door at the end. Adolf slid a key card through the lock. The lock clicked and Adolf opened the door.

CHAPTER EIGHTEEN

Inside the penthouse I was led to the main room; a living area decorated in black and white and silver. There was a distinct absence of color except for a few decorative items placed on glass top tables and a couple of pieces of artwork on the walls.

The eight of us stood in a circle between the black leather sofa and the fireplace. Ladon had positioned himself directly in front of the fireplace. He pulled out a pack of cigarettes from the inside pocket of his suit jacket. He tapped the top of the packet against the palm of his left hand and a couple of cigarettes protruded from the top of the foil pack. Ladon removed one of the white sticks from its brothers and placed it between his lips. He produced an antique silver lighter from his jacket pocket.

Ladon looked my direction, pulled the cigarette from his lips and laughed, "Chad, can you believe it? I almost asked if you minded if I smoked! How ridiculous of me."

Ladon returned the cigarette to his lips, lit it, and inhaled deeply. He exhaled and pushed a gray cloud into the center of the room as he locked his cold gaze on me.

"Chad, I brought you here for a little demonstration.

Adolf will now bring our guest while I set the stage.

What you need to understand is that I have a very active and limitless imagination. He took a drag on his cigarette. I also have none of the ethical and moral weaknesses that you and so many humans have. With my imagination, ethical freedom, and the vocal talents equal to the El-yanin I have no limits in how I can bring pain, suffering, and death. I have the freedom and power of a god!"

I had no motivation to hold my tongue. "My God gives life. You only take life and your parlor tricks don't work on me! If you had the power to truly create anything, then I *might* be impressed."

Ladon chuckled, "Chad, my boy, you've stumbled upon what this is all about. With what you are going to take for us, with the abilities you have that we will make our own, we will be both destroyers and creators. Our godhood will be complete."

Adolf returned, leading someone to the center of the circle. It was Special Agent, Sandra Ellis. Sandra's hands were bound with a leather strap, and she was gagged with something I had never seen before. It was a black leather cord with a black rubber ball wedged in her mouth.

Sandra's lower lip was split. There was dried blood on her upper lip that had come from her nose. Her face was starting to show fresh bruising. There was blood on her white blouse. Her black slacks terminated in bare feet.

I glared at Ladon, "You sick, son-of-a..."

Ladon cut me off, "Now Chad, you can't call me anything I haven't heard before. And besides, my boys here wanted to have a little fun. Why should I deny my own children a few simple pleasures?"

With a nod from Ladon, Adolf released Sandra's hands and removed the ball gag. Sandra coughed and shook her arms to return the flow of blood to her hands. She took in the faces in the room before speaking.

"I'm an agent with the FBI. You've all made a horrible

mistake!"

The group laughed and Ladon spoke.

"Chad, now you're going to understand my special powers and abilities. I don't need to point a gun. I don't need to get my hands dirty with a knife. I don't have much use for poisons or explosives. I can accomplish everything I want by uttering just a few simple words. Just imagine your mother or uncle getting a phone call from me."

Ladon flicked his cigarette into the fireplace and then put his focus on Sandra Ellis. He gazed at her in silence for a few seconds. I heard the high pitched whistle of the El-yanin voice as he spoke, "Sandra Ellis. You are on fire. You're burning to death."

I heard Sandra inhale and fill her lungs to their capacity. There was no mistaking what was coming next. Sandra's voice shattered the air. She screamed at the top of her lungs as she beat her arms, legs, and chest with the palms of her hands. She dropped to the floor and rolled around trying to extinguish the flames that no one else could see or feel.

I yelled, "Ladon! Stop it! Stop it now!"

Ladon and the other spectators stood laughing as I continued yelling for this to stop. Sandra rolled on the floor, screaming.

What happened next was pure instinct. There was no planning and no forethought. I must have moved so fast that my own mind had to catch up with what was happening.

I found myself standing behind Ladon. His left wrist was in my left hand, and was pushed up between his shoulder blades. My right hand was crossed in front of him and I had a grip on his throat. I could see that my hand was red and scaly. The claws of my hand were pressing on his throat near the carotid arteries.

My voice came out through clenched teeth, "Put a stop to this! Now!"

My demand went unanswered.

"Ladon! Put a stop to this now, or I'll rip out your throat!"

I saw the men in the circle drawing guns and pointing them my direction. I yelled out, "If anyone fires, I rip out his throat!"

I felt the muscles in Ladon's throat tighten. I heard the whistle while the words passed through his lips, "Sandra, you're OK. Everything is fine. You're not burning."

Sandra stopped rolling on the floor. She gasped and coughed a few times. She pulled herself slowly to her hands and knees. She looked at her arms, and looked at her surroundings.

I called out, "Sandra! You're OK. Get their guns. We need to get out of here!"

Sandra shook her head, and slowly stood to her feet. She looked my direction. Her gaze became fixed on Ladon and me. She stood there staring as if she was trying to understand what she was seeing.

I called out again, "Sandra! Get their guns. We've got to go! Now!"

Sandra made a noise, sort of a grunt, and nodded. She went to the man to my right, took his gun from his hands and placed it under her waistband, against her spine. She moved to the second man, took the gun, removed the clip and dropped it on the white carpet. She hit the release and pulled the slide and barrel from the pistol and let the pieces fall. It was a scene she repeated around the circle.

When she finished with the last man, I asked Ladon, "What's the best way out of here?"

Ladon rasped, "The service elevator; the way we came."

I smelled onions, I knew he was lying. I also knew what we needed to do.

Sandra looked at me, at my hands, and at Ladon. She asked me, "Now what?"

"Now we leave."

I kept my grip on Ladon. I turned and backed through

the room toward the door, dragging Ladon along. Ladon made a few noises and with each noise I pushed his left arm up between his shoulder blades.

Sandra reached the door first and held it open. I backed through with Ladon in tow, followed by Sandra. Sandra closed the door quickly and blurted out, "Which way to the service elevator?"

"We're not going that way. Ladon lied. We won't make it out if we do that."

"Lying? How do you know?"

"I smelled onions. I'll explain later."

As I backed up, I gave Ladon's wrist a little twist, "Which way to the elevators?"

He rasped softly, "Down the hall, first left."

As we backed up a few more steps, the penthouse door opened and out came Adolf followed by his companions. We continued down the hall, and on toward the public elevator. Ladon's men followed, but kept their distance. Out of the corner of my eye I saw that Sandra Ellis had pulled the gun from her waistband and was pointing it in the general direction of Adolf and party. That explained why they were keeping their distance.

We made it to the elevators. Sandra pushed the button, and we waited. While we waited, I watched the group of six following us leave in pairs. Soon only Adolf and one other man remained. Adolf glared at us, "You won't make it out of here, Fury."

Ladon answered, "Keep calm, son. I'm fine. He's not going to kill me. He thinks he needs me as a shield."

I put a little added pressure on Ladon's wrist and he winced as I barked out, "Shut up!"

A bell chimed and the elevator doors opened behind us. The three of us entered the car. As the door began to close, a set of fingers caught the edge of the doors from the outside. Sandra hit the fingers with the butt of the gun. I heard Adolf yelp. The doors closed and the car started to descend from the fortieth floor. Sandra pushed the button for the ground floor.

Sandra was staring at my hand as I held Ladon's throat. She spoke without taking her eyes off of my hand, "What are we going to do? They'll be waiting at the bottom."

"I know. I don't think we should be there."

I looked over Ladon's shoulder and at the panel of buttons. There was a large oblong button marked "Tower Bridge".

"Ladon, what's that, the Tower Bridge button?"

Ladon hesitated and answered, "There's a walkway on the fourth floor. It connects the Dillinger and Capone towers."

I quickly blurted out, "Sandra, push it. We'll get off and take the bridge to the other tower."

Sandra pushed the button. The car began to slow as we approached the twenty-seventh floor. The doors opened to reveal two young women and their dates facing us. The black haired woman started to get on; her tall blonde friend reached his hand out and stopped her. When she saw us, she screamed and jumped back. The doors closed and we continued down.

"Sandra, when we get to the fourth floor, I'll go out first. Ladon's men are likely to be there. Whatever happens, keep your gun trained on Ladon. If you have the urge to shoot anybody, make sure it's him."

Sandra nodded in agreement and the elevator slowed as we approached the fourth floor. The car stopped, and the doors opened to reveal three men in pinstriped suits waiting with pistols drawn.

I changed the grip I had on Ladon. I grabbed his suit collar with my left hand and his waistband with my right. With a sufficient hold on him, I pushed him forward, hard, as I stepped off the elevator. Ladon went crashing into the two men to my left. I spun hard to my right and took hold of the gun arm of the third man.

I had the man's wrist in my left hand and the top of the gun barrel in my right. I pushed both of my arms toward the side of his head. As the man's wrist came close to his ear, the gun broke free of his grasp. I kept my grip on his wrist and pulled his arm back over his shoulder and down toward the ground. The man followed his wrist and landed on the ground. My right foot found his right knee, and I heard a disturbing snap as I stepped down on it, hard.

As the man cried out in pain, I turned toward the other two men. Sandra had left the elevator and was pointing her gun at the two men lying on their backs. Ladon was lying across them. Sandra was barking, "Don't move! Stay down!"

The men's guns were on the floor, and I kicked them away. I put the gun I was holding into my waistband. I pulled Ladon to his feet, removed his belt and used it to tie his hands behind his back. I did the same with the other three men.

Sandra relaxed her grip on her pistol and asked, "Is it Chad or Drake?"

"Chad will do."

"Well, Chad, go call the police. I'll stay here."

"Nothing doing."

"OK, you stay and I'll call."

"No. Is your memory that short? Do you not remember what happened in the penthouse just a little while ago?"

"I, well, I...I don't understand. How did they do that?"

"Ladon and his *family* can tell anyone anything and make them believe it."

Sandra looked curiously at the men and then at me.

"Chad. How is that possible?"

"I'll explain later. But, for right now, if the police come, Ladon and his men will end up as free as if nothing ever happened."

"What do we do?"

"We get out of here."

"How?"

I pointed to my right, "Like this. See that window over

there? I think it looks down over the street."

I took the gun from my waistband and pointed it toward the window. I fired four shots through the glass. This wasn't the movies, so the glass didn't shatter and rain down in shards. Instead there were four holes with break lines radiating from the bullet holes like spiderwebs.

I picked up the trash can next to the elevators, walked over to the window and used it to break out the glass.

I walked back to the elevator and pushed the down button.

"Now, Sandra, we wait."

When the elevator arrived, Sandra and I dragged the four men into the car. I pushed the button for the lobby, and exited the car back onto the fourth floor.

"What was that all about, Chad?"

"They'll think we went out through the window."

"That's ridiculous. We're four stories up."

"For most people, yes. But, you saw my hands. My feet do the same thing. They know I've climbed up and down walls before."

"You're nuts. But we still need to get out of here."

"Let's head to the other tower. We will find the elevator, then we will make our way out through the casino."

We ran down the hallway and followed the signs to the Capone tower. When we reached the elevator bank I pushed the button and waited. We didn't have to wait long.

When the car arrived I got in first. Sandra stood outside for a moment, and I saw her hand reach up to the wall. A second later alarms were going off, and lights were flashing in the hallway.

Sandra jumped into the elevator, the doors closed and we started moving down before I pushed the button.

"What did you do, Sandra?"

"I pulled the fire alarm. That ought to create enough confusion for us to get out of here."

In about ten seconds we were on the ground floor. The elevator doors opened. We stepped out and into a river of humanity sweeping us along into the casino and out onto Fremont street.

CHAPTER NINETEEN

The light from my cell phone illuminated the surroundings just enough to ward off total darkness. Sandra Ellis sat against the concrete wall of the storm sewer and sobbed. I supposed that this was a natural reaction to her mind trying to make sense of what had happened to her.

After making our way onto Fremont Street, Sandra and I had argued for a moment about what to do next. She wanted to go to the police station, but I told her she needed to get out of Las Vegas.

When I saw that I wasn't going to win the argument, I grabbed her wrist and dragged her along the street to the nearest manhole cover. I inserted a claw into the slot in the round plate, lifted the cover, and made Sandra climb down through the opening.

Sandra had demanded explanations and I tried to explain, but it didn't seem to help. I tried putting a hand on her shoulder, but she recoiled against the concrete wall.

I had given up trying to comfort her, and now my priority was getting Sandra out of Vegas. I made a call to Lisa, she answered on the fifth ring.

"Lisa, it's Chad. I need your help."

"Chad, do you know what time it is? Why are you calling?"

"Uh, not exactly, I'm guessing it's after midnight, and I just told you, I need help."

"What happened to you, Chad? Why didn't you call me? What went on at the university? Is everything OK?"

"Uh…I'll try to take all of that in order. I couldn't call because I was being held by Ladon. A student was murdered in my office. And no, everything's not OK.

I'm in the storm sewer beneath Fremont Street. I need to get to London. But I don't have the transresinator; it's in my office, in my desk, in the top-left drawer. Would you please bring it to me?"

"Why don't you have the transresinator? I told you to keep it with you at all times. If you'd just listened to me then…"

I cut Lisa off sharply, "Lisa, let's not do this now! I'll explain everything later. Just come to the portal and bring the transresinator. I'll listen for your motorcycle and come find you. Please, I need you."

I ended the call and turned my attention back to Sandra Ellis. She had stopped sobbing and was sitting with her shoulders against the wall, looking at me. I walked over and sat next to her.

She started asking questions again, "What's going on, Chad?"

"Let's try this a different way. You didn't like my explanation, so what do you think happened?"

"I…well…I was drugged."

"OK, you were drugged. Who did it? When, and how? And, are you still drugged?"

Sandra blinked in the dim light from the phone, "No. I'm not drugged, but…I don't know. I just want to wake up. I want this all to be some horrific nightmare."

I reached over and put my hand on the back of her hand, resting on her knee. This time she didn't recoil. She turned her head and looked at me.

I spoke softly, "Tell me what happened to you. I only know what I saw in the room."

Sandra closed her eyes and let her head rest against the wall. She was silent and pursed her lips for a few seconds.

"Alright, Chad. I was in the car with Sean, my partner. We were at the campus, sitting in the parking lot. We had followed you from the diner.

A man came to my car window. He knocked. I rolled the window down. The man told Sean to stay in the car, and me to get out. I did. I did everything I was told. I didn't want to, I just had to."

I squeezed Sandra's hand gently, "They can do that. They can make you do whatever they want by just speaking."

Sandra inhaled deeply and continued, "The man drove me to the hotel. I was taken up to the room and…and they…"

"I know they beat you."

"They did more. They…I'm…too ashamed. They told me to…I let…them…use me. I didn't want to."

"I know. Like I said, they can make anyone do anything."

She opened her eyes and looked at me, "But you? Why weren't they making you do things?"

"I'm the only one they can't control with their voice. I was there because they were threatening me. They made it clear they would kill me, and people around me, if I didn't come."

We continued talking, and she asked questions about me and my situation. I told her, but I don't think she believed me. She was polite and didn't question my explanation too forcefully.

It was an hour before we heard the sounds of a motorcycle ringing through the tunnel. I helped Sandra to her feet and we walked toward the sound. In a few minutes we saw a light and Lisa slowly pulled up to us. She stopped, dismounted and walked up to us.

She gave me a quick hug and backed up a step. She looked us over before speaking.

"Chad, I'm glad to see you're alright. What's going on?"

"It's a long story."

"I'm sure it is, and I've got time."

"Oh, Lisa, this is Special Agent Sandra Ellis."

Sandra stuck out her right hand toward Lisa, "Glad to meet you."

Lisa took her hand, "We've met."

Sandra screwed up her face, "No, I'd remember."

Lisa let go of Sandra's hand, "No, we've met, and you wouldn't remember."

Before the conversation could continue, Lisa turned away and went to the rear of her motorcycle. She opened a pouch by the seat and pulled something out. She walked back to me and handed me a familiar small glass cube.

"Chad," Lisa looked at me very seriously, "Keep the transresinator with you at all times. I mean it."

I replied back, "I know, but everything happened too fast for me to think about grabbing it."

Sandra butted in, "What are the two of you talking about?"

"This." I held out the cube in the light of motorcycle's headlight.

"And that would be?" Sandra asked.

I sighed, "Another long story which will have to wait. Right now we need to get you to safety."

Lisa put a hand on my arm, "Chad, wait. You mentioned London on the phone. You're not planning on taking Sandra to the Sisterhood, are you?"

"Yes I am."

"Chad, you can't. They won't do it. They're not a rescue mission for wayward Federal Agents."

"If they want my help, they will. Maybe they could get her to an Embassy or something."

Sandra piped up, "London? Do you mean England?"

Lisa and I ignored her.

"Chad," Lisa hesitated, "OK. But you stay. I'll take her. The authorities may want to talk to you, and Ladon will probably try to contact you. You need to be here."

"Alright, but you will take care of her?"

"Yes. I'll take care of her."

Lisa looked at Sandra, "Are you up for a motorcycle ride?"

"If it gets me out of this smelly hole, sure."

"Hop on."

Lisa mounted the motorcycle, and Sandra got on behind her.

Lisa spoke before starting the bike, "Chad. Be careful. Call me when something happens."

"I will. You be careful. It's a long trip." I winked.

Lisa started the bike and headed forward a few yards. I heard Sandra yell as the bike turned toward the tunnel wall and disappeared into it.

CHAPTER TWENTY

It was nearly five-thirty in the morning when I finally laid my head on my pillow. I set the alarm on my phone for nine a.m. and hoped that whatever rest I could get would be enough. I turned over on my side, reached over to the nightstand, and dropped the phone just within reach of my fingertips.

I closed my eyes. My mind raced, replaying the events of the day. Genuine sleep proved itself to be elusive. It taunted me, running just ahead and calling back to me. My mind stumbled between awareness and slumber like a drunken man trying to walk a straight line.

Through the haze of semi-consciousness, I heard my cell phone ringing. I stretched my arm to retrieve the phone, blinked several times, and tried to read the caller ID in vain. I answered, "Hello."

I heard a soft, alto voice coming through the speaker announcing itself to be Ellen Chambers, the dean of the university. I shook off the sleep and gave as much sobriety as possible to the moment.

"Dean Chambers, what can I do for you?"

"Mr. Manning. I wanted this call to come from me, and

not Human Resources. Let me begin by saying how sorry I am for your situation. There's no way I can understand what you're going through and how this must be affecting you."

"Thank you, Dean. I appreciate that."

"Drake, the reason I called... You're being put on leave through the remainder of the semester."

"But, finals...I've got classes and..."

"And, Drake, you've been through something none of us can imagine. Your office is a crime scene. It's taped off and no one is allowed inside. Also, this whole affair is traumatic for your students as well as the entire campus. Counseling is being made available for your students and anyone else who wants it, including you."

"Thank you, but I'm alright. I need to take care of my classes."

"Drake. If you show up to give final exams, the students will want to talk. They will be distracted. This isn't a normal situation, and we shouldn't expect everything to suddenly return to normal.

I want you to call human resources today. They will give you instructions on how to schedule counseling through your medical benefits.

I want you to email your final exams to your department chair. We'll arrange to have your tests proctored."

"Thank you dean. I'll take care of it today."

The conversation ended with an awkward exchange of courtesies.

It was eight forty-seven. I made sure my alarms were off, returned my phone to the night stand, and laid my head back on my pillow.

When I opened my eyes again, I realized that I had been dreaming. I looked at my cell phone and saw that it was almost noon.

As I sat on the edge of the bed I tried to recall the details of my dream. It was a dream I hadn't had since the day I had gotten the dragon tattoo. It started exactly the same as back then. I was a dragon. I ran through green fields. I was with a pack of dragons. I fought with the other dragons to become the leader of my pack. Then the hunters came and I destroyed them.

But this time there was more. I returned to my pack, and there in the middle of my brother dragons was a woman in a brown robe. She held out something and I approached to inspect the thing she held in her hands. The thing was rectangular, and old looking. It was a book with a leather cover. I sniffed it.

The woman spoke to me in a soft melodic voice, "Find them. Find the books. Kill those hiding the books. Lead your brothers and bring me the books, my faithful servant, my protector."

As I thought about the dream I remembered what Ladon had told me about the El-yanin's project and plans. A sick ball of acid filled my stomach. Ladon had believed what he had told me; I had not smelled onions while he talked. But, that didn't mean it was necessarily true. All that meant was that he believed it.

I picked up the phone and called Lisa. On the sixth ring, a voice I knew better than most said, "Hello."

"Lisa, it's Chad."

"Hello, *Chad*." Lisa sounded a little irritated. "Sandra is fine. I'm getting her settled in and…"

I cut her off, "And that's not why I called."

"What's wrong?"

"Ladon's told me quite a lot, and I need to discuss it with the Matron. No, wait, not just her, but also whoever she reports to. I remember hearing something about a 'Grand Council'. I need to talk to them."

"Chad, you're out of your freakin' mind! No one makes that kind of a demand."

"Well, I do. I talk to them or I don't help them."

"What's this all about, Chad? Why the attitude?"

"Look, Lisa, Ladon told me a lot of stuff. I expected

him to lie, but he didn't. Everything he told me, he believes. But, that doesn't make it true. I need to know the truth."

"What could Ladon have possibly told you?"

"He…told me about…the history of the El-yanin, here, on Earth. He told me about their plans for leaving."

"What did he say?"

"No. Not over the phone. I'll tell the Grand Council. And, I'll tell you in person; face to face."

"OK, Chad. I'll try. And, I'll come back to Vegas as soon as I can."

We said our goodbyes and I put down the phone.

I was tense and decided a workout might help. I packed a bag, put on some clothes, and headed for the gym.

When I arrived at Frank's Octagon, Frank and the gym staff greeted me like a long lost relative. They asked where I had been. They asked about the shooting on campus. And, to be quite honest, I liked the attention. I needed to believe that someone was interested in me and my well-being. I needed family, and this was the closest thing I had in Vegas.

A few minutes later I was changed, wearing fingerless gloves, and standing in front of a heavy punching bag. I looked at the bag suspended by its chain. I thought about what Ladon had told me, how the El-yanin had manipulated humanity's DNA. I got angry and threw a punch at the black vinyl. The 'thud' was, satisfying.

With each thought about the El-yanin, I delivered a series of blows in rapid succession.

Then my mind turned to Ladon. I thought about his threats against my mother and uncle. I hit the bag harder, and it started swinging. With each swing of the bag toward me, I threw a punch that stopped its forward motion and sent it back away from me again.

I remembered Stacy Adams dying in my office. I paused. I let my shoulders slump, and I felt a lump in my throat as I remembered her blood on my hands. I tensed up, made my hands into fists and hit the bag.

I thought about the scene with Special Agent, Sandra Ellis. I moved from angry to very angry and let myself slip over the edge into rage.

I attacked the bag with a ferocity I had never let myself experience before in my life. I poured my rage into the helpless bag.

I heard profanities slip through my lips as I abused the passive target of my wrath. An unplanned, explosive kick swung the bag nearly to the ceiling, and it was over. Calm began to flood my being.

When I stepped away from the bag I saw a group had gathered around me. Some were strangers, most were friends and staff at the gym. I felt a strong hand gently rest on my shoulder; I heard Frank's voice.

"Drake, are you OK? Is there anything you'd like to talk about?"

"I'm fine, Frank."

"No, you're not. That...what just happened...was, well...disturbing."

"I'm sorry. I didn't mean to cause a scene."

"It's OK. But, are you OK? Who's Ladon? And who's Sandra? And what's uh… 'El…ya-nan'?"

"Was I talking?"

"No. It was louder than talking. Drake, we're all your friends here. If there's anything you'd like to talk about, we're all here for you. All you have to do is ask."

"Listen, I appreciate that more than you could know. But you're better off not knowing about this."

"Drake. One thing I do know, finally, is why you refuse to get in the ring professionally. If you ever let go, you'd kill somebody."

I excused myself and headed off to change. I was just about finished putting on my street clothes when my cell phone rang. I answered and a raspy baritone came through the speaker, "Hello, Chad."

I let out a string of profanity.

"How nice to hear from you too, Chad."

"Ladon! What do you want?"

"We have some unfinished business. By the way, you really should have ripped out my throat. I would respect you much more if you had."

"That doesn't even make sense."

"No, I suppose not. However, you did surprise me. Even though things did not go exactly as planned, I still think I made my point. I did make my point, didn't I?"

"You did."

"Good. Then here's what's about to happen. There's a museum at the university: the National Atomic Testing Museum."

"Yes, I know it."

"You're going to buy a ticket. There's a small theater inside. You're going to be in the theater, alone, at two o'clock tomorrow. If you can't be there exactly at two, be early."

"Ladon, you…"

"Chad, before you get all belligerent, here are the rules. You disobey me, someone you love gets hurt. You fail to successfully carry out anything I tell you to do, and someone you love gets hurt. If you irritate me or make me angry, someone you love gets hurt. Do we have an understanding?"

"We do."

"Good. I *will* see you tomorrow."

I ended the call and headed home.

CHAPTER TWENTY-ONE

I looked at my watch; it was sixteen minutes before two as I walked up to the ticket counter at the National Atomic Testing Museum. The white-haired woman behind the glass looked up at me without smiling. I handed her a ten dollar bill and showed her my faculty ID. She handed me back my ticket and some change.

I left the ticket window, crossed over to my right and up a ramp to a white door with a chrome vertical bar for a handle. I pulled. The door opened and cold air rolled out over my body. I crossed the threshold and found myself standing in a room covered in gray carpeting. The gray walls caused the corners in the room to disappear and blend in with the shadows. Spotlights were placed just so as to draw attention to the exhibits on the walls.

I proceeded along the perimeter and glanced at the pictures. The photographs formed some kind of timeline leading to the develop.m.ent of the first atomic bomb.

I paused at the end of the timeline and stared at a list of names that ran from the ceiling to the floor. It was list of atomic tests that had been carried out since the first atomic explosion.

Although the surroundings were gray and bleak, it was interesting. I would like to have stayed if there had been time.

I continued on until I came to an alcove with two gray swinging doors. I pushed on the doors and entered a small theater. The room was covered with the same gray carpet. The seating was nothing more than benches covered in the same carpeting. The room probably couldn't accommodate more than twenty people.

At the back of the room were three men seated in the shadows. I couldn't make out their features. At the front was a solitary figure. The entire room smelled of burnt cinnamon. I spoke, "Hello Ladon."

The man at the front turned slightly, "Come sit here, Chad."

I walked to the front and sat. Ladon's face was grim; he was silent for a moment and then looked at his watch.

"It's one-fifty-five. I'm glad you showed up on time."

"What do you want, Ladon?"

"I want to give you an assignment, and I need to fill in a few details."

"I'm all ears."

"Alright then. I, we, The Company, want you to bring us a quantum computer."

"The Sisterhood's not going to let go of one very easily."

"You're not going to take it from the Sisterhood. I'm sending you after the Stone of Destiny."

"What's a Destiny Stone?"

"It's not the Destiny Stone, it's the Stone of Destiny."

"I say potato you say…"

"I say shut-up, Chad. You can hear much better with your mouth closed."

I gave Ladon a dirty look and he continued.

"Chad. The Stone of Destiny has a long and interesting history. When the El-yanin came to Earth long ago, they used quantum computers to redirect evolution on this planet. When they left, they left a quantum computer behind. It served as a beacon of sorts, to allow them to reopen a doorway here.

After the El-yanin returned, they lost track of that quantum computer. It was stolen, and it was venerated by superstitious people as a magical object.

To the people of the time it looked like an oblong sandstone block with a metal ring on each end so it could be carried. It's a little more than two feet long and just over fifteen inches tall. It weighs a little under three-hundred forty pounds."

"So, where is this hunk of rock now?"

"In the Tower of London, near the crown jewels..."

"You're out of your ever-loving gourd! I'm *not* breaking into the Tower of London."

"No, you're not. You didn't let me finish. The stone in the Tower of London is a fake. You can find pictures of the stone on the internet. I'm telling you so you that will know what you're after. It's also called the Coronation Stone.

The real stone was stolen long ago and lost. We have reason to believe that it was found and brought to the United States. We believe the military was studying it, just after the Second World War. But something happened and the stone was lost, again. You're going to find it and bring it to us."

"Why? I know you'll kill people if I don't, but, why do you want *this* stone?"

"I told you, it's a quantum computer. And it's one that's not currently in the possession of the El-yanin."

"Yes, but what are you going to do with it, Ladon? You've told me that if I help the Sisterhood, I'm killing humanity. What if I help you? What will you do with the stone? I'm not helping you if I don't know your plans."

Ladon leaned back, looked around the room, and sighed as he refocused his gaze on me.

"Very well. We will use the stone to make more

quantum computers, some of which will be very special. We will make computers that are the size of a grain of rice. Those computers will be more powerful than the computers sitting on people's desktops today. We will implant the computers under the skin of every person on Earth.

With a quantum computer inside each person, we will be able to control all of humanity. Humanity will become our spies and our army, doing our bidding at our every whim. They will be our slaves and they *will* worship us."

"That's insane. People will never let you, and you can't control enough people with your voice to make it happen."

"That's where you are wrong. We won't start by controlling all people, only governments. Every government wants to control its people, to varying degrees of course. But all government leaders feel the need to control people. And we will give the nations of this world the ability to control every person."

"People won't stand for it. They'll rebel. There will be civil wars."

"Once again, Chad, you fail to understand. We are going to solve every major problem people *think* they have today.

Each quantum computer will have its own identifying number. This will give each person on the planet a unique ID. The ID will be used with every financial transaction; it will eliminate identity theft.

Parents will want it because the quantum computer will be used with the global network to find the location of any person. There will be no more missing persons. No more children stolen. No more runaways disappearing and never being heard from again.

The police will want it. The identities and locations of criminals and terrorists will be immediately known.

And, there will be health benefits. The computer will monitor the vital signs of each person. If a person is having a heart attack or other life-threatening emergency, an ambulance will be called for them. Otherwise, their health will be monitored, and medications will be immediately prescribed without the need for a doctor's visit."

"Oh, my God, they will accept it."

"Yes, they will gladly throw away their freedoms and accept us as their gods in exchange for peace, safety, and prosperity."

"Chad, side with us, and humanity lives. Side with the El-yanin, and humanity dies. Refuse to work with me, and the people you love will suffer. Find, and bring me the stone."

"You'll have to give me more to start with than the military had it after World War II."

Ladon stood, turned toward the back of the theater and motioned for three men to come to the front. As they came down the aisle, there was enough light that I could make out their features. I recognized the man in the middle; I ground my teeth.

"Ladon, what is Sirhan Jadiddian doing here!"

I blurted it out, not as a question but as a statement of dismay and disgust.

Ladon grinned, "Chad, Sirhan is your first clue to the location of the stone. Among his various businesses he acquired things for his second-hand store. Often he bought the entire estates of the recently deceased.

One such estate came into his possession, and we believe that clues to the location of the stone are there, in the former belongings of one U.S. Army Colonel, Roger Evans.

All of Sirhan's assets were seized by the FBI, and will eventually be sold at auction. You need Sirhan's help to find the clues to the location of the stone.

After you're done with Sirhan, do with him as you will. I don't want him back."

Ladon turned to leave, and stopped. "Oh, I nearly

forgot," he said as he turned back toward me. He reached inside his suit coat, pulled out a cell phone and handed it to me.

"What's this?"

"That, Chad, is a cell phone. You will keep it with you at all times. I will be using it to track your location. I will occasionally turn on the microphone and listen in on your private conversations.

Whenever I call, you *will* answer."

I held the phone and watched Ladon leave. Sirhan stood next to me and laughed.

CHAPTER TWENTY-TWO

I had driven back to my apartment in silence with Sirhan in the passenger's seat. Well, the drive was almost silent. Sirhan tried to talk, but I ignored him. When ignoring him didn't work, I told him to shut up. To my surprise he didn't speak for the rest of the trip.

When we arrived at my apartment, I opened the door and shoved Sirhan Jadiddian through ahead of me. He stumbled, but managed not to fall. I turned on the lights and pointed toward my sofa. Sirhan moved silently and took a seat. He grinned. His oily, slimy grin displayed his yellowing teeth.

Sirhan looked very much the same as when I had seen him the first time. He had the same pencil thin mustache, the same light-olive complexion, and the same brown hair and brown eyes. But, he did seem a little thinner; I supposed that was due to prison life. His teeth were a little more yellow. It was possible that personal hygiene had recently become an issue for him.

"Sirhan, you're the last person I expected to see, ever."

"It's a pleasure to see you too…What should I call you? The first time we met, you introduced yourself as Charlie

Fenton. After I was arrested I was told your name was Chad Fury. Now I hear that you go by Drake Manning. What do I call you?"

"Call me Chad. But, Sirhan, what am I supposed to do with you?"

"You heard Ladon. You need my help to find the Stone of Destiny."

"Right. But what am I supposed to do with you right now? You can't stay here."

"You could put me up in a hotel. There are plenty of nice places around here."

I made a huffing noise, "Not on your life. I'm not spending my hard-earned money on your comfort."

"Well, how about letting go of a little jingle for some food. I'm hungry; I haven't eaten since yesterday."

"You have a lot of nerve!"

Sirhan's demeanor changed and he let me know he had a little backbone left. "Chad! I don't care much for this *arrangement* either. You set me up! Because of you I lost my business, my wife, my kids, and everything I own! It's *all* gone! Because of *you*, I was going to spend the rest of my life caged up with nothing but disgusting people. I spent most of this last year trying to keep from playing pick up the soap with strange men in the showers!"

"You can't blame *any* of that on me! *You* made a career out of selling arms and drugs. My God, you even ran that Dark Realms website where children were being sold. Children! Just where did you think all of that was going to land you? You were headed to prison, eventually. Were you just too dense to realize it?"

"Chad. Every night last year I went to sleep dreaming of killing you and Vitaly Dimitrievich. The two of you ruined my life. And now that I'm out, I *can't* kill you. Those men, The Company, they're forcing me to work with you. Believe me, if I could, I'd kill you where you stand!"

"I'd love for you to try, believe me! You'd find killing me a lot more difficult than you could imagine."

We exchanged a few more words, but the energy behind our dispute eventually faded and the conversation changed.

"Sirhan, I think we're both hungry. I'll call in a pizza. We'll talk about this Destiny Stone while we eat."

"That's Stone of Destiny."

"What's the difference?"

"Ladon corrected me too. The Destiny Stone is a piece of fiction from those movies about magic and sorcery. You know, the Harvey Porter movies?"

"So that's where I've heard it."

"According to Ladon, the Stone of Destiny was used in ceremonies for the crowning of kings. Whatever else it is, I don't know."

I picked up the phone and called in a pizza. We continued to talk while we waited. Sirhan asked me questions about The Company and how they could control people with their voices. I told him less than I knew, and no more than I thought he knew already.

I asked Sirhan about The Company. I was curious as to how many of its members he had seen and what he knew about how it was run. He knew very little. But it was obvious there were a lot of them here in Vegas.

Sirhan did know one thing that I stored away for future reference. It seems that the members of The Company select a name to be used for Company business. Ladon was The Company name of one Lawrence Thorne. Lawrence Thorne was the owner of a hotel chain that included the Old Chicago Hotel and Casino.

The pizza arrived and I pulled some beer out of the refrigerator for us. Sirhan consumed the food greedily. I asked questions and interrupted Sirhan's chewing.

"Tell me, Sirhan. This army colonel. How did you get his stuff, where is it, and what are we expected to find?"

Sirhan chewed a little more, swallowed, and washed it down with a mouthful of beer before answering.

"Colonel Roger Evans. He retired in Oklahoma, over

by Lake Eufaula. When he died, his kids tried to get rid of his stuff.

His son called me. I bought all the contents of the home, sight unseen. I hired a moving company. They packed up the house and delivered everything to my warehouse."

"So everything is at your warehouse."

"It was, but not anymore. The FBI seized all that. I'm sure it's been moved to wherever stuff sits that will eventually be sold at government auction." Sirhan laughed pathetically, "It's ironic. I used to buy stuff from those auctions."

"So where is it now?"

"I don't know. Maybe somebody at the FBI knows. You'd probably need to ask someone at the Oklahoma City office."

"Oh, great," I sighed, "just how much better is this going to get?"

"It could get a lot better. For starters, I don't know what it is we're supposed to find."

I stared blankly at Sirhan, "Just what do you mean, by *'you don't know'*?"

Sirhan unbuttoned and removed his shirt. His chest and back were covered in scars and cuts. My jaw went slack at the sight and Sirhan explained, "I'm like this all over. They cut me and asked me questions. They told me they could take my memories by touching my blood.

They gave up trying to find out anything I knew about where the stone is. They couldn't find out because I don't know."

Sirhan put his shirt back on and I discovered that I had no appetite.

"Sirhan, when you've finished eating, you can sleep in my bed. I'll sleep out here, on the sofa."

"Why would you give me your bed?"

"Two reasons. I actually feel a little sorry for you, and I don't trust you. I'm a light sleeper. If you leave the bedroom, I'll know it.

CHAPTER TWENTY-THREE

I woke to rapping at my door. I realized very quickly that I was angry, the clock on the wall showed three-thirty. I hadn't been asleep long and I had to move the sofa before I could answer the door. I had put the sofa in front of the door to block Sirhan's exit or anyone else's entrance.

As the rapping continued, I withheld what I was actually thinking and called out, "Just a minute!" I threw on my jeans. I didn't bother with a shirt. I pulled the sofa back to its home and went to the door.

I opened the door just a crack to see who it was that wanted my attention. On the other side was Lisa. I opened the door and she started inside. I put up my hand and gently pushed her back outside, closing the door behind me.

Lisa looked at me a little confused. "Chad, what is it? Why can't I come inside?"

"Lisa, I need to explain something first. I'm not alone."

"Who is she, Chad?" Lisa's face showed a hint of scorn.

"It's not like that. It's a man, not a woman."

Lisa let her words flow quickly. "Well! Chad, I didn't

think you went for that! I guess you really don't know how you feel about anything…"

I interrupted, "Lisa! Stop! Stop right now! I can't let you inside for several reasons."

"Chad, why are you so angry?"

"Because I'm boxed in a corner, and I can't get out. If I don't do what Ladon says, my mother and uncle will be tortured and killed. And who knows what else he'll do if I don't do what he says."

"Just what does he want?"

"He wants me to find something called the Stone of Destiny and bring it to him."

Lisa backed up a step and grabbed the railing on the walkway. I watched her steady herself as she whispered, "No. You can't."

"So you know about the stone? That must mean that you know all about the El-yanin's plans."

"Chad, we need to talk. Can we go inside, please?"

"I don't know. The person inside is, well…"

"Is this person one of the Abomination, or is he human?"

"Oh, he's human alright."

"Then he's not a problem. I can deal with him."

Lisa moved to the door and turned the knob. I stepped between her and the doorway.

Lisa looked me in the eyes and whispered, "Chad, please."

"Alright, but give me a second."

I was worried about the cell phone Ladon had given me. I knew it was possible for him to turn on the microphone at any time and eavesdrop. The only thing I could think of was to put it in the refrigerator, so that's what I did.

After going inside and putting the phone in the refrigerator, I went to the front room and turned on a light. Lisa was already inside, sitting on the sofa with her legs crossed and a frown on her face. She patted the cushion next to her, and I went and sat.

"Chad, tell me what's going on. Who is that in your bed, and what's happened?"

"I'd better start with what's happened. Ladon had me meet him at the Atomic Testing Museum on campus. He told me a lot of things. He believes them, but I need to know if they're true. I need to talk to the El-yanin in charge."

"Will it matter? Will anything they say really matter?"

"You're damned right it will matter."

"I came here to tell you that they're willing to meet with you. The Grand Council agreed to talk to you. But, what are you going to talk to them about? Maybe you should tell me; I might be able to help."

I related everything Ladon had told me about how the El-yanin had come to Earth in its ancient pre-history. As I related what I had been told about the El-yanin creating humankind just to harvest DNA, Lisa objected.

"Chad, if any of that were true, at the very least there should be something about that in my memories. But this is the first I've ever heard about this."

"Lisa, Ladon believes it, and it makes sense. The odds of two species from two different worlds looking so much alike, let alone being able to interbreed is astronomical. It's downright impossible!"

"I don't know, Chad. Even if it's true, does it matter? Shouldn't you just be glad you exist?"

"Maybe not, but there's more. Ladon claims that before the El-yanin leave they will unleash all of the creatures they created to scour the Earth for the missing books and kill the Abomination."

Lisa shifted in her seat and looked more than a little uncomfortable. I pressed her for what she knew.

"So, what is it Lisa? The creatures like you tried to make me into…what happened to them after you were done with them?"

"Chad," Lisa bit her lip and turned away for a moment.

"Chad, they are in stasis. We're waiting until we need them."

"In stasis? Waiting until you need them? What does that mean?"

"Stasis. It's kind of like being frozen. They're not dead, but they're not asleep either. They will be revived before we leave…to…deal with the Abomination."

"You mean hunt and kill them."

"Well it's more like…OK…yes. To hunt them and to lead us to the books."

"Lisa, what is the plan for the creatures after you're done with them."

"I never actually asked."

"That doesn't mean you don't know. What *is* going to happen when you leave?"

"They're going to guard us until we've finished going through the portal. They'll make sure no one stops us from leaving."

"And then?"

"And then nothing. We're gone and they're still here."

"So, you're going to leave how many wild, dangerous, nearly indestructible animals running loose on Earth?"

"There had to be enough of them to search every continent. There's less than three thousand."

I raised my voice, "Three thousand vicious monsters are going to be unleashed on unsuspecting humanity!?"

"Chad, calm down! It's just…"

Our heated discussion had disturbed my guest. A voice from the direction of the bedroom interrupted. "Hey, guys. What's going on in here? I'd like to get some sleep."

Sirhan Jadiddian was standing in the doorway, wearing nothing but a pair of briefs.

Lisa stood up, faced him, and inhaled. She inhaled so deeply that it could be heard from the next apartment.

Then came the scream. There were no words, and nothing that was in the range of normal hearing. It was a high pitched whistle which varied in pitch and intensity.

I winced in pain. Sirhan grab the door frame. His knees buckled. He fell to the floor, on his side, and began to convulse.

I tried to run to him, but I could only stagger in the midst of the intense pain piercing my skull. It was like a white-hot knife going through my head. I yelled out, "Lisa! Stop! You're killing him! Stop!"

Lisa ran out of air, and started inhaling again. I leapt to my feet and ran to her. I put my hand over her mouth. "Lisa! No! I need him alive! If he dies, so does my mother and uncle!"

Lisa slowly let the breath out of her nose. I took my hand from over her mouth.

"Chad! What's *he* doing here!?"

"Ladon seems to think I need him to help find the Stone of Destiny."

"Do you have any idea what he did to me while I was in that warehouse?"

"What do you mean? Do you mean he…" My words fell off as I saw the look in Lisa's eyes there was no mistaking what Sirhan had done. Only one thing could explain that look, and the thought of it filled my chest with rage.

I turned to face Sirhan. He was staggering to his feet, pulling himself up by the door frame, and coughing. I went to him, made a fist, and hit him in the mouth. He fell backwards. He laid there on the carpet, breathing, but not moving.

I turned back, went to Lisa, took her, and lead her to the sofa.

"I'm so sorry, Lisa. I had no idea."

Lisa wiped an eye. I pull her toward me. She crumpled and buried her head in my chest. She sobbed as I held her tight.

CHAPTER TWENTY-FOUR

After the way the encounter with Sirhan affected Lisa, I couldn't make myself push her for more answers. I decided to leave my questions for the Grand Council. Lisa, on the other hand, turned our conversation to how the meeting with the Grand Council would proceed.

The council agreed to meet me in an undisclosed location. Lisa used the mapping program in my cell phone to enter the location of several portals across the globe. I was to use the portals marked as destinations in the map. When I crossed through the final portal I would be at the meeting place.

This was Saturday morning and the meeting was set for Friday evening, my time. According to Lisa, that didn't allow much in the way of extra time. I was going to be on my own, in foreign countries, trying to make my way from one map point to another. I didn't have a passport, and like so many other Americans, I didn't speak anything except English.

Lisa helped me prepare for the trip. I was grateful for the help. She suggested that I buy a backpack with a bedroll. According to Lisa, it would be suitable camouflage if I appeared to be an American backpacking across any country where I happened to be.

I was at one of those large sporting goods stores looking at backpacking supplies when the phone Ladon had given me started ringing in my pocket. I answered it.

"Hello, Ladon."

"What are you up to, Chad." It was a short terse statement, and not a question.

"What do you mean?"

"I mean, Chad, according to the GPS in the phone you are running all over Vegas, and *not* headed to Oklahoma. You have a job to do, and I expect you to do it!"

"Back off, Ladon! You dumped Sirhan in my lap without so much as a toothbrush. Now I'm expected to take him with me to Oklahoma, and only God knows where else. I've got to get some basic things for him like clothes and a razor. And, I can't just pick up and leave without taking care of a few things for myself!"

"Don't take too long, Chad. I gave you a job to do and I expect you to do it."

"Yeah, well, you said that already and I…"

Ladon ended the call before I could fully express my opinion.

I angrily grabbed the things I was after, threw them in my basket and proceeded to the checkout.

I hurried through the remainder of my errands and returned to the apartment where Lisa was waiting and keeping watch over Sirhan.

When I arrived home I found Lisa sitting on the sofa with a laptop computer. I sat down the package in my arm and I held up my index finger toward Lisa. Neither of us said a word while I went to the refrigerator and put Ladon's phone inside.

I went back to the front door and picked up the package I had placed on the floor.

"Hey, Lisa. What are you up to?"

"I'm catching up on some work," she said as she closed

the lid of the computer. "Did you get everything?"

I pulled out my new backpack from the sack, held it up and displayed it proudly.

"I did indeed. I have a backpack with a bedroll, three thousand dollars in cash, and a power converter. I even stopped by my office at the university and picked up the two watt laser and the lock pick set you gave me last year."

I looked around the room. "Oh, and I picked up some clothes and a toothbrush for Sirhan. Where is he?"

"Sirhan? She's in your bedroom, having a tea party with imaginary guests."

"She? What? What the hell?"

"He thinks he's a five year-old girl. It was easier that way."

I went to my bedroom, opened the door cautiously and peered inside. Sirhan was sitting at the head of the bed with his legs folded, clapping his hands and giggling. He put his right arm out in front of him, made some kind of a waving gesture and spoke to the empty air, "You silly!"

Sirhan turned his head and saw me. He spoke in a soft, childlike voice, "Hello, mister. Who are you? My name's Shirley."

"I'm Chad. This is my home…my bedroom."

"Oh. Nice to meet you Mr. Chad. Would you like some tea?"

"Uh, no. Thank you."

Sirhan continued to talk while I pulled the door closed and retuned to Lisa.

"Lisa, I repeat. What…the…hell? Will he be OK?"

"He'll be fine, just as soon as I tell him who he is."

"Will he remember any of this?"

Lisa pursed her lips. I could see fire in her eyes as she spoke slowly, "I…haven't…decided."

"Lisa, we have a problem." I sat on the sofa next to her. "Let me rephrase that. I have a problem, and I could really use your help, please."

"What's wrong, Chad. If it's Sirhan, I promise you, he'll

be fine."

"It's not that. It's Ladon. He called while I was out. He was tracking me with the GPS in the phone he gave me. He knew where I was and he was insisting that I get started finding the stone."

"Well, Chad, I guess you have a choice to make. Either you do what Ladon wants, or you meet the Grand Council. You can't do both."

"What if I took Sirhan with me to meet the council?"

Lisa pointed toward the bedroom, "Really? Do you want to go globe-hopping with that thing in there? Besides, if you go to meet the council, and you take Ladon's phone with you, he'll have the GPS coordinates of every portal you used. The council won't stand for that."

I exhaled heavily. "I figured as much. I can't take Ladon's phone with me when I meet the council, and Ladon wants me in Oklahoma. I don't know what to do."

"Chad." Lisa reached over and put her hand on my thigh. "Maybe *you* don't need to go to Oklahoma. Maybe only Ladon's phone needs to go."

"What are you suggesting?"

"I'll clone Ladon's phone, and give you the clone. I'll keep the original. When Ladon calls, both phones will ring and you'll answer."

"That might work." I put my hand on top of Lisa's, and squeezed it gently. "You'd do that for me? You'd take Sirhan and the phone and go search for the stone?"

"Yes. For you, I would."

CHAPTER TWENTY-FIVE

It was six in the morning, on Sunday, when I found myself standing in the empty spillway. I was staring into the dark opening of the storm sewer that Lisa had taken me into before. While I was peering into the blackness ahead of me, I felt Lisa's hand on my shoulder. I turned to face her. As we looked at each other, I tried to figure out what she was feeling. I settled on concern.

Lisa blinked and said softly, "Hey Dragon Boy, you be careful out there. You've got a long journey ahead."

"I will be careful. You do the same. Will you be alright traveling with Sirhan?"

"I'll be fine. You watched me put him to sleep before we left. I plan for him to stay that way most of the time."

"I'm still concerned about Ladon," I said as I shifted my weight from one foot to the other. "Are you sure we can pull this off?"

"Just do like we planned. When he calls, I'll have the phone he gave you, and you'll have the clone. You answer on the clone and talk to him. I'll be listening."

"And what if I need to describe where I am and what I'm doing?"

149

"Just take out your other phone and read the text messages. I'll be texting what we're doing. And, if worse comes to worst, I'll answer for you."

"That's the part I don't like. Are you sure you can imitate my voice?"

Lisa replied in a voice that was definitely not hers, "Yes, I can. Don't worry."

"That was close, Lisa, but I don't think it sounds like me."

"That's because you hear your voice from inside your own head. Believe me; that was perfect."

"And what about cell reception? I may not be near any cell towers."

"I've set your transresinator to act like a cell tower. You'll never be without a signal. Now, do you have everything you need?"

I took off my backpack and bedroll to take one last inventory. In the main compartment, on top, were some protein bars and some bottles of water. Underneath was a change of clothes and a plastic rain poncho. Further down was an old towel hiding the presence of my two watt laser, lock pick set, and three thousand dollars in cash. I would need cash for food and shelter, but mostly I had it for bribes. I would be traveling in foreign countries without a passport. I was hoping that the right amount of money might put people around me at ease.

I pulled the transresinator from the outside pouch of the backpack and showed it to Lisa. I patted the right and left pockets in my jeans, and looked at Lisa. "My personal cell phone is in my left pocket and the clone of Ladon's phone is in my right."

"OK, Chad. I think you have most of it. What about batteries and a current converter so you can plug your stuff in overseas?"

I looked one more time in the backpack and found the things Lisa had mentioned and showed them to her.

"Lisa, I think we're stalling. We both need to get

going."

I put out my arms to hug her goodbye, and something happened. Somehow, our lips met in a long farewell kiss.

We both backed up a step from each other and exhaled in unison. Lisa turned and started up the embankment without a word. I took out my flashlight from the bag. I turned and watched Lisa ascend the slope and get into my car. I didn't look away until she was out of sight.

I stepped into the dark hole ahead of me while I put my backpack on my shoulders. I had a bad feeling about this trip, but I didn't have a choice. I needed information that only the El-yanin had. I needed to find out who had the truth, and then decide what to do with it.

I walked slowly in the darkness several steps before I turned on my flashlight. The beam cut through the black and revealed graffiti on the walls. As I walked, the graffiti soon ended, but the odors remained.

It wasn't entirely quiet in the tunnel. There was the sound of dripping water and a faint dull roar similar to what happens when you put a seashell against your ear.

I walked on, going deeper into the tunnel until it felt as though the blackness ahead and behind were infinite. As I approached the first connecting tunnel I heard something moving. It was too big to be a rat. I bristled. I hoped I was not about to meet some of the people Lisa said lived down here.

I walked about thirty or forty more feet and my eyes caught motion at the end of my flashlight beam. I called out, "Hello!" I waited a second and walked forward a few more steps. I heard the sound of footsteps ahead of me. I called out again, "Hello! I just need to walk through here. I don't want to bother you!"

A voice echoed off the walls ahead of me, "Go away! This is our home!"

"My name's Chad. I don't want any trouble. I don't want to go to your home. I just need to come through this tunnel. I need to get underneath Fremont Street."

There was a pause. I heard nothing so I continued walking. I had taken no more than five steps when the voice returned, "You with the city?"

"No. I'm not. I just need to get to Fremont Street."

"Why?"

I kept walking as I talked.

"There's a door down here. I need to go through it."

"Ain't no doors. Just concrete."

"If you let me, I'll show it to you. A friend took me through it."

I took a few more steps and saw the outline of a man move into the beam from the flashlight. I moved the beam so the light would not be in his eyes. As I took another step the figure moved and I could tell he was holding something the way a ball player holds a bat.

"I'm unarmed. All I have is a flashlight. I just want to pass. I have twenty dollars in my pocket. Would that be enough to let me pass?"

"I don't want your money. I want you gone."

"I can't do that. I have to keep going."

I was getting close to the man, close enough I could tell that he hadn't shaved in a few days.

"Listen, friend. I'm harmless," I said as I turned the light on myself to show him who I was.

That turned out to be a mistake. With the light no longer on him, he rushed toward me. I turned the light back in time to see him swinging a pipe toward my head.

I dropped my light and caught the pipe with my left hand. I turned my body. I took his wrist in my right hand. I continued to turn until my back was to the man. I dropped to a squat with my arms above my head and I pulled my arms forward, hard and fast. The man sailed over my head and hit the concrete floor several feet ahead of me. I heard the pipe hit the floor further in the distance.

I stood up, "Are you alright?"

The figure on the ground moaned, and I stepped toward him. When he saw me coming, he scrambled to his feet and ran away.

I retrieved my light and headed quickly in the direction of the portal, listening carefully for more residents of the darkness.

I met no one else along my path and eventually I found myself standing under the grate where Lisa had brought me. I took the transresinator from my backpack and looked at it. There was a red arrow pointing at the opposite wall.

I adjusted my backpack. I tilted my head from side to side and heard my neck crack. I reassured myself, "You can do this, Chad. Lisa said it gets easier. You won't be as sick this time...I hope."

I inhaled, held my breath, and started walking toward the wall. I came to the wall and continued forward. I pierced the concrete like walking through tissue paper.

CHAPTER TWENTY-SIX

I laid on the floor, face-down. The stone surface was cool against my left cheek. I needed the coolness of the hard stones beneath me; it was keeping the nausea at bay. As I lay there, I became aware of a sound, someone groaning. When I realized the sound was coming from me, I forced myself to stop.

It wasn't long before the world righted itself and was no longer spinning out of control. I sighed at the thought that I had to keep doing this to get where I was going. "This has to be the *suckiest* way to travel," I heard myself say as I pulled myself to my knees.

I looked around the room. It hadn't changed since Lisa brought me here. I took off my backpack and let it fall to the floor. I crawled to the wall beneath the window and sat with my back against the wall. As my head cleared, I looked around the room. I hadn't taken the time before to notice the mural above the fireplace which was, for me, the portal I had just come through.

The mural was faded, but it seemed to be a picture of demons and angels struggling against each other. The longer I looked, the more it made sense. The angels were

154

feminine and the demons were masculine. A few of the angels were holding cubes in their hands. And they seemed to be fighting over some books. Whoever painted this had to know something about the Sisterhood and the Abomination.

With my head finally clear, I pulled out my cell phone. The time had automatically updated. It showed the local time to be a few minutes before five P.M.. I sent a text to Lisa.

"I'm in London. I hope your trip goes well. I wish you were here."

I waited, but there was no reply. Lisa was probably on the road so I shouldn't expect an immediate reply.

I put my cell phone back in my pocket and picked up my pack. I went to the door on the opposite wall and turned the handle. I pulled on the door and opened it slowly. I stuck my head through the opening, watching and listening. The hallway seemed empty. As I pulled the door open a little further, I heard footsteps. I closed the door quickly and moved to one side.

The footsteps stopped at the door and a key scratched at the deadbolt lock above the doorknob. I heard the lock turn and I clenched my teeth together. There was no little latch to turn on this side of the deadbolt, only a slot for a key.

I put my pack down and dug out my lock pick set. I worked on the lock a few minutes while nothing happened. I started cussing. I convinced myself that this lock must have a profanity requirement because the pins didn't seem to stay in place unless I was using the right swear words.

After a sufficient amount of cussing and swearing, the lock conceded the contest and turned for me. Once again I pulled the door open cautiously and this time I stepped through.

The halls were empty and I made my way quickly out the exit. The last of the day's guests were leaving the tower grounds and I joined them.

Out by the street I stood and thought for a moment. With each portal I used I would be passing through various time zones and I would, without a doubt, lose track of my deadline. I figured I had roughly one hundred hours to get through the final portal. I took out my cell phone and created an appointment on my calendar for Friday afternoon, Vegas time.

I turned my attention to the map in my cell phone. The map was directing me to something called the Callanish Stone Circle. It appeared to be somewhere on an island north of Scotland. According to the map, driving would take about sixteen hours. I had no time to waste.

I ran along the street until I saw a cab. I knew I would sound crazy, but I had to start somewhere. I hailed the taxi and the car pulled up next to me. I leaned down toward the open window.

"Excuse me. I need to get to the Callanish Stone Circle."

The driver laughed. "You're out of your bloody tree! Americans! Ha!"

"I'm sorry, I know it's quite a distance. But I really need to get there as fast as I can."

I pulled a couple of one hundred dollar bills out of my pocket and displayed them to the driver.

"I'll make it worth your while if you can help me."

The driver's expression changed and he replied in his thick accent, "Ah, well then. There's no good way. There's only slow, slower, an' no bloody way."

"Callanish is an island. Could I take a boat?"

"I suppose you could, from Liverpool. I could drive you to the train station and you can take the train to Liverpool. But, I'd take the buses all the way to the Skye Ferry."

"How long will that take?"

"Two days."

"That's too long. Please take me to the train station. I'll

try Liverpool."

I got in the back of the cab and we started off. The ride only took a few minutes. When we arrived at the Fenchurch Street Station, I paid the driver with the credit card the sisterhood had given me.

Outside the cab I took in my surroundings. The train station building stood in stark contrast to the modern glass buildings surrounding it. The gray stone face of the train station was the only structure I could see that looked as though it belonged to the early nineteen hundreds.

I looked up at the large clock sitting beneath the arched roof. The clock showed the time to be six forty-five. I began to realize my body still thought it was around ten in the morning.

If I went to Liverpool, that would take another two or three hours and I'd have an awful time finding a boat in the middle of the night. I considered that the trains might be a better option.

I entered the glass doors under the awning of the stone building. The station's exterior had kept the secret of how modern the interior was. I felt like I was standing in any large airport in the United States.

I made my way to the ticket counter and found someone who could help me with train schedules. The young brown-skinned woman behind the counter was quick to correct me and let me know that the Callanish Stones are located on the Isle of Lewis. It seems there is no such thing as a Callanish Island. It was only after she concluded my geography lesson that she was willing to help me with tickets.

"I'm sorry, sir, but there are no connections to the Isle of Lewis."

I took note of the woman's name tag, "Dana, just how close can you get me?"

Dana's brown fingers flew across her keyboard at speeds I didn't think were possible. She peered into her computer monitor and was transfixed for a number of seconds.

"I can get you to either Fort William or Inverness. Oh bollocks!" Dana looked at me surprised, "Oh do forgive…I'm trying to watch my language in front of customers. Really, I am."

"That's alright, I don't even know what you said. But back to the trip…"

"Oh, yes. I can get you to Inverness. The Fort William Station is closed for repairs for the next three days, and the private sleepers are sold out. I'll have to book you in a shared sleeper."

"I don't care. Just get me as close as you can, thank you."

"Your train leaves at nine. You'll be in Inverness at eight-thirty in the morning."

Dana printed up two tickets, it seemed I would have to change trains along the way.

After passing through a set of turnstiles I found myself in a food court. I ordered a sandwich and fries. The pimple-faced boy behind the counter had great fun at my expense.

It turned out I was being entirely inappropriate by ordering fries. No one orders "fries." I was informed that they sell "chips." When I told him I didn't want a bag of chips, I was further informed that they don't have bags of "chips," they have bags of "crisps."

At the height of my frustration I demanded to have pieces of potato boiled in oil, like I saw others around me eating.

I took my food and found an empty table. As I was sitting down, the phone in my right pocket, the clone of Ladon's phone, started ringing.

I dropped my paper sack of food on the table and pulled out both phones, Ladon's clone and my own phone. I hit the answer button on Ladon's phone, put it to my ear, and said "Hello".

"Hello, Chad. I've been tracking your progress with

your phone's GPS. I'm glad to see that you're on your way. Just where are you right now?"

I looked at my own phone. Text messages from Lisa were showing up on the screen. Lisa was telling me that she and Sirhan had stopped for lunch in Flagstaff.

"We've stopped for lunch. We're in Flagstaff, Arizona. But you know that. You're tracking my GPS."

"What are you eating?"

"Ladon! Cut the crap! What do you want?"

"I want you to know that I've got you on a leash! What are your plans? Where are you looking first when you get to Oklahoma City?"

I looked at Lisa's text messages.

"We're not stopping in Oklahoma City. We're going to Lake Eufaula."

"Why are you headed there? You need to find the stone."

"Yes, and Colonel Roger Evans knew something about it before he died. I'm going to look around his home. I'm going to find his children and see if they know something or took something that might tell us where the stone is."

"That's a waste of time. Go to the FBI and look through their files, their evidence storage, and the warehouse where they keep things that will eventually be auctioned."

"Ladon, you told *me* to find the stone. I'm going to do it *my* way. If you could have found the stone without me, you would have done it; so just let me do it!"

"Very well. But don't waste any time. I'm watching you."

Ladon ended the call abruptly. I retuned the phones to my pockets and sat down to eat.

CHAPTER TWENTY-SEVEN

My train pulled into the Inverness station Monday morning at eight-thirty. It had been an uneventful trip, and I was tired. The time change was catching up with me; my body was convinced it should be midnight and not early morning.

I got off of the train and looked around the platform. The station was modern, but not nearly as large as the Fenchurch Street Station. I found the exit signs and followed them as they led me out to the street.

I turned back to look at the station. Above the doors hung a sign reading "Inverness Scott Rail" and above that was a clock. I decided that must be a thing; it must be expected to have a clock above a train station entrance.

What I saw of Inverness looked like any other modern city. As far as I could see there was the normal hustle and bustle of people going in and out of office buildings and shops. Across the street was a restaurant with a sign that read "Beathan's - Open for Breakfast." I trotted across the street. It wasn't that I was hungry, I was more tired than anything. But, I was hoping that eating breakfast and drinking coffee would help my body adjust to the time

160

change.

The inside of Beathan's looked like many other restaurants where I had been, but the smells were different. They weren't bad smells, just different. I could recognize some of the smells, like the smell of sausage. But, there were other smells that I could not identify. I decided to take my chances. At the very least, I knew I needed coffee.

I waited as a girl about my age approached. She was carrying menus and wearing a cream-colored blouse and a tartan skirt. She pulled a strand of black hair away from her blue eyes and smiled. She said something to me that I didn't quite understand.

"Forgive me, my American ears aren't used to your Scottish brogue."

"Well!" she exclaimed. "Heets no' a brogue. Heets a burrr. A brogue's Irish. A burrr is Scah-ish."

"I do apologize," I looked at her name tag, "Muria. Please forgive an awkward American."

"Ah, heets all good. Table for one?"

"Yes, please."

Muria turned and I followed the tartan skirt to a table at the far corner. I found myself wishing that the walk to the table had taken just a little longer.

Muria left me at the table to study the menu while she tended to other customers. Some of what was on the menu I didn't understand, so I closed the menu and waited until Muria returned.

"So, my new American friend, what can I bring ye?"

I sat in awe of her accent, the soft roll of the "r" was either a trill or possibly something a little more guttural.

I opened the menu and pointed, "I'll have the 'Complete Breakfast'."

"Ye don't look big enough to eat all that, but, that's no' my concern."

"And, bring me coffee. Lots and lots of coffee."

"The meal comes with breakfast tea."

"I don't want tea. I'd like coffee."

"Ye don't want coffee with a real Scah-ish breakfast. Ye'll 'ave tea."

"Then, please bring both."

"I'll 'ave to make the coffee."

"Please, if you don't mind too much."

She made a little "hmpf" sound and turned. I watched the tartan skirt disappear into the kitchen.

Muria returned in a few minutes with orange juice, coffee, hot tea, and a small bowl of something. All of which, she arranged carefully in front of me.

I looked up at Muria, "What's all this?"

"Heet comes with juice and porridge."

I stuck my spoon in the bowl and pulled it back out, "Oh, it's oatmeal."

Muria looked sternly. "Heets porridge."

"What's it made of?"

"Oats."

"I see the difference."

Muria left and I ate.

A few minutes later Muria returned with a tray and several plates. My mouth fell open as I realized everything on the tray was for me.

She explained what I was getting as she sat each item on the table. First there was a small plate with what looked like a slice of ham, which she called bacon. Next came what looked like a napkin holder with four slices of nearly black toast standing straight up. I was told not to complain about the toast, that it's the Scottish way.

The main plate was overflowing, and the combination of items on the plate did not say "breakfast" to me. There's not any time of day that I would have said was right for what I was seeing.

Nearest to me was something Muria called a tattie scone. I decided it was a potato pancake, and it wasn't bad. To its right were baked beans. Yes, baked beans for breakfast.

Next to the beans was a respectably sized sausage link and beside it was a pile of whole, cooked mushrooms. Finishing off the plate were two eggs, sunny-side up and a round black disk, about half an inch thick.

"Excuse me, what's this?" I pointed to the black mass on the plate.

"Heets black pudding."

It was most certainly black, but it didn't look like pudding.

"What's in it?"

Muria hesitated and then listed the ingredients, which included pig's blood.

Muria left. I tasted everything except the congealed pig's blood, and I ate only what appealed to me.

When I had finished eating Muria presented the bill and I asked her what was the best way to get to the Callanish Stone Circle. She suggested I rent a car. It seems I could rent a car, drive to the Skye ferry and leave it at a rental station before boarding the ferry. According to Muria, there are tour vans on the Isle of Lewis waiting at the ferry dock to drive visitors to the stones.

I left a large tip for Muria and headed out of the restaurant, across the street, and back inside the train station. Inside were car rental stations just like I was used to seeing inside airports.

It was a simple matter to rent a car and get directions to the ferry. In less than an hour I was in a car and on my way. It did feel awkward with the steering wheel on the opposite side from what I was used to. But, it didn't take long to adjust to driving on the left-hand side of the road.

It was a three hour drive to the ferry. With the help of my cell phone I arrived at the ferry dock just before two in the afternoon. It had taken me nineteen hours to get here, and according the map on my phone, I was still almost four hours from the stone circle. I understood what the cab driver meant when he said there were three ways to get there, "slow, slower, and no bloody way."

I ran from the car rental station to the Skye Ferry terminal. It was a mile away, and for me, that was a quick jog. I bought my ticket at the terminal and waited forty minutes to board so that I could take a thirty minute ride across the water.

The boat docked at the Tarbert Ferry Terminal. I debarked and looked for the tour vans that I was told would be waiting. There were no vans. I found three buildings with tour signs, and two of them were closed. I went inside the open one.

It was a small office with three uncomfortable looking metal chairs near the door, and a long counter on the opposite side. The walls were lined with dark wood paneling. Hanging on the walls were colored posters of various resort destinations. The large, overweight man behind the counter completed the picture.

The man behind the counter was unshaven. His dark eyes looked as though they were trying to take shelter beneath his unkempt black hair.

I spoke first, "Hello. I'm wanting to get to the stone circle."

The man responded in something I could not understand. I supposed it was Gaelic. I had never actually heard Gaelic, but I guessed that's what it was.

When I didn't respond, the man spoke in words I could, with great effort, understand. There's no way I could duplicate his accent, so I'll not try. I'll only tell you what I think he was saying.

He looked at me and said, "Aye, you're out of luck for today." That was followed by some words I did not understand, but I think there was something in there about stones rolling up hill.

I pleaded my case to the man. "I was told there would be vans waiting to take visitors to the stones."

"Aye, there would be, but not this time of day. The last van leaves at noon. If ye left now, it would be dark when ye got there. Come back in the morning. The stones will still be there."

I left the building and entered the street. I looked up and down the asphalt lane. I saw a small grocery store, and not much else worth mentioning. I had two choices. Wait until tomorrow or go on foot.

I pulled out my cell phone and looked at the map. By car, the trip would be just over an hour. According to the map it looked like thirty-eight miles of winding road to the stones. It would be far shorter if I could follow a straight line. But, there were so many small lakes and small bodies of water in the path that a straight line wasn't possible. It looked like following the road would be best.

I took off my backpack and checked my supplies. I had plenty of bottled water and protein bars. I took off my shoes and put them in the backpack. I checked the time on my phone. It showed four-thirty in the afternoon. In another hour I would be at the second portal. After that, only one more portal.

I put the phone in my pocket and put the backpack on my shoulders. I oriented myself with the afternoon sun on my left. I was facing north when I started my jog. After a few seconds I was at a full run.

I was focused on the roads and staying out of the way of traffic for the first few miles. Then, as the traffic cleared, I began to notice the countryside.

The green hills were breathtaking. The lakes and streams were crystal clear. I thoroughly enjoyed the run. Most fun of all were the dogs that chased me and tried to keep up. By my best guess I outran the fastest dog by ten miles per hour.

As I approached the end of the road I saw a building with a sign reading, "Visitors Center". From the distance I could tell that the lights were off inside the building. I trotted closer and saw a red and white sign on the door that read "Closed."

I walked northward across the gravel parking lot and up a grassy knoll. From the top of the knoll, in the evening light I could see the stones. There was an inner circle of grey rocks. At the center stood a large grey monolith. Coming out from the circle, like the four points of the compass were rows of stones. The entire structure formed a sort of a cross with the circle at the center.

Amongst the stones were people. A pair stood in the center, one in all white. A third person stood in front of the pair. Rows and rows of people sat in chairs watching the trio. It was a wedding.

I continued to sit and watch. I took off my pack, sat down on the grass, drank two bottles of water, and ate a protein bar.

I considered that it only seemed proper for a Christian wedding to be conducted in the center of a cross. I also became a little sad as I realized I had planned to be married by now. I started to think about Lisa. I pulled out my phone to send her a text.

My cell phone showed the time was a quarter 'til six. I decided I could wait until the wedding ceremony was over, but I wasn't going to wait any longer than that.

I saw that I had missed a text from Lisa. She was informing me that they had arrived in Oklahoma City, and would spend the night there. She had convinced Sirhan that she was me, and she had also made him sleep most of the trip.

I typed out, "Lisa. Glad to know you are OK. I have arrived at the Callanish stones. It's almost six P.M. here. There's a wedding in progress. I will go through the portal ASAP."

I waited, but there was no reply.

Another twenty or so minutes passed before it was obvious that the bride and groom were now husband and wife. But, the crowd was not leaving.

Instead, tables had been set up and food was being brought out. Torches were being lit. Generators were being started and electric lights were casting their glow over the stones, a portable dance floor, and banquet tables.

I was about to crash my first wedding. I proceeded down the hill and onto the field. As I approached the circle, two men in kilts and black suit-coats approached. They took up positions between me and the stones, just a few feet away.

The man on my right said sternly, "Aye, sonny. Ye can't be here. Tis a private affair."

The other man chimed in, "Ye best be on your way."

I decided against a fight, and opted for something a little more theatrical.

"Gentlemen," I said in my most dramatic voice, "You don't understand. I'm the entertainment!"

"We've goh' a DJ," said the first man, "now run along. I've noh' 'eard a word a'bou' anyone else."

I crouched to one knee, raised my right hand, and brought my fingertips hard onto the ground. I raised my hand up to their faces, and said, "I am the great acrobat and magician, Chad Dragon Fury!"

After speaking my hand began turning back from the red scales and claws, and became normal flesh.

The second man spoke up immediately, "Right this way, I'll introduce ye."

I walked to the center of the circle and removed my backpack while the two men got the attention of everyone there. With every eye in the crowd fixed on me, I introduced myself.

"Ladies and gentlemen! I am the great, the one and only, magician and acrobat, Chad Dragon Fury!

I've come all the way from America to be here, at this precise moment because this night, this time, and this place is full of magic and wonder!"

I took both hands and hit the center monolith. My hands changed and I displayed them proudly to the onlookers. I asked the bride and groom to step forward and examine my hands. The couple stroked my fingers gently as they transformed back into normal flesh.

I counted thirteen stones around the circle, each

appeared to be about ten feet high. I jumped to the top of the nearest stone, and did a backflip off of the top, landing on my bare feet.

I did handstands and flips on the stones and the crowd loved it. They applauded and cheered. And after a bit, I decided it was time for me to bring on the grand finally. I went to my backpack and pulled out the transresinator. I held it up for all to see.

"Ladies and gentlemen. Many people have wondered about the purpose of these stones, and other stones like them all around the world. Tonight you will see the stones' real purpose. Tonight you are privileged to see how the ancients used them.

The stones are a gateway to other places around the globe. And in a very few moments, I will be whisked away to a far off land.

In my hand I hold the key. A simple glass cube."

I held the cube in my right palm, and placed my left index finger on the top. The cube glowed with orange light, and began pulsing with my heartbeat.

I removed my finger to find that the red arrow was pointing me toward the face of the center stone.

"To the bride and groom, I wish you a lifetime of happiness. To the rest of you, I bid you a good night."

With my backpack in hand, I turned and stepped through the surface of the largest stone.

CHAPTER TWENTY-EIGHT

The world was tilted, and a distorted swirling panorama of images blinded me. But, I was standing, and I was hearing sounds. I heard voices, very excited voices. The world righted itself quickly this time; it was only a matter of seconds. My eyes caught up with my ears and I was able to see my surroundings.

I was in a room painted with reds, oranges, yellows, and gold. Directly in front of me was a large doorway leading outside and into the night.

Between me and the door were three men with shaved heads. Each man was wearing a burnt orange robe. The center man was holding smoldering incense sticks. The three were looking back and forth at me and at each other, and jabbering wildly.

I don't call it jabbering out of disrespect, it's just how it sounded to my foreign ears. And since my words might sound just as unintelligible to them, I opted not to try and explain my sudden appearance.

I put the transresinator in my backpack and dropped the backpack on the floor. I squatted to the ground and hit the concrete with the fingertips of both hands. I raised my hands over my head. I let out the fiercest roar I could make. The sound even frightened me a little.

The three men fled, making excited noises as they ran. I chose to run too, but a little more quietly. I snatched up my backpack, put it on, and jogged cautiously into the night.

I crossed through a courtyard and under a stone archway. I found myself on a city street, surrounded by modern buildings, artificial lights, and traffic. I picked a direction and ran full speed along the sidewalk, dodging the occasional pedestrian.

When I stopped, I pulled out my cell phone to get my bearings. The phone had reset the time and the display was showing one in the morning. I pulled up the mapping program. The portal had dropped me in Beijing China, at the Zhihua Buddhist temple.

A hotel on the map caught my attention. I noticed it because the name was English, and it was the name of a hotel chain that I recognized. It was also only a mile away. I headed for the hotel. Nothing sounded better than a hot shower and a warm bed.

I ran full speed toward the hotel, and I was there in just minutes. I took a moment outside the hotel to put on my shoes before entering.

Inside, the lobby was opulent. It rivaled the finest of hotels I had seen on the Las Vegas strip. I made my way across the marble floor and underneath the massive chandelier to the lobby counter. There, a young man with black hair and wearing a black suit was doing something behind a computer.

When I arrived at the counter, I dropped my backpack to the floor and the young man looked up at me. He said something in Chinese. I replied back with a question, "English?"

The man stood a little straighter and his face looked as though he was thinking carefully about what he was trying to say. He spoke very slowly and deliberately. "Ah. Yehsss sssihr. I heyrp you?"

I could tell this was going to be difficult, so I did as much as possible with as few words as possible. I pulled out a credit card and placed it on the counter. "I want a room. One night."

The man looked confused.

"Checkout e-rev-in, today. Two nights?"

I understood his meaning. It was one in the morning. If I checked in now, I would be charged for a full night. If I wanted to stay past eleven, I'd have to pay for two nights.

It had taken me about twenty-seven hours to get here. I had one more portal to go through, then I would be at the meeting sight. For the moment, I felt like I had some time. But, as I looked at the map through weary eyes, I couldn't tell if I had two hundred or four hundred miles to go. I opted for a short stay.

"One night. Please."

In a few short minutes I was in possession of a key for room number twelve twenty-nine. I picked up my backpack and the man looked at me puzzled.

"Rug-age rohst at aihr pohrht?"

"That's right, Scooby. Ruggage Rost," I said as I turned my back toward him. I crossed to the elevators and made my way to the twelfth floor and room number twenty-nine.

The room was nice. I put my bag down and checked the room service menu. The restaurant was closed, but would reopen at six, less than five hours from now.

I pulled out my cell phones and plugged them in to charge. As for me, I showered, set an alarm for nine a.m., turned out the lights and crawled into a nice, warm bed.

CHAPTER TWENTY-NINE

I woke up just before the alarm went off. I dressed quickly. I looked at both phones before putting them in my pockets. There were no messages.

I headed out of the room and descended in the elevator to the lobby. The restaurant was calling my name and it would have been rude to ignore it. The menu was in both English and Chinese, for which I was very grateful.

I found a traditional American breakfast and ordered. After the previous attempt at breakfast, I had no desire to chance finding out that something on my plate was made with something else's blood.

As I ate my breakfast and drank my coffee, I looked at the map on my cell phone. The last point Lisa had set in the map was on a little outcrop at the Bohai Sea. The location was called the Old Dragon's Head, and it was in Qinhuangdao City. According to the map it was over two hundred miles away.

I didn't have a clue about the trains and busses here. And trying to take public transportation when I couldn't read the signs or speak the language seemed like I was asking for trouble. Renting a car seemed risky. I could run it in five or six hours, but that seemed like a last resort. I decided to ask for advice from the hotel concierge.

I paid for my meal and found the concierge's desk. The desk was occupied by a lovely lady with black hair, brown eyes, and flawless skin. I introduced myself. She bowed her head slightly and extended her hand. I took it gently in mine.

As I took my seat, I started talking. "I'm trying to get to Qinhuangdao City, the Old Dragon's Head."

The lady looked at me and spoke sweetly, "You must to see Great Wall?"

I noted that throughout our conversation her pronunciation was near perfect, but her choice of words was off. She did not have a grasp of when to use words like "the," "a," and "an" so she didn't bother with them.

"Yes. The Old Dragon's Head."

"Have you seen Great Wall here?"

"No, I have not."

"You must to see here. Much closer than Bohai. Much more to see here. From here to Great Wall, seventy-five kilometer. Much closer. Bohai three hundred-thirty kilometer."

"I know it's a long way. How is the best way to get there?"

The lady frowned as she appeared to be thinking. She turned and took a brochure from a holder next to her and pushed it across the desk to me.

"Great Wall tour. You see wall here, then First Gate of Heaven, then Old Dragon's Head. Tour leave in two day."

"I won't be here in two days."

"No good way to Dragon's Head. Too many train, too many bus. You rent car?"

"I suppose I could rent a car."

The lady pulled out a printed map and made an "X" on it.

"You here," she said, and made a circle a little distance away. "You go here. Take passport. No passport, no car."

173

"I don't have a passport."

The flawless face looked concerned. "You have trouble. You need Embassy." She drew another circle on the map.

"I probably do need the Embassy, but later."

She leaned back a little, "You take airline ticket to Embassy. They help you."

"I don't have a ticket."

"You have much trouble. You have money?"

"Yes, I have American dollars."

"You need Yuan. You go to bank. Have Dollar made to Yuan. Tell bank trouble. Bank will help."

"But what about the Great Wall?"

"You have too much trouble. You get Yuan. You need Yuan for cab, for train. Then you go to Embassy."

"Where is the bank?"

"Down street." She pointed on the map.

I thanked her, took my pack in my left hand and exited the hotel. She had been right about one thing. I would need local currency if I wanted to take public transportation. I decided it wouldn't hurt to get some.

It was my mistake to make, and I made it. There, on the sidewalk, next to the busy street I sat down my bag and dug through it until I found my cash. I pulled out three, one hundred dollar bills and stuck them in my pocket.

At that moment, with my hand in my pocket and my pack on the ground a young man on a bicycle rode past, grabbed the bag and rode away as fast as he could.

I experienced a moment of shock that cost me a few precious seconds. I yelled, "Stop! Thief!" The crush of people was oblivious to my words.

I kicked off my shoes. The transresinator was in that bag and I needed it. I could lose everything else, but I had to have the cube.

I exploded into a run directly into the street and oncoming traffic following after the bicycle ahead of me. The thief was riding between cars but I was gaining on him.

A car on my right began pulling over to where I was running. I sprang upward and found myself crouching on all fours on the roof of the car. Another small leap and I was crouching on the hood of the vehicle; the claws on my hands and feet dug in and pierced the metal.

The car swerved, and I leapt off just before it collided with another.

I leapt from car to car like an animal, on all fours. I was leaving a string of panicked drivers crashing into one another behind me.

The man on the bicycle was moving as fast as he could. I leapt back to the asphalt and ran. I got close. I reached out a clawed hand and swung at the rear wheel. The bike turned, and I caught empty air.

A car struck me from behind. I heard screeching tires as I sailed through the air. I landed about twenty feet away and rolled. As I stood to my feet I saw uniformed men blowing whistles and yelling at me. I ignored them and ran after my bag.

I leapt on top of two wrecked cars and looked for the bicycle. I spotted it at the end of the alley directly in front of me. I leapt off and ran.

The bike turned out of the alley. When I got to end of the alley, the bicycle was lying on the sidewalk. There was no man and no backpack.

Instead, I was looking at a near solid mass of people around me, moving in two directions down the sidewalk. I was looking for one man, whose face I had never seen and who looked to my eyes to be very much like the people all around me.

My eyes strained to see something, anything, in any direction that looked anything like my precious backpack. But all I got was disappointment. My heart sank into my stomach as I realized my backpack was gone and each passing second was placing it further out of reach.

My disappointment turned to anger and I yelled out

"Thief! Come back thief!" Well, that's not actually what I said, but I don't want to repeat the words I used.

The people around me stopped and stared. They may have not understood my words, but anger and frustration are universal. My outburst caused people to back away and give me some room; it was clear they didn't want to be too close to a crazy man.

I picked a direction and just ran. I ran a couple of blocks, dodging and pushing people out of my way as I went. I turned down an alley and paused. I leaned against a wall and let my head fall back against it with a thud.

My racing thoughts, consumed me with only one question, "What am I going to do *now*?" I was obsessed with my own thoughts for a few minutes, and true reason was keeping its distance from me.

I calmed down enough to start thinking again, and I took inventory of my situation. I patted my pockets. I had the two cell phones, my billfold with the credit cards, and some cash.

I pulled out my cell phone. The screen was cracked. My heart skipped a beat, but relief flooded me when I saw that it still worked. I checked the cloned phone, and it was fine.

I took my phone and dialed the only number that offered any hope. The phone rang eight times; there was no answer. I waited another few seconds and hit redial. Lisa's voice settled into my ear after the third ring, "Hello?"

"Lisa, it's Chad."

"Chad, do you know what time it is?"

"Here in Beijing it's almost noon."

"Well in Oklahoma it's almost ten P.M.. I had just gone to bed. Why are you calling?"

"I've lost the transresinator; it was stolen."

"What? No, Chad, How?"

As I related the events I was interrupted by needless commentary on my intelligence. Under any other circumstances I would have defended myself. But, I needed help and I let all that pass and kept the focus on my current predicament.

"Alright, Lisa. What do I do?"

"Can you get to the Dragon's Head?"

"I guess, but I need help with the busses and trains."

"Forget the trains. How far are you from the Great Wall?"

"I don't know, exactly. Maybe forty miles, maybe fifty."

"Alright, Chad. Let's call it fifty. From the Great Wall at Beijing to the Dragon's head is two-hundred fifty miles. That's about three-hundred miles in all. How long will it take you to run that?"

I tried to do the math in my head, but ended up giving Lisa my closest guess. "Between seven and eight hours. But that's without stopping. I'll have to stop."

"You also need to get some supplies before you start. You'll need to take some food and water. There's literally nothing between here and there."

"I don't suppose you know where I can buy a few things like shoes?"

"Chad, Beijing is one of the most modern cities in the world. You can get anything you can think of there. You'll find something.

But that brings up a good point. I need to figure another three or four hours before you start the trip. It could take that long since you don't know your way around."

"Lisa, what about the portal? When I get there, what do I do? Without the cube, I'm stuck."

"Leave that to me, Chad. I'll do my best to have someone meet you in about twenty-four hours from now. You just get yourself to the Old Dragon's head and wait."

"How will she know me; the woman you send?"

"Let's see. You're an American male, about six feet tall, and you'll be loitering at the end of the Great Wall. I don't think that will be a problem. Someone will find you."

"How will I know her?"

"Chad, this isn't a spy movie. Trust me, it won't be a problem."

"OK, Lisa. Is there anything else I should do?"

"It's pretty simple. Buy what you need; shoes, food water, and so-forth. Then run."

We wished each other luck and said our goodbyes. I put the phone in my pocket and headed back to the busy street.

I tried to get the attention of a man headed my direction.

"Excuse me...I need help...I'm an American...Can you help me?"

The man kept his gaze forward, and never slowed. He never let his eyes look directly at me.

I tried with several others, and it was the same. I was either ignored or entirely avoided. I began to think I should try to find help inside one of the buildings.

The building next to me was a modern glass and steel structure. I walked a few feet and found the entrance. I pushed the revolving door and went into the marble floored lobby.

My bare feet padded up toward the security desk where two men in uniform sat frowning at me. One of the men started making noises at me. I didn't know what he was saying, but the message was unmistakable; I wasn't welcome here.

"Please...Help me. American. English. Help."

One of the guards stood, pointed and gestured back the direction I had come.

"Please. Help. American."

The other guard stood and they both came around the desk to confront me. In a few moments they had me by the elbows and were guiding me backwards the way I had come.

I didn't fight. I went through the revolving door and back on the street. I couldn't imagine why no one was making an effort to help me. That is, I couldn't imagine until I saw my reflection in the glass of the office building.

I was a mess. My hair was uncombed, my face was dirty. My shirt was torn. My jeans were ripped. And, I had no shoes on my dirty feet. If I saw me, and I couldn't understand me, I'd stay away from me too.

At least now I knew what I had to overcome. I reached into my pocket and pulled out a twenty dollar bill. This time I waved it at a passersby as I asked for help. "Please...Help...American."

The third man to pass stopped. I will always think of him as the most intelligent man in all of China. He saw my real problem and solved it for me in a matter of seconds.

The man was well dressed, wearing a suit and tie. He looked at me. His eyes went up and down, from my head to my toes, taking in my current state. He looked into my face and asked, "Ameh-we-can?"

I responded hopefully, "Yes. American."

The gentleman reached into his suit pocket and pulled out a cell phone. He tapped the screen a few times and after a few seconds he spoke into it. He turned the phone where I could see the display.

The cell phone was showing two boxes. One box was filled with Chinese characters. The second box had English words reading, "American you are. Help need you."

I was seeing the online translation utility created by my favorite internet search engine. I was both relieved, and I felt like an idiot. Here I was struggling with the language when I had a translator in my pocket.

I touched the microphone icon under the box with English words and spoke, "Yes. I am American. I need help. I was robbed. I have some money. I have credit cards. Where can I buy shoes and clothes?"

The man turned the phone back toward him, and read the text. He spoke into the phone and showed it to me. I read, "Call police can I."

We repeated the process for a little bit, but the long

and short of the story is that I convinced him that what I needed first was to buy clothing and get something to eat.

The man put his phone in his pocket and gestured for me to wait. He hailed a cab. When the cab stopped, he spoke to the driver and gave him money in local currency.

I reached into my pocket and took out a one-hundred dollar bill. I put it in my rescuer's hand and thanked him profusely. I know he didn't understand the words, but I'm certain he got the message.

I climbed into the cab, and we rode for about twenty minutes. The driver pulled the cab over to the side of the road and stopped. He said some things, none of which I understood, but I supposed that he meant I should get out.

I opened the door of the cab and stepped out onto sidewalk. Before closing the door, I stuck my head back inside and thanked the man. He nodded and said something back. I replied, "How 'bout those Cowboys; Go Sooners," just to be polite.

I stood on the sidewalk and looked around, as if it was even possible I could get my bearings. Where I was standing could have been the heart of any modern shopping district in any metropolis, in any part of the world.

The buildings were huge, dwarfing the people and the traffic. High above were large electronic billboards scrolling through advertisements targeted to the shoppers down here on the sidewalk.

At ground level, the windows of the buildings were massive displays of the latest goods arranged in the most enticing manner. The building where I was standing appeared to be a department store. The mannequins in the windows were models of the best dressed men and women posed for a night on the town or a fancy dinner party.

I spent some time looking at the display. I had never seen mannequins so life-like. While I watched, two figures, a man and woman started to move. The gallant gentleman took the young lady's hand and they began dancing in time to music coming through speakers on the street.

I stood, enthralled as the couple danced. I wondered what their resumes would look like. Was this a career with a lot of upward mobility? Then I noticed my feet and my clothes. I had a deadline, and I needed to focus on my own problems.

I made my way down the street, past the rows of street vendors selling foods of all kinds. The aromas called out to me and I drooled like one of Pavlov's dogs. There were bowls of noodles, varieties of fruit, and pieces of grilled meat on sharp bamboo skewers. There was one cart offering live scorpions. I lost my appetite and moved along quickly.

My wanderings proved fruitful. I soon discovered I was standing in front of what appeared to be a sporting goods store. I went inside.

I won't bore you with the details of my shopping. I had learned my lesson from my benefactor and, with the aid of the translation application on the internet, I was able to get everything I needed. I left the store wearing a new jogging suit and carrying a backpack filled with supplies. Plus, I had one other item which was an impulse buy, a bicycle.

I had seen so many bicycles in Beijing that it occurred to me that it might be the best way to travel. This particular bicycle caught my attention because it folded in half. It also came with a carrying case that could be slung over the shoulder.

I waked on for a few more feet, hoping to find a bank so that I could turn a few dollars into Yuan. What I did find was an automated teller machine. I swiped my credit card and was relieved to see instructions in both Chinese and English. And in a few seconds I had Yuan in my pocket.

My final stop was to get some food from a street vendor. I sat on a bench, ate a bowl of noodles and drank soda from a can.

I sent a text to Lisa.

"I'm ready to leave for the Great Wall.
The time here is four-thirty."

CHAPTER THIRTY

The map on my cell phone showed that the Great Wall was fifty-two miles to the north. I put my phone in my backpack next to the clone of the phone Ladon had given me.

I picked up Ladon's phone and spent a moment looking at it. It had not rung for a while, and that bothered me. I hoped nothing was wrong. It seemed to me that I was overdue for a call from him. I put the phone back and put it out of my mind. I had a trip to complete.

I mounted my new bicycle and headed north. I hadn't been on a bicycle in years, and it showed. But, after a few minutes I was peddling smoothly. What I wasn't comfortable with, was shifting gears. Removing a hand to shift was, well, awkward.

I made myself keep pace with the other cyclists. I rode with a group northward, through the busy city streets. After a while I was riding with a much smaller group and the surroundings changed. The modern glass and steel edifices had been replaced by more traditional looking buildings. I pressed on, and the number of bicyclists dropped even further. Now the streets were filled with mostly cars and busses. I kept pace with the traffic.

The scenery changed again. The buildings gave way to more open spaces. This was much more rural, and the landscape could have been almost anywhere, including Oklahoma.

The traffic was light, and the road was broad. I shifted into the highest gear and peddled hard. A once forgotten feeling returned. The last time I felt this, I was twelve or thirteen years old and riding my ten-speed bicycle. I felt like I was flying above the asphalt.

Back then, I was riding down the streets of Tulsa, Oklahoma. I would find the biggest hills and peddle as hard as I could, until gravity propelled me faster than my legs could keep up. That, for a kid, was freedom.

I reveled in the moment. I let go of the handles, straightened my back, and stretched my arms out at my sides. I coasted and threw my head back. The wind roared in my ears and pulled the hot sweat from my body. I was lost in the moment until a car horn sounded from behind; it startled me. A car passed with a driver jabbering at me through an open window.

With my mind back on what I was doing, I stared noticing signs on the highway. I was now seeing that the signs were written in multiple languages, including English. One such sign informed me that I should take the next exit to see the Great Wall.

It was only a few more minutes and I was riding into a parking lot filled with cars and tour buses. People were getting on the busses, and cars were leaving.

At the far end of the lot was a single building. It was average in appearance, which made it seem out of place sitting here in the Orient. It had beige walls, a flat roof, and glass double-doors facing the parking lot. There was a red sign written in several languages. The white letters I was able to read said, "Gift Shop - Tickets"

I rode up close, stopped, dismounted, folded the bike and put it in its carrying bag. With the backpack on my back, and the black canvas bag with the bike slung over a shoulder, I must have looked a sight.

I went through the doors and got my bearings. I crossed through the gift shop to the opposite side. I approached the ticket counter. The woman on the other side looked at me wide-eyed.

I leaned close to the glass separating me from the woman dispensing tickets.

"Hello. How much to see the wall?"

"We crose-ing. You come back tomorrow."

"I won't be here tomorrow. I came all this way. Please."

"We crose sunset. People take picture of sunset, then we lock gates."

"I'd like a ticket."

"No discount. You pay full day."

"That's fine. I'd like a ticket, please."

"That one-hundred seventy Yuan."

I clumsily dug out the local currency from my pocket and slid the bills one by one under the gap between the glass and the countertop. I stopped when I saw the woman's expression change. She took the bills and gave me change.

I took the change and nearly laughed. I found it amusing that I had no idea how much I had paid for the ticket, and no way of knowing if the change was correct.

The woman pushed a brochure under the glass.

"This your ticket. Gates crose sunset. You hurry. No one let you out after gate crose."

I thanked the lady and headed through the double doors near the ticket counter.

Outside, I was standing on an asphalt path. A few feet ahead of me was a very large chain-link fence with a large gate that could be pulled across the path. Past the gate the asphalt trail led to a set of stone steps that were part of the Great Wall. I craned my neck and bent my head back to see the top.

The wall was over twenty feet high, and sitting on the wall, at the top of the stairs, was a square tower. The tower was easily as tall as the wall itself.

I ascended the steps. I could kick myself for not having counted the steps. The number of steps would have made one of those fascinating little details to make the telling of this all the more interesting. If I had counted the steps, I could throw the fact casually into a conversation. "Did you know there are exactly one hundred-thirteen steps up to the Great Wall?" But, I missed my opportunity to acquire that little piece of trivia.

The wall was clearly an elevated highway, it was about twenty feet across, and there were no less than one hundred people milling around. Most of the people appeared be selecting a spot from which to take pictures of the approaching sunset.

I turned my back to the sunset and began walking. I proceeded through the square tower, without taking time to read the signs placed around for the benefit of the tourists.

I walked casually on until I was past the crowds. Ahead of me the wall meandered gently down the landscape to the foothills of a mountain. From there it ascended gracefully until it disappeared over the mountain top.

I turned back to watch the setting sun. I sat down my backpack and the bag with the bicycle. I had to take out my cell phone and get a picture.

The sky was painted with orange fire that danced and played against the clouds. The backdrop was turning rapidly from blues to purples. I wanted to stay in this moment of silent solitude. With my feet planted firmly on stone, I felt anchored, secure in this timeless moment.

The darkness came on quickly and the magic and awe faded with the receding sun. I unfolded my bike, mounted it, and began silently coasting downhill, slowly picking up speed.

My eyes were adjusting to the low levels of light, and

the moon shown from overhead, making it simple for me to see where I was going. I congratulated myself for buying the bicycle.

I have no idea how fast I was traveling, I was moving my legs as fast as I could, and the wind was whistling in my ears. The best thing about this was that I didn't have to watch for cars, people or anything. This was a smooth track leading to my destination.

When I got to the mountains, my pace slowed. The climb was incredibly steep, and eventually I had to stop. I stopped, not because I couldn't push the pedals, but the smooth road had been replaced with stairs. There were two sections of stairs in the up-hill climb.

At the very top of the mountain was another of those square towers. I stopped there to drink water, eat, and rest. I checked the time. It was just after nine P.M.. I had no idea how fast I had gone, or just how far. There was no cell signal. I put both cell phones in my backpack.

After my short twenty minute break, I continued my journey and began my descent down the other side. I hit one section of stairs, and afterwards it was smooth coasting all the way down.

The landscape was dramatically different at the bottom of this side of the mountain. The surroundings were more arid. The vegetation was thin, and it was becoming increasingly desert-like. The wall changed too. The type of stones were different. The road was not as wide, it had narrowed to half of its previous width.

I pushed on as fast and hard as I could. Still it was a little boring and my mind wandered. That was a mistake. While I was pondering the troops that must have marched along the top of the wall and the battles to defend against invaders, the road ran out.

To my shock, I saw open air directly ahead of me; there was no wall. Approaching at break-neck speed was nothing but empty space.

I applied the brakes, desperately. But, the brakes could

do very little against my forward momentum. I was slowing, but not enough. As I approached the chasm, I decided to separate myself from my bike. I leaned to my left and pushed off.

The bike fell away to my right. My left foot hit the solid surface of the road. I began stumbling forward, with my legs unable to position themselves beneath my forward moving mass. I fell and rolled over the edge.

I would call the experience of falling over the edge and flailing uncontrollably in the air, awesome, if awesome meant something entirely different. The experience was punctuated by a sudden stop as the earth slapped me on my back.

A feeling like electricity and fire passed through my limbs. Every joint screamed at me as every nerve ending had something to say about the sudden stop. I laid there taking inventory of my body parts as I heard myself say, "*Ouch.*" It seemed satisfying, so I said it again, "Ouch."

I didn't have time to think about retrieving my bicycle. I lifted my head and looked back to where I had come from, and there was my bike faithfully following after its master. It landed across my stomach. I repeated myself, "*Ouch.*"

I let my head drop to the ground, and I laid there. I waited until my strength returned and replaced my humiliation.

I pushed the bike off of me, and sat up. There was rubble all around. Rubble was all that was left of the wall. I undid the latches on the bike and folded it up. I removed my backpack to retrieve the canvas carrying case. Beneath the canvas bag, the contents of the backpack were wet. Two of my water bottles had burst. I had plenty of water left, but my clean, dry clothes were no longer dry.

I pulled out the empty and crushed plastic bottles and threw them on the ground with disgust. I inspected my two cell phones. Both of them were shattered. I tested the phones. Neither would turn on. Disgust, disappointment, and frustration mingled into a new feeling for which I have no name.

I took the phones in my right hand and threw them as hard as I could, away from me. Words flowed past my lips. Words that if taken literally, would mean the Almighty would be sending those phones to an eternal fiery damnation.

CHAPTER THIRTY-ONE

I was off and running again. The broken remains of the wall made for decent path markers. The hard-packed earth served as a good solid running surface for my bare feet. The backpack and bike pouch were fastened tightly, and bounced very little as my feet pounded into the ground.

I don't know how long or how far I had run before I felt the need to stop. I slowed to a walk. Around me was a significant amount of trash; cans, bottles, and other debris illuminated by the moonlight. There was also a little pile of charred wood. Someone had made a campfire.

The scene reminded me of the lakes back in Oklahoma. Teenagers would drive out to the lake shores for parties. There would be drinking, a bonfire, and music. I wondered if that had happened here.

I stopped, dropped my burden, and dug water and protein bars out of my backpack. I sat on the hard earth by the burned out fire. I drank my water and ate a protein bar in the chill air.

I stood up and relieved myself. I only mention that because of what happened next. As I was finishing, I heard a noise and a light from a distance lit up the area. I turned to see a vehicle of some kind headed my way.

I hurried to make myself presentable. I didn't know who that could be in the distance, but I imagined I would be charged with trespassing and, pardon the pun, violating the penal code.

The vehicle was a jeep, and it was headed rapidly toward me. I didn't have any chance of grabbing my things and running away. I chose to stay and face what was coming.

The jeep pulled to a stop just a couple of feet directly in front of me. The harsh lights made it so I could not see any details. I made out the outlines of two men getting out of the jeep. The driver was making noises at me. I made some back. "American. English."

There were more noises from the driver, and then some noises from the other man. The driver stepped into the light and I could tell he was wearing a uniform of some kind. He pulled out a pistol and pointed it my direction. He made more noises. I repeated my noises, "American! English!"

Another man in uniform stepped into the lights on the other side of me. He was carrying handcuffs in his right hand.

Reason was out of the question. I didn't have time to experience the local legal system. I decided to try and scare them off. I turned toward the jeep like I was about to put my hands on the hood for a pat-down. I raised my arms and brought my hands down, hard, on the jeep. My hands changed.

I let out the most animal-sounding growl I could manage as I spun around. I displayed my hands to the men. The two started making very excited noises. The man holding the gun pulled the trigger repeatedly.

The bullets stung, but did no damage except to make holes in my clothes. I leapt toward him and knocked the gun from his hand.

The man's partner was getting back in the jeep, on the

driver's side. I ran to him. I took him by his shirt collar and pulled him out on the ground.

The men took turns trying to get into the jeep. I made a game of pushing them out, pulling them out, and generally playing king of the mountain.

The two men finally ran off in fear as I slapped a hand on the passenger seat and used my claws to rip it to shreds.

With the men gone, I gathered my things, put them in the jeep and started driving east. I was able to push the jeep at a decent speed; I think I averaged about fifty miles per hour. It wasn't the most pleasant ride; there were no seatbelts, and my body left the seat countless times. By the time the ride was over the jeep was going to need new shocks, and who knows what else.

About the time I thought my teeth weren't going to be able to handle any more of this, I saw the wall. I slowed and drove up to it. It was less of a wall, and more of a pile of crumbling bricks. I drove on, knowing there had to be more of the wall in better shape.

After what must have been another twenty minutes, I saw more of what I expected the Great Wall should be. It was high, and wide, and made of cut stone. I stopped the jeep and got out.

I took my things and put them over my shoulders. I went to the wall and hit it with my fingertips. My claws held nicely to the surface. It was a simple climb to the top where I pulled myself up and over the edge.

I unpacked and unfolded my bicycle. I examined it closely for damage from the fall. There were scratches, but fortunately there was no real damage.

I thought about what had happened. I decided right then and there my bicycle deserved a name. I spoke to it, "Well, Humpty Dumpty, let's both try and stay on the wall this time."

I was off again, pedaling as fast as I could. My old friend, the moon, was behind me in the west, still providing light for my journey. The road on the top of the wall turned out to be in decent shape, and after a while widened to about twenty or so feet across.

As the first rays of sunlight appeared ahead of me, I saw a very large structure in the distance that seemed to swallow-up the wall. As I got closer I could see the structure was a two story building a little wider than the road I had been traveling. The road divided and went around the square building on both sides.

There was also a group of men in burnt-orange robes standing around the building, facing outward. Their hands were steepled, as they nodded and chanted. Someone, somewhere nearby, was striking a gong. The men would chant in unison, pause, the gong would sound, and the worshipers would begin again.

I rode close to the group, dismounted Humpty Dumpty, and walked while looking for a way around the mass of worshipers. There wasn't enough space for me to get through. I walked over to the edge of the road, sat on the edge of the wall and rested. I ate a protein bar and drank my last bottle of water as I waited for the men to finish.

I suppose I could have pushed my way through the orange robes, but that would have been just too rude. It's not that it was totally beyond me, but unless they were going to be there several hours, I would make it to the Dragon's Head in plenty of time.

When the sun had fully risen, and the bright orb was no longer obscured by anything sitting on the horizon, the men left. They departed in total silence, in an orderly procession slowly descending the broad stone stairway to the city below. Humpty Dumpty and I resumed our journey in the direction of the newly risen sun.

It was an easy ride, and compared to the rest of the journey, it was nothing. I rode all the way to the end where there was a small square tower standing watch over the ocean.

I got off of Humpty and put him away. I walked the

perimeter of the tower. I stuck my head inside a doorway. There was nothing, and there was no one. I was early, and I wanted food, water, and rest.

I walked back the way I had come and descended a set of broad stone stairs. At the bottom of the stairs was a fairly modern city, but with the oriental color and architecture the average tourist might expect.

I didn't have to walk far until I found it. The building's architecture made it right at home with the other structures around, but the sign and logo were unmistakable. It was the American paradise, the real symbol of home, the true American Embassy, the most famous of fast food restaurants.

I ran up to the sign with the gently curving yellow arches and stood in awe. I didn't know whether to salute and say the Pledge of Allegiance, or offer some kind of prayer to a benevolent God who placed this here just for me. I did none of that.

I went to the entrance and pulled open the door. Inside, I was home. Well, it was a reasonable facsimile of every memory I had of being inside this particular restaurant chain.

At the counter, I was greeted by someone who spoke no English. I didn't care. I pointed greedily to a picture on the plastic covered mat on the counter. I tapped the picture of the breakfast sandwich, coffee, and hash browns. Then I tapped the picture of orange juice.

In a few minutes I had a tray of hot food that looked and smelled like home. I carried my tray past the other patrons to an empty booth. I put my things in the seat across from me.

The breakfast sandwich was manna to me, and the juice was ambrosia. I must have taken all of four minutes to consume everything except the coffee. After swallowing my last bite, I turned sideways on the bench with my back against the wall and stretched out my legs.

I took my time finishing my coffee. It was boiling hot,

strong, and bitter. I loved it; it was liquid strength and vitality that I sipped from the Styrofoam cup.

As I sipped, I watched the people around me. I tried to imagine their conversations and what their days might be like. It was all relaxing, harmless amusement until a worker took my tray with the empty wrappers and indicated I should move along.

I did move. I gathered my things and went to the restroom where I washed my face and put on the fresh change of clothes I had in my backpack. The blue tee-shirt and jeans were still damp from the busted water bottles, but I didn't care. I knew they would dry. At least I looked a little less like a homeless person, and I felt better.

CHAPTER THIRTY-TWO

I had spent my morning not wandering very far from where I'd had breakfast. I discovered a souvenir shop nearby and I bought a cheap watch. The clerk who sold me the watch was kind enough to set the time for me.

After a hamburger, fries, and a shake for lunch, I walked back to the Dragon's Head.

Standing at the end of the Great Wall, overlooking the ocean, I felt very, very, alone. There were a few tourists milling around, but they chose not to stay. Even with the few people around I felt isolated and powerless. I had no way home, and I was possibly the only man on the planet that knew humanity's future was at risk. I scanned the ocean. It was empty. It looked as empty as I felt.

I took off my backpack and put the bicycle in its bag. I sat on the stone pavement with my back against the outside of the small square building. I let my skin soak up the sunshine and I closed my eyes.

I awoke to something tapping against the bottom of my right foot. I looked up, startled, to see a man kicking the sole of my shoe. I looked him in the face, he said, "Chad, Chad Fury?"

"Uh, yes," I said and stood.

"Lisa sent me. My name is Oother-ben-taka. You can just call me Oother."

From the way he said it I couldn't tell if that was one name or three names. But it probably would have been impolite to ask, so I didn't.

"OK, Oother it is."

I took in the sight of this strange man. I had expected I would have been met by a woman, part of the Sisterhood. But this was a man, about my height, and about two hundred pounds. He had a crop of straight black hair that was a little too long, parted on one side. His eyes were dark brown. His skin was too white, as though it had not seen sunlight in years.

He was dressed in a light brown shirt with slacks that seemed to be something of a grayish brown. I determined very quickly that he was about forty-years-old and had zero fashion sense.

As I put out my hand to shake his, I caught the scent of sweet cinnamon. "It's very good to meet you. I think you have something for me?"

Oother took my hand, gripped it firmly, and pumped twice. "No, I'm not here to give you anything. I'm here to take you the through the portal."

I nodded and bent down to get my things. I put my backpack on my shoulders and took the bag with the bicycle in my hand.

Oother gave me a puzzled look and asked, "What's that?"

"Oh, that's my new friend, Humpty Dumpty. I'll introduce you later, if you like."

I followed Oother into the square tower. There was a family inside, Two parents and three children consisting of a teenage boy and two young girls; all being typical tourists. Oother started toward a wall.

I grabbed his arm, "Hey, aren't we going to wait?"

"Why? What are they going to do? Besides, it will give

them a story to tell about their vacation. That's what people want, stories. Now take my hand."

I took Oother's hand and we walked through the wall.

I blinked my eyes a couple of times at the sudden change in the amount of light. I was not, however, dizzy or sick. It seemed I had finally adjusted to portal travel. I looked at my new surroundings.

I was standing in a small room with gray metallic walls. The floor was white and almost rubbery. As I shifted my weight, the surface gave slightly.

The lighting was puzzling. There was no discernible light source. There were no windows, and there were no light bulbs or glowing panels, yet the room was full of soft, white light. I looked down at the floor. Neither Oother or I were casting a shadow.

"Welcome, Chad. You can let go of my hand now."

I drooped Oother's hand. "Oh, sorry...Where are we?"

"We are in our facility. It serves as a base, a command center, housing, or anything else we may need.

The Grand Council will convene in approximately eight hours. That gives you some time to cleanup and to rest."

"I would appreciate that. Thank you."

"Please follow me."

I followed Oother to the opposite wall. A door panel slid open sideways and disappeared into the wall.

"That's very cool," I said. Oother ignored me.

I followed Oother through the door, and we turned right. We walked down a hallway past several other doors that all looked the same.

As we went, we came upon a man and woman in the hallway. The two were dressed alike in black slacks and yellow shirts. They both looked very similar to Oother; pasty white skin, brown eyes, and straight black hair. They stopped and spoke to Oother in a language I had never heard before.

After their brief exchange I asked, "Oother, where are we? I tried to imagine where the last portal would take me.

I was betting on either South America or Antarctica."

Oother stopped and turned to face me. "Chad, where this facility is, isn't important. It has nothing to do with you."

I smelled onions. "Oother, you don't believe that. It is important, and you know it."

"I was warned about you, but frankly, I didn't believe it; that you could tell when someone was lying.

You're, well...we are, well...I think I'd better just show you. This way."

Oother turned and led me back in the direction we had just been until the hall ended abruptly at an orange door. The door slid open. I could see that the room was tiny; just large enough for a few people.

"What's this?"

"It's an elevator, Chad."

I followed Oother inside and the door closed behind us. Oother put the palm of his hand on the wall and a panel of buttons made of pure light appeared and floated in the air in front of him. Oother stuck a finger through the top button. The elevator car moved smoothly upward.

After a few seconds, the door slid open. Oother exited and I followed. We were standing in a very large circular room. Round white tables with four to six chairs each were clustered throughout the open space. Each table was supported by a single white cone. The chairs matched the tables. I blurted out, "the nineteen-sixties called, they want their furniture back."

To my right was something that looked like a cafeteria buffet line. At the end of the line was an indentation in the wall; I couldn't tell what the indentation was concealing.

I counted eleven people in the room seated at various tables. They were all dressed alike and looked like the people I had seen in the hallway. Some were eating, some were talking, and some were just sitting.

I walked forward about ten feet, and looked up. My jaw went slack, I dropped Humpty and stumbled backward.

Oother steadied me so I didn't fall.

Above me was a clear dome revealing a black sky. There were stars, and the most prominent feature was a huge reddish ball. I recognized the reddish orb from countless pictures taken through telescopes. I stared in disbelief at the scarred surface and the craters.

"That's...we're on...that's really…?"

Oother looked at me and smiled, clearly amused.

"You know it as Mars."

I removed my backpack and dropped it. I walked to the nearest chair and sat with my jaw hanging limply.

Oother joined me.

"Oother, you mean we're on a space ship?"

"No. Mars has two moons. We are on the larger moon, Phobos."

"Please explain *all* of this. Why?"

"I won't explain all of it, at least, not until after you meet with the Grand Council. Afterwards, I'll tell you more. Until then, how about something to eat?"

Oother didn't wait for my reply. He got up and headed toward the indentation at the end of the buffet counter. He returned carrying a tray which he sat in front of me.

"This is ulchar soup. Next to it is sliced chartan fruit."

I pointed to the amber glass on my tray and asked, "What's that?"

Oother smiled, "That's water."

I took a spoon and lifted some of the soup. It looked creamy and kind of greenish, and there were little black bits floating in it. I smelled it before putting it in my mouth.

I deposited a spoonful of the warm liquid in my mouth. Flavors exploded on my tongue. There was something nutty, something citrus, and something a little like cheese. I swallowed.

"That's very good."

"You'll want the chartan."

"Oother, tell me about this place. Why put it here,

on...Phob..." I coughed. I couldn't make words. My throat was closing quickly. I panicked. It felt like I was inhaling through a soda straw.

Oother pushed the chartan close to me.

"I told you, you'll want the chartan fruit. Ulchar is poisonous. Chartan is the antidote."

I looked at Oother, stunned. I managed to rasp, "Can't breathe!"

Oother leaned close, "Take the chartan."

My hand shook as I quickly took a slice of what looked like raw potato. I bit into it. The taste was horrendous! It was bitter and sour at the same time. I forced myself to swallow. The taste made me imagine black ink filling my mouth and coating my throat. Almost instantly I began breathing easier.

I choked and coughed out a question "Why?"

Oother cocked his head, "Why Phobos?"

"No," I coughed, "Why…poison?"

Oother leaned in close. He lowered his voice to a whisper.

"Because I've learned something. I have to be very selective who I talk to. You need to be careful too."

I nodded as though I understood, even though I didn't.

"Chad, ulchar and chartan need each other. Which one of those two would you call good, and which one would you call evil?"

I swallowed hard. "I'm more concerned about you right now."

"This is important, Chad. Is ulchar good or evil?"

"I don't know. The ulchar tastes very good, but it's still poison. The chartan is awful, but it stops the poison. I guess it's all in how you define good."

"Exactly. You need to be *very* careful, Chad. Don't be taken in by anyone's definition of good. Don't be too quick to put anything in a box and label it good. That could be a catastrophic mistake. Not everything is as it seems."

Oother leaned back in his chair and resumed speaking normally. "Now, finish your soup and then I'll get you settled until the Grand Council convenes."

"I think I'm done with the soup."

"Very well, Chad, follow me."

Oother stood, and headed back toward the elevator. I grabbed my things and followed.

CHAPTER THIRTY-THREE

Oother had taken me to a small room that, in my opinion, would have doubled nicely as a prison cell. The bed was a metal plate fastened to the wall. On the plate was an orange mat, about three inches thick. There was one small, white, round table with a matching chair. Sitting folded on the table was a change of clothes. A brown shirt, jeans, socks, underwear, and tennis shoes all in my size.

Oother had left me alone, told me to rest, cleanup and change into fresh clothes. He said he would come get me before the meeting.

I did clean up and put on the clothes, but I couldn't rest. My mind was spinning with questions. I was sitting in a room, on a moon orbiting Mars, and the man that was supposed to be my guardian had deliberately fed me poison as some kind of an object lesson. His reason? He wanted me to be suspicious of everyone and everything. He definitely succeeded.

I must have fallen asleep, because I was unaware when Oother entered the room. I was startled when I heard his voice. "Chad. It's time."

I sat up on the bed and stayed there for a moment as I

oriented myself.

"Oother, what should I expect?"

"The Grand Council has fifteen members. Normally, when they meet it's a very formal and boring affair. They read notes from the previous meeting, they discuss and argue details of the current projects, and the Council Master gives out assignments.

I don't know what this meeting will be like. Just be polite. Tell them what you need to and ask the questions you want to ask. If you don't like the answers to your questions, don't push too hard. Remember, you don't have any way to get home without help."

I nodded, stood, and followed Oother out of the room. We walked down a couple of hallways, took an elevator up a couple of levels, and then down a couple of more hallways before arriving.

I was brought into a large room with theater seating. I didn't count, but guessed it would seat about two hundred people.

Across the platform, at the front, was a long table with fifteen chairs behind it. At the foot of the platform was a smaller, rectangular table with four chairs facing the platform.

Oother guided me to the small table with the four chairs and we took our seats. I turned to Oother and stated nervously, "I feel like I'm on trial."

"You may be. Everything you say certainly will be."

I swallowed hard and fidgeted a little. "Oother, about what you were telling me with the soup..."

Oother lowered his voice to a whisper, "Not now, Chad, not here. Later."

We sat in silence for just a little longer before a brown-robed procession came in through the door. The leader of the procession was a man with straight, black hair and pasty-white skin. He took the central seat behind the long table.

The Matron was number four in the procession. She

took a seat at the far end of the table. There were a total of three men in the group, and the rest were women. As far as race was concerned, the women looked like a smattering of every race on Earth. There could not have been a more diverse looking group. The men, however, looked like Oother; far too pasty-white, dark brown eyes and straight black hair.

After everyone was seated, the man at the center thumped the table.

"Thank you all for coming to this special convocation. I know we all have things we need to be doing. We will, therefore, dispense with the usual formalities and attend to the matter at hand."

The man looked down at me.

"Mr. Fury."

"Yes, sir."

"I am Council Master, Garthon."

I nodded, "Pleased to meet you, sir, and thank you for having me."

The man nodded to me. "I trust you were made comfortable?"

"Yes, sir."

"Good, now to the matter at hand. It is my understanding that you have information about the Abomination which you would like to share with us. If you will consent to us cutting you, we can take that information quickly and efficiently."

"With all due respect, Garthon, ladies and gentlemen, I would prefer to share the information verbally. I do not have your ability to acquire memories. Therefore, I would prefer to conduct our business on a more even field."

Garthon looked a little irritated. "Humans. So very foolish. Very well, I'll not try to convince you. If we tried to take your memories, and you were unwilling, it would make the process longer and more difficult.

Please tell us what you know."

I started to stand and Oother pulled on my shirtsleeve.

I remained seated and looked up and down the panel. I related everything that Ladon had told me in my two encounters with him. After I had finished, the brown-robed group began discussing something, in what I assumed to be, the El-yanin language.

As the pace of the conversation slowed, Garthon spoke and the group fell silent.

"Mr. Fury. Everything you said could have been related through Lisa. Why are you here?"

I opted for honesty. "Garthon, ladies and gentlemen. Ladon believes everything he was saying to me. But, just because he believes it, that doesn't make it true. I need to know the truth. Just as you are compelled to save your people, I will not be a party to the destruction of mine. I need to know if anything Ladon said is true; will you unleash thousands of monsters on earth, and do you plan to destroy humanity when you leave?"

Oother kicked my leg, but I didn't react. I knew exactly what I had done the very moment I did it. I had committed myself. For all I knew, Garthon might throw me into space just to be rid of me. I watched Garthon. But, I could not tell if my statement had affected him one way or another.

Garthon shifted in his seat, then stood and began speaking. "Mr. Fury. You've had contact with Lisa and Tatriana-shar-dasa; you know her as the Matron."

Garthon turned toward the end of the table where the Matron was seated.

"Tell me, Tatriana, have you ever told Chad our departure plans?"

The Matron looked calm and relaxed as she said, "No, Council Master. I have not."

Garthon gave her a nod, and turned back to me. He said nothing for a few seconds. Then he spoke.

"Chad. I believe one of your religious books says, 'out of the mouth of two or three witnesses, let every word be established.' I'm going to let others in this room tell you our plans. Atvana-sur-tarventa, please tell Chad about our plans to depart."

Garthon seated himself and a young, woman with African features stood to her feet. She cleared her throat.

"Chad. After we have the books, we will gather at..." The woman looked at Garthon, "Council Master, shall I disclose the departure location?" Garthon shook his head from side to side. The woman continued, "We shall assemble at a particular location. The knowledge of the books will be loaded into a cartoosh. I think you would call a cartoosh a quantum computer.

Regardless, the data will be loaded, and we will sing the traveling song. The cartoosh will destabilize the kartal-dashar in a certain volume of water. Your people call it the *Higgs Boson*.

The destruction of the matter will be a controlled reaction, much like your nuclear reactors. A portal connecting to El-yana will open. We will take the genes we have harvested and we will depart. The portal will close, and we will never return."

The woman sat and Garthon stood. He looked at me and spoke slowly, "Tell me, Chad, did you detect any deception?"

"No, Council Master Garthon. I did not."

"Good. Now, Oother, it is your turn. Tell Chad about our departure, and feel free to add anything that you feel was left out."

I was stunned by Garthon's request that Oother corroborate what I was just told. Garthon knew I could detect lying. Oother knew it too.

I turned in my chair to face Oother, and Oother faced me. He spoke slowly and deliberately. "Chad. What you have heard is planted deeply in the memories of all of us."

I inhaled, there was no change in the odors in the room. Oother continued, "Every single one of us believes the account you have heard." I smelled onions.

"Chad, before we depart, we will destroy the

Abomination. The Protectors will play that role. As they hunt the Hunters, the Abomination will attempt to relocate with the books. That is how we will find our missing books."

There was no sign of deception; Oother believed what he was saying. He continued, "The Protectors will gather around us before we depart. They will ensure that no one will interfere with our plans. After we exit through the portal, the portal will collapse, and the energy from the collapse will destroy the protectors."

I smelled onions, strong onions. Oother had told a lie, and it was a whopper.

Garthon interrupted the interaction. "Tell me, Chad, are you satisfied that you have been told the truth?"

I swallowed hard and decided it was best to play along with this charade. "Yes. I am."

"Very well. Then let me ask you some questions. We cannot allow the Abomination to get the Stone of Destiny. Either we send the Protectors to locate the stone, or you commit to keeping the books and the stone from their hands. If they have the stone and even one book, it will be disastrous for all of us.

My question is simple. Will you help us? What are your plans now?"

I knew it was against protocol, but I stood to my feet. "Council Master Garthon, and members of the Grand Council. I promise you this. I will do everything I can to keep the stone out of Ladon's hands. If I can destroy the stone, I will. If I can't destroy it, then I will make certain that it is where he can't get it."

Garthon smiled, "This Council is adjourned. Oother, please see to it that Chad is returned."

CHAPTER THIRTY-FOUR

Following the council meeting, Oother led me to what he called his lab, saying that he needed to make a new transresinator for me. I tried to ask questions along the way, but he silenced me, and whispered that I should wait to ask.

Inside Oother's lab, I took a seat on a white stool behind a shiny black tabletop mounted along one wall. Against the wall was a glossy black panel about six feet wide and four feet tall. Oother sat next to me.

"Chad, I thought you might want to see how we make things. Let me start by sealing the door. We can't compromise the room during the process."

Oother tapped the tabletop once, and a series of dots lit up on the black surface. He tapped three of them.

"Alright Chad, the room is sealed and soundproofed. We can talk freely here."

Oother tapped a few more glowing symbols, and a black block, about three feet tall, six feet wide, and three feet deep, rose from the floor in the center of the room.

"Chad, it will take about two hours for the quantum computer to make a new transresinator out of waste material here in the complex. We have that long to talk freely."

Oother tapped a few more symbols as he sang a few notes; it sounded as if he was practicing scales. When he finished singing and tapping the symbols on the tabletop, I spoke.

"Oother, I don't even know where to begin. Rather than me ask you a bunch of pointless questions, why don't you just tell me what it is you think I need to know?"

Oother agreed, "I can do that. What you need to know first is that what is happening on Earth is neither the first nor the only operation of its kind. This whole thing has been going on for longer than you can imagine, in more places than just Earth."

"What do you mean?"

"Chad. The *original* Oother came here with expedition number twenty-nine. I am aware of forty-seven total past or on-going efforts similar to this one. There are eleven such efforts in this universe, three of which are in this very galaxy."

"I thought the traits you were looking for were rare, and so are the potential planets with compatible life."

"You're right, Chad. They are rare; so rare that we had to make it happen. We couldn't rely on just stumbling upon what we needed."

"So you did what, exactly, Oother?"

"The first expedition to your solar system found two planets capable of supporting life compatible with our own; Cerrous, you know it as Mars, and Earth.

The first expedition helped evolution along. They seeded the planets with genes that would eventually develop into creatures that look like us.

That group of El-yanin returned home. Then the current group arrived. We entered at a different point in your time; a time in which life should have developed to the point that we could begin experimenting with cross breeding.

Our group consisted of two-hundred female volunteers and forty scientists and technicians. On your calendar, that was about four-thousand BC."

"Whoa, wait a second, Oother. Lisa told me you came to Earth about fourteen-hundred years ago."

"Yes, that's what most of us believe. I used to believe it too. But we have been given false memories. The reality of what we did is horrific. Too many of us would rebel if the truth were known."

"What is the truth?"

"When we came, Cerrous was more developed than Earth. They were noble creatures; slender, tall, bronze skinned, and talented in mathematics. We chose to focus our efforts on the Cerrans.

The first pairings between El-yanin and Cerrans were disastrous. The offspring were deformed, savage brutes.

We released viruses that inserted new traits into the population. With each release of new traits we would make a little progress in one area, but fail in others. The more we added new traits to the population, the more disease we created. After a few generations the population was riddled with cancers and mental disorders."

"So they just died out?"

"No, Chad. It was decided that we should cleanse the planet. A few that were not diseased were sent to Earth. It was hoped their traits would mix favorably with the inhabitants of Earth. After they were re-settled, we set about cleansing Mars.

We destroyed the Higgs Boson in the water. The water burned; it was a nuclear fire. All of the water burned; the oceans, the rivers, the plants and animals, and even the water vapor in the air.

The surface of the planet became so hot that the thermal currents in the planet's molten metal core stopped. When the currents stopped, the magnetic field around the planet collapsed. Solar radiation poured onto the planet eliminating the possibility that life would ever exist here again."

Oother hung his head. It was obvious he had mourned over the death of the planet, many times. What had been done seemed to still weigh heavily on him.

"Oother, I can't begin to take in what you're telling me. Did everyone go along with this?"

"No. There was a revolt, an attempt to put a stop to the destruction. But, the revolt was futile. It was crushed and the instigators were killed. False memories were created and seeded into the clones of all El-yanin. Every clone now wakes with the false memories. They have no memory of what happened on Mars. For them, everything started with Earth."

"Are you the only one that knows the truth?"

"No. Garthon and the Matron know the truth. I don't think they ever got the false memories. It was their decision to destroy Mars. They are the ones perpetuating the false memories. And they are the ones driving events toward a similar end on Earth."

"Tell me about Earth."

"After Mars was destroyed, we went into stasis for a time. Most of us awoke about fourteen-hundred years ago. But, Garthon and the Matron would wake up every few centuries to check the progress of their experiment. When the population needed a correction, they would introduce wars and disease to thin out different populations. The black plague was their invention."

"Oh my God, Oother! The black plague killed over fifty-million people!"

"Yes. Add to that influenza, and small pox."

"That's horrible!"

"In their minds it *looks* like they may have succeeded in getting viable traits. That's why they have not destroyed the Abomination."

"I don't understand. Why do they need the Abomination?"

"Because ulchar needs chartan. The El-yanin need

them. If the Abomination are crossed with the hybrids we have created, and the offspring are normal, then we will have succeeded."

"Why are you telling me this, Oother?"

"Because it won't work. I've seen too much. I know what has happened on other worlds. In every case, we failed. I've come to believe that you only solve spiritual problems with spiritual answers."

"What do you mean?"

"Every planet with intelligent life tends to do exactly the same thing. They start with cultures that believe in many gods, and eventually monotheism takes hold. Within the monotheistic religions, the issue of personal sin comes to the forefront, and so does a solution."

"Are you telling me that only God can fix your problems? I think my uncle would like to talk to you."

"What I'm saying is, intelligent species recognize evil. And every one of them comes to the same conclusion. It is a problem that can only be fixed by something bigger than themselves."

"I'm not sure what to say to all of that. In order to make yourselves better, you're creating and destroying entire species."

"Yes, Chad, entire worlds. And, if necessary they would destroy entire universes. Our problem, the El-yanin problem, has no solution. But they don't see it. They will keep on doing this for as long as they exist. Every living thing in every universe eventually dies. If it is our time, then so be it."

"Oother, what do I need to do?"

"Keep the stone out of the hands of the Abomination, and the books away from us."

"What about those books, Oother? Ladon seems to think they may not be all that important."

Oother cracked a mischievous smile. "Chad, the pages in the book are meaningless. The words are a deception. A ruse.

We needed to hide something and keep it safe. The best way to do that was to convince our enemy that he needed it. He ended up protecting it for us."

"So what is it that the Abomination is keeping safe for you?"

Oother got up and crossed over to the other side of the room. He pulled something from a cabinet drawer and returned. He handed me a crystal rod, cut in half, lengthwise. The rod was about seven inches long, and two inches wide. It was curved on one side and flat on the other.

"What is this, Oother?"

"That is a data crystal. Think of it as one of your USB storage devices. In the spine of each book is a data crystal. They contain maps of the universes all El-yanin have been to, and the coordinates needed to return to El-yana.

Place any data crystal in contact with a quantum computer, and the computer will access the data in the crystal. We need all of the data crystals to get home. Keep the crystals on Earth, and Earth will not be destroyed."

"But how did they come to be in the hands of the Abomination, and why are they in the books rather than here?"

"That, Chad, is a very long story that will have to wait for another time."

The humming in the room subsided, and I looked at the table in the center. In the middle of the table was a transresinator. Oother tapped a couple of symbols on the counter.

"Chad, our time's up. I'm unlocking the door."

The door panel slid open to reveal someone standing there; a young woman with pasty white skin, dark eyes, and straight black hair. She spoke to Oother in a language I didn't understand.

When their conversation ended, Oother looked seriously at me. "Chad, we have to go. Lisa needs to talk to you. It's important."

CHAPTER THIRTY-FIVE

Oother led me to another room that looked similar to his lab. A pasty-white woman sat behind a single table at the front of the room. Her job seemed to consist of tapping symbols that appeared and disappeared on the black tabletop. Occasionally she would speak to a voice that seemed to come from nowhere.

Oother approached the woman and they exchanged a handful of words, again in a strange language. Oother turned to me and said, "I've asked her to contact Lisa. Please, come stand next to me."

Oother took a position about a third of the way into the room, facing the back wall. I stood to his right, and we waited silently. I heard the woman behind me tapping the countertop a few times, and saying something. A moment later Lisa appeared, standing, facing us.

I stared for a second, then turned and asked Oother, "A hologram?"

"Yes, Chad. Give it a few seconds more."

I waited, and after about five more seconds, the image nodded its head, and spoke, "Hello Oother, Chad."

Oother and I both said, "Hello," in unison.

Lisa started in and monopolized the conversation. She was in high gear, and had no intention of showing restraint. She spoke sharply, "Chad! How could you be such an idiot! I mean, of all the bone-headed, thick-skulled, moronic and imbecilic things!"

I interrupted, "What are you talking about? What did I do?"

"What did you do!?" Lisa's eyes flashed at me, "How can you even ask that? You! You moron!"

Lisa was continuing to rant as I turned to Oother.

"Oother, can she see me?"

"Yes, Chad, she can."

I took a step closer to Lisa's image, extended my arm, turned my palm up, made a fist, and displayed a single finger in front her face.

Lisa's image momentarily froze with a look of shock. "Chad! That's rude! How could you?"

I lowered my arm. "Now that I have your attention...berating me isn't solving anything. You haven't even said what you're upset about! I *strongly* suggest that you put away your anger so we can have a *useful* conversation. Now tell me what happened!"

Lisa shifted her weight and scowled, "Ladon called. I had to pretend to be you."

"We expected that. Did he buy it?"

"Not entirely. He knows something's up."

"Why?"

Lisa hesitated, "Ladon's been monitoring your bank account and credit cards. A charge came through on your credit card. It seems you paid for a hotel room in Beijing with your *personal* credit card."

I was stunned. "I...I what?"

"Chad, you used your personal credit card, twice in Beijing. You paid for a hotel room, and you bought something at a sporting goods store."

I exhaled in disgust, "How could I have done that? I'm such and idiot!"

Lisa jumped in quickly, "Well, at least we agree on something!"

"What's this all mean, Lisa?"

"Ladon's coming to Oklahoma City to get an update from you, face to face. He'll be here, at our hotel, in about twenty-four hours."

"It's over! Lisa, there's nothing I can do! It will take days to get back to Vegas the way I came. And I can't get a plane from Beijing; I don't even have a passport."

"I know, Chad." Lisa shook her head slowly, "It's hopeless."

Oother touched my shoulder, "Excuse me."

Lisa and I kept talking, and Oother tried again, only louder, "Excuse me!"

I turned to Oother, Lisa and I said in unison, "What!"

Oother asserted himself. "If the two of you will calm down, I can have Chad back in the United States in less than five hours."

Lisa looked stunned. "That's not possible!"

Oother inhaled and exhaled as if he had something important to say. "It is possible. I'll have Chad explain when he gets there. I'll send you coordinates after I get Chad on his way."

Lisa agreed, and the image disappeared.

Without looking at me, Oother turned and started walking. He commanded, "Chad, follow me."

We proceeded quickly to the elevator which took us to what I assume was the very bottom, several floors down. When the doors opened, we were in what appeared to be an older, more unused part of the complex. It almost looked like we were in access tunnels. The walls and floor were gray, and there was dust on large pipes running the length of the ceiling.

Oother turned and led me down the tunnel to a large room. Inside was filled with shelves and containers. Against one wall was equipment that I did not recognize, and on another wall was what looked like orange-colored space suits, hanging on racks.

Oother went to the suits and started examining them. He turned and looked me up and down one time. He rifled through the suits until he found one he liked. "Come over here, Chad."

I went, and Oother selected a suit and pushed it into my arms. The suit was extremely light weight, and the fabric seemed very thin.

"What's this for, Oother?"

"Occasionally we have to do work outside. You'll need it to get back to Earth."

I followed Oother to a shelf with boxes. He pulled out a box, and opened it. Inside was a helmet to match the suit I was holding. He handed me the helmet, while he went to another box and retrieved boots and gloves.

Oother exited the storeroom carrying the boots and gloves, and I followed. We walked down the hall, made a couple of turns and ended at another empty room.

"Chad, put on the suit, quickly."

I tried, but needed Oother's help. As I was being put into the suit, Oother gave me instructions on how to lock and release the clamps for the boots, gloves, and helmet. He gave me more instructions to help me get where I was going.

Before Oother put the helmet over my head, I had to say something. "Oother, thank you."

"You're welcome, Chad. Just put a stop to this mess, if you can. Don't let the Sisterhood have the books, and keep the stone out of the hands of the Abomination."

"I'll try."

"Another thing, Chad. If Garthon or the Matron find out what I'm doing, or what I've told you, I'll be replaced by a clone with different memories. There's every possibility that I won't be here to help you if you need anything. If you see me again, realize that it may not be me."

I took Oother's right hand in mine, and placed my left

hand on his shoulder.

"Thank you Oother. I sincerely hope that doesn't happen. I'd like to keep you as a friend."

Oother nodded, "I hope so too."

I don't know where he'd been carrying it, but Oother produced a transresinator and showed it to me.

"Here, Chad. When I made this, I sync'd it with your biometric signature. It will open the portals for you, but not much else until Lisa programs it."

He put the cube in a pouch attached to the waist on my suit. Then, he slipped the helmet over my head. When it sank into the suit's collar, there was a hissing sound and the pressure in the suit increased.

Oother patted me once on the shoulder, and I turned toward the gray wall behind me. I walked through it.

CHAPTER THIRTY-SIX

I scanned the horizon. If I had not been told differently, I could have easily believed I was standing in a desert on Earth. The sky was grayish orange from the dust hanging in the air. There were mountains on the horizon, in every direction. The sun was just above the horizon; I didn't know if it was setting or had just risen. I wished I'd had a camera; I was the first man on Mars and I had no way to prove it.

I looked down at my feet. I was standing on what looked like loose, orange sand. I bent down and rubbed my gloved hand over it, it was finer than sand, it was almost dust.

I stood up and looked at my immediate surroundings. I was standing just inside a large circle of crumbled and broken black rocks. In the center was a short black column, a pedestal about three feet tall, and two feet across. I took a step toward it, and yelled out as I stumbled forward and fell on my face.

I knew Mars had less gravity, but to go immediately from normal gravity to this was ridiculous. My muscles had no time to adjust. Instead of a little step I had made a leap of about eight feet.

I stood up carefully and oriented myself back toward the column in center. I stepped again, very cautiously. Gingerly, I approached the black stone.

Obeying Oother's instructions, I placed the transresinator, silver edges down, on the center of the pedestal. The ground vibrated under my feet, in regular, rhythmic pulsations. The sandy dust formed ripples radiating from the column. It looked as though someone had dropped a stone in a pool of water.

The circle of crumbled stones yielded to something pushing its way up from underneath. I counted twelve giant slabs of what looked like black, shiny obsidian taking their places on the surface. I was soon surrounded by a stone circle similar to the ones on Earth. The monolithic slabs were easily fifteen feet tall and possibly five or six feet thick.

I turned my attention to the center pedestal. I placed my gloved hand on top of the transresinator. White images appeared on the surfaces of the black monoliths. One of the stones was covered in symbols, writing that I could not read. According to Oother, I needed to orient myself to that stone.

I went to the stone and found the symbol he had described to me about six inches above eye level. It was a curved line, bowl shaped, with two parallel lines forming a stem beneath the bottom of the bowl. There were three vertical dots between the lines. I reached up and touched it with my index finger. The symbol flickered and glowed yellow.

I turned my attention to the stones at my left. Oother said it would be either the third or fourth stone, he couldn't be sure which.

On the first stone to my left was a galaxy; pinpoints of white dots representing stars slowly turning around a central axis. I counted six arms radiating from a dense ring of white dots with a black void in the center. Toward the center of one arm was a red triangle.

The next two stones were similar. Each had images of galaxies of different shapes. Each galaxy had one or more red triangles in them. On the fourth monolith was a spiral galaxy with a bulging disc at the center. The disc sat on its edge. From the edges of the disc were two arms spiraling outward. Between the two spirals were two wispy arms, not connected to the disc. There were three red triangles in the arms. I was very glad I had taken an astronomy class in college. If anyone had tried to tell me that I would one day *need* the class, I would have laughed at them.

I recognized the galaxy as our ours, the Milky Way. I touched the triangle that seemed to be furthest from the center, where I assumed our solar system was.

I turned back to look at the pedestal at the center of the circle. Floating above the transresinator, was a glowing image of Earth, slowly turning in midair. I approached the image. There, over the North American continent was a large, red triangle. I put my finger through the triangle.

The image stopped turning, it rose to a height of what I guessed to be fifteen or so feet. It changed to a ball of yellow light, and started moving to my left.

I picked up the transresinator and put it in the pouch on my spacesuit. I walked toward the glowing ball. As I walked, it moved forward. When I stopped, it stopped.

As I went, I became used to the change in gravity. I couldn't run like I did on Earth. Running on Mars was more like hopping. I lengthened my stride and found I was able to do a type of exaggerated running motion. I wasn't moving my legs as rapidly as running, but I was covering more ground with each step. I would have loved to know how fast I was going, it felt like the ground was flying by beneath my feet.

The landscape was pocked with craters. Most of which were small enough that I could leap from one edge and land somewhere near the center of the crater. On the larger ones, I was in and out of the crater in a matter of two or three hops.

I don't know how far I ran, but it was long enough I got bored with the lack of scenery. The craters and rocks tended to look very much alike from one place to another.

At long last, I saw something in the distance; it was a mound of some kind. It wasn't a mountain, or really even a hill. It was a solitary object and the glowing orb was leading me toward it.

As I approached, the structure grew in size and I saw that it was pyramid shaped. It was hard to recognize at first because sharp edges had been worn away and rounded by the blowing sand.

The pyramid was made of large reddish stones fitted together tightly. I don't know how the size compared to the pyramids of Egypt, since I had only seen pictures of those. But, even from a distance this one seemed massive.

The yellow orb stopped in front of the pyramid, and hung motionless near the face. I approached the face slowly and stood directly beneath the glowing orb.

I took a minute to look closely at the stones and when I looked up again, the orb had vanished.

"Well, I guess I'm here," I said aloud. "I wonder what I do next? Oother left this part out."

I patted the face of the pyramid. It was solid. There was no portal. I pulled out the transresinator and looked it over. A small red arrow pointed directly at the wall in front of me. I held the transresinator against the wall momentarily. Something started to happen. I felt the ground beneath me vibrate, and the soft sand sank beneath my feet.

I took a step back and fell. I pushed myself back and scrambled away from the hole rapidly forming at my feet. I sat at the edge of the hole until the moving sand slowed and stopped. Thankfully, I still had the transresinator in my right hand.

I was staring at a dark hole that seemed to lead inside of the pyramid. I can only assume that over the passing years sand must have piled up and covered the entrance. When the transresinator touched the wall, a door had opened and the sand poured through like an hourglass.

I put my cube in my pouch and lowered myself feet first into the hole. It was just large enough to squeeze through. Inside, it was pitch black. But light from my suit came on automatically when I entered the darkness.

I was in a large main room. I took a moment to examine the walls. They were covered in elaborate paintings and gold artwork. I have no idea how all of this survived the intense heat Oother described, but it must have been protected for some reason.

The longer I stared at the paintings and the gold wall hangings, the more I decided that it looked like Aztec or Mayan artifacts. I mused over a thought. If this connected to the Mayans, just how many other civilizations had connections to other planets in our universe? After all, the stone circle that led me here pointed out doorways to other worlds too. But, there was no time to daydream no matter how compelling the mystery. I needed to locate the portal to Earth.

A quick walk around the room showed three doorways. Only one of the doorways seemed to lead deeper into the pyramid. I went through it.

The doorway turned out to be a tunnel leading down a sloping path. The entire passageway was lined from floor to ceiling with grotesque little figurines standing only five or six inches high, all sitting in little alcoves, standing guard over the path. There must have been hundreds of the figures keeping a silent watch over the corridor. Each little figure appeared to be made of gold and was adorned with various precious stones set in the eye sockets.

I took a couple of the figures and put them in free pouches in my suit. I don't know if that counts as stealing, or maybe some kind of desecration, but there was no way I was leaving Mars without taking something with me.

The passageway continued on, guiding me downward,

and turning a few times before depositing me in a small chamber.

I found myself standing in a simple room with nothing but a vertical, black stone slab in the center. I didn't have to speculate or second guess. It had to mark the portal. I walked up and touched the surface. It rippled like a pool of water

.

CHAPTER THIRTY-SEVEN

I had gone immediately from a dark room with a black stone slab to a dark room, without a stone slab. I turned my head from side to side, taking in what I could see of my surroundings. The lights in my suit were showing the walls to be stone. I just hoped this was Earth.

I took a step, but my leg didn't move the way it was supposed to. My toes drug the floor, and I stumbled. I felt much heavier here. My legs still wanted to move like they had done in the Martian gravity. I took that as a good sign, and hoped that I could breathe the air.

My right hand moved to the collar holding the helmet. My fingers found the three buttons Oother had shown me. I pressed the two outer buttons and then hesitated before pressing the center one. There was a click and then a hiss as the pressure changed. I twisted the helmet a little to the left; it clicked again. I held my breath, and lifted the helmet just above my mouth.

I exhaled slowly, paused, and readied myself to put the helmet back if I needed it. I inhaled slowly through my mouth. The air *seemed* fine. I exhaled and inhaled two more times before I pulled the helmet the remainder of the way over my head.

It was only after I had taken the helmet off that I wondered about the light still coming from my suit. I couldn't imagine how that was possible since there were no bulbs or individual light sources. The fabric of the suit seemed to be the source of the light.

I walked the perimeter of the room while examining the walls. They were solid rock that had been roughly hewn out into a rectangular space. There was no artwork, there were no cave paintings or any other sign of what this room might have been used for over the passing years. There was, however, a doorway. I had to duck to pass through.

On the other side was a passage, leading left and right. I would have been much happier to have been dumped into an open field. I had no idea if I was in a dungeon, a cave, or just what. I had a moment of worry that wanted to push itself into panic as I considered that wherever I was could be buried deep underground, and there might not be a way out.

"OK, Chad. Think. Think like a scientist. How can you know which way leads out of here?"

I turned to the right and yelled out, "Hello!" I listened. There was an echo. An echo could only mean something solid was in that direction.

I turned to the left and repeated, "Hello!" I waited and there was no reply. I thought it was rather amusing. I had never actually read Dante's Inferno, but I remember being told that the book's main character made his way out of Hell through a series of left turns. I started walking.

I hadn't proceed more than fifty feet before I smelled pine needles. What a welcome relief! Pine needles meant Earth, fresh air, and a way out somewhere ahead.

I went forward at a little faster pace. In the distance I saw a pinpoint of light. I jogged forward; it was a star. There were stars through an opening ahead. And, there was the sound of a breeze rustling through trees. My heart pounded, and I let out with a "Thank you, God."

I stopped at the opening to survey my surroundings. I was in a cave, in a cliff face, about fifty or so feet above the ground. I peered out, there were other openings in the cliff. The openings had wood ladders leading to the ground. I had no such luck as to have a ladder.

I removed my space suit. I had no intention of leaving it behind, so I put the gloves, boots, my shoes, and the helmet inside the body of the suit. I tied the arms together. I put my head between the arms. I let the suit dangle from my back like a limp doll.

It was an easy climb down. My claws had no problem holding to the rock face. On the way down, I peered into one of the cave openings. There was a house made of clay bricks in the entrance. That's when I knew, kind of, where I was. This had to be an Anasazi dwelling, and that meant I was in Colorado or New Mexico.

At the foot of the cliff, I retrieved my shoes, the transresinator, and the helmet. The remainder I laid out on the ground to fold carefully. With the suit face down and the arms to the side; I folded all of the material over the air tanks and tied the bundle off using the suit's arms.

I stood up with my bundle in my left hand and my helmet in my right. I proceeded away from the cliff face. I hadn't realized it, but I was standing in a gravel parking lot. At the far end of the lot, a car flashed its headlights.

I approached the car with a degree of caution. The driver rolled down his window and the head of a Hispanic looking young man peered out the window. "Are you Chad Fury?"

"I am."

"I need to take Chad Fury to the airport. I was told to take Chad Fury to the airport, and now I have to."

"I'm Chad Fury. Please take me to the airport."

I went to the passenger side of the old white sedan and let myself in. I sat down with my bundle in my lap and placed my helmet at my feet.

Gravel crunched under the tires as the car moved forward.

"Thank you for coming. You know I'm Chad, and you are?"

"I am taking Chad to the airport. I have to."

I laughed, "So much for conversation."

I watched the man drive. I felt a little sorry for him because of what Lisa had done to him. He was using his gasoline and losing sleep.

"Let's try this again, my name's Chad. What's your name?"

"Rafa. Rafa Morales."

"Alright, Rafa. You're taking Chad Fury to the airport. Which airport?"

"Cortez Municipal Airport."

"Is that in New Mexico, or Colorado?"

"Colorado. I'm taking Chad Fury to the airport."

"Yeah, I got that already."

I looked at the dashboard. "Hey, the clock in the dash, is that the right time?"

"No, it's seven minutes fast."

I did the math and set the time on my watch to two thirty-eight and settled in for the remainder of the ride.

At ten minutes after three a.m., we pulled to a stop in front of the Cortez Municipal Airport. Rafa turned to me, "You have a ticket waiting at Southern Airlines."

I opened the car door and stepped out. As soon as I was out, Rafa seemed to be more aware of what was happening.

"Hey, who are you? What are you doing?"

I reached back into the car for my things. "Rafa, I was stranded, and you gave me a lift to the airport. Thank you."

Rafa blinked a couple of times. "Yo! Man! Rafa don't do nuthin' fo' free."

I put my stuff on the ground and dug through my pockets. I found a couple of twenties and tossed them on the passenger seat. I suddenly had a lot less compassion for the man.

Rafa sped away and left me at the main entrance. I went to the door and pulled on the handle. The door didn't move, and I could see through the glass that the terminal was dark and empty. I looked at my watch, again. I figured it might be another couple of hours before I could go inside.

I sat on the concrete with my back against the door and closed my eyes. I know that I could have been upset over all kinds of things, but I was just so glad to be back on Earth, and back in the United States, that nothing else mattered.

I may have been there for about fifteen or twenty minutes before I heard a voice. "Hey, is everything OK, do you need anything?"

I opened my eyes to see a gray-haired man in a blue security guard's uniform looking down at me.

"I'm fine. I'm just waiting until the doors open."

"You picked a mighty uncomfortable place to wait. The doors don't open until five."

"I didn't have much choice. I was stranded and I hitched a ride here."

"That's just down-right unfriendly, leaving a man stranded out here." The guard shook his head from side to side. "Why don't you let me buy you a cup of coffee while you wait? Follow me, son."

I got up, gathered my things, and followed the man around the side of the terminal. The guard selected a key from a large ring bursting with keys. He opened a gray metal door and I followed him.

The door lead directly into a break room of some kind. The guard walked over to a counter where there was a stained coffee pot beneath a stained brewer that had definitely seen better days. He selected a Styrofoam cup and poured a far too-black liquid from the darkly stained pot.

"Here." He handed me the cup. "It's probably not as hot as you'd like but at least it's bitter."

"Thank you," I said. I dropped my orange bundle to the floor and took the cup. I took a sip and made a face. "I know one thing, you're an honest man."

The security guard motioned me to a long table and pulled out a folding chair. I sat down, and he went back to the counter. He returned with a box of donuts and some napkins.

"Try one of these, they make the coffee go down easier."

"You know," I said as I lifted my cup, "I think washing out the pot would help."

"We tried that once, a couple of years ago. It changed the taste too much. It was a full year before the coffee tasted right again."

I laughed. "Well, we can't have that."

The guard pulled up a chair. "My name's Keith."

I thought about whether to use my real name, and decided it didn't matter. "My name's Chad."

"So how did Chad end up stranded in Cortez, Colorado?"

"Now that's a long story. Too long for one cup of coffee."

"I've got some time."

I almost told him the truth, but decided to spare him the drama.

"I was hiking across country. My backpack was stolen. I have a little cash, credit cards, and drivers' license. But I lost everything else. I called a friend and she arranged for me to pick up a plane ticket. I hitched a ride, so here I am."

"Well, that didn't take so long to tell."

"No I guess it didn't. What about you? What's your story?"

"What makes a young fella like you think an old codger like me has a story to tell?"

"Call it a hunch."

"I lost my Carolyn twenty years ago, tomorrow."

"I'm so sorry."

The man just nodded and continued, "I was a doctor back then. But, without my Carolyn I became depressed. I didn't go to work and I started prescribing pills for myself. Eventually I lost my license. And, here I am."

"That's rough. I'm so sorry."

"Don't be. I wouldn't change a thing. I'm glad I had my Carolyn. A single day spent with someone who loves you is worth all of the pain and suffering of an entire lifetime. Carolyn and I had exactly seven thousand, three hundred fifty-two of those days together. I cherish every single one of them."

Keith and I sat and talked, well he mostly talked. I listened until the terminal opened for business.

After saying my farewell, I went to the Southern Airlines ticket counter where a middle-aged woman printed my tickets. She put my space suit into a box and checked it as baggage. I put the grotesque little gold figures and the transresinator into my space helmet and carried them with me.

The terminal was small, and I went through the only security checkpoint in the building. I performed the customary airport striptease and placed my shoes, belt, and other things in bins to go through the x-ray machine.

I walked barefoot through the metal detector while keeping an eye on my helmet and statues. After I passed through the metal detector, a TSA agent pulled me aside. He was holding my gold statues.

"Uhm…Are these real?

"What do you mean by real, sir?

"They look like gold."

"I know. I think they're lead in the center. I picked them up at a souvenir shop in Denver."

The TSA agent stood there in his blue uniform eying me suspiciously for a few seconds.

"What are they for? What are you going to do with them?"

"They're door stops. They scare away evil spirits."

"*Really.*"

"Oh yeah. If you think your house is haunted, you put a few of these around and it drives the ghosts away."

"Are you serious?"

I tried to keep from cracking a smile, "*Entirely.*"

The agent looked them over one more time and handed them back to me. "Good luck with that."

I took my statues and headed straight for an old black vinyl and chrome seat at one of the only two gates in the airport.

My flight boarded at six a.m., and flew out a few minutes later. We touched down in Denver, picked up a few people before continuing onward to Oklahoma City. I took the opportunity to sleep.

CHAPTER THIRTY-EIGHT

The Oklahoma City Airport doesn't change that much. There's always construction; new vendors seem to constantly rotate through the bays, and something is always being repaired. That's what doesn't change. It always seems like the airport is never finished.

It was one-thirty in the afternoon when I made my way down the concourse along with the rest of the travelers to wait at the baggage claim. While I was waiting for the conveyer belt to start depositing luggage on the carrousel, I felt a warm hand rest gently in the small of my back and I heard a welcome voice. "Hey there, Dragon Boy."

I turned to face Lisa. I hugged her and exhaled in relief. As I released the hug, I paused and let my lips say hello to her lips for a few seconds.

Lisa pushed me back and looked at me. "You certainly look like hell."

"Thanks. You're actually a sight for sore eyes."

"Come on, Chad. Let's get out of here. We've got a lot to tell each other. And I want to start with just how you got here."

"Not yet, I have to get my luggage."

"Luggage? You have luggage?"

"Not exactly, it's a box."

"What's in it?"

I lifted my right arm and showed Lisa my space helmet. "The rest of this. I checked the suit."

Lisa looked puzzled, "Just why do you have...I mean, where did you get...a space suit?"

"That, my dear, is part of the long story I have to tell. I needed the suit to get here."

I turned back to see my cardboard box coming toward me on the stainless steel carousel. I handed Lisa the helmet. She made a noise like it was heavy.

"Careful Lisa. What's inside is pretty heavy."

Lisa looked inside the helmet. "Chad, are those solid..."

I cut her off, "Shhh...Yes, I think they are. I'll tell you about them in a minute."

I took my box from the parade of luggage and took my helmet from Lisa. She started immediately toward the exit; I followed.

Lisa led me to my car, where she opened the trunk and I deposited my things. She tossed me the keys and I smiled. I couldn't wait to get behind the wheel of my baby once again.

I put the key in the ignition and turned it. The roar of the engine was a gentle, warm purr in my ears. I patted the dashboard, "Good girl."

Before putting the car in gear I adjusted the seat and mirrors. And, I noticed something. I sniffed the air. I sniffed again.

"Lisa, what's that? What did you do?"

"What are you talking about?"

"That smell, what did you do to my car?"

Lisa reached under her seat and pulled out a little round container that looked like a chewing tobacco tin. It was yellow and white with little vent holes in the top.

"Chad, Sirhan stinks! He smells like old socks and moldy cheese. I *had* to do something. The scent is lemon chiffon butter cookie. Do you like it?"

"Let me see that."

Lisa handed the thing to me. I opened the car door and threw it out.

"Chad, after you have Sirhan in the car with you, you'll want that back."

"I can roll down a window."

As we left the parking lot Lisa gave me directions to the hotel. And, she pumped me for information.

"Chad, spill it. How did you get here?"

"Through the portal on Mars."

"There is no portal on Mars. I would know."

"Then, Lisa, tell me why I have a space suit and two gold statues I took from a temple on Mars?"

"Chad, back up and tell me everything."

As we pulled onto the highway I told my story. I began with meeting Oother at the Old Dragon's head. When I got to the part about the soup, it started to rain. I turned on the windshield wipers and slowed down.

By the time we reached the hotel, I was finishing my story, and the rain was coming down in torrents. I parked the car and Lisa suggested waiting until the rain let up before getting out. I agreed.

"So, Lisa, what do you think?"

Lisa shook her head, "I don't know what to think. You show up here telling me that everything I know is a lie, and I can't even trust my own memories? I don't know *what* to do with this."

"Welcome to my world! About this time last year, you were asking me to believe a whole lot that I couldn't swallow."

"I get it, Chad…shoe's on the other foot. But give me something besides just this story!"

"I already did. The gold statues. Why do you think I took them? And, there's the space suit…analyze it. Do whatever you need to. I ran across Mars in it; it's covered with Martian dust. And then there's Oother. Get in touch with him. Find out what he has to say. And lastly, check out your own memories. Oother said the false memories are 'flat', whatever that means."

"Fine! I've got a lot to think about! But, you know what bothers me most?"

"No, what?"

"You're telling me I can't trust the very people that raised me, took care of me, and taught me everything I know."

"No, I'm telling you can't trust *some* of them. Most of them have been lied to, just like you."

Lisa frowned, "The rain's letting up. Let's go."

We got out. I grabbed my things from the trunk and followed Lisa inside the hotel. She led me up to the third floor and down a hallway to room three-eleven. She slid the key card into the lock, opened the door and walked inside. I followed. Lisa dropped the key card on the desk and took a seat in the chair. I dropped my things on the floor and sat on the bed, facing her.

"Chad, this is your room. I took the liberty of buying you a few clothes. They're hanging in the closet, they're in the drawers. You've got a razor, toothbrush, etcetera, in the bathroom. I wanted to make it look like you've been here a couple of days already."

"Thank you. I didn't know what I was going to do about clothes and things."

"Sirhan is in the adjoining room." Lisa nodded at the door next to the dresser. "Whenever Ladon asks for details about what you were doing, let Sirhan fill that in. Here's what you need to know.

You went to Lake Eufaula. You went to the home that used to belong to Colonel Roger Evans. The new owners were gone, and you broke in and looked around. You were interested in seeing if there was anything left in the attic. Sirhan found a shoebox wedged between the ceiling joists; it had these in it."

Lisa handed me several sheets of old, hand-written

papers that had been lying on the desk.

"What am I looking at?"

"These were all written to Colonel Evans, from someone named Ray. There were no envelopes, and Ray's last name isn't in the letters."

"And...Just what makes these important?"

Lisa reached out a hand and I handed the letters back to her. She rifled through them and read aloud. "Roger, you can't blame yourself. None of us knew what that block of stone could do, or how to use it."

She flipped through the letters again, "I'm looking after Eddie. Tell your lovely bride that her nephew will have only the best care. I won't let anything happen to him."

Lisa found another page and read, "Eddie isn't right. I don't think he ever will be. But I promise you, as long as I live, I'll make sure that he's taken care of. The facility he's in is top-notch and I'm visiting him every day."

"Wow, so Lisa, you think this Eddie had something to do with the stone?"

"I'm certain of it. There was some kind of an accident. Several people died very horribly. Eddie was injured, and this Ray person was taking care of him."

"Who is this, 'Ray'?"

"That's still part of the mystery we have to solve. Sirhan and I located Roger Evans' oldest son. He's living in Catoosa, Oklahoma. We had a talk with him and tried to find out if he had any friends named Ray that he ever talked about. We came up empty.

We did find out about Eddie. His name is Edward Scofield. Eddie went into the service and Roger used his influence to get Eddie into the kinds of positions that he thought were good for him. Eddie was injured in the service, and was never seen again.

Roger Evans blamed himself for what happened, and never was the same after that. His wife divorced him and died a few years later."

"What you're telling me, Lisa, is we don't have a clue

who Ray is, what happened to Eddie, or how to find the stone."

"That's mostly true. We don't know anything more about Ray or Eddie, but we know what we're looking for. We're looking for those names, and any reference to the accident."

"What's the next move, Lisa?"

"We go to the FBI. We look through the things confiscated from Sirhan's business. Hopefully, somewhere in there is something that will tell us about these people, and possibly the stone.

But, First, you need to read these letters and get cleaned-up. Get some dinner for you and Sirhan, and get ready to meet Ladon. He'll knock on your door at nine. I'm going to be in my room, directly above you. You can fill me in after he leaves."

I watched Lisa leave the room. I picked up the letters, laid back on the bed and started reading.

CHAPTER THIRTY-NINE

There was a knock at the door. I looked at my watch; it read nine-twenty. I leaned forward, adjusted the pillow against my back, and leaned back against the headboard. After a few seconds the knock came again. I turned off the television and went to the door. I undid the chain and opened the door. A surly looking Ladon was standing in the hallway.

"Ladon, I'm glad to see you're punctual. Won't you come in?"

Ladon replied with a scowl, "Ass."

I gestured toward the desk chair next to the window, "Please take a seat."

Ladon sat himself down and I returned to my nest on the bed and settled my back against the headboard. Ladon spoke first. "I want the truth, Chad. Tell me what you were doing all week."

I leaned forward to get up. "I'll get Sirhan. He can verify everything I say."

"Don't bother, Fury. I just came from his room. I cut him, and I have his memories. There's something wrong. You have one chance to tell me the truth or someone you love *will* die."

I swung my legs over the edge of the bed, and leaned forward. I narrowed my eyes and gave Ladon my coldest look.

"Hear me, and hear me *well*, Ladon. If anyone I care about dies, or is hurt in *any* way, then I *will* hunt you down! I will rip out your throat with my bare hands, and *you know* I can do it."

Ladon reached into his shirt pocket and pulled out a cell phone. He dialed. "Let's just see how your mother likes talking to me."

I pulled off my right shoe and threw it. It sailed like a bullet at the phone in his hands. There was a crack and the phone went sailing over Ladon's right shoulder. He yelped and shook out his hands.

"Fury! What the Hell!?"

"Ladon, you're an idiot if you think I'll help you if you hurt my mother. You're insane if you think threatening my family will get you anywhere. If you hurt anyone, there's no power in the universe that will stop me from killing you."

Ladon leaned back in his chair and calmly laid his right ankle on his left knee.

"Chad. I want the truth. Sirhan's memories don't add up. He remembers you, but he spent far too much time asleep this week. He seems to have gone to sleep on command.

Then, there's the business of your credit card being used in Beijing. I've got a guess as to what happened, but I want to hear it from you."

I sat up straight. I thought for a moment. If I didn't tell the truth, it might just make Ladon scrutinize me even more. Plus, he might decide that he was willing to risk killing mom.

"Ladon. I was in Beijing."

"Very good, Chad. Now what were you doing there?"

"I needed to verify what you told me about the plans of

the El-yanin."

"I thought you could tell when someone lying? I told you the truth, you should have known."

"All I knew, Ladon, was that you believed what you were saying. That didn't make it true."

"I concede your point, Chad. What did you determine?"

"That the El-yanin will destroy Earth, and everything on it when they leave."

"And that means, Chad, that you will..." Ladon let his words hang in the air as he waited for me to finish the statement.

"Ladon, I have no choice. I cannot let the El-yanin wipe us out."

"I take that to mean that you will deliver the stone to us."

"I will find the stone."

"You will locate the stone, and you *will* deliver it to us, Chad!"

"I haven't decided if I will give it to you. After you have the stone, you'll kill Mom and Uncle Allan."

"Sniff the air, Chad. Tell me if I'm lying. I promise you that if you deliver the stone to me, I will not kill your mother or your uncle."

I did sniff the air. There were no noxious odors. He believed what he was saying.

"Ladon, answer me this. Have you ever changed your mind and broken a promise?"

Ladon sat silent. He didn't answer.

"That's what I thought, Ladon. Your word's no good! Depending on which way the wind blows, you could justify breaking any promise."

"Let me give you a little clarity, Chad. The reason you're torn as to what to do is that you can't see any other way to stop the El-yanin. You know we're the best chance to keep everyone on this lousy little planet alive. If you had another option, we wouldn't be talking right now. It's true you don't like the option, but it's the *only* option you have."

I sat there motionless, and silent. Ladon was right, but I didn't want to admit it. I remembered Oother and his lesson with the soup. The El-yanin were the soup and the Abomination were the bitter antidote.

"Lost your tongue, Chad? Very well, let's move on to the search for the stone. How's that going?"

"Sirhan found something. Some letters. They're on the desk next to you."

Ladon pointed to his head, "I know about the letters. I know what's in them. Sirhan read them. What I want to know is what you're doing next."

"I'm going to the FBI. I'm going to ask Saysha Givens to give me access to everything they collected of Sirhan's"

"The FBI is not going to just give you access to everything."

"Normally, I would agree, but I have something they want. Sirhan."

"Well, that's a surprise."

"Why? You said you don't want him back, and I certainly don't want him around."

"Very well. Keep me updated."

Ladon stood and started toward the door. I got up and retrieved his cell phone from across the room. I went and handed it to him. Ladon reached out a hand and slapped me.

CHAPTER FORTY

My phone rang and jarred me awake. I rolled over and looked at the clock. Five fifty-three. Someone was calling the room phone at five fifty-three in the morning! I reached over and slurred out a "Hello."

"Chad, it's Lisa. We need to talk."

"Really?" I rubbed my eyes, "We need to talk before seven a.m.? What do you think we were doing past two this morning?"

"I'm serious, Chad. Throw some clothes on and get up here."

"Give me ten minutes."

I hung up the phone without saying so much as a goodbye, and got out of bed. In eleven minutes I was knocking on Lisa's door.

The door opened and revealed Lisa. She was dressed in loose fitting sweats. Lisa motioned me inside and I went.

On the far side of the room was a rolling table and two chairs. Breakfast for two was sitting on the table. And to my delight, there was a fresh pot of coffee.

"Lisa, if you wanted to have breakfast with me, all you had to do was say so. You didn't have to make it sound so urgent."

"It is urgent, at least for me. Breakfast was a courtesy. I wanted you to have a clear head for what I have to say."

"Look, if you're still upset about me telling Ladon that I was in Beijing..."

Lisa cut me off. "No. You did the best thing. Our little act was over. This is about Oother."

"What about Oother?"

Lisa went to the table and sat. I joined her.

"Chad. Just like you had to talk with the council and decide for yourself what's true, I need to find out what memories of mine, if any, are a lie."

"How can you do that?"

"I've been going over my memories. I don't see anything that looks *fake*. I think I need some help from the memories of other people in my head.

Remember last year when you needed to be in two places at once, and I said I needed to *talk* to my memories?"

"Sure, I remember."

"I need to do the same thing, only much more intensely."

Lisa poured some coffee for us. I took my cup and sipped.

"Chad, this time I need total quiet, and I'll need you to come check on me periodically."

"You're scaring me a little. I don't understand."

"If I'm this deep in my own head, there's a chance I could get lost. I might not be able to tell what's a memory versus what's real."

"Maybe you shouldn't do this."

"I have to, Chad. I have to know what memories I can trust. It's one thing to be told a lie and act on it, it's another thing entirely to have memories in your head that seem real, but are total fiction.

I am, who I am, because of my memories. That's how I make decisions and carry out my life. I base everything I do on my memories. I have to know what's real and what isn't."

"I think I understand. What can I do for you?"

"To keep myself anchored to reality, I tap a finger. As long as you see me tapping a finger on either hand, I am aware that I am reliving memories. The finger taps will stop if I've slid too deep into the memories. I'll need you to bring me back by whatever means possible."

"I don't think you should do this, Lisa."

"I have to. Just be here for me. Snap me out of it if I go too deep."

There was a little more conversation, but ultimately, I agreed. Lisa handed me her room key and I left.

I went to Sirhan's room and told him that I would be out. I left him with instructions to find a computer and research the names in the letters he had found. Besides just keeping him busy, I was hoping he might be able to dig out a little more information about those names.

I headed directly to the FBI office on Memorial Road, stopping only to replace my cell phone. The entire time I was mulling over what I would say to Agent Givens. If Lisa were here, this would be simple. Lisa would use her vocal talents to make Agent Givens give us access to whatever we want. But, I would have to do this the human way.

I pulled into the parking lot and stopped the car in a spot nearest the front entrance. I looked at my watch. It was just a few minutes past nine. The last time I had gone through those doors, my attorney had been with me. I found myself wishing I could consult with him right now.

I pulled open the door of the curved entrance and entered the lobby. It hadn't changed at all since I was there last. There was the same wood paneled security desk, the same fichus trees, and the same uncomfortable looking teal and chrome furniture in the lobby.

The man at the desk eyed me and spoke as I approached. "May I help you?"

I looked at the man and wondered if he was the same person who sat behind that desk when I was here a year ago. It was possible; he did look familiar.

"I'm here to see Saysha Givens."

"Is she expecting you?"

"No. Please tell her Chad Fury is here to see her."

The man raised his eyebrows in a way which seemed to me that he recognized my name. He picked up the phone and punched four numbers.

"Director Givens, this is the Security Desk. There's a Chad Fury here to see you...Yes ma'am. I understand."

The man lowered the receiver, and placed his palm over the mouthpiece. He looked me and cracked a small grin. "Director Givens wants me to ask you 'What the *hell* are you doing here?'"

"Director Givens? I always thought she was Agent Givens?"

The man sat silently and waited for an answer to my question. He cocked his head to one side as if he was gesturing for an answer.

"Tell her it's about Sirhan Jadiddian. I know where he is."

The man put the receiver back to his ear, "Director Givens, he says he knows the location of Sirhan Jadiddian...Yes, ma'am. I'll tell him."

The man cradled the receiver and said, "Take a seat. She will be a few minutes."

I went to the chairs in the lobby. Most of the seats were uncomfortable looking chrome and teal chairs. The one piece of furniture that wasn't chrome was a black leather love seat against the wall, and it looked even less inviting than the chairs.

I selected a chair and pulled out my new phone. I entertained myself by downloading my apps from the cloud, and getting all of the settings on the phone just the way I like them.

I was editing my contact list when Saysha Givens

approached.

"Well, Mr. Fury. I never expected to see you here today."

"Good morning Agent Givens, or should I say Director?"

"Agent is fine. Director seems a little pretentious. I've been doing the job of Facility Director for the last eighteen months. It was supposed to be temporary, but the title became official three days ago. It's not nearly as impressive as it sounds."

"Congratulations anyway, Director."

"You didn't come here to flatter me. You said you have information about Sirhan? Follow me. We can talk in my office."

Saysha Givens turned and went toward the far side of the lobby. I put away my phone and followed. She led me through a hallway, past a cluster of cubicles, and to an elevator. We took the elevator to the top; the third floor.

There were several conference rooms on the third floor plus one very nice office with the name "Saysha Givens" on a shiny brass plate on the door. We went inside, and she closed the door.

Saysha Givens took a seat behind the large wood desk. I took a chair in front of the desk.

"Mr. Fury. Before we talk about Sirhan Jadiddian, there are some answers I'd like from you."

"What can I tell you?"

"I've heard what's been happening in Vegas. The office there has kept me informed.

A little more than a week ago a girl was shot in your office at the university. Shortly after that Agent Sandra Ellis disappeared.

On Thursday of last week Special Agent Sandra Ellis turned up at the United States Embassy in London. She was telling a wild tale about the two of you fighting your way out of a Vegas hotel. And, she's even claimed that a girl on a motorcycle drove her through a wall in the sewer.

She says that's how she ended up in London. Special Agent Ellis is currently undergoing psychiatric evaluation.

Since her story involves you. I'd like for *you* to tell *me* what happened."

Director Givens leaned back in her chair, steepled her hands, interlaced her fingers, and let her arms drop to her lap. She sat and waited.

"Director Givens. You've never appreciated what I've told you, I don't think you're going to like this very much either."

"Oh, *please*, do go on. I can't *wait* to hear this one."

I told her about Stacy Adams coming into my office, and how she was on the phone with Ladon relaying what he was saying to me.

I told her about the shooting, about meeting Ladon at the hotel, and about being brought up to the penthouse for a demonstration of what he could do.

When I came to the part where Agent Ellis was brought into the room, Director Givens interrupted.

"Chad, tell me, as best as you can remember, how she was dressed, about her physical appearance, and any other details."

I described her clothes, the bruising and other signs of abuse, including the ball gag that was in her mouth. Director Givens pursed her lips and shook her head.

"Director, is there something wrong?"

"No, please continue, Chad."

I did. I described everything up to and including watching Lisa drive her motorcycle through the wall, taking Agent Ellis with her.

"Chad, this is very important. Just where, assuming you know, did Agent Ellis end up? Where did that so-called *portal* drop Lisa and Agent Ellis? Please be very specific."

"The other side of that portal is in the Tower of London, the Byward Tower."

"Damn it, Chad!"

"What's wrong?"

"You can't believe just how much I wanted to be able to dismiss at least *part* of Agent Ellis' story. But everything you've said goes right along with her story.

Do you know how many people come into this field office every month telling wild tales of aliens, conspiracies, and even Big Foot sightings?"

"Uhh...no."

"Trust me when I say, it's a lot, and almost every one of them should be wearing a tinfoil hat! Now, *I'm* starting to believe you! I had put you in the same group as those people until..."

I finished her sentence, "Until now."

Saysha Givens fell silent. She shook her head from side to side a few times and said nothing.

"Listen, Director. I'm here because I need your help."

"No, Chad."

"No? But you haven't even heard..."

"And I don't want to hear it. I have a nice, sane, rational little life. I don't want to put any of that at risk by involving myself in *your* problems."

"Director Givens, I'm sorry, really I am. I am sorry that you've been dragged you into this nightmare. But, like it or not, I'm here and you're here. I'm trying to get out of it."

"Let me guess. The fate of the world *hangs* in the balance!"

"As a matter of fact, Director, yes it does. But, here's what's about to happen. You can cooperate with me willingly, or I can bring in someone who will tell you what to do, and you'll do it. Remember the cut on your arm?"

Saysha Givens rubbed the inside of her arm and a moment of fear flashed across her face.

"Director. Saysha. Please. If you help me out, I'll turn Sirhan over to you. If you don't, you'll receive a visit from someone who can make you help me, and then I'll turn Sirhan over to the U.S. Marshals."

"What is it you're after, Chad?"

"When Sirhan was arrested, all of his things were

confiscated. Somewhere in his things, or in the evidence you collected, is a clue to the location of the Stone of Destiny."

"No. No. No. Do you expect me to give you access to Federal evidence so you can search for a magic rock?"

"The Stone of Destiny is a quantum computer. Ladon sent me to find it. If I don't turn it over to him, he will kill my mother and my uncle. If he gets the stone he'll enslave humanity."

"Chad." The way she said my name sounded pathetic. She shook her head and repeated, "Chad."

"Director, please. All I want is to look. I don't want to take anything."

"I can't give you access without a reason; a *believable* reason.

I suppose I could say that you're looking at everything because it might give you a clue where Sirhan is hiding. Even that's a stretch, but I could sell it.

Come back here tomorrow morning, at eight. I'll have everything ready. Now please. Go away. I want to spend the rest of my day calmly and peacefully dealing with terrorists, cyber criminals, and bomb threats."

Saysha Givens got up and escorted me all of the way out of the building.

I went directly back to the hotel and straight to Lisa's room. I was hoping that she would be done with her memory exercise and we could talk. I wanted her help looking through the FBI's evidence.

I went to her floor and to her door. The "do not disturb" sign was hanging on the door handle. I started to knock, but decided against it. I slid the key card through the reader and slowly turned the handle. I walked quietly inside and softly closed the door behind me.

In the room, Lisa was lying on the bed, fully dressed in a pair of sweats, a tee-shirt, and tennis shoes. She was breathing slowly. The index finger on her right hand tapped slowly. Tap tap...tap tap...tap tap...tap tap. It reminded me of a heartbeat.

I left the room quietly and returned to my floor. On the way I stopped in to see Sirhan. He was propped up on the bed staring at the television.

"Sirhan, good news. I've got an appointment to look through the FBI's evidence."

"Great. Wonderful." The sarcasm was unmistakable, "Trust me, I'm under-whelmed."

"Look, I know it's hard for you."

"Hard? Let me tell you what hard is. When this is over, if you send me back to Ladon, he'll kill me. You're not going to let me go free, so that means I'm headed back to prison.

In the meantime, I'm stuck here, bored out of my skull, watching television and surfing internet porn until the Feds show up to drag me away."

"I'm sorry you're bored. I don't care what you do. Keep yourself entertained. Just stay out of the way until I'm ready for you again."

I left, pulling the door firmly behind me.

CHAPTER FORTY-ONE

I looked at my watch. It was four-thirty in the afternoon. I had checked on Lisa nearly five hours earlier. I decided that it was time to look in on her again.

I left my room and headed up to hers. I saw the "do not disturb" sign still hanging on the door. It made me anxious. If Lisa had started going through her memories after I had left for the FBI office, that would mean that she had been lying on the bed in that state for about nine hours.

I rapped softly on her door and listened. I heard nothing. I slid her key card in and out of the lock, it clicked. I opened the door and crossed the threshold. I didn't have to take but one step and I could see her feet and legs on the bed. I walked quickly to her side.

Her red hair caressed her cheeks as it flowed gracefully on the pillow. Her eyes were closed, but they were moving rapidly. It reminded me of video I had seen in college of people in REM sleep.

I looked at her hands. They were motionless. I held my breath and waited for the tapping to return. There was nothing. I took her hand and patted it as I called to her,

"Lisa, Lisa, it's Chad. You need to wake up."

I put her hand down and patted her face. "Lisa. It's Chad. It's time to get up." She was motionless except for the fluttering of her eyes beneath closed lids. I panicked, just a little.

I ran to the bathroom, found a hand towel, and ran it under cool water. I squeezed out some of the excess.

I went back to Lisa's side and rubbed her face with the wet towel. I rubbed her arms and hands too. The entire time I called out, "Lisa! Lisa! Get up!"

I dropped the towel on the floor, straightened my back, and raised my eyes to the ceiling. I tried to think calmly.

An idea flashed across my mind and I ran out of the room, down the hall, and pressed the button on the service elevator.

I took the elevator to the basement. When the doors opened I was looking at a gray hallway with cement floors. I followed the hall past the laundry room where two women and a man were putting sheets and towels into industrial washing machines.

I went on quickly, trying doors until I found the janitor's supply closet. I looked at all the bottles. I stopped looking when I found what I wanted, ammonia cleaner. I unscrewed the cap and put the bottle to my nose. I jerked my head back at the noxious, sharp odor.

I replaced the lid and ran back. I passed the elevator and found the stairs. I ran up the stairs, taking the steps two at a time. I bolted out of the stairwell, and down the hall. I nearly knocked over a man dragging a wheeled suitcase behind him.

Back in Lisa's room, I went to the bathroom and grabbed a clean washcloth. I poured copious amounts of the cleaning fluid onto the white cloth.

I went to Lisa and laid the cloth over her nose. I couldn't believe it. She just laid there. She didn't move!

I pulled the cloth away and dropped it on the floor. I took two fingers and found the carotid artery in her neck.

There was a pulse, but it was slow. I looked at my watch. I counted her pulse as the watch's second hand clicked off fifteen seconds. I counted ten beats. That's only forty beats a minute! I counted again, but this time while the second hand swept past thirty seconds. I counted nineteen beats. That's thirty-eight beats a minute!

My emotions welled up in my throat. I inhaled. The air flowed into my lungs in short halting spurts as I struggled against my emotions.

I pulled out my phone and dialed nine-one-one. The phone rang twice, "Nine-one-one. What is your emergency?"

"My, uh, friend. She's unconscious."

I was asked a series of questions about what she might have taken or some medical condition that might account for Lisa's state. The voice on the other end of the phone told me she was dispatching an ambulance, and she would stay on the phone with me.

I was on the phone for an eternity of fourteen minutes before two men with a gurney arrived.

The paramedics took Lisa's pulse and blood pressure. Her pulse was thirty-nine beats a minute and her pressure was sixty-five over forty. The men looked concerned as they called the station and reported the situation.

As the paramedics put Lisa on the gurney, I thought to take her purse with me. We were headed to the hospital, and I would need her ID and insurance card, if she had one. I rode with Lisa in the ambulance.

At the hospital, Lisa was taken into emergency while I was detained at the admitting desk by a woman in her mid-thirties. She asked me for details. Details were something I had in very short supply. I pulled out Lisa's ID and cards, and made up a story as we went. The biggest, bold-faced lie I told was that I was her husband.

If I had told the hospital I was a friend, I would have had very little access to her, and almost no information from the doctors. I also had no one I could contact on

Lisa's behalf. If I were to tell anyone in the Sisterhood, they would find out what Lisa was doing and that could be bad for Lisa and Oother.

After giving the lady mostly fiction and a credit card, I was allowed to go to the ER where Lisa was being treated. That's where I met Dr. Lee, the emergency room physician.

Doctor Lee spent some real, quality time explaining his diagnoses and his inability to give me a prognosis.

"Mr. Fury. By all definitions that I know, your wife is in a serious coma. And, there's not much we really know about the human mind and how to wake it up from a state like this. The mind has to heal itself.

There may be some physiological or biochemical factors that brought this on, but ultimately, her own mind will have to wake her up. There will be a neurologist assigned to your wife's case. But, he or she will tell you the same thing. Whatever happens will be between God and Lisa."

It took hours, but Lisa was moved to a room on the fifth floor. I stayed with her until about two a.m., after which, I told the nurse at the nurse's station I was leaving. I gave the weary looking nurse my cell phone number to call if there was anything they needed.

CHAPTER FORTY-TWO

Tuesday morning found me standing in the Oklahoma City FBI office at exactly eight a.m. as requested. The attendant at the security desk called Director Givens to let her know I was here. And, I didn't have to wait long. It was less than a minute before I saw Saysha Givens appear through the hallway to the right of the desk.

"Fury, we need to talk."

Saysha Givens looked very intense. She held her lips pressed tightly together. But, I smiled and responded to her terse greeting. "Good morning to you too, Director."

Saysha turned quickly as she said, "Follow me."

I followed. We proceeded down the hallway to a conference room. Unless I was badly mistaken it was the same room I had occupied the previous year with my attorney.

I took a chair at the far side of the table, and Director Givens took a seat directly across from me.

"What are we talking about, Director?"

"We're talking about you."

"Just what about me?"

"After you left my office yesterday, I called the field

office in Las Vegas. I told them you were here and that you had come to see me. That conversation caused quite a stir.

It seems that you dropped off of the face of the Earth. Both the Marshals' Service and the FBI were keeping you under surveillance. Both of them lost you. And that doesn't happen."

"Yes, I went away. I had to verify some information I had been told."

"What information?"

"Stories that Ladon had told me about what the El-yanin were going to do when they left Earth."

Saysha Givens sneered. She sucked some air in through her teeth before she spoke.

"These…*stories*. I can't do anything with them. And, I am not sure *what* to believe. I half expected you to tell me you've been on the moon for the past week."

"Mars, actually. It was only a few hours there. I've also been on Phobos, one of the moons of Mars, and…"

"Chad! Stop it!"

I sat up, blinked, and stayed quiet.

"Chad, you seem to think that you can come in here and tell me how things are going to work, and the only thing you need to do is feed me some wild tale!

Well, here's how things are going to be! You *will* tell us where Sirhan Jadiddian is. If it turns out that you don't know, or that you've helped him to evade capture, then you *may* be arrested!"

"Director Givens, I need to know where the Stone…"

"Chad, no! You're not going to look at any evidence, or anything related to the case against Sirhan Jadiddian."

Saysha Givens reached forward and touched a button on the phone at the center of the table. She said rather loudly, "We're ready for you."

After about fifteen seconds, a man I recognized walked through the door. It was Special Agent, August Milton whom I had dealt with during the incident last year.

Saysha Givens never took her eyes off of me, but addressed Agent Milton. "Agent Milton, you will accompany Chad Fury everywhere he goes. You will not leave his side until we have Sirhan Jadiddian in custody."

Agent Milton responded, "Yes ma'am."

Director Givens leaned forward. "Now, Chad. Where is Sirhan Jadiddian?"

I thought for a moment. I had honestly believed that Saysha Givens was going to help me out. I hadn't detected that she was lying yesterday. I could only assume she had changed her mind after we talked. I saw no choice but to go along with this, at least for now.

"He's at my hotel. He has the adjoining room."

Director Givens looked at me with stern eyes. "And, just how did you come to be staying at the same hotel in adjoining rooms?"

I opted for telling the truth, but only the parts that would not sound crazy. "I was traveling alone last week. Three days ago, on Saturday, I was in Colorado and needed to get here. Lisa arranged a flight for me. On Sunday morning I caught a flight from Cortez, Colorado to Oklahoma City. I arrived Sunday afternoon. Lisa had taken Sirhan to a hotel and put him up in a room. I took the room adjoining Sirhan's"

Director Givens pointed a long, sharp index finger at me. "Let me get this straight. You're claiming that you had nothing to do with aiding and abetting Sirhan."

"That's right. On Monday morning I came directly here, and spoke to you."

"That's enough, Chad! You could have called the police on Sunday. You came here trying to use Sirhan as leverage to get me to let you look through evidence related to his case. Tell me the *truth*!"

"You're right. I intended to use Sirhan. I need to look through his things."

Director Givens turned to Special Agent Milton. "Agent Milton, escort Chad to his hotel. Find out when he arrived, and then arrest Sirhan Jadiddian. Bring both of them back here. I'm going to get to the bottom of this game they're playing."

Saysha Givens stood and left the room. I stood and walked with Special Agent Milton out of the building and to his car.

We rode most of the way to the hotel in silence. The entire time I was thinking about Lisa. I began wondering if I had missed a call from the hospital. I pulled out my phone to see.

"What are you doing, Chad?"

"I'm checking my messages, is that OK?"

"No. It's not. Put the phone away."

I gave Special Agent Milton a dirty look and put the phone back in my pocket. "You're still smoking as much as ever, I see."

Agent Milton returned the dirty look, "I don't smoke."

"You're a smoker and a liar," I said as I settled into my seat for the rest of the trip.

When we arrived at the hotel, we went directly to Sirhan's room. I knocked on the door and called out, "Sirhan. It's Chad. We need to talk."

We stood there and waited, but nothing happened. I knocked again. "Sirhan. Open the door. It's Chad."

Again, nothing happened. Agent Milton looked irritated, knocked, but kept silent. He turned to me. "Try the door in your room."

We went into my room, and I opened the door between our rooms. I stepped through into Sirhan's room. There was no Sirhan. There was no suitcase on the floor. There were no dirty clothes lying around. The closet was open and empty. Agent Milton opened and closed the dresser drawers; they were empty.

The reality that Sirhan was gone hit me and the blood drained from my face.

"Chad, where's Sirhan?"

"I don't know. He *was* here."

"Follow me."

We left the room and I followed Agent Milton to the front desk. Agent Milton pulled out his badge and displayed it as he got the clerk's attention. "I need some information."

The man behind the desk turned and halted when he saw the badge. His eyes got wide and his mouth opened slightly.

"Yes sir. What can I do for you, sir?" the man said as he took a step toward the counter.

"Rooms three-eleven and three-oh-nine. Tell me about the occupants."

"Yes sir. Well, three eleven is occupied by him," the clerk said as he nodded his head toward me. "A very attractive redhead rented the room for him. He checked in on Sunday."

"And the other room?"

"It was occupied by Matthew Jones. He checked out this morning. He also left something for him." The clerk nodded my direction.

"Let's see it."

The man excused himself and disappeared through a doorway in the wall behind him. He returned carrying a white envelope with "Chad Fury" written on the front.

The clerk handed it to me, but Agent Milton took it from my hands and opened it. He read it silently then handed it to me. Agent Milton was pulling out his cell phone as I read the hand-written letter on hotel stationery.

"Chad,

Ladon released me from you and The Company. Thanks for nothing. Watch your back!"

I looked up from the letter and Agent Milton was talking into his cell phone.

"Put me through to Director Givens. It's urgent."

Agent Milton stared at me coldly as he waited on the

phone. After a moment he spoke. "Director Givens, it's August Milton. Sirhan Jadiddian is in the wind."

The conversation that followed was pretty intense, but the long and short of it was that Director Givens wanted me back as soon as possible.

This was absolutely more than I thought I could stand. Lisa was lying in a hospital bed, unconscious. Sirhan, my only leverage with the FBI, was God-knows-where. And Saysha Givens was being uncooperative. I swallowed hard and ground my teeth. Agent Milton barked at me, "Get your ass in the car Fury! We're headed back."

I went with Agent Milton back to the car, but the truth is, I almost ran the other way. I'm not sure what kept me from running. Perhaps it was only because I didn't know where to run.

When we arrived at the FBI office, Director Givens was waiting in the lobby. As soon as we came through the doors, she spoke. "Agent Milton, you and Fury. My office. Now!"

Director Givens marched off across the lobby and badged in through the door. She held the door for the two of us. We passed through ahead of her and she followed silently behind.

When we reached her office, she pushed the door open, ushered us through and closed the door very firmly behind us. She strutted all the way to her desk like a woman on a mission.

I watched her smooth her navy skirt, point her chin high, and settle into her chair. Agent Milton and I seated ourselves.

Director Givens looked at me, then at Agent Milton. "Agent Milton. Tell me what happened."

Agent Milton related everything as faithfully as a tape recorder. He missed nothing, he included little details that I had missed such as the name of the clerk at the front desk.

Saysha pursed her lips, inhaled and exhaled noticeably.

"Agent Milton. Get your team together. I want Sirhan Jadiddian found. He's probably still in Oklahoma, and I don't want to find out that he's crossed the state line."

"Yes ma'am. I'll get the BOLO out immediately."

"Do that. Then keep me updated. I want him found, and fast!"

Agent Milton left the office. I turned back to Agent Givens and asked, "Now what?"

"Now *what*? You have some kind of nerve, Fury! You march in here and expect to use Sirhan to make a deal? And, you don't even try to secure him! You are unbelievable!"

I raised my voice. "Me! What about you? You told me you were going to help me. They you changed your mind. Instead of letting me look through the things you confiscated from Sirhan, you practically arrest me and go charging after Sirhan! What does that say about you?"

"How dare you, Fury!"

"Let me tell you how I dare. I've told you the truth! You've seen some of it for yourself, and you keep refusing to believe. This has *nothing* to do with what I'm telling you, it has to do with the fact that the truth is *too* uncomfortable for you. You keep trying to dismiss the truth, hoping it will go away because if you believe it, *you'll* have to change. You'd have to put out the effort to *make* others believe it too.

In the meantime, Ladon has threatened me and could kill my family at any moment!

You once told me that keeping secrets would cost too much. You've been hearing the truth, and you can't handle the cost of that!"

We sat and stared at each other for several seconds. Director Givens spoke first.

"Chad. I can't tell people the stories you've told me, even if I do believe them. Others won't believe and I'll end up sharing a room with Agent Ellis.

But what I can do is go after Sirhan. We can track him

down and put him back in the hole he crawled out of."

"Director, that's not enough. The Company, and Ladon, are still out there. They can't be stopped by you. Arresting Sirhan won't do any good. You'll still have to deal with The Company, and to do that you've got to accept who and what they are."

"Do you think *you* can stop them?"

"I don't know. But I know it will be very bad if they get the Stone of Destiny. I have a *chance* of finding the stone first and keeping it out of The Company's hands."

"What about Lisa? Chad, can she help?"

"She's in the hospital. In a coma."

"Do I even want to know why?"

"Probably not."

"Chad, I don't know what to do either. Let's work on finding Sirhan first. That seems like a more urgent priority. You go back to your hotel. Try to think of something, anything that might help find Sirhan. I promise you, we'll take care of the other matter *after* that."

CHAPTER FORTY-THREE

Saysha Givens had told me to go back to my hotel, but I
didn't. Instead I went to the hospital. I went to Lisa's room
and pulled up a chair next to the bed. I gently took Lisa's
hand in mine. I stroked the back of it with my free hand.

"Lisa, I need you. Please find your way back to me."

I felt something hot run down my cheek. I reached up
with my free hand and wiped tears from my eyes.

"Damn it! Why did it take *this* for me to know how I
feel about you?"

I heard someone clear their throat behind me. I wiped
my eyes, stood, and turned. A pudgy man in his forties was
standing in the doorway. He was wearing a white lab coat
and a blue shirt. A stethoscope was hanging around his
neck. I couldn't read the name tag.

"I'm sorry to interrupt. I'm Doctor Stenson, the
neurologist."

"I'm Chad Fury. It's..." I choked up for a moment and
recovered. "It's good to meet you."

"Mr. Fury. I'm glad you're here. I need to talk to you
about your wife's treatment. You'll need to sign some
release forms."

"Treatment? What kind of treatment are we talking about?"

"We've run blood work and a full toxicology panel. Under any other circumstances I would be thrilled to say everything came back perfect. There were no drugs in her system, no poisons, and her blood chemistry is perfect. Everything is textbook normal.

We need to start ruling out other possible causes for her condition. Has your wife had any memory lapses or blackouts?"

"No. She's been fine."

"I want to schedule an MRI and an EEG. The MRI will reveal any tumors or structural abnormalities. The EEG will provide a baseline of her brain activity so we will be able to know if she's improving."

The doctor handed me the clipboard he was holding. He gave me a pen from his shirt pocket. I signed the papers and handed them back.

"Mr. Fury, there's a fifteen-point scale we use to describe a coma. At one end is like what we've all experienced; we're trying to wake up, we know we're trying to wake up, but we can't get fully conscious. We try to speak and there's nothing; we just can't. We try to move, but can't control it. At the opposite end of the scale is total unresponsiveness to any stimulus, including pain.

Your wife is somewhere near the most severe end. She's not responding to pain, but her eye movements have me confused. Her eyes are moving like she's in REM sleep. We need to understand her current level of brain activity."

"What about prognosis, Doctor? Is there anything you can do?"

"At the moment, I don't know what we can do. If we can find a chemical or physical reason for her condition, we can work on that. But, she's perfect. This battle looks to be hers, and hers alone.

If she doesn't wakeup within two weeks, there's a higher probability of long-term brain issues. If she's like this for more than a month, the odds start increasing that she's not going to come out of it.

I'm sorry to be so blunt with you, but I want you to know exactly what it is we're facing."

I thanked the doctor and then left the room for him to examine Lisa. While I stood in the hallway I began wishing I had someone to talk to. I pulled out my phone and called Uncle Allan. After the fifth ring, a voice answered, "Hello."

"Uncle Allan, it's Chad."

"Chad! It's good to hear you!"

I sighed, "You too, Uncle. You too."

"You don't sound good. Are you alright?"

"No. Not exactly. I'm at the hospital. In Oklahoma City. Lisa's in a coma and I'm in a mess."

I told Uncle Allan which hospital and the room number. He said he'd be there in about half an hour.

When Allan Fury arrived, I was having a long, one-sided conversation with Lisa. I got up from my chair and crossed to the door. I hadn't seen Uncle Allan in about a year, and that's the kind of hug I gave him.

Uncle Allan backed up a step and cupped each of my shoulders in his hands.

"Let me look at you, Chad! I can't believe it's really you!"

"It's good to see you too."

To my eyes, Allan Fury looked almost exactly the same as he did a year ago. I was trying to decide if I could see even a tiny hint more of gray in his temples, but he looked exactly the same as I remembered.

"Have a seat, Uncle."

We went to the sofa and sat.

"Chad, tell me what's happening."

I told him everything. It would have been a much shorter story, but Uncle Allan is one to ask questions and pull out every last little detail. He had issues with the idea of the dimensional portals. He went off on a tangent about space being an n-dimensional superfluid, and I had to reel him back on topic.

"Chad, I don't know. *I'm* having a hard time accepting all of this. I can't imagine how impossible it is for Saysha Givens."

"Uncle, I know that. And I don't know what to do. Sirhan is out there somewhere, I can't make Saysha Givens help me, Ladon wants me to find the stone or he'll kill mom, you, and everyone I care about. Lisa's lying in a coma and there's no way to know if she'll ever come out of it. And, the El-yanin could decide to leave at any time. When they do, they'll destroy all life on Earth.

This whole thing sounds like a very bad sci-fi movie. I'm stuck in the middle of all of this, and there's nothing I can do, about *anything*. Am I supposed to just sit back and watch everything fall apart?"

"Chad, when I look at you I can tell a few things right off. First, you're tired and hungry. You don't realize it, but you are. You need to eat and to rest.

Next, you're too close to all of this. There's too much emotion involved. You'll never be able to do anything as long as your emotions are filling your head. Don't get me wrong, emotions aren't bad. But, sometimes our minds don't have the capacity to think and feel at the same time. Pure, raw emotion disrupts thinking.

Chad, let's go get something to eat. I'll buy, and then let's start talking this out."

I suggested that we eat at the hotel restaurant where I was staying. It would be quieter than most restaurants.

Twenty minutes later Uncle Allan and I were sitting at a table in the far corner of the hotel's bar looking over a menu. We both ordered a beer, a burger, and a platter of fries to split.

Uncle Allan took a sip of his beer, sat the glass on the coaster, and exhaled loudly. "Chad, you need faith."

"Not now, Uncle, I can't talk about religion right now."

"I'm not talking about religion."

"You said I need *faith*."

"Chad, most people think faith is some mystical force that can change the world. It's not. Faith is a force that can change you; not the world around you."

"Cut to the chase. I'm too tired to try and follow where you're going."

At that moment our waitress brought our food. But, it didn't stop Uncle Allan. He had a point to make and he insisted on making it.

"Chad, you need to do probably the hardest thing anybody ever has to do, and to do it, you need faith."

"I took a bite of my burger, swallowed, and asked, "What is it you think I need to do?"

"There are things in life that you can fix, and things you can't. You need to put all of your effort into fixing the things you can, and let all of the other things fix themselves. That takes faith."

"I don't like what you're saying. You've just gone the long way around to tell me to forget about Lisa."

"No, Chad. I didn't. I'm saying you can't help Lisa. Spending your energy worrying about her is, well, it's counterproductive."

"Uncle, I can't bear the thought of losing her."

"No, I'm sure you can't. But every day that you spend caught up in thoughts of losing Lisa is a day spent grieving while she's still alive. You're experiencing her loss before she's gone. It takes massive amounts of faith to let her go, and let God, or fate, or whatever take care of her."

"I can't do that."

"You've got to. If you don't then everything you've been fighting for is meaningless. You may as well give up."

I thought about it for a moment. "OK, I'll try."

"Good. Now let's talk about you. What is it that you want, besides Lisa being well?"

"I want to find the Stone of Destiny."

"And what's preventing you from finding the Stone?"

"I need Saysha Givens' help at the FBI. I can't go

through the things they took from Sirhan without her help. But, if I know where they were keeping Sirhan's stuff, I suppose I might be able to break in..."

"No, Chad. You don't know what you're looking for. Breaking in isn't a good idea. You probably wouldn't have time to look through everything if you did that."

"No, I suppose not. Not to mention that it's illegal too."

"You're right, Chad. You need Saysha Givens' help. Can you motivate her to help you?"

"No. I can't."

"You can't because?"

"I've told Saysha Givens the truth. She's seen my hands change right in front of her eyes. She's been visited by Ladon or one of his men, and her arm has been cut. She remembers the event.

I really thought she was going to help me, and then she changed her mind."

"Chad, every corporation, every group, every social structure has its own politics. Saysha Givens is at the top of the political structure in the Oklahoma City FBI office. But she's nowhere near the real top.

Saysha Givens has to conduct herself in such a way that she'll have the respect of those beneath her and those above her. She can't put that at risk if she wants to continue to be a part of the FBI."

"I know you're right. Somehow helping me has to be a low risk task for her."

"Exactly, Chad. Saysha Givens is putting too much at risk by helping you."

"I need to find a way to make helping me to be not so risky."

"Chad, how do you do that?"

"I don't know."

"OK. Think about it. Let's work on that, later. It can be put on the back burner for now.

What about Sirhan? Is there anything you need to be

doing there?"

"Sirhan told me to watch my back. He told me he spent every day for the last year behind bars planning revenge against me and Vitaly Dimitrievich."

"Is there something you can do about that?"

"I *might* be able to. If Sirhan is obsessed with revenge, then he won't be leaving Oklahoma City for a while. He'll go after Vitaly *and* come after me.

If I can catch him and turn him over to the FBI, It might make it easier for Saysha Givens to help me."

"Maybe, Chad. But I wouldn't count on it. Saysha Givens would still need to have a reason for letting you look through the things they confiscated from Sirhan, and that reason should not look too unusual."

"I agree, but going after Sirhan is something I *can* do, and maybe the other things will take care of themselves."

CHAPTER FORTY-FOUR

Wednesday, at noon, I was sitting in the office of Vitaly Dimitrievich, at his nightclub, The Port. It had been a year since I had been there. The club had been given a facelift in the form of a fresh coat of paint, but his office was still the same. The same lawyer's book cases, the same leather chairs, and the same green Berber carpet.

Vitaly looked the same too. The same gray hair and steel blue eyes looked at me across his large desk. But this time his body guards were not present, and he actually smiled. It took me off guard. He spoke to me in his Russian accent.

"Mister Fury. It is good to see you. How have you been?"

We exchanged pleasantries before he changed the subject and got down to business.

"Chad, I am not thinking that you came here to talk as friends. From what I understand, you are in Witness Protection, in Las Vegas, I think. Is that not still correct?"

"Um...I am, sort of. But how did you know..."

Vitaly made sort of a clicking sound with his tongue against his teeth. "How is not important. I hear things. I make it a priority to stay...informed."

I nodded in appreciation for the secrets that needed to be kept. "Mr. Dimitrievich. I'm here because of Sirhan. He's free."

Vitaly frowned. "Tell me more."

"Several weeks ago, The Company broke Sirhan out of a Federal facility in Texas. Later, someone from The Company, a man named Ladon, approached me and forced me to work with Sirhan to find a particular object for him."

I watched Vitaly for any sign that he recognized Ladon's name, but I saw nothing.

"Chad, please continue."

"Ladon wants me to find an artifact, and he seems to think that clues to its location are somewhere in the items seized by the FBI when Sirhan was arrested."

"And you came to Oklahoma to look through Sirhan's property that is in the possession of the FBI."

"That is correct."

"And, Chad, what has transpired that brings you here, now?"

"In one of the conversations I had with Sirhan, he mentioned that he spent the entire last year fantasizing about getting revenge. He blames me *and* you.

Yesterday, Sirhan bolted. He left me a note saying that Ladon had released him from working with me, and I need to watch my back."

Vitaly took a deep breath and exhaled slowly. "That is good news."

"Good news? Seriously?"

"Yes, my friend. It is good because a man consumed by revenge is a driven man. Sirhan has spent a full year fueling and tending the fires of rage..." Vitaly made a fist and beat the center of his chest twice, "...in his heart."

I leaned forward. "That doesn't sound good to me."

"It is very good. A driven man cannot make his own decisions. He is compelled to act out what he has planned.

273

We have no need to find him. He will come to us."

"Mr. Dimitrievich, you seem to know a lot about how Sirhan thinks."

"In my business, I have to know…people. I know that you played a larger role in Sirhan's arrest than I did. That means he will most likely come after me first."

"Why come after you first? He hates me more than you. I was the one working with the FBI."

"Because he will want you to know how dangerous he is. If he succeeds in killing me, he will boast about it to you.

But, tell me this. Did Sirhan mention what he was most upset about losing?"

"He seemed to be more upset about losing his wife and family."

Vitaly reached across his desk and lifted the receiver on his phone. He punched a button and put the receiver to his ear. After a moment he said, "Please send in Pavel."

Vitaly cradled the phone and we both waited in silence. We only waited fifteen or twenty seconds before Pavel entered the room and stood in front of Vitaly's desk next to my chair.

"Pavel, please go to my home. I would like you to watch over Serena. Sirhan Jadiddian is free, and he may be wanting to visit my Serena. If he comes near my wife, make certain he stops breathing."

Pavel said something in Russian, Vitaly responded. Pavel patted the gun under his sport coat and left.

Vitaly leaned forward in his chair.

"Mr. Fury, my friend. There are some things you need to know."

"About what?"

"About Sirhan, and how he will act. Sirhan is a weasel, but he is no fool. He knows you will tell the FBI he is missing, if you have not already."

"They know. I was going to turn him over to the FBI in exchange for looking at what they confiscated."

"I'm sure Sirhan figured that out. He knows the FBI will find him, *eventually*. It may take weeks, or much longer, but they will find him.

The rage burning in his heart will make him do certain things. He will go after my family, me, anyone you love, and finally you; in that order.

He will not use poisons. They are not personal enough. He will want us to know that he is the one killing us. He will want to cause us as much pain as possible before he kills us.

Sirhan must also move quickly. If he does nothing in the next three days, it becomes more likely that he will not do anything."

"But you don't think that will happen, do you Mr. Dimitrievich? You think he will come after us."

"I'm certain he will. Very soon."

The remainder of our conversation was ordinary. I made sure Vitaly had my cell phone number. He said he would call if anything happened.

I left Vitaly's club and headed to the hospital. I planned to spend the afternoon and evening sitting in Lisa's room. I'm glad I did because I was there when the neurologist stopped by late, that afternoon.

Dr. Stenson looked the same as the previous day, except he had changed his shirt from blue to red.

"Mr. Fury. I'm glad to see you. I wanted to give you an update."

"What can you tell me, Doctor?"

"We've run a CAT scan and an MRI. I'm having difficulty understanding what I'm seeing."

"Why is that?"

"The MRI was able to pinpoint activity in her brain. With it, we saw what areas are active and what are not.

In most coma patients we don't see this kind of activity. Let me rephrase that. We never see this kind of activity in coma patients."

"What you talking about?"

"Every area of her brain is firing. The kind of activity in her brain is the same kind, same amount, and the same areas that we would see in a person who is up, awake, and actively doing things.

Her visual centers are active, just as though she were watching a play or a movie. Her motor centers are firing, but she's not moving. For all I know her brain could be telling her body to run a race.

Every part of her brain is like that. Active and doing something. This is extremely unusual."

I looked over at Lisa on the bed, "Lisa is an unusual lady."

"I'm certain she is...Oh, and we found some other things. They're unrelated, I'm sure, but they are unusual.

The CAT scan. We were looking for tumors or anything that might account for Lisa's condition. We injected her with a radioactive dye, and it let us see what organs were the most metabolically active. We discovered this."

Doctor Stenson pulled an x-ray film from a folder he was carrying. He went to the window and held the film up to the light.

"Mr. Fury, this is your wife's throat. It's not serious, it's just unusual. It appears that she has two fully formed sets of vocal chords. I've never seen that before."

I looked at the film, and saw it. I think I smiled as I replied, "That is unusual."

"And then, Mr. Fury, there's this. You may want to have an endocrinologist look at her when she recovers."

Doctor Stenson pulled out a second piece of film and held it up to the glass.

"Mr. Fury, this is Lisa's thymus gland. It's unusually large and it's very metabolically active. The thymus gland is the triangular mass below her throat. It's a vestigial organ, similar to the appendix. Long ago the appendix may have had a function in humans, but now, it behaves like lymph tissue.

The thymus gland is really only active until puberty. It plays a role in the develop.m.ent of T cells in the blood.

Lisa's thymus gland is very active. It's as active as her liver. I can't explain it.

But, she has more serious problems than her thymus gland. Her biggest issue is that I can't find a reason for her to be like this. That means there's nothing for me to treat. All we can do is watch her and wait."

CHAPTER FORTY-FIVE

I woke to my cell phone ringing. I had been asleep on the sofa in Lisa's hospital room. The phone vibrated in my hand as I sat up and touched the red button on the face of the phone.

"Hello?" It came out as a question, because I was wondering who would be calling me at one in the morning.

Vitaly's voice came through the speaker, "Mr. Fury. I have news about Sirhan."

"Really? What?"

"I am at my home. Sirhan has been here. Pavel is dead. There's a bullet hole in the back of his head, and my Serena is missing."

"Oh my God! Did you call the police?" I was stunned. I didn't know what else to say.

"I do not call the police. The people I work for would not take my working with the police, favorably. Mr. Fury, you owe me a favor. I'm calling it in."

I swallowed hard, "What do you expect me to do?"

"You are going to help me kill Sirhan and get my Serena back."

"Mr. Dimitrievich, I'm not going to kill anybody."

"We will discuss that later. You're going to do whatever I say. And, for now, all you need to do is wait."

"I don't understand. Your wife is missing and you're telling me to wait?"

"Yes. Sirhan is playing a game. He wants to make me sweat. He took my Serana, and I don't think he'll harm her; not yet."

"You're much more calm than I would be."

"I am older than you Mr. Fury. Serena and I have always known something like this was possible. We've prepared for it. Serena knows how to act. She is a strong woman. And if she and I keep our heads, we will come out of this alive."

"What happens next?"

"Sirhan will keep Serena safe, at least for a while. Eventually he will send me a note, or make a phone call. He will not contact me until he thinks I am overcome with worry. That should be late this evening, or tomorrow morning.

Sirhan will arrange a meeting at someplace where he thinks he can be in control. He will want to make the execution of my wife and me, theatrical, a performance."

"What do you want me to do?"

"Chad. You never did tell me what you did to Kane when I handed you over to him. How did you deal with him? Did you take his gun from him and shoot him?"

"No, sir. I beat the crap out of him. Then I tied him up and delivered him to the women he was hunting."

"Good. You handled the situation like a man. Be prepared to beat the *crap* out of Sirhan. When the time comes, I will tell you what to do."

Vitaly ended the call abruptly, without so much as a "goodbye".

I sat on the sofa for a moment looking at Lisa in the hospital bed. Uncle Allan had been right. I must not let my emotions over Lisa cloud my thinking. The situation was serious. Sirhan had started killing, and more people were going to die if I did the wrong thing.

I got up and left to find a cup of coffee I could sip on while I drove back to my hotel room. I needed real rest, in a comfortable bed, if I was to think clearly enough to help anybody.

It was seven-thirty a.m., on a Thursday, when I woke-up in my hotel room. I took a quick shower. After which, I headed down to the breakfast buffet in the hotel lobby. I allowed myself just enough time to eat some scrambled eggs and drink some coffee while I decided what to do.

I understood why Vitaly couldn't afford to go to the police, but my situation was different. I already had a relationship with the FBI and the U.S. Marshal's service.

It was obvious I was in over my head, and a wise man would ask for help. I thought it best I should go back to the FBI and give Saysha Givens another opportunity to help me. If she refused, or I didn't like the help she had to offer, I would contact the U.S. Marshals.

I finished my last swallow of coffee and headed for the car. It was rush hour, so my fifteen minute trip turned into thirty. I probably could have gotten there faster if I ran. Still, I found myself walking into the FBI office on Memorial Street just after nine a.m..

Inside, I approached the man at the security desk and asked him to tell Director Givens that Chad Fury needed to talk to her.

There was a brief exchange between the man behind the desk and the voice on the phone. He hung up and told me, "Someone will be down in a moment."

I retreated to the teal colored chairs and waited patiently. After about five minutes, Special Agent August Milton showed up and spoke to me. "Chad, the Director will see you in her office."

I followed Agent Milton through the door and down the path I had followed before. If it wasn't for needing a badge to open the doors, I could have found my own way.

Agent Milton left me in Saysha's office and closed the door as he left. I took a seat in front of Saysha's desk.

"Mr. Fury, what do you want?" I detected a hint of sarcasm and a lot of exasperation in her voice.

"It's about Sirhan."

"I'm sure it is," she said flatly. "But, don't waste your breath. We're on top of it. We are expanding the search outside of the city. Our profiler tells us it is probable that he's headed to Houston, Texas."

"He's not. He's here."

"And you *know* where he is? That worked out so well last time."

"I know where he's been, and I'm going to know where *he's* going to be."

Saysha Givens raised an eyebrow, "Well, do go on."

I told Saysha about going to Vitaly's office to talk with him. She interrupted with a burst of emotion, "Hold on! What *the hell* are *you* doing talking with *that* man? Do you know who he is and who he's involved with?"

"I know. There are some things I never told you about him, about..."

"Let me guess. He's an alien!"

"No, he's Russian, and last year he helped me contact Sirhan Jadiddian. He suggested I setup Sirhan and turn him over to the FBI so I could make a deal."

Saysha raised her voice, "Why didn't you tell us that last year?"

"That was part of my deal with Vitaly; that I would keep him out of the sting."

Saysha Givens sat there and shook her head. "Chad, Chad, Chad. Just how deep are your ties with the Russian mafia?"

"I don't have ties with the Russian mafia. I never knew any of them until last year. When Lisa went missing, I found clues that let me know The Company had her and was possibly holding her at a place called 'The Hub'. When I went looking for information about The Hub; that led me to Vitaly."

"Chad. Enough about ancient history. What about now? Why were you in Vitaly's office?"

"Because Sirhan told me he spent a year in prison planning revenge against Vitaly and me. I thought I should warn Vitaly.

And, I came to you this morning, Director, because I don't think Sirhan is going to leave Oklahoma City. He wants revenge too badly."

Saysha Givens started to speak, but was interrupted by the cell phone ringing in my pocket. It was the phone Ladon had given me.

"Excuse me Director, you'll want to hear this."

I pulled out the phone, laid it on the desk and answered it in speaker mode.

"Hello, Ladon."

Ladon's voice cut through the air in a slow rhythm that was just, creepy. "Hello, Chad. I'm so glad to see that you're finally back on task."

Saysha Givens recoiled and pushed herself into her chair. She looked terrified, and stuttered, "Tha...that voice. It...it's him. The man who cut me!"

I watched her grip the chair arms, lock her elbows, and force her body deep into the chair.

Ladon's voice filtered out of the phone, "Saysha Givens, what a surprise to hear your voice again. I'm so glad you remember mine. I left a suggestion in your mind that you would always be *terrified* of my voice. I imagine you're trembling all over right now.

Here's something for you to think about. You have some delicious secrets in that head of yours. I *will* come back someday and explore those with you."

Saysha just muttered softly, "No. no. no."

I stared angrily at the phone, "Ladon. What do you want?"

"I want to make sure you are on task. You need to be searching for the Stone of Destiny."

"It would have been a little easier if you had not released Sirhan."

Ladon laughed. "Oh, that was good, wasn't it? You and Lisa deceived me. You went on your little trip to China while you were supposed to be here.

I thought you should have an obstacle to contend with for your disobedience. Besides, I'm not done with your training."

"What are you talking about?"

"I told you that one day you will bow to me as your master. One day you *will* do everything I say, without question.

I intend to make you into a weapon. A weapon that has no feelings about killing. You have too many feelings.

Sirhan will come for you. He won't stop coming. Chad, the only way he can be stopped is for you to kill him. And after he's dead, I will send others. You need the practice killing. I will create a trail of blood and death around you."

"Ladon, I'm not playing your games. I will find the stone, but I'll never be a killer!"

Ladon laughed and ended the call.

I looked up at Saysha. Her feet were pulled up in her chair and her arms were wrapped around her knees. Tears were flowing down her cheeks.

I went around the desk and put a hand on her shoulder. "Saysha. You're alright. Everything's fine."

"That voice. I can't..."

"Saysha, it was just sounds coming through the phone. You're OK. Ladon got into your head. You're stronger than that. You can pull yourself together and *be* the Director of this facility."

Saysha lowered her feet to the floor. "Chad, could you bring me some water? There's a break room to the right and down the hall."

I went. I found the break room. It had a table and chairs, two refrigerators, two microwaves, vending machines, a machine dispensing ice and water, and a coffee maker.

I took two Styrofoam cups from a dispenser. I filled one cup with ice water, and I poured myself a cup of coffee.

When I returned to Saysha Givens' office, she was more composed. She was looking into a mirror and touching up her makeup. I closed the door behind me.

Saysha looked up and said, "Thank you, Chad."

I approached and placed the water on her desk. I sat and sipped my coffee while Saysha put her makeup away.

"Chad, I believe you. I believe all your stories."

My jaw went slack. "Director, will you help me? Will you help me find this stone that Ladon wants?"

"Answer me this, Chad. Can you stop him? Can *you* stop Ladon? The FBI can't."

"I don't know. But I am going to try. I can't let him have the stone. If he gets it, it will be very bad for everyone."

"I will help you. There are three types of things we've confiscated from Sirhan. There are financial records, which probably will not help you. There's the contraband: weapons, drugs, and other paraphernalia. And, there are his assets from his home and business. Where do you want to start?"

"I want to see what was confiscated from his business."

"I'll arrange for Agent Milton to escort you and give you access to all of it. Is there anything else I can do for you?"

"Possibly. Lisa and Sirhan searched the former home of Colonel Roger Evans. Colonel Evans was somehow involved. Sirhan found some letters with some names. I don't actually know, but my gut tells me the names are related to the stone. I'd like to bring you the letters. You might be able to find out who these people are."

"I'll look into it."

Saysha told me that she needed a little time to compose herself. And, we agreed that I would return at two P.M..

At exactly two in the afternoon I was sitting in Saysha Givens' office, handing her the letters across her desk. Special Agent August Milton was seated to my left.

I let go of the stack of letters and commented, "Director. Here, are the letters I told you about. They were all written to the late Colonel Roger Evans. The author is someone named Ray. I don't know who Ray is. The subject of the letters is someone named Eddie. Lisa and I believe he's Edward Scofield, Colonel Evans' nephew by marriage."

Director Givens flipped through the papers quickly. "Do you need these back?"

"No ma'am. I took pictures with my cell phone."

Saysha Givens nodded.

Agent Milton interrupted, "Excuse me, Director, but what is this about?"

Saysha turned to Agent Milton. "This is about The Company. We have a possible lead to their organization.

A man calling himself Ladon has been in contact with Chad. He's extorting Chad into finding an artifact that The Company wants."

I watched the expression on August Milton's face. It was pure puzzlement as Saysha continued, "Ladon believes that the artifact, or more likely a clue to the artifact's location, is somewhere in the things confiscated from Sirhan Jadiddian 's business."

"Excuse me, Director. What is this *artifact*, and why does the Bureau care about it."

"Let's take that in reverse order. The Bureau doesn't care about the artifact. But, the fact The Company is searching for it gives us an opportunity to find out more about The Company and their criminal activities. As to the artifact, Chad, please give Agent Milton a *reasonable* description."

I understood Saysha's use of the word, reasonable. Now was not the time to introduce Agent Milton to anything he would have a difficulty believing.

"The Company, Ladon in particular, believes the artifact is a quantum computer disguised to look like a block of stone."

August Milton turned to Saysha Givens and asked, "Is it time for the tinfoil hats?"

Saysha, frowned, "Agent Milton, Auggie," she inhaled and exhaled. "I know how this sounds. But, you know as well as anybody that the truth is often less important than what people believe to be true.

The Company has made very few mistakes, and if what they believe about a hunk of rock makes them want it, that gives us an opportunity and I would hate to pass it up.

Also, Sirhan Jadiddian is in the wind. Our profiler believes he's on his way to Houston. But, Chad thinks he could come after him. Maybe he will.

Chad's supposed to be in Witness Protection, yet, here he is, sitting in my office.

Auggie, here's what's going to happen. I'm not burning a bunch of resources looking for supposed clues to a hunk of rock. Since those clues are thought to be in the items confiscated from Sirhan's business, I'm authorizing Chad to look through them. Those things are less sensitive than the evidence we've compiled. You will go with him to make certain that he has access *only* to Sirhan's things, and that he doesn't touch anything he shouldn't.

Also, you or a member of your team will stick with Chad twenty-four by seven. Until we know that Sirhan is not in Oklahoma City, we will keep him safe. Have I made myself clear?"

Agent Milton replied, "Yes ma'am," in an almost military sounding tone.

"Alright. Auggie, Chad, go do some work."

Agent Milton stood and I took my cue from him. As I stood I said "Thank you" to Saysha. She nodded. I turned and followed Agent Milton.

Agent Milton stopped at the elevator and pressed the button. "Chad, we need to stop at my desk. I have some things that will make the job a little easier."

I nodded, "Whatever you say."

We rode down one floor and I found myself standing in a maze of cubicles. The entire room was wall to wall gray-colored, half-wall cubicles each equipped with a phone, a computer, and filing cabinets.

Agent Milton navigated the maze, deftly. We were soon standing in a three-sided box with his name on the outside. Agent Milton dug through a desk drawer and pulled out two felt-tipped pens, two ball point pens, and two flashlights. He opened a file cabinet and pulled out two new legal pads. He handed everything to me and said, "Make yourself useful."

Agent Milton guided me to the elevator, down to the first floor, and out the back of the building to the employee parking lot. I followed him to a white sedan which had seen better days.

I got in the passenger side, as Agent Milton started the car. "Gee, Auggie, I would have thought you could get something a little nicer on your salary."

August Milton gave me a dirty look. "This car belongs to the Bureau. It's one of our surveillance vehicles. I was told to keep an eye on you, so I'm saving some time and taking this car now."

We drove silently for a while. From what I could tell, we were headed to the south side of Oklahoma City. Agent Milton was silent until we were on the I-35 interstate.

"Tell me, Chad, what's this all about, really?"

"What do you mean?"

"I can't seem to figure you out. Last year, when I first met you, I expected to see a wild-eyed young man fitting the profile of a terrorist. Then, I saw you. You were scared and disoriented. I ruled out drugs, and it was obvious any connection between you and terrorists was ridiculous.

Then we found the fingerprints of a murdered school teacher in your car. Suddenly, I hear you escaped from the

Cleveland County Jail. How did you do it? How did you reach that access hatch in the shower room ceiling? That's fourteen feet. How?"

I thought for a moment and told him the truth. "I jumped."

August Milton took his eyes off the road and looked me up and down once. "Liar."

"Hey, it's up to you whether you want to believe the truth. Do you have a better explanation?"

"No."

We drove the rest of the way in silence along I-35, through Norman, Oklahoma and almost all the way to Highway Nine. We pulled off the interstate and drove to an industrial park. Agent Milton pulled up to a set of warehouses that were surrounded by chain link fence with razor wire running across the top. The grounds looked more like a prison than warehouses.

Agent Milton drove the car slowly up alongside a keypad mounted on a pole near the gate. He punched in an eight digit number. After a moment the gate slid to one side and he drove through.

The building we wanted was at the far end of the facility. Agent Milton parked the car near a set of concrete steps. We exited and he led the way up to the door.

There was another keypad, and Agent Milton pressed the keys eight times. There was a loud click and he pushed the door open.

It was dark inside. Agent Milton located a light switch by the door. Lights flickered overhead for a moment and then burned steadily.

"Chad, wait here. I'm headed to the breaker box to start the exhaust fans."

I was left alone, staring at the inside of the warehouse. I was facing unending isles of shelves, crates, pallets and furniture. The concrete floor was cordoned off in rectangles of yellow tape.

Agent Milton returned while I was still staring at all of

the stuff.

"Pretty amazing, isn't it, Chad. I've seen this so many times that I forget how overwhelming it is to see it for the first time."

"So what kind of stuff is in here?"

"Everything. Everything from dishes to computers. You name it. The only things not here are vehicles; cars, boats, etcetera.

That reminds me. I forgot to lookup the space numbers for Sirhan's stuff."

Agent Milton pulled out his phone and typed out a text message. We didn't have to wait long before the reply came.

"Part of it's this way." Agent Milton started off to the right. I followed as he counted off six rows and turned down the isle of the seventh. We walked what seemed to be the length of a football field before he stopped and turned to face a stack of cardboard boxes.

"This is it Chad. Our first stop on the never ending trail of all things Jadiddian."

I stared upward at the mountain in front of me, "Oh...My...God! How much is there?"

"I really don't know. I just know it's a lot. That's where the pens and lights will come in handy. Let me have one of the markers and a light.

I handed him what he asked for, and he led me to a box. "Watch this."

Agent Milton uncapped the marker and made a checkmark on the side.

I didn't see anything. I said, "Your marker must be dry. Here, let me get you the other one."

Agent Milton smiled, "No. Look here." He held up the flashlight and a circle of blue light hit the box. There in the circle, in white, was the checkmark he had made.

"Now that's cool, what is it," I asked?

"It's ultraviolet ink, and the light is an ultraviolet light source. You can mark anything and no one will see it without the light. It's a little tagging trick. Use the markers to keep track of what you've looked at."

I pulled a box from the top of the stack, placed it in the isle, and removed the lid. "There's nothing here but old paperback books."

I started to put the lid back when Agent Milton stopped me, "Whoa. Hold your horses. You really don't know the first thing about searching."

I gave him a funny look, "There's nothing here."

"Don't be so sure. I've found a lot of things stuffed between the pages of books. And, you know that old trick you see in the movies where people cut the pages out of a book to hide something inside?"

"Sure."

"Well, sometimes it's really done. If you're serious about looking through this crap, pick everything up, look it over, leaf through the pages, and look for anything that shouldn't be there."

I pulled out a book and did as he said. On the very first book, when I fanned through the pages, a folded piece of paper fell out. I unfolded it, and read aloud, "Eggs, sugar, milk, green beans..."

Agent Milton smiled, "Sometimes it goes like that. Here, let me help."

Agent Milton took another box and started going through it. I worked silently until the boredom became too great and I tried making conversation.

"Agent Milton, can I call you something other than 'Agent'?"

"Sure. I go by Auggie."

"So...tell me about your time in the Marines, and how you got hooked up with the FBI."

"How did you know I was in the Marines?"

"I spent some time in the Army. You carry yourself like every Marine I ever met."

Auggie gave me a dirty look.

"Auggie, I didn't mean anything bad by that. You stand

straight and have that *look*. It's almost like a Marine can leave the service, but the service never leaves a Marine."

Auggie nodded, "You're right. The training never leaves.

After I got out, I went to college. My degree is in criminal justice. Afterwards, the police and regular law enforcement just didn't seem like where I wanted to be. A friend who had become a State Trooper suggested the FBI. I applied and was accepted.

Mine's a pretty dull story. But yours is probably a lot more interesting. There's a lot that you've kept secret."

"You're right. I have kept it a secret, mostly because people would treat it the way you did when you asked how I broke out of jail. I don't have any burning desire to be called a liar."

"Then prove it. Prove just that one thing; that you can jump high enough to reach an access panel fourteen feet overhead."

"Seriously?"

"Why not? The shelving across from us is at least that tall."

"Tell me this. Is this place under surveillance? Is there a camera somewhere that will record it?"

"No. There are no cameras."

I smelled onions. "I can safely say, Auggie, you're a liar."

"OK. Explain that. How do you know when I'm lying? Last year you insisted that I smoke, and I kept telling you I don't. And just now. There are cameras, and they're motion activated. How did you know?"

"When people lie, they give off an odor, kind of like onions. I can smell it."

"You're full of shit."

"I think I'd smell that too. But no, it's the truth."

We continued working in silence until we had cleared every box in the fifteen by fifteen square foot space. I looked at my watch. It was six-thirty.

"Auggie, I'm hungry and tired. Take me back to my car."

"Chad, you want to come back here again tomorrow, right?"

"Sure. I'm going to find something. I have to."

"Then your car's fine where it is. I'll take you back to your hotel and pick you up at seven in the morning."

We left the way we came and Auggie drove me to the hotel, parked the car, and followed me to my room.

"Auggie, I need to tell you, you're not coming in. I like you, but not in *that* way."

"I'm staying in the hallway until my partner arrives. Director Givens told me to stick to you."

"Do you want me to call room service and have something brought to you?"

"Thanks, but no. I'll be fine."

"I'll see you in the morning, Auggie."

I slid the key card in the reader, and opened the door.

CHAPTER FORTY-SIX

I hadn't been asleep long when I heard someone pounding on my door. I jumped up out of bed, threw on a pair of jeans, and went to the door. As the door opened I heard a familiar Russian accent.

"Mister Fury. You have much to do. Get dressed."

"Hello to you too, Mr. Dimitrievich, won't you come in?"

I turned and went to the closet. Vitaly let himself in while I picked out a fresh shirt, shoes, and socks. "What's happened?"

"I heard from Sirhan this afternoon. He's being very theatrical. He told me to meet him tonight, at midnight. He said I am to come alone and to bring two hundred and fifty-thousand dollars in cash if I ever want to see my Serena again."

I let out a whistle, "A quarter of a million in cash? That's a lot to get on short notice."

"It is not as much as you think. But, I am very glad he said this. It means he is making a *big* production out of my murder. The more he builds it up, the more time he will take in killing my Serena and me. That gives you more opportunity to kill him."

"Hey, I'm not onboard with killing anyone; no matter how much they deserve it."

"Chad. You owe me. You will do what you need to do."

I knew Vitaly was right. I would do whatever I had to do if it meant saving a life. But I was not going to head into this believing I was going to kill someone.

"So what's the play here, Mr. Dimitrievich?"

"The play. That is an excellent choice of words. This is theater.

Sirhan wants me to come to the old Hub location; the warehouse where he was arrested. I am to bring the money. He will underestimate me. He will expect me to do something stupid. I *will* do something stupid and make him believe he has the, as you say...upper hand."

"What are you going to do?"

Vitaly reached behind his back and handed me a pistol. "Take this. You will need it."

I did not reach for it. "No. I don't need that."

"Take it. Put it in your waist band."

I took it reluctantly, and placed it under my waistband against the small of my back.

"Chad, I will have a pistol. Mine will be empty. I will let Sirhan take it from me. He will be so consumed with revenge that he will not be able to refuse killing my Serena and me with my own weapon. That will buy us a few more precious seconds. Use those seconds to kill Sirhan."

"But, he told you to come alone. How do I get there?"

"Come with me."

I followed Vitaly to the parking lot and to a large, expensive looking sedan. Vitaly opened the trunk. "Chad, get inside."

I balked, just like all thinking people would do. "Uh, I'd rather not."

"Chad. It is all good. See, here?" Vitaly pointed to a latch on the inside of the trunk lid. "When we get to the warehouse, you will open the trunk and slip out."

"Getting out, I have no problem with. It's getting in that I don't like very much."

"Chad. You will stay inside until I turn off the engine. You will not get out until it is quiet; until you are sure that no one is around. Do not wait too long. My Serena's life depends on it."

I climbed into the trunk, and the lid closed before I had a chance to change my mind. A moment later the engine started, and the car began rolling forward. I made myself as comfortable as possible, which was not comfortable at all. The minutes crawled by. I was nervous about this plan of Vitaly's, and the constant jarring of the road didn't help my nerves.

At long last, the car slowed and I heard gravel crunching beneath the tires. We came to a stop. The car engine purred into silence. A moment later a car door opened and closed. I heard voices.

"Vitaly, you old wolf. How good of you to come."

"Nyet! Let's get this over with."

"You have the money?"

"I have it."

"And you came alone?"

"Do you see anyone? Are you a blind durak?"

"That, Vitaly, is not an answer!"

I heard the crunch of gravel under feet. The sound seemed to be getting closer. Then, Sirhan's voice came loud and clear; he was next to the trunk.

"Open the trunk!"

"Nyet. No."

"Very well."

A shot rang out, and something burning hot hit me in the stomach. I clenched my teeth to keep from making a sound. Five more shots rang out in succession. With each shot, fire struck a different part of my body and I clenched my teeth tight. I laid there motionless; my ears ringing from the noise. Even with my ears ringing I could hear the conversation outside.

"Well, Vitaly, opening the trunk is needless now. Why do you look so sad?"

"I've grown to like that car."

The crunching of gravel under foot started again. I heard the sound of a door open and close. I counted off thirty seconds and pulled the release on the trunk lid.

I crawled out of trunk and took off my shoes in hopes that my approach would be a little more quiet. I ascended the concrete steps to the warehouse and listened at the door. I heard voices.

I pulled the door open slightly; no one seemed to notice. I peered inside. Three figures were in the center of the large, mostly empty room. Sirhan had his back to me.

There were a few crates and pallets around, but not much else. I crept into the room and ducked through the shadows. I moved deep into the shadows to Sirhan's left. I hid myself behind a stack of boxes on a pallet. I waited a moment and listened.

"Sirhan, you have the money. Now let my Serena go. You want me. She is nothing to you."

"In a word, no. I want to see you beg. I want to hear The Wolf plead for the life of his beloved and sob for his own miserable existence."

"You will get none of that from me."

"Oh, but I think I will."

I moved closer to the trio and perched myself behind a stack of old wood pallets.

"Sirhan, a man on your path does not live too long."

"Perhaps not, but I *will* live long enough to see you die."

The surrounding darkness was thick, and inky black. I moved slowly, and low to the ground like a predator inching toward Sirhan. Sirhan's attention was on Vitaly and Serena. He was not looking my direction, and even if he were, it was doubtful that he would see me in the darkness.

Sirhan pointed his weapon at Serena. It was pointed

low, as if he was aiming at her legs.

"Vitaly, you are going to watch as I take your wife's life from her, inch by inch."

There was no more time. Sirhan was about to start firing, and I did not know if he was holding Vitaly's empty gun. I forced the knuckles of my right hand firmly onto the concrete floor. I tightened my legs. I could feel the muscles in my thighs strain against the denim material of my jeans. I let out an inhuman roar.

Sirhan turned, and fired. The shot went wild and to my left. I sprang forward out of the darkness. Two more shots rang out; searing heat hit my chest. I ran forward.

Sirhan yelled out, "Stop or she dies!" Sirhan pointed his gun at Serena. I continued forward, but my target changed; I headed for Serena.

At that moment I heard Vitaly yelling something in Russian. Sirhan hesitated just long enough for my charge to make a difference. I took two more steps and leapt with all my strength. I flew through the air, caught Serena in my arms, and rolled over on my back. My back hit the concrete and Serena landed on top of me as bullets sailed overhead.

I pushed the stunned woman off of me and charged toward Sirhan. Three more bullets hit me in the chest, then his gun went "click".

I heard a gunshot from directly ahead of me. Sirhan went limp. I caught him in my arms and lowered him to the concrete.

Two men came jogging toward me. Vitaly from behind, and Agent August Milton from directly in front.

Both men asked in unison, "Are you alright?"

I answered, "Yeah, I'm fine."

Agent Milton looked me up and down, "What is it I just saw? There's no way Sirhan missed you."

"He must have missed. I'm fine." I shook my shirt, and three spent slugs fell from inside my shirt and made little pinging noises as they hit the concrete floor.

Vitaly ignored it and called for my attention.

"Mister Fury. Things turned out rather well. I am thinking that you still owe me a favor..."

A female voice with a thick Russian accent cut Vitaly off in mid-sentence, "Vitaly, you old wolf! Behave yourself!"

Serena walked calmly up to her spouse and took his hand. She looked into his eyes and continued, "This man owes you nothing. I owe him my life, and since you owe me..."

Vitaly smiled, and kissed her gently on the forehead. "Yes my dear, but..."

"But nothing! Remember whose money built your club, and whose brother it is that you answer to."

There was a pause, and then a simple, "Yes, dear."

Serena turned to me. She appeared to be a graceful woman in her late fifties. Her face showed a few lines, but they only made her features more interesting.

She held out her right hand, "And you would be?"

"I'm Chad Fury."

"Chad, Vitaly and I are in your debt. If you need anything, nothing will be too great to ask. If it is in our power to do, it will be done."

"That is very generous of you."

"Generosity has nothing to do with it. It is only right."

Agent Milton interrupted, "Chad, if you're through ingratiating yourself with these people, we need to have a talk. In just a few minutes this place is going to be crawling with Federal Agents. I need something to tell them about what I've seen."

"I can't help you with that. I suggest you call Director Givens. She might have some ideas."

Agent Milton stared at me in disbelief.

CHAPTER FORTY-SEVEN

Director Givens looked at me across the conference table. Neither of us had said anything for what seemed like several minutes. I had no intention of being the first to break the silence. I had already told Saysha what had happened, several times. But the truth wasn't anything that, as she put it, she could use.

"Chad, please help me out here. I have three people all claiming to have seen you shot, multiple times. Sirhan Jadiddian was firing a Glock. The magazine holds fifteen rounds. And, if there was a round already chambered, that means the weapon could have been fired sixteen times. Vitaly has already stated that you may have been hit *at least* ten times.

Auggie, who I trust more than any other agent, claims to have seen you shot point blank, three times. I can't dismiss Auggie's statement.

A wanted fugitive is dead, and I need something that everyone can agree upon, and won't be questioned. The truth will make us *all* residents of the rubber room hotel."

"Director. Saysha. What is it that you want me to tell you? I know how ridiculous the truth sounds, I'm the one living it! But, maybe you could run with this. You'll need Vitaly's cooperation if he's ever questioned."

"Oh no! I'm not getting in bed with the Russian mafia, no *matter* what."

"Hear me out. Vitaly was bringing an unloaded pistol into the warehouse. He was betting that Sirhan would not pass up the opportunity to kill him and his wife with his own gun. It was a diversion, meant to buy a little time while I used the Glock he gave me to take out Sirhan.

What if the gun wasn't empty, but instead it was full of blanks?"

"That's absurd. What about the spent slugs lying all over the warehouse?"

"Then we're back to 'he missed', or the slugs came from a different gun on a different day. Either way, there's no way you can spin the story to explain everything."

"Maybe, I don't have to."

Saysha Givens reached for the speaker phone on the conference table and pushed four buttons. A phone rang somewhere, twice. Auggie's voice answered, "Hello, this is August Milton."

"Auggie, I'm ready for you. Please come to the large conference room on the first floor."

We waited less than a minute before the door opened and August Milton stepped through.

Auggie looked the same as he did about eight hours earlier in the warehouse, except a little more tired and he needed a shave. I empathized as I watched him take a seat on my side of the table.

Saysha turned her chair slightly to address Auggie directly.

"Auggie. We need to have a talk about last night's events. There's a little matter of the truth; what needs to be documented."

Agent Milton had a concerned look on his face. "Ma'am, I don't understand."

"Auggie, I know why you claim you don't smoke..."

Agent Milton interrupted, "I don't smoke."

I probably raised an eyebrow. I shifted in my chair and made myself comfortable as I settled in to enjoy the show.

Saysha raised a hand and displayed her palm. "Stop. Just save it.

A lot of people in this building smoke. They have stressful jobs, and they smoke. Most of them claim not to smoke for the same reason. Their health insurance would go up by seventy-five dollars a month. It saves them nine hundred dollars a year to claim they don't smoke.

If the insurance company finds out they do smoke, their rates go up and they pay a two hundred dollar penalty. So just where is the incentive for honesty?"

Agent Milton had slipped down in his chair a couple of inches. I almost laughed as he stammered, "Well... I... I... There's..."

"Quiet, Auggie, I'm not finished. Do you know why I don't tell the insurance company? Don't answer that. It's rhetorical.

If I told the insurance company about all of the people here who smoke, they would send a team to perform saliva tests for the presence of nicotine.

Everyone here would know I was the one who told about the smokers. Everybody in the building would have an opinion. Most of the opinions would be negative. I would end up with a largely *disgruntled* workforce.

Where, then, is my incentive to expose the truth?"

August Milton looked uncomfortable as he replied, "Excuse me, ma'am. But I thought we were going to talk about last night?"

Saysha let her shoulders relax, and she leaned back in her chair.

"Auggie, we are talking about last night. Let me put it another way.

Chad has been in Witness Protection, in Las Vegas. Some things have been happening in Vegas, related to Chad, of which I have been made aware.

I have been told about a field agent, Sandra Ellis, who had been assigned the task of keeping Chad under surveillance for his own protection.

Last week, Special Agent Sandra Ellis showed up at the United States Embassy, in London."

August Milton sat up in his chair and leaned forward, "London? As in England? What was she doing there?"

"Oh, you'll love this. This story is so much better than bullets bouncing off of Chad."

Saysha glanced my direction and gave me a quick frown before she continued.

"The way Agent Ellis tells the story, she was keeping an eye on Chad when she was abducted. She was taken to the Old Chicago Hotel in Old Las Vegas. There, she was beaten and sexually assaulted by a group of men she had never seen before.

Later that evening, one of the men dragged her out of the room where they had been keeping her and brought her into another room. The men stood in a circle around her. There were two new faces in the group. Someone named Ladon, and Chad."

Agent Milton turned and looked at me, but he spoke to Saysha, "What was Chad doing there?"

"Auggie. You're going to *love* this part. Ladon spoke to Agent Ellis. He called her by name. He told her she was burning to death. Agent Ellis claims that she burst into flames and couldn't put the fire out. She burned until Ladon told her that she was OK; that there was no fire."

Agent Milton looked puzzled, "Was there a fire?"

"No, Auggie. Sandra Ellis has no burns on her body. But that's only a small part of the story. Chad took Ladon hostage with his bare hands. Agent Ellis claims that Chad had Ladon's throat in his right hand and was twisting Ladon's left arm behind his back.

But this is the really good part. Chad's hands didn't look human. They were red and scaly, with two fingers, a thumb, and yellow claws."

August Milton screwed up his face and looked at me. I raised my right hand over my head, curled my fingers, and heard Saysha givens yell out, "Chad! Stop! Put your hand down *very* slowly."

I lowered my hand to my lap and listened to Saysha tell the rest of her story.

"Auggie, the way Sandra Ellis tells the story, Chad dragged Ladon out of the room and into the elevators. Agent Ellis followed. They stopped on a floor and three of Ladon's men were waiting for them. Chad threw Ladon out of the elevator and subdued the men.

Chad and Agent Ellis found another bank of elevators. They pulled the fire alarm, and took the elevator to the ground floor. They escaped the building in the mass of people exiting the hotel."

Agent Milton folded his hands and took turns looking at both of us, "That's pretty unbelievable."

Saysha continued, "Oh, you haven't heard the most unbelievable part. Out on the street, in front of the hotel, Chad took Agent Ellis by the arm and drug her down a manhole and into the storm sewers."

"What? The sewers?"

"That's right Auggie. Chad dragged Agent Ellis into the storm sewers and made a phone call to Lisa. The same Lisa who right now is lying in the hospital, in a coma.

Anyway, Lisa came riding in on a motorcycle, through the sewers."

Agent Milton laughed, "This is a joke. Right?"

"No, Auggie. This is Sandra Ellis' version of the truth."

"You're saying, Lisa took Agent Ellis to the airport."

"No. Agent Ellis got onto the back of the motorcycle and Lisa drove the motorcycle through a concrete wall. The next thing Agent Ellis recalls is finding herself in the Tower of London."

August Milton leaned forward, "Director, where is Agent Ellis now?"

"Agent Ellis is undergoing psychiatric evaluation. I

expect that she will be found unfit for duty, released, and given the opportunity to find other employment."

August Milton leaned back in his chair and just said, "Hmmm."

"Auggie, I'm not telling you to falsify your report. I'm asking you to carefully consider what facts to include so that you don't win both of us a free trip to the laughing academy.

At a high level, the facts of last night are believable. You entered the warehouse. Sirhan Jadiddian was discharging a weapon. You fired. Sirhan died, and no one else was injured."

"Even that might be questioned. The distance between Sirhan and his targets was measured in feet, not yards. It was a can't-miss range."

"Auggie, did you hear about the Carson brothers last year?"

"No. What about them?"

"They were small time drug dealers who wanted to make it big. Jake and Frank Carson began exporting their product across state lines. They laundered money and committed wire fraud.

That's when we got involved. Jake and Frank had a falling out over the way the business was being run. One night they met in a field over by Arcadia Lake. They both brought pistols, they both fired. They kept shooting and kept missing.

When they were both out of ammunition, they threw their weapons at each other. That's when it turned into a bare-knuckled fight. Finally Jake picked up a rock and bashed in Frank's skull."

"Hmmm. OK. I get it. I won't lie, but I'm not going to write the report to where anyone will ask questions that we'd rather not answer."

Saysha Givens sighed, "Thank you. Now there's one last matter. I've promised Chad he could continue looking through Sirhan's things. I intend to keep that promise. I know you're both tired. It's up to you whether you continue today or go get some rest. But, mind you, I'd like this finished as soon as possible."

August Milton replied, "Understood."

I chimed in, "I am tired, but I've got a few more hours in me."

Saysha smiled, "Good. Let's get this done. And then, Chad, let's get you back to Las Vegas and Witness Protection."

CHAPTER FORTY-EIGHT

Agent Milton drove us back to the warehouses. We made one stop at my insistence; a drive through for overpriced coffee and sandwiches. The food was from one of those places you would recognize by name, where they don't sell coffee in small, medium, and large sizes. They make up their own names for the sizes. Anyway, I paid for both of us.

When we arrived at the warehouse, Agent Milton got out of the car and stopped. He pulled out a cigarette.

"No use hiding this any longer," he said and laughed.

I held up my coffee and said, "I'll join you in my addiction."

Agent Milton took a long slow drag on his cigarette and exhaled. "I want to know, Chad, the stuff Director Givens said about you and Agent Ellis. Is it true?"

I thought a moment. I didn't want to drag anyone else into my drama, but Auggie was already a part of it. "Every last syllable."

"I'd appreciate a little proof."

"No you wouldn't. You'd just try to explain it away. And, if you did believe it, you might become a target for

Ladon and his people."

Auggie took another drag on his cigarette. He held the smoke for a moment, then exhaled. "You may be right, but still..."

"Auggie, let's change the subject. Just how much of Sirhan's stuff is left to go through?"

"There's a lot. On the other end of these grounds there are cars, boats, motorcycles, RV's and trailers. Then there's furniture. Beds, sofas, tables and chairs; you name it. And, there's a section of office equip.m.ent and electronics. Fax machines, printers, computers, stereo equip.m.ent, and anything else with an electrical cord."

"I'm too tired to think about all of that. What would be the easiest group to eliminate? I'd like to feel like I accomplished something today."

Auggie took a last drag on his cigarette. "Probably the electronics. Unless there's a need to do forensics on the computers, it will be the easiest."

"Let's do that. I vote for easy."

Auggie flicked his cigarette butt on the ground and crushed it with his right foot.

I followed him to the warehouse door. He entered the access code, and I followed. In a few moments he had the lights switched on and the ventilation fans running.

I followed Auggie down the furthest isle and to the back of the warehouse. After a while I was standing in a section that looked like an electronics warehouse had blown-up.

"We're here, Chad."

I sighed, "OK, let's get started."

"Not so fast." Auggie reached into a pocket and pulled out a pair of blue surgical gloves. "Here, put these on."

"Why? Are you worried about finger prints?"

"No, you've obviously never searched this kind of stuff before. It's filthy. The printers and copiers will get your hands black, and the computers are just nasty."

Auggie pulled out a second pair of gloves and went to a

large printer on wheels. "Come over here, Chad. I'll show you how to search electronics for contraband."

I put on my gloves and stood next to Auggie.

"This is a multi-function device. It's a printer, scanner, fax, and copier all in one. If there's a panel or a door, open it."

Auggie pushed a square button on the side of the device, and a large panel fell open. "Now reach your hand in and feel around all the crevices and open spaces. Criminals look for all kinds of free spaces to hide things. They call these hiding places 'slicks'."

Auggie demonstrated. He stuck his hand inside and felt around. He pulled his hand out and displayed it. Black powder was all over the glove.

"Now you can see why I gave you the gloves. That's toner powder. Go to work on the other stuff, when you get to the computers, wait for me."

I searched eleven printers and six fax machines. I came up empty except for a few mouse droppings and a lot of black toner powder on my gloves.

Auggie moved to the computers and waited for me. He picked up a desktop computer and sat it on a nearby rolling cart.

"Chad, you wouldn't happen to have a screw driver?"

"Actually, I do. I pulled out my Swiss style knife."

"Good. The older computers will have screws holding the cover. The newer ones, like this, have a latch or lever that releases the cover so you can lift it off."

"You don't really find things stuffed inside computers, do you?"

"You wouldn't believe what people hide inside of them. I've found marijuana, hard-core drugs, and a gun. I even found a brassiere once."

I gave Auggie a funny look.

"Chad, before you ask, the answer is 'I do not know why it was there and I did not ask'."

"At least your job is interesting."

"Sometimes it is."

Auggie pulled the latch on the computer's cover. He removed it. I saw what he meant when he said computers were nasty. The thing was full of lint and dust. He moved the dust balls around and looked. There was nothing there that looked like it didn't belong.

I set to work looking through the machines. I was opening computer number eight when Auggie called me over to him.

"Chad. Come take a look at this."

I made my way around the pile of computers and printers over to him. Auggie lifted the cover panel from the side of the computer sitting on the rolling cart. He turned the panel toward me. There was something large, covered in black plastic, fastened to the panel with gray duct tape.

Auggie handed the panel to me and said, "Here. You'll want to do the honors."

I took the panel and laid it on a stack of computers next to me. I took out my pocket knife and unfolded the largest blade. I cut through the duct tape where the black plastic met the metal, and lifted the object.

"Chad, what do you think it is?"

"It feels like a book."

Auggie stood close to me and watched as I carefully unwrapped the plastic, revealing a light blue card-stock paper cover on a book that must have been almost two inches thick. The side I was looking at had no writing. I turned the book over. There was printing on the front.

At the top, in red ink, there were letters made by a large rubber stamp spelling out "SECRET." Beneath that was a white square of paper with the typed words.

"Nuclear Testing Summary 1962 - 1969
Nevada Proving Grounds
Nye County, Nevada

Property of the United States Army"

I held the book in both hands and looked Auggie in the face. "This has to be it! This had to have been put here by Colonel Evans. Auggie, please tell me I can take it with me."

"I don't know, Chad. I should really tell the Director."

"Look. This was hidden in all this junk. Nobody knew it was here. It wouldn't be like I was taking FBI property."

"Oh, come on Chad. I can't let you just walk out with that, especially since it's stamped 'secret'. I know you don't have any kind of security clearance."

"Auggie, what would you do with it?"

"I'd put it in an evidence bag and hand it over to Director Givens."

"Alright then. Let's do that on Monday morning. This is Friday. Let me take the book, look through it, and see if there's anything here that leads to the artifact Ladon wants."

"Chad!"

"Auggie! I could take this book, run out of here right now, and you would never see me again."

"I'm calling Director Givens."

"No, Auggie. Don't."

August Milton stepped away a few feet, pulled out his cell phone and dialed. In a moment he was speaking to Saysha Givens. I listened carefully to hear both sides of the conversation.

"Director, we've found something."

Auggie described the exterior of the book and then told Director Givens that I wanted to take the book. I heard a very loud, "Damn, damn, damn!" come through the phone.

There was a long pause, and then I heard her say, "Auggie, you didn't find anything today. If you find something later, you're to hand it over immediately. If something like that were to be found, we could discuss the contents with Chad. But today, you came up empty."

Auggie put the phone away and started to speak, but I interrupted.

"I heard everything she said, Auggie. We never found anything. Perhaps we'll have better luck on Monday.

Now please take me back to my car."

"How did you hear...oh never mind." Auggie just shook his head and muttered to himself as we straightened up the area to leave.

The ride back started silently. I couldn't tell if Auggie was upset or if he was tired. He finally broke the silence.

"Chad, I want to know one thing. How did all of this start, how did you get mixed up with these people? What really happened?"

I told him. I told him about getting the tattoo last year, meeting Lisa, the abduction and all of it right up to the point that I was arrested.

That's when we pulled into the parking lot at the FBI office. Auggie stopped the car. He looked at me for a moment, "Chad, did you ever have a normal life?"

"Yes, I did. It seems like a very long time ago. I'm starting to think I'll never have one again."

I got out of the old white sedan and walked over to my baby, my black Ford Interceptor. I unlocked the door and threw the book on the passenger's seat. I gave Auggie a friendly salute, and got in my car.

I didn't drive back to the hotel. Instead, I headed to the hospital. Now that Sirhan was dead, and I had this book to digest, I didn't want to be alone. There was only one person I wanted to be with, and it didn't matter if she could talk to me or not. I still wanted to talk to her.

Inside the hospital room, I took in the sight of Lisa lying there in the bed at the center of a bundle of wires and tubes. I laid the book on the sofa, and pulled up a chair next to Lisa. Before I sat down, I leaned over, stroked her red hair, and lightly kissed her forehead. I sat, held her hand, and talked.

"I'm sorry about being gone. I had to take care of a few things. Mainly, Sirhan. He's dead by the way. The FBI shot him. And, I think I found something that may help us find the stone. It's the book over there," I nodded toward the sofa.

I told Lisa my story. I was interrupted by a nurse who came in to check on her. The nurse and I talked for a moment while she checked Lisa's tubes and wires. She drew a little blood and left.

After the nurse was gone I went to the sofa, placed the book on the floor, laid down, and slept.

CHAPTER FORTY-NINE

I woke at ten minutes after seven in the morning. The phone in my pocket was ringing. It was the phone Ladon had given me. I made a face. I thought about not answering, but I answered.

"What do you want, Ladon?"

"Good morning, Chad." The tone of the voice was as creepy as ever. "I'm given to understand that Sirhan is dead."

"He is."

"I'm disappointed."

"You wanted him dead, and he's dead."

"Yes, but I wanted *you* to kill him, with *your* bare hands."

"Oh, shut up!"

"Chad! I have to continue your training. But first, tell me, have you found anything among Sirhan's things?"

I lied. "No. And thanks to your stunt with Sirhan, I wasted a lot of time that could have been spent looking."

"Perhaps you'll have better luck today."

"I'm taking the weekend off. I can't get into the warehouse until Monday."

"That's not true. I expect..."

"Ladon, the agent that's been escorting me in and out of the warehouse won't be available all weekend."

"You're hiding something from me, Chad. And I don't like secrets."

"Ladon. Let me remind you that you told *me* to search for the stone. If you want it done a different way, *you* can do it yourself!"

"You really shouldn't be arguing with me, Chad. Perhaps you need a partner on this. Take your weekend. I'll work on finding you a companion."

Ladon hung up the phone.

I put away the phone. I looked at Lisa lying in the bed, then I bent down and picked up the book from the floor. At least I had the weekend to figure out what this book might tell me.

"Lisa, I'm sorry I can't sit here and keep you company. There's too much to do, and I wish you could help."

I took my phone out of my pocket and dialed Uncle Allan's number. The phone rang six times before I heard a familiar voice say, "Hello."

"Uncle Allan, it's Chad. I'm sorry to bother you so early."

"That's quite alright, Chad. What can I do for you? Is anything wrong?"

"I've found something that may help me locate what Ladon's after. But, I've only got the weekend to work on it. I was wondering if you would take a look at it and we could work on this together."

"Have you had breakfast?"

"No."

"Then come over. I'll have breakfast ready and we can talk about whatever it is you found."

I stood, put the phone in my pocket, went to the bed and gave Lisa a kiss on the forehead. I left the room and headed for my car.

Given that it was Saturday, it was an easy drive to

Uncle Allan's house. In a short twenty minutes I was standing on his doorstep, ringing his doorbell.

The door opened to reveal my uncle in blue jeans and a tee-shirt, holding a spatula in his left hand.

"Come on in, Chad. Sorry to run. The bacon's about to burn."

Uncle Allan ran off to the kitchen. I crossed the threshold and closed the door behind me. When I entered the kitchen, Uncle Allan was taking bacon out of a pan and laying it on a paper towel.

"Can I help you, Uncle?"

"Sure, the table's set. Bring the coffee."

I took the glass carafe from beneath the maker and followed Uncle Allan into the dining room.

We took our seats and Uncle Allan did his customary praying before eating. After which, we filled our plates and Uncle Allan started asking questions.

"Tell me Chad, what is it you found?"

"It's a book." I nodded toward the blue book I had placed on the table. "It's a collection of reports on nuclear testing that was done in the sixties, in the Nevada desert."

"That's interesting." Allan took a bite of scrambled eggs and a swallow of coffee before he continued. "And why do you think that's related to the stone that Ladon wants?"

I took a bite of toast and swallowed. "Because, it was hidden inside a computer, wrapped in plastic and taped to the inside cover. I think it's pretty likely, especially since whatever I needed to find was supposed to have belonged to this Colonel Roger Evans. And the book is an Army document."

"That's good. I just want to rule out any spurious correlations."

I gave Uncle Allan a puzzled look, "You want to what?"

"I want to make sure finding the book wasn't a coincidence."

"Why didn't you just say so?"

"I did. You should really work on your vocabulary, Chad. You're teaching at a university. You have an obligation to make your students think." Uncle Allan reached up and tapped his temple with his index finger.

I shook my head and continued eating. Allan changed the subject. He wanted to know more about my trip through the portals, and especially my time on Phobos and Mars.

After breakfast, we cleared the table and went to the den to look over the book. Uncle Allan took the book from the coffee table where I had placed it. He leafed through the first several pages with what I interpreted to be a look of appreciation. When I had done the same thing, all I felt was overwhelmed.

"Uncle Allan, what do you think it is that we should be looking for in there?"

"I'm not sure. You said you had some names in the letters you found. We need to keep our eyes open for those. Still, I don't know if they will even be in there."

"I understand, but still. There's got to be something."

"Agreed." Uncle Allan bit his lower lip. "Maybe we shouldn't start with what's written in the book. Maybe we should start with what the book itself can tell us."

"You just lost me, Uncle. What do you mean?"

"I'm thinking about Benford's Law."

"What's that?"

"Benford's Law was discovered by Simon Newcomb. He was an amateur astronomer. He never got credit for his discovery. Another man, Benford, got the credit. Anyway, the law demonstrates that naturally occurring numbers don't show up with equal probability."

"What? And did you know that the price of tea in China is about to take a sharp increase?"

"Chad, be serious. The way the law was discovered is that Simon Newcomb was using log rhythm tables for his calculations. He noticed one day that some of the pages in his book of log rhythm tables were more well-worn than others. That's because he needed information from some tables more often than others."

"Where are you going with this, Uncle?"

"Human nature, Chad. Human nature."

"I still don't understand."

"Hand me my Bible. It's on the shelf over there." Uncle Allan nodded toward the opposite wall.

"No. I'm in no mood for one of your Sunday School lessons."

"Neither am I. Indulge me."

I got up and retrieved the book. I handed it to Uncle Allan, but he refused to take it.

"Chad. Tell me what my favorite Bible passage is."

"I don't have any idea."

"Look at the book. The pages should be more well-worn where I read more often."

"Oh, I see! What you're saying is that if Colonel Evans put that book in the computer, he did so, because it was important to him. And he probably spent time reading the section that was important to him, more than any of the other sections."

"Exactly!"

"Why didn't you just say so?"

"I thought I just did."

I shook my head as I returned his Bible to the shelf. By the time I had returned to the sofa, Alan was examining the edges of the book. He bent the book gently from top to bottom, making the long edge of the book fan out slightly. The wear and discoloration from handling seemed to show up just a little better that way.

"Chad, I think whatever we're looking for is in the last half. See how worn the edges of those pages are?"

I nodded. The smudges where the book was handled began at the last half of the volume. Uncle Alan turned to the middle of the book. My heart skipped a beat as I saw the title on the page.

"Uncle, look at that, 'Operation Whetstone 1964-1965', could that be the Stone of Destiny?"

"I don't know. There's only one way to find out. We've got some reading to do."

We spent hours reading and talking, and I won't bore you with all the details. But, we found out Operation Whetstone consisted of a total of forty-six nuclear tests.

It was an odd thing about those tests. The bombs were called "devices". The whole thing seemed a little less dangerous talking about a "device" rather than a bomb.

The devices had been "activated" in a variety of numbered places around the Nevada desert. Operation Whetstone was conducted primarily in areas fifteen, nineteen, and twenty. The only exception was a single test conducted near Lumberton, Mississippi.

The first twenty devices had been constructed to the exact same specifications. They did not vary at all in weight or the amount of nuclear material used to construct the bomb.

The first ten of these devices comprised the control group. They were detonated underground, in tunnels and shafts. The explosions were carefully monitored and the radiation was measured for several days following the blast.

For the next ten tests, the conditions were repeated, with one exception. Something they referred to as the "Omega Device" was placed at varying distances from the center of the blast zone.

From the physical description of the "Omega Device" I knew it had to be the Stone of Destiny. And from the report, I could see why the military was so interested in the stone. The results of every test were the same. The stone somehow absorbed the blast energy.

It was as though the stone took all of the power of the nuclear blast and nullified it. Wherever the stone was, the entire area was unharmed. The blast had no more effect than a firecracker. And, there was no residual radiation.

"Chad, this is amazing! Do you realize what the military was doing?"

"I think so. It looks like they were hoping to have a defense against nuclear weapons."

"If they could duplicate this effect, the threat of nuclear war would be eliminated!"

We continued to talk for a while before we turned our attention to the next section. It was titled "Operation Opera 1966".

We both got excited when we read the report, me, more so than Uncle Allan. The report described different kinds of tests designed to help them understand the stone and how it worked.

From what we gathered from the report, every attempt to look inside the stone failed. X-rays could not penetrate it. Every attempt to cut it open resulted in the same effect; material cut or chipped away reformed on the stone.

It had been noted in other tests that the stone reacted to sound. It was the goal of Operation Opera to exploit that observation in hope that insight would be gained into how the stone worked.

Someone on the project had a sense of humor. A machine was created to produce sounds and direct those sounds at the stone. The machine was named Fat Lady. Uncle Allan and I both commented that the Opera's not over until the Fat Lady sings.

Fat Lady would play a tone and any observed effect on the stone was meticulously recorded. After playing single tones, the tones where an effect was observed were combined in various patterns.

The effects from playing single tones ranged from changes in the temperature of the stone to bursts of light and energy emanating from the stone. When the tones were combined, the effects became more intense, and in one experiment the mass of the stone decreased to almost nothing.

The final experiment of Operation Opera was

disastrous. Fat Lady had been prepared to play sets of tones together, like musical chords. The entire experiment was, essentially, a song for Fat Lady to sing.

When Fat Lady sang her song, light filled the test chamber. It seemed to rotate and coalesce into what was described as broken shards of a giant mirror. But the effect wasn't limited to the test chamber. The same thing was happening across the entire test facility.

The giant shards swirled around the stone. As a mirrored shard touched an object, the object seemed to fall into the shard and disappear. This included people who were in paths of the moving shards.

The people and the objects didn't stay gone. They reappeared in various places. When they reappeared, people were dying or dead. Some were corpses, charred beyond recognition. Some reappeared alive, fused with the walls and floors, and some onlookers were fused with the tables and chairs swept up by the shards.

The report mentioned one brave soul, E. Scofield, a technician on the project. E. Scofield ran into the test chamber, dodged the swirling shards, and ran to Fat Lady. He tried to stop Fat Lady's song. He pulled the plug, but the shards remained for several seconds more. E. Scofield was swallowed up by a shard and deposited face down on the stone as the shards faded into nothing.

A total of seventy-eight people were swept up by the shards. Sixteen disappeared and were never found. Another six appeared somewhere in the facility, dead. Twenty died slowly as they reappeared fused with the walls, floors, and furniture in the facility. Another twenty appeared, fused with each other; there were fused masses of two, three, and four people combined into new grotesque shapes with heads, arms, and legs in places they should not be.

The final eight were alive. Some were discovered wondering around the facility, some were in shock. All of them proved to be mentally unstable. Seven of the eight died within a week. Only E. Scofield survived, and was placed into a psychiatric facility.

Following the accident, Operation Opera was abandoned, and all experiments regarding the stone were suspended, indefinitely.

After taking all of this in, Uncle Allan and I sat silent for a time. He finally spoke, "Chad, I think we've had enough for today. Why don't you come back in the morning? We'll go to Sunday Mass, and then take this up again after lunch."

"After all of this, I don't think I can do Mass."

"After all of this, Chad, I think I need to. You're welcome to come. Otherwise, come back tomorrow afternoon, around two."

CHAPTER FIFTY

Sunday afternoon I was sitting in Uncle Allan's den, holding the blue book. Our moods had improved, and we were ready to start tackling this job again.

"Well, Uncle, now we know where the stone was, how do we go about finding where it is?"

"Sorry, Chad, but you're wrong."

"About what?"

"We don't know where the stone was, not really. Every place listed in that book where tests occurred is listed as a numbered area. The index at the back lists all of the areas and the names of the tests. The list goes from Area One through Area Thirty. And we don't know where those are. We only know it was in the Nevada desert, and that's no small place to be searching."

"So what do we do?"

"I have an idea."

Uncle Allan left the room and returned with his laptop computer. He fired it up and went immediately to a search engine where he typed "Nevada Nuclear Test Sites." In a flash we were seeing a large list of web pages on the subject.

The first website was pure gold. We were looking at a list of all of the test sites, by area number. It included a map with geographic coordinates.

What the website didn't include was Area Thirteen where Operation Opera had been conducted. There was only one reference on the page to Area Thirteen. It stated that Area Thirteen does not exist.

"Well that's just great, Uncle! What are we supposed to do now?"

"I don't think there's much we can do, Chad. Think about it. We have a government experiment that went so badly wrong, that not only was it covered up, but the entire region was removed from the list of test sites."

"Uhh...You mean that's it? We're done? It's a dead end?"

"It is, unless..."

"Unless what?"

"Unless you can get someone with the right government connections to help."

"I don't know anyone with government connections."

"Yes you do. Think about it."

I thought and then it struck me, "Saysha Givens."

"Right. Tell her everything you know. She might be able to find something out about what happened after Operation Opera. If you're lucky, someone will tell her what happened to the stone."

Other than that, the only thing to do is turn this all over to Ladon and let him take it from here."

"If I do that, Ladon gets the stone and we all lose."

We talked a little while longer, and I eventually left to return to my hotel room. There seemed to be nothing to do but see Saysha Givens first thing in the morning.

It was around five-thirty when I arrived back at my hotel room. I slid the key card in and out of the lock. The lock clicked; I turned the handle. When I pushed the door open, an odor hit my nose. It wasn't burnt cinnamon, but it was someone familiar.

I called out into the room, "Jim Clayton? What are you doing here?"

There was no reply. I walked in to find Jim, in uniform, sitting on my bed with his back against the headboard. His hands were folded in his lap.

"Hello, Chad. Pull up a seat. We need to talk."

"Just what are you doing here?"

"I came to have a talk with you. I see you're carrying something. That must mean you've found something important. Ladon will want to know."

I stood there at the foot of the bed, stunned, unable to respond to the words that had come out of Jim's mouth.

"Chad. Really, take a seat. Grow up and get your head in the game."

I pulled out the chair from behind the desk and turned it to face Jim. I sat and looked him in the eyes.

"Jim. Why are you here and how do you know Ladon?"

"Second part first. I don't know Ladon. I know Adolf Thorne.

About eight years ago, Adolf approached me. He told me to do something for him. He wanted me to make the Marshals look the other way in a manhunt we were conducting. I didn't seem to have a choice.

After that, he made requests, I complied, and he paid me well. Now, I do what he asks and I get paid. If I don't, my family will be hurt.

As to why I'm here. Adolf tells me that Ladon sent you on a job for him. You were to recover something from Sirhan's things that are currently in the custody of the FBI. I'm here to make sure you're doing your job. I was told to stay by your side and not leave until your job was finished.

By the way you're clutching that book, I assume you've found what Ladon wants."

"Ladon wants me to find a stone block. This isn't a block of stone," I said as I put the book on the desk. "But, it *was* you, Jim, wasn't it?"

"It was me, *what?*"

"You fed all the information about me to Ladon."

"No. I had never heard the name Ladon until you said it at the police station. Adolf explained the situation to me. I bought a plane ticket and came here.

Now. What have you found?"

I sat silent for a moment thinking. I had caught a light scent of onions when Jim mentioned the manhunt. I think there was more to that story. But I dismissed that for now.

More importantly, Ladon sent Jim to keep me in line. Jim seemed to know a lot about my situation. I also wondered if Ladon intended for me to kill Jim as part of the so-called *training* that Ladon seemed to think I needed.

"Speak up, Chad."

"OK. Ladon wants a stone, the Stone of Destiny. The U.S. Army experimented with it in the sixties. I found this book hidden inside a computer among Sirhan's things. The book lists tests that were conducted using the stone.

Tell Ladon we need to know everything about Operation Opera, Area Thirteen, Eddie Scofield, and possibly someone named Ray."

"And what were you planning on doing with this information?"

"I was going to take it to Saysha Givens first thing in the morning."

Jim was silent. He pulled a cell phone out of his shirt pocket and dialed. After a moment Jim spoke and I listened in on the conversation.

"Adolf, it's Clayton. I'm here with Chad."

I heard the voice on the phone reply, "That's good. How are things?"

"Things are fine. He's actually got something. There's a book of some kind that mentions tests the U.S. military conducted using the stone Ladon wants."

"Good. Does it say where the stone is now?"

"No. But Chad was planning on taking the book and a couple of names to Saysha Givens. He was going to ask her for help in finding out about the stone and the people."

"That sounds fine. Do that. Make sure you don't let Chad out of your sight. I'll make some calls so that Saysha Givens doesn't have any problems finding out what we need to know."

Jim ended the call. "Well, Chad, it seems that..."

"I know. I heard it all. We're to turn everything over to Saysha, just like I had planned."

Jim gave me a questioning look, but didn't comment.

"Chad, I'm hungry. Pick up the phone and call room service I want their best steak and potato."

I made the call and ordered for both of us. I kept silent until the food came.

After the food arrived I discovered I wasn't very hungry, and I only picked at it. Jim, on the other hand, devoured his plate.

After dinner Jim barked at me, "Whatever it is that you do to get ready for bed, do it now."

"I'm not tired. And by the way, where will you be sleeping?"

"I'm in the adjoining room. The hotel was quite accommodating and moved the occupants out for me so I could track my fugitive."

"Oh, really. That's what I am? A fugitive?"

"That's how we're going to play this, Chad. Now get ready for bed. When you're done, I'm going to handcuff you to the headboard so you don't wander off in the night."

"No. We're not doing that."

Jim pulled his gun and stroked it with his free hand. "Chad, I was told that you might not have much respect for guns. I was told I should tell you I was given titanium tipped bullets to use. Why that makes a difference, I don't know."

I swallowed hard and kept silent.

"Chad, get ready for bed. Now."

I complied. I brushed my teeth and performed the

necessary functions. When I returned Jim was holding handcuffs in one hand and his gun in the other.

"Put these on, Chad."

Jim tossed the handcuffs to me. I put one shackle on my left wrist and the other on the headboard frame.

"Chad, I'll be in the next room. If you need something, it's just too damn bad."

Before Jim left, he moved the room telephone out of reach and made sure I couldn't get to my cell phone or anything else. Jim turned out the lights and closed the door behind him.

CHAPTER FIFTY-ONE

Jim Clayton came into my room just before seven a.m.. I hadn't slept well. There was too much going on in my head, not to mention that my left wrist had been pinned above my head all night long.

I could have broken free with enough effort. But, it would have bought me nothing. If I was going to keep the stone out of Ladon's hands, I needed to play along.

Jim came over to the bed and unlocked the cuffs.

"Time to get ready, Chad. I'll call up room service while you get dressed."

I rubbed my left wrist and moved my left arm in circles to release the stiffness out of my shoulder.

"Jim, none of this was really necessary."

"I'm afraid it was. Adolf says you're slippery. I was told not to let you out of my sight, and that's what I'm doing."

"You've certainly learned to follow orders."

"You can judge me all you want, Chad, but it won't change anything. I'm doing what I have to do to protect my family."

I showered and dressed; breakfast arrived. As we ate, I asked, "What's the plan, Jim?"

"We check out of the hotel. We go to the FBI and *encourage* Saysha Givens to find out about those names and that project in that book. Then we catch a flight back to Vegas and wait."

I was upset with myself for how foolish I had been. I had assumed it would be so easy to fool Ladon; to find the stone and keep it away from him. Now, I had no idea if keeping the stone out of Ladon's hands was even possible.

"Jim, I want to ask you one favor, please."

"The answer's no."

"You haven't even heard it."

"I don't have to. It probably involves altering the plans in some way. I do as I'm told."

"It has to do with my car. I don't want to leave it abandoned here in Oklahoma. My uncle's not far away. Either on the way to the FBI, or before we go to the airport; I just want to leave it in his driveway where it will be safe."

"We're taking your car to the airport, and you'll leave it there. You can mail your keys to your uncle."

I exhaled, and I'm certain I grimaced, "I guess you're in charge."

"Pack your things, Chad. I'm not wasting any time."

I packed. While Jim had his back turned to me I put the gold statues inside the orange spacesuit and folded it tightly.

We took our bags to my car. Jim commented on the orange spacesuit when I put it in the trunk next to the suitcase. I dismissed his comment by saying it was a souvenir from a movie set.

It seemed like a long ride to the FBI office. The trip was made even more uncomfortable by the fact that Jim *drove* my car!

Still, we arrived and soon were seated in Saysha Givens' office. Saysha looked angry.

"Chad, I know why you and Deputy Clayton are here. I had a phone call yesterday from someone named Adolf."

Jim Clayton smiled, "Good. I understand it's Director now?"

Saysha nodded, "Facility Director."

Jim continued, "Then, Director, I want to make it clear that *I* was never here. This conversation never happened."

Saysha Givens leaned back in her chair. "Whatever. Play your silly games all you want. You realize that whatever investigation we make into The Company will eventually lead back to you."

Jim placed an ankle on his knee and shifted in his chair. "The people in charge of all of this know how to make things...go away. I've come to accept that. What I know, and you don't, is they can make anyone do whatever they want. It's just simpler, and more profitable, to go along with their wishes."

Saysha turned her attention to me. "Chad, is that the book I was told about?"

I handed the book across the table. "Yes. About three quarters of the way through, there's a section on Operation Opera. I need to know more about it.

In nineteen sixty-six, the military conducted tests on the stone in a place referred to as Area Thirteen. It might help to know where that is. There was a horrific accident, and there's no mention of what happened to the stone afterwards.

The report mentions a name, E. Scofield. I think that's Eddie Scofield. Colonel Evans' nephew. Eddie may have talked to someone about the stone. Anything you can find out about Operation Opera, Area Thirteen, and Eddie Scofield would be appreciated."

Saysha dropped the book on her desk. It made a thud.

"Chad, I can't believe you're going along with this. For that matter I can't believe I am either.

Alright. I'll make some calls. I'll tell you what I find out."

Saysha turned to Jim. "Get out. Now. I don't want to see you ever again."

It was a short trip to the airport. Jim drove. He parked my car in the lot marked as long term parking. We got out of my car and went to the trunk. Before he got his bag, he opened a side pocket and pulled out a large, clear plastic bag with the word "Evidence" printed in white letters on one side.

"Empty your pockets and put everything in here. Your watch too."

"And why would I do that?"

"Because we're taking a plane ride, and we're not walking up to the ticket counter and buying tickets."

I complied. I dropped everything into the bag, and Jim put it in his small suitcase. We put our bags on the ground. I left the orange spacesuit in the trunk and closed the trunk lid.

Jim pulled out his handcuffs.

"Jim, no. *Please.*"

"Sorry, Chad. This is the price of your ticket. Now hold out your hands."

I couldn't believe I was doing it, but I held out my arms and let Jim put the silver shackles on my wrists.

Jim carried our luggage into the airport terminal. It was oddly humiliating walking in front of him, handcuffed. People stared, children pointed, and I heard whispers.

Jim directed me past the ticket counters and straight to the TSA checkpoint. When the TSA officer at the front saw us, he escorted us around the lines, past the baggage scanners, and into a side room. The officer left us alone and we waited.

"Chad. While we're in the airport I expect you to play your part."

"What does that mean?"

"You're a captured fugitive. Be quiet and submissive. If you make a scene, I'll treat you like a real fugitive. You'll be restrained."

I held out my wrists, "What do you call this?"

"You haven't seen anything, yet. Say one thing out of line and you'll get to experience leg shackles and belly chains."

About that time a man in his late fifties with a crew cut walked into the room. He put out his hand toward Jim. Jim took his hand and shook it firmly.

The man introduced himself to Jim and ignored me like I was a piece of furniture.

"I'm Air Marshal, Bill Ransom."

"Deputy Marshal, Jim Clayton. Good to meet you."

Bill nodded and looked my direction, "What do we have here?"

Jim answered for me, "His name's Chad. He also goes by the name Drake Manning. He likes to murder hookers and rob casinos. He got away from his keepers, and I'm taking him back to Vegas to stand trial."

"We'll make some room on a flight. Let me take your bags." Bill looked at the luggage, "You're not traveling very light."

Jim looked at me as he spoke. "The large bag is his. I decided not to leave it. There are some things in there that used to belong to his victims."

Bill frowned and took the bags. He looked at me. "No wonder you got caught, son. Nobody ever taught you to travel light."

Once we were alone, I turned to Jim, "What the *hell*? I murder prostitutes!?" Really!?"

"What do you care? You'll never see him again."

I went to one of the black and chrome chairs against the wall and dropped myself into the seat with a thud.

"I can't believe how mad I am at myself, that I actually *liked* Jim Clayton. I thought he was one of the good guys, a real stand-up kind of guy. But no. He's one of The Company's lackeys, a real..."

Jim cut me off, "Shut up, Chad! You don't know what you're talking about."

I held out my wrists to him, "Oh really. I don't know what *I'm* talking about. I don't know that Jim Clayton *can't* be trusted."

Jim came over and sat next to me. "Chad, believe me,

you don't understand."

"Educate me."

Jim glanced furtively around the empty room before speaking.

"Eight years ago we were looking for a man named Carson Little who had broken out of prison. He crossed three states to get to Nevada.

The manhunt had just gotten underway when I got a phone call from a man calling himself Adolf. He said that when we found out where Carson Little was hiding, I was to cover it up and call him back with the location.

I didn't want to do it, I just had to. I tried not to do it, but I did it anyway. I altered the reports to lead the Marshals to the wrong side of town. Then I called Adolf.

Adolf told me to come pick him up and take him to Carson Little. Once again, I did. I drove Adolf to a seedy little motel on the outskirts of Vegas.

When we got to the motel I went into the room with Adolf. He gave me a knife and told me to kill Carson. I tried to put the knife down. I *tried* to walk away. I *tried* to drop the knife, but my hand clung to it. The more I tried to let it go, the more tightly I gripped the knife. There was nothing I could do except what I was told.

But, Adolf didn't just tell me to kill Carson, he told me to rip him open and cut his guts out. I was told to clean and dress his carcass the way I would a deer."

"Oh...my...God."

"The next day the body was found by the cleaning crew."

"Jim. I'm so sorry."

"Chad, I've had to do other things. Things just as horrible. Trust me, if I could put an end to all of this, I would."

I turned to look him squarely in eyes, "Jim, why did you just tell me all of this? You could have kept it a secret."

"Because now they have you. I don't know what they

want with you, but whatever it is, you won't like it. They'll manage to get you in a position where you don't have choices. You'll be like me, trapped into doing whatever they say."

"Jim, if there's any way I can put a stop to this, I will. Somehow, I'll bring them down."

Jim looked at my wrists and the handcuffs. He pinched one of the cuffs and raised my hands a few inches.

"Sure you will, Chad. You'll just step right out of those cuffs and take out Adolf, Ladon, and everyone else in The Company."

Jim and I stopped talking, and after a few minutes of awkward silence, Bill retuned. He informed us that they had found two seats for us on a plane leaving in twenty minutes.

We were escorted by airport security through the concourse to the gate. Jim took my elbow and guided me onto the plane. A stewardess pointed us to two seats in first class. I was made to sit by the window.

The flight was uneventful except that I found it's difficult to flirt when you're in handcuffs. When the stewardess came to take our drink orders, I held up my wrists, winked and said, "I'm innocent. Really, I am."

The stewardess stammered and Jim told me to be quiet. He apologized for me.

I leaned into the corner of the seat against the window and closed my eyes. I wasn't tired, I just wanted to shut out the entire situation.

CHAPTER FIFTY-TWO

It was mid-afternoon when our flight landed at the Vegas airport. We were the last ones to get off of the plane. Jim Clayton took my elbow and directed me up the gantry and into the terminal where we were met by four men in airport security uniforms. One of the men smelled like burnt cinnamon.

The man with the burnt cinnamon odor put out a hand to Jim. Jim took it.

"Officer Clayton, I'm glad to see that you were able to get your fugitive. I hope he didn't cause you too much trouble."

"I didn't give him the chance."

We started down the concourse toward the baggage claim, two men in front, two behind, and Jim guiding me by gripping my elbow. Along the way we stopped at a stainless steel door. One of the men produced a key and we entered.

We walked down the hallway for a while. The hallway was lined with doors. The doors had name plates that corresponded to the airport restaurants and shops. We continued through the maze until we came to another stainless steel door. On the other side was the baggage claim.

Jim and the man smelling of burnt cinnamon went to the baggage carrousel while I waited with the three airport security guards. Jim took our bags, and we were on our way again.

Outside the building, Jim left us waiting with the luggage. The four men stood around me and the man smelling of burnt cinnamon spoke.

"Well Chad, Ladon is not happy with you."

"I've figured that out."

"People who cross Ladon don't usually live as long as you have."

"Lucky me!" I said as I rolled my eyes and threw my head back for effect.

"You realize who, or rather what Jim Clayton is, don't you?"

"What do you mean?"

"Jim Clayton is part of your continued training. Ladon expects you to kill him."

The man pulled out a handcuff key and released my wrists. He took the handcuffs.

I rubbed my wrists and looked the man in his gray eyes, "Not on your life. I'm not killing anyone."

"You can kill him now, while we watch, or later. It's your choice. But you will kill him. If you don't do it of your own free will, Ladon will create a situation where you don't have a choice."

"I don't know why it's so important to Ladon that I become a murderer, but no matter what he does, he can't make me into a murderer. The next time you see Ladon, tell him that he can send whomever he wants after me. He can create any situation he chooses, but he can't change who I am, inside."

"Very well. Have it your way. We will do this the hard way. When Ladon decides it's time, Jim Clayton will turn on you. You won't have a choice either he will kill you, or you will kill him. We've given him titanium tipped bullets and a knife with a titanium blade. He can kill you."

"Ladon wants me alive. He's not going to have Jim Clayton kill me."

"Ladon would prefer you alive. But he wants you to be trained. If you refuse to be trained, well, that's the price of your education."

About that time, Jim pulled up in his car. He got out, took the bags, and put them in the trunk. Ladon's man returned Jim's handcuffs to him and said, "Watch yourself. I wouldn't trust Chad."

"Don't worry about me. Chad's a pussycat."

Jim got into the car, and I let myself into the passenger's side. When I closed the door, I turned to Jim and said, "Meow."

"Oh, get over yourself, Chad."

"Where are you taking me?"

"Back to your apartment. We're going to wait there until Saysha Givens calls."

"It's been a while since I've been home. The food's probably spoiled. We'll need to stop for something."

"No. You can have anything delivered that you want. I'll make the phone calls."

"You don't have to treat me like a prisoner, Jim."

"Yes I do. I have my orders."

Jim pulled away from the airport and we headed toward my apartment. After a few minutes, I picked up the conversation again.

"Jim, Ladon wants me to kill you."

"And you're telling me this because?"

"Because I don't want to. But if you keep this up, if you keep obeying The Company's orders, I may have to."

Jim gave me a quick, awkward glance, as he passed a truck on the interstate.

"Chad, no offense, but you can't pull off that bluff."

"It's not a bluff. The airport security that met us, one of those men was one of Ladon's men."

"You recognized him?"

"No. I smelled him. All of Ladon's men have the same odor. The man who was talking to you was Ladon's man. The others were just doing what they were told."

"What about him? Ladon's man."

"When you were gone to get the car, he told me that Ladon wants me to kill you. And, if I don't Ladon will create a situation where I have no choice."

"Chad." Jim paused, "If that's true...there's nothing you or I can do about it."

"But there is, Jim. Get out of Vegas. Take your family and leave."

"I can't do that. There's no place I could go that they wouldn't find me."

"I think there are some places. You could be in London in less time than you'd believe possible."

"And so what if I left? If I took my family and ran? It's just not possible."

"Jim, I can get my hands on three hundred-thousand dollars. It's yours if you'll take your family as far away as you can get."

Jim looked shocked and then laughed out loud, "Chad, you almost had me. I almost bought it hook, line and sinker!"

"What? It's true!"

"Adolf was right, you are slippery! There's no way you have that much money! What's next, you have your own secret gold mine?"

"It's not so much a mine as well...oh forget it."

I sank back into the car seat and kept silent for the remainder of the ride.

CHAPTER FIFTY-THREE

I woke up Tuesday morning in my own bed. Jim had spent the night on the sofa. I had closed my bedroom door and put a chair against it. I laid there in bed thinking, actually hoping. I hoped that somehow I could convince Jim to take his family and go away. If he didn't, I knew what would happen. I knew what had to happen. Ladon would make it so that one of us would die.

While I was still considering how I might get Jim to leave, I heard a cell phone ringing in the next room. I heard Jim Clayton answer. Less than a minute later, there was a knock on my door.

"Chad, get up. Saysha Givens is on the phone. She needs to talk to you; to us."

"Give me a minute!"

I grabbed the jeans lying on the floor at the foot of the bed and put them on. I moved the chair and opened the door.

Jim was standing on the other side holding my cell phone. "What is it?" I asked as I pushed my way past him. I went to the kitchen to make coffee.

Jim followed and put the phone on speaker.

"Saysha, I have Chad here. I've got you on speaker."

Saysha's voice came through the phone as I turned on the tap and filled the glass coffee pot. "Chad, I've got some information. I must say, I don't understand how, but Adolf opened a number of doors that should have remained closed. I received a flood of calls yesterday and all through the evening. People, people in very high places, were calling and volunteering information.

Still, I don't know what can be done with it; it's pretty thin."

"Go ahead, I'm listening," I said as I poured fresh water into the coffee maker.

"Alright. Let's start with Area Thirteen. There is no Area Thirteen, at least not today. Area Thirteen was subsumed into the area known as the Nellis Air Force Range."

Jim Clayton answered for me, "That's good. That's something to go on."

The voice on the phone answered back, "No. it's not. The Nellis Air Force Range is over eight thousand square miles of open desert. I've been assured that there are no surviving records of where Area Thirteen used to be."

I measured out the coffee and put it in the filter basket before speaking. "Then, Director, there's nothing we can do with that information?"

"No, Chad, there's something, just not a lot. The testing was carried out in a building. And, the people doing the testing did not live at the facility. Both army personnel and civilians worked at the facility where the object was being tested. All of the civilians were taken to and from the facility by bus, every day."

I hit the button to start the coffee maker, "I don't follow, what good does that do us?"

"The busses didn't travel across open desert, they drove down roads. If you can get your hands on a satellite map of the area, you might be able to see the roads. Even if the military destroyed the roads, there might be traces of the roads. It's at least something.

But if you find the roads and the facility, assuming it still exists, that's only where the thing was. It doesn't tell you where it is now."

"I understand. Did you find out anything about the names I gave you?"

"Chad, the names, that's another issue. I was given a list of names by someone at the Pentagon. I'd rather not say who."

"I understand. What about the names?"

"I have names, addresses, and phone numbers of most of the people directly involved in Operation Opera."

"Wow. Now I'm impressed."

"Don't be. I had my people run down the names and addresses. Chad, the names on the list fall into three categories; missing, dead, and very old.

What you're looking into happened forty-nine years ago. Your chances of finding someone alive who remembers anything about what happened to the stone are slim and none."

"Tell me this, please, Director. The names in the letters I gave you. Did you find out anything there?"

"I did. Edward Scofield worked on the project as a technician. He was injured in the accident, and he was the only survivor. He was placed in a psychiatric facility. He was there until nineteen seventy-two, and then he disappeared."

"What do you mean disappeared?"

"That's all anyone knows. They don't know if he escaped or someone took him out. He was just gone and never heard from again. He's on the list as one of the missing."

"Director. And, what about Ray, the man who wrote the letters?"

"We think that's Doctor Raymond Freeze. He was an army physician. He's on the list in the old category. He's ninety-three or ninety four years old now. He's living in the

Silver Seniors Sunset Center. It's a nursing home in Henderson, Nevada. I've been told he has dementia."

I pulled a coffee mug out of the cabinet. "You're right, Director Givens, this all may be a fool's errand."

"Chad. I've got the list of names in a pdf document. I'll email it to you. And, good luck Chad. I hope I see you again."

"Me too, Director. Thank you."

Jim ended the call and I poured myself some coffee. I pushed past Jim on my way out of the kitchen.

"Where are you going, Chad?"

I didn't hide my irritation. "I'm going to take a shower. Then, I'm going to brush my teeth. I *might* even floss. If any of that's particularly interesting to you, then you're welcome to watch."

I plodded off into the bathroom and slammed the door behind me. While I cleaned up I thought about what it might take to get Jim Clayton to run away from all of this. My mind was spinning, but very few possibilities presented themselves.

Still I felt I had to keep working on Jim. If he could be convinced that I could get him and his family far away, he might just go. I had to try, for his sake and mine.

After I had dressed, I went on a search through my combination bedroom and office. I found a padded envelope and a notebook. I went into living room where Jim was sitting on the sofa with his shoes off, eating a plate of eggs and bacon.

"That's right Jim, help yourself. Make yourself at home. No need to ask for anything."

"What are you doing, Chad? What's that you're carrying?"

"You said I should mail my car keys to my uncle. Let me have my keys."

I addressed the envelope while Jim dug my keys out of his luggage. I scribbled out a note to Uncle Allan.

"Chad, what are you writing?"

I showed it to Jim. He grunted and handed it back. I placed the keys and the note into the envelope and sealed it.

"Jim, I want my billfold back, along with the keys to my apartment, and everything else you took from me."

Jim was reluctant, but gave in to most of my request.

"Chad, I'm keeping the cell phones. I don't want you calling anyone that I don't know about."

"Fine, Jim. Whatever."

"You look like you're ready to go somewhere. What's the plan?"

"Well, Jim, I thought you would drive me to Henderson. I want to talk with Ray Freeze. But first, you'll take me to the bank and the post office."

"What do you need with the bank?"

"You'll see when I get there."

Jim finished his last bite of eggs, got up and put his dishes in the kitchen sink. I went to the door and waited.

Jim went back to the sofa. He put on his shoes, loaded his pockets with his paraphernalia, and checked the cartridges in his pistol.

I insisted on stopping at the bank. I didn't actually need anything, but Jim needed to see that I wasn't a liar. We both went into the bank lobby and I asked Jim to stand next to me at the teller window.

The woman behind the counter seemed a little nervous. I can only guess it was because it was unusual to have a U.S. Marshal in uniform escorting another man to do his banking.

The teller gave us both an awkward smile, "May I help you, gentlemen?"

I pulled out my billfold and extracted the debit card the Matron had given me and my drivers' license.

"Yes, please. I would like five hundred dollars, in fifties. Please take it from the account attached to this card."

The young lady took the card and my license. Soon she

was counting out the money. When she finished, I asked, "Oh, and by the way, what is the balance in that account? Would you write it down and give it to my friend here?"

She looked a little confused at the odd request, but answered back, "Of course, sir." A moment later she was handing Jim a slip of paper with a number written on it. "Here you are, sir. That's before this withdrawal."

Jim looked at the number. I didn't have to look to know what it was, but I glanced. It was three hundred-thousand dollars. The Matron had been good to her word and was keeping the account funded.

Jim looked at me, his lips parted and he closed them quickly. It was clear that he was trying not to react.

Back in the car, the questions came flooding out.

"OK, Fury. Spill it. Just where did you get that kind of money?"

"Technically, it's not mine, per se. It's an account that's been funded for me to use as needed while I'm working."

"That makes no sense, whatsoever."

"It's a long story, if you want to listen."

"I'm all ears. Tell me what's going on here."

I told Jim my story starting from the murder of Stacy Adams in my office. I didn't tell him everything, I just told him about my meetings with Ladon. I stressed Ladon's plans for the stone.

Jim was so intent on my hearing my story, and I was so involved in the telling that we never made it to the post office. Instead we headed directly to Henderson, Nevada to find Doctor Freeze at the nursing home.

CHAPTER FIFTY-FOUR

It was the middle of the afternoon when we drove up to the Silver Seniors Sunset Center nursing home. We exited the car and walked up to the entrance. I pulled the handle, and the door didn't move. I looked at Jim.

"Chad, you've not been to many nursing homes, have you?"

"As a matter of fact, no."

"Well, you have to be let inside. They do that for the protection of the inmates, uh, I mean residents."

Jim pushed a button beneath a speaker mounted by the door. A bell rang, and a voice came through the speaker panel, "May I help you?"

Jim answered, "Yes, we're here to speak with someone."

"Just a minute."

There was a delay of at least fifteen seconds before we heard the lock click. I pulled the door handle and this time the door conceded to my request.

Immediately, odors hit me in the face: bleach, disinfectants, bodily fluids, and food. It all combined to make a unique "nursing home" scent. Jim was unaffected by the odors, but my sensitive nose complained to my stomach and I had a moment of nausea.

"Are you OK, Chad?"

"I'm fine. It's just the odors. Let's get this over with so I can start inhaling again."

We walked across the linoleum tiles to the nurse's station. A blond haired woman in red hospital scrubs greeted us. "Hello gentlemen. What can I do for you?"

Jim did the talking. It was a little dangerous for me to be opening my mouth until the nausea passed.

"I'm Officer Jim Clayton. We have some questions that we need to ask a patient here. May we speak to Raymond Freeze?"

"Of course, officer. I'm Julie. If you'll just follow me."

As we followed Julie, the odors seemed to let up and I was able to focus a little better. We were led to the end of the nearest hallway. About half way down, an old woman behind a walker pushed her way in front of me. She stopped and looked up into my face.

Her eyes were brown, and the left one was clouded over with a cataract. She licked her lips and said, "You look just like my fourth husband!"

I was a little embarrassed, and asked, "Really? How many times were you married?"

She licked her lips again. "Three times." She laughed, "Get it, three? Three times?"

Julie interrupted, "Now, Agnes, please don't bother these men. They're here on business."

I moved around Agnes and left her standing and laughing in the hallway.

Julie looked at me, "I apologize, she tells that same joke all day long to every man she sees."

"Well, at least she's happy."

Julie stopped at the last room. "Mr. Freeze is in here. If you need anything, someone in the lovely red uniforms will be close by."

We thanked Julie and knocked on the door. A weak

voice called from inside the room, "Come in!"

Jim pushed open the door and went through. I followed. On the far side of the room was a skeleton covered in skin, lying on a hospital bed. The head of the bed was raised so that the occupant could watch the television mounted on the wall.

"Mr. Freeze, I'm Jim Clayton. This is Chad Fury. We would like to ask some questions if you don't mind."

The man in the bed nodded and coughed. He raised his gnarled fingers and wiped his chin. He rasped out, "Sure. What can I do for you?"

Jim and I pulled up a couple of chairs and sat by the bed. Mr. Freeze looked a little confused. "Now, how do I know you?"

I answered, "You don't. We're here about Colonel Roger Evans."

"Oh my, Roger. How is my old friend? Is he here?"

"No, he passed away last year."

"Oh dear." A tear ran down from the corner of Ray's eye. "I'm going to miss him. I was just talking to him...was it yesterday?"

Jim interrupted, "Mr. Freeze, Ray. We need to ask some questions about Colonel Evans' nephew, Eddie Scofield. We need to know about the accident. Anything you can tell us will help."

"No, no." Ray almost whimpered. "Can't talk about it. It's top secret. I was sworn to secrecy. Talking is treason."

I looked at Jim, "Let me try."

"Ray, what happened at Operation Opera is top secret."

"That's right. Can't talk about it."

"Ray, why is it a secret? Why was it covered up?"

Ray turned his head and looked at me, "Because it's too terrible. The stone isn't from this world. It's too powerful. Too dangerous.

Now just who are you young man? And how do I know you?"

"Ray, I'm Chad. I'm a friend of Roger Evans."

"Roger, my dear friend, Roger. How is Roger?"

"Roger is fine. He's concerned about his nephew, Eddie. He wants to know that Eddie is alright."

"Oh, Eddie." A tear rolled down from Ray's eye. "That was terrible, what happened to Eddie. It's top secret, you know."

"Yes I know. It's top secret. But, Ray's worried. You're in here, and he wants to know that someone is looking after Eddie. Where is Eddie now? Roger wants to know."

"My phone." Ray coughed. "Get my phone."

Jim got up and went to the night stand. There was a cell phone next to a glass of water. He handed it to Ray. Ray shook his head, "No. In contacts. My son. Call my son, Cameron. He's a doctor."

Jim found the name in the contacts and dialed. Jim started speaking. "Hello, Cameron Freeze? My name is US Deputy Marshal, Jim Clayton."

I listened in on the conversation.

"This is Cameron Freeze. What can I do for you?"

"My partner and I have been talking to your father. It's about Edward Scofield. Your father can't seem to answer very many questions about Eddie. I was hoping we could talk with you."

"I wondered if this day would ever come. Can we talk in person? Can I come to your office?"

"My office is in Las Vegas. My partner and I are in the room with your father. Is there some place else we could meet?"

"I'll come to you. I'm six miles away. I'll be there in ten minutes."

Jim thanked Cameron and ended the call.

Jim looked at me, "You heard that?"

"I did."

"Good. I don't have to repeat myself."

We waited and I continued to talk to Ray. Ray must have asked who we are at least four more times before there was a knock at the door.

Jim got up and answered the door. Standing on the other side was a slender man, just a little less than six feet tall. He looked to be in his late-forties. He also looked worried.

He spoke first, "Gentlemen, would it be possible for us to speak in the courtyard? It would be simpler."

Jim agreed, and I stood. I said goodbye to Ray, turned and left.

Cameron led the way to the courtyard. The building formed a square around an open space in the center. There were a number of patio tables and chairs sitting on concrete slabs around the perimeter. We seated ourselves at the nearest table.

Jim began the conversation. "Mr. Freeze, Cameron. Thank you for coming. My name is Jim Clayton, and this is my associate, Chad Fury. I take it you live close by?"

"I do. I was going to come see Dad today, so this wasn't an inconvenience. Now what is this about?"

Jim laid his palm on the table and leaned forward. "I remember you saying you wondered if this day would come. What did you mean by that?"

Cameron looked anxious. "I probably shouldn't have said that. I didn't mean anything."

I smelled onions, so I interrupted, "Come now, Cameron. You did mean something. What?"

Cameron shook his head, "I may as well talk. I knew this could blow up in our faces, someday. It's just been so long that I thought we had a chance. But, at least you can't arrest dad. He won't have to stand trial for treason. But, me..."

Jim looked at me, then at Cameron. "I can assure you, we have no plans of arresting anyone. What we want is a little difficult to explain. We are looking into a matter that led us to Operation Opera and Area Thirteen. We simply need to know everything we can about what happened at Operation Opera."

Cameron stood to his feet, "Gentlemen, I cannot help you. Area Thirteen is a myth, and Operation Opera is top secret. I don't know anything."

Jim stood and nodded to me. I stood and moved to block Cameron from leaving.

"Cameron," Jim said strongly, "The way you keep from being arrested is to cooperate. You've admitted to treasonable action. We can pursue that course, if you wish."

Cameron returned to his chair, and I returned to mine. I attempted getting something out of Cameron.

"Mr. Freeze, please tell us about Eddie Scofield. What happened to him? Is he still alive?"

"You don't know?"

"No, we don't know. But we need to find out. Where is he?"

Cameron relaxed a little. His pupils constricted then dilated. His eyes looked up and to the right. "He's dead. He died."

I smelled onions. "You're lying, Mr. Freeze. Please be honest with me. Let's try this again. Where is Eddie Scofield? What have you and your father been hiding?"

Cameron put his elbows on the table, bent his neck, and rested his forehead in the palms of his hands. He didn't respond.

"Cameron," Jim said, "my associate asked you a question. We need an answer."

Cameron raised his head, and pushed himself back into his chair. "Alright. Alright." He looked at Jim and me. "You have me. Just promise me you won't disgrace my father before he dies."

"We promise," I said.

"Very well gentlemen, Eddie Scofield is alive. He's in Las Vegas. But as to what he knows or can tell you, that's even more of a gamble than talking to my father."

"What do you mean?" Jim asked.

"I mean his mind is scrambled. He was never right

after the accident, and there were other changes too."

"What kind of changes?" I asked.

"The kind that no one would believe. The kind that the world is better off not knowing about. But then, I don't know how many lifetimes this can go on."

Jim looked at me and then at Cameron, "Just what are you talking about?"

I couldn't tell from the looks of Cameron if he was about to pass out, or about to cry. He spoke softly. "My father and Roger Evans were the best of friends. After Roger's nephew, Eddie, was in the accident Roger never got over it. My father swore to look after Eddie for the rest of Eddie's life.

Dad made sure that Eddie had the finest hospital care in the world. Even after Eddie was institutionalized, Dad would look in on him, sometimes daily.

Because he was looking after him daily, he started noticing the change over time. He decided that Eddie couldn't stay there. He couldn't let the doctors, or anyone else see him. If Eddie stayed, he would eventually end up being experimented on for the rest of his life, however long that might turn out to be."

"I still don't understand what you're talking about," I said. "Please get to the point. Tell us straight, what happened to Eddie?"

Cameron bit his lower lip, then relaxed his jaw. "Dad took Eddie Scofield out of the psychiatric ward and brought him home."

Jim leaned forward, "Why did he do that? I mean break him out?"

Cameron looked at both of us. "Because Eddie Scofield wasn't aging. From nineteen sixty-six until today, Eddie Scofield looks exactly the same. He still looks twenty-eight years old."

Jim sneered, "That's absurd."

I interrupted, "No, Jim. Wait. Give him a chance. I've seen enough strange things that I am willing to at least hear this out.

Cameron. Will you tell us where Eddie is? We need to talk to him."

"If I tell you, and you go, he won't be there. He doesn't trust people. He'll know you're coming and he'll leave."

"How will he know we're coming?" I asked.

Cameron looked me in the eyes, "I don't understand it, but he seems to know things. He won't be there if you go alone."

Jim asked, "Cameron, will you take us? Will he be there if you take us to him?"

Cameron paused, his eyes momentarily looked straight up. "Yes, he might. It would be the only way."

CHAPTER FIFTY-FIVE

Cameron had agreed to take us to see Eddie that very afternoon. But first, he said he needed a few things from his home. He drove to his house and we followed. We waited in his driveway until he returned.

Cameron got into the passenger's seat and I rode in the back. He had with him a small brown paper sack and a package of chocolate cookies which he held in his lap.

"What's all that?" I asked.

Cameron spoke without turning around. "It's for Eddie; medicine and cookies. He's a little easier to handle when I have cookies."

Jim asked, "Where are we headed, Cameron?"

"Take us to highway ninety-five, where it crosses Lone Mountain Road."

Jim shot Cameron a quick glance, "What's the address?"

"There isn't one. Just park the car. We'll walk from there."

It took more than thirty minutes before we arrived. Jim parked by the side of the road next to highway ninety-five. Cameron got out of the car. Jim and I followed.

I looked around. There was nothing special here. A shopping center sat on the north side of the road and a set of apartment buildings occupied the south.

While staring at the apartment buildings I asked, "Cameron, why didn't we drive to the apartments?"

"Because we're not going there. Follow me."

Cameron walked east a few feet and it became obvious where he was headed. He was walking toward a concrete building several feet off of the road. It was a square structure, six feet in all directions, and it had a single gray metal door.

Jim asked, "What the hell is this, Cameron? Where are you taking us?"

"This is an access port to the storm sewers."

Jim stopped in his tracks. "You're kidding me. You mean to tell me that you've been keeping Eddie Scofield in the storm drains for the last fifty years?"

Cameron turned to face Jim. "No, it's more like forty years. Dad tried keeping him in apartments and even our home, but he was too much trouble. He tore the places up. He wrote on the walls, ruined furniture, and he scared people. He can't hurt anything down there."

Cameron went to the door and pulled a key from his pocket. He put it into the padlock hanging from the door. After opening the door he dropped the padlock into his pocket.

I saw Cameron reach into the paper sack and pull out a small flashlight. He motioned for us to follow, and we did. Jim went first. When I came through the door, Cameron and Jim were half way down the metal ladder. I pulled the door closed and followed.

This section of the storm sewer was just like the others I had been in recently, dark and very smelly. Cameron was waiting for us at the bottom of the ladder.

"Jim, Chad," Cameron said in hushed tones, "Try not to make too much noise. To your left is the exit to the spillway, maybe two hundred fifty or three hundred yards. Some dangerous people live down there. Try not to let them hear you. Even the city workers don't go there without a police escort."

Cameron headed off in the opposite direction and we followed. We walked for three or four minutes before I whispered, "Cameron, can I ask you something?"

Cameron whispered back, "Go ahead."

"Just what ever made your father think of putting Eddie down here?"

"He didn't. According to dad, it was Eddie's idea. Eddie seemed to know about the entire storm sewer system. He seems to know where things are."

Jim spoke up, "Cameron, I've had enough; I'm calling B. S. on all of this. The storm sewers were built in the nineties."

Cameron stopped walking. "That's not entirely true. There have always been storm drains beneath Las Vegas. But, in the nineties there was a major project to make them larger and interconnected. As the city grows, so does the drainage system.

By the way, we're almost there. I want to show you something."

Cameron pointed his flashlight at the wall. It was covered in graffiti, but not the ordinary gang symbols and foul words. This was bright yellow paint, and it looked like mostly algebra and calculus.

Jim spoke first. "What am I seeing?"

Cameron moved his light slowly along the wall. "This is the first stop on your tour of all things Crazy Eddie."

"Whoa, stop there!" I said with some excitement. "What's that?"

Cameron stopped moving the light. I was looking at curved, bowl-shaped line with two parallel lines forming a stem beneath the bottom of the bowl. There were three vertical dots between the lines.

"I don't know, Chad. It looks like a lot of the other crazy things written on the walls. Why? Does it mean something to you?"

"I've seen it before, but I don't know what it means."

We continued on and the math and the symbols didn't seem to stop. They covered the walls and the ceiling.

Soon Cameron started calling out in a gentle voice, "Hey, Eddie. It's Cam. I've come with your medicine. I have cookies; your favorite. Nice round cookies."

There was no answer; we took a few more steps. Cameron called out again, "Eddie, it's alright. I'm here with friends. These are good men. Don't be afraid. Come out and talk to us, and you can have your cookies."

There was an answer this time. "Cam, can Eddie have cookies?"

"Yes, Eddie. You can have your cookies."

"Eddie doesn't like man with gun. Man with gun come if man with claws says OK. Man with claws is good."

Jim turned to Cameron and me, "What the hell?"

Cameron answered, "I don't think he likes you, Jim. I don't know why."

"Can he see me? How does he know I'm carrying a gun?"

"He seems to see, everything. I don't understand it. But, he's never wrong.

Chad, I think he wants you to say it's alright for Jim to come along. Although, I don't know what he means about you having claws."

I spoke loudly into the darkness, "Eddie, It's alright. I won't let the man with the gun hurt you. I'll keep you safe."

The voice came back through the darkness, "OK... Bring cookies."

We walked a few more feet and turned a corner. Cameron's light filled the area. There, in the middle of the concrete floor was a man sitting on a stack of three old mattresses. He was rocking forward and back, clutching his hands.

The man looked to be no more than twenty-eight years old. His hair was long and stringy. His fingernails were long. He wore an old set of army fatigues. The sneakers on his feet were falling apart.

Cameron approached the man. "Eddie. Eddie. It's Cam."

"I know."

"I have your cookies." Cameron handed the package to the Eddie.

Eddie tore open the package greedily. He grabbed two of the cookies and shoved them in his mouth. He spoke with his mouth full, "Eddie like'th cookie'th. Cookie'th are round."

Jim said, "Chad, I think this is hopeless."

"It certainly looks that way."

Cameron kept talking to Eddie. "Now, Eddie. These men want to talk to you. Will you take your medicine so you can talk to them?"

Eddie shook his head violently, "No! No shot! Eddie doesn't like shots!"

"Now Eddie, you like the way the medicine makes you feel. It stops the noises in your head. You want the noises to stop."

"Yes. Make noises stop!" Eddie thrust out his arm and Cameron put the flashlight on the floor. He pulled a syringe and a rubber hose out of the paper sack. He held the syringe between his teeth as he tied the hose beneath Eddie's bicep. Eddie whimpered.

"Now, Eddie," Cameron said soothingly, "this will only pinch a little. Then you'll start feeling better. The noises in your head will stop. Think about how good you're going to feel."

Cameron pushed the needle into Eddie's arm and released the rubber hose. He pushed slowly on the plunger of the syringe. Eddie whimpered.

Cameron put the paraphernalia back in the paper sack, picked up the flashlight, and backed up a couple of paces.

He turned to Jim and me. "Jim, Chad. Give it about ten minutes. He'll start getting better soon. Then you can talk to him."

I had to ask, "What did you give him?"

Cameron hesitated, "It's...kind of an...opiate cocktail. It's a mixture of heroin and morphine. And yes, before you ask, it's not legal and it's enough to kill a normal man."

Jim exclaimed, "Just what the hell did we walk into?"

Cameron was quick to answer, "My father started giving this to him right after he brought Eddie into our house. It settles him down. He's a *little* closer to normal with it."

Eddie called out in the darkness, "Cam. Cam. Eddie feels better. Eddie will talk now. First, Eddie wants light."

I heard movement. From the sounds of it, Eddie got up and was moving papers around. A moment later the area lit up from the striking of a match. Eddie was lighting a candle. The candle was sitting on a milk crate.

Eddie went around the area lighting more candles. Soon the room was lit well enough for anyone to see. There were folding chairs next to the mattresses. There was a table made out of a stack of wood pallets. And there was a stand made of plastic pipe that had some shirts and a jacket on hangers.

Eddie held a candle and approached us. He walked up to me. "Eddie likes you. What's your name?"

"Eddie, My name's Chad. It' nice to meet you."

"You have claws. Can Eddie see your claws?"

"Maybe later. Right now we have questions."

Eddie turned toward Jim. "Eddie doesn't like you." He turned back to me.

"You walk through walls. I want to go to the tower. Take Eddie to the tower. Eddie grabbed my hand and started pulling me toward the nearest wall."

"Eddie, I can't. It won't work on that wall."

"Eddie show you something. Eddie did good."

Eddie walked past the mattresses, motioning for us to follow. We did.

After we walked for about five minutes, Eddie began lighting more candles. He must have lit at least a hundred.

The section of the tunnel we were in was now brightly lit. The walls, ceiling and floor had been painted black. White and yellow paint on the walls, ceiling and floor looked like stars. We were standing in a reproduction of the Milky Way galaxy. The candles Eddie had lit seemed to represent more stars in the open space.

Eddie stood in the center and swayed, "Eddie hears them. Eddie hears their songs. They sing too loud. That's why Eddie needs medicine."

I couldn't help it, I didn't mean to say it out loud, but I did. "I think we just took the bullet train to Crazy Town."

I walked up to Eddie. "Eddie, tell me about the songs. What do you mean you hear them?"

"The stars. Stars sing songs. Eddie knows where they are. Eddie knows where everything is."

"What does that mean, you know where everything is? How do you know where everything is?"

"Everything sings. Chad has thirty-eight cents in his pocket. Eddie hears it. Chad has a quarter, two nickels and three pennies. That's thirty eight."

I checked my right pocket. Eddie was right.

"Eddie. I need to talk to you about Operation Opera. I need to know about the accident."

Eddie dropped to the floor and folded his knees to his chest. "No. That was bad. Eddie can't talk about it."

I squatted on the floor in front of Eddie.

"Please, Eddie. I have to know. The stone, the Omega Artifact. I need to find it."

"No. No find it. Stone is bad."

"Eddie, some bad men are looking for the Omega Artifact. They *will* get it. I need to stop them from getting it. If you tell Chad where it is, Chad can keep them from having it."

"Will Chad use his claws?"

"I might have to."

Eddie stood up. "OK. Eddie will show you. Eddie can't tell you. Eddie will show you. Not now. Tomorrow. You come back tomorrow. Eddie will show you tomorrow. Bring round cookies."

CHAPTER FIFTY-SIX

After our visit with Eddie, Jim had driven Cameron home. During the drive back to Vegas, Jim was in a talkative mood.

"Chad, you realize that I have to report all of this to Adolf."

"I know that you *think* you do. But, you do have options. You can still run away from all of this. The three hundred-thousand is yours for you to go away and take your family. There are parts of the world where that kind of money will last several lifetimes."

"Chad, you just don't understand."

"What is it that I don't understand, Jim?"

"Eddie may be nuts, but he's still right. He called you good, and he said he didn't like me. He's right not to like me."

"Jim, you're not a bad person. You just got caught up with the wrong people. Adolf got in your head and you didn't have a choice."

Jim looked over at me, "Chad. I could take my family and run away. I'd always be looking over my shoulder wondering when The Company was going to find me. But more importantly, I could never run away from myself.

Do you know what my involvement with Adolf has done to me?"

"No, Jim. I don't."

"It's made me a liar. Every day I lie to somebody. I lie to the Marshals Service and to my wife about what I do after hours. I lied to Peggy. I told her I was on official business when I was out working for The Company."

"Jim, she will forgive you. You lied to protect her."

"Working for Adolf has made me a murderer. It all started with a murder, and it's never going to end. If Adolf wants someone silenced, there's a good chance he'll call on me. He told me it was because my badge can get me places others can't go."

Jim looked at me again. "And Chad, when Adolf called and told me to find you in Oklahoma City, he told me to kill you if you double-crossed Ladon."

"Let me put your mind at ease, Jim. You can't kill me. I'm a lot tougher than I look."

Jim shook his head, "Chad, Chad, Chad. I know you have a little military training, well, so do I. I also have continued training with the Marshals Service. And, I have experience killing.

I've met a lot of punks who think they're tough. I'm telling you right now that you don't have any idea what you're up against.

I'll tell you what, Chad. If running away is such a good idea, then you do it. You take that money in the bank and run. You go far, far away and never come back."

"I can't do that, there's more at stake than you realize. But, I have an idea. Hand me my cell phone."

"Who do you want to call?"

"I want to call my gym. I want to arrange for us to get into the ring, after hours."

"Why?"

"Because, I'm going to prove to you that you can't kill me. I'm going to show you that if you try, you could end up dead. But more importantly, I'll make a wager. If I win, if you tap out, then you take the money and your family and you get out of Vegas."

"And if I win?"

"Jim, if you win, then you get the money and I shut up about all of this. I will cooperate with you and The Company. I'll turn the stone over to Ladon."

"Chad, you're saying that if I fight you, I get the three hundred-thousand dollars, win or lose?"

"That's right. I'm paying you three hundred-thousand dollars for the chance to open your eyes and let you see the truth."

Jim remove a hand from the steering wheel and dug my cell phone out of his pocket. He handed it to me, "Chad, put it on speaker. I want to hear the conversation."

I found the number for Frank Campbell, the gym owner, in my list of contacts. I dialed and put the phone on speaker. Frank answered on the fourth ring.

"This is Frank. What can I do for you?"

"Frank, it's Drake Manning."

"Drake, are you alright? We've missed you around here."

"I'm fine. I've just had some things to take care of. But, the reason I called...You said before that if there was anything I needed, you'd help?"

"That's right. And, I will if I can, Drake. What's up?"

"You close the gym at ten tonight, right?"

"That's right we close at ten every night."

"I'd like you to keep the place open another thirty minutes longer. I need the ring, and I don't need any spectators."

"Well...uh...OK. It's only a half hour. Sure. You'll have the ring, and your privacy."

"Thank you, Frank. I owe you."

Jim took my phone back, and we headed straight for the gym. We arrived at nine-thirty. Inside the gym we made a stop at the pro shop where Jim picked out shorts, shoes, and other gear. I insisted that he get headgear and a mouthpiece. I paid for everything using the credit card the Matron had given me.

At exactly ten P.M., Jim and I were standing alone in the main ring. I stood there in my red shorts, without shoes, without gloves, and no head gear or mouthpiece. Jim faced me, about six feet away in his blue headgear, fingerless padded gloves, and blue shorts. He held his mouthpiece in his fingertips.

"Chad, are you sure you want to go through with this? I've mopped the floor with men better than you."

"Jim, why did we stop at the bank this morning? It was so I could prove to you that I wasn't lying; that I could lay my hands on three hundred-thousand dollars in cash.

We're in this ring right now so I can prove to you that if you stay on the path you're on, you'll end up dead. There's no way this is going to end well for you. I'm trying to get you to run from this for your sake, not for mine."

"Chad, I won't say the money isn't tempting, but I need to teach you a lesson. You've accused Adolf of getting into my head. And, he has. But that's what you're trying to do. All your stories, all the claims that if I don't take the money and run; that's nothing! I'm tired of you trying to manipulate me. I intend to shut you up!"

I stretched out my right arm, turned my palm up, and curled and released my fingers a few times. "Come on. Shut me up, if you can. I'm right here."

Jim inserted the mouth guard and we both closed the distance. I let my arms hang at my side and waited. Jim stood there, fists up, ready to begin.

"Go ahead, Jim. Teach me a lesson. Shut me up! I'm going to keep running my mouth until you shut it! Or, do you want to keep hearing how following The Company will make you dead?"

Jim let fly with his right, squarely in my teeth. My head snapped back. I grinned. "Come on, Jim. You've taken down tougher than me. I'm still talking."

Jim gave me another jab and landed it on my nose. My head snapped again. It would have broken anyone else's nose, but luckily for me, my bones don't seem to break.

Jim relaxed his shoulders when he saw I wasn't fighting back.

"OK. Jim. I've shown you I can take a punch. You've hit me only because I let you. That's over now."

Jim came at me again. He poured it on with everything he had. I've seen very few men throw punches as fast as Jim Clayton.

I played strict defense. We moved around the ring. I deflected the punches or else I moved out of the way. I didn't let Jim land a single shot. We kept this up for a good two minutes; enough time that Jim was getting tired. I wasn't.

I backed away and held up my palms. Jim spit out his mouthguard and heaved, catching his breath. "What, Chad? Are you quitting?"

"Nope, not me. I'm giving you a chance to get your second wind. Plus, I'm a teacher and I'm announcing the next lesson. You've seen I can take a punch. You've seen you're not going to touch me unless I let you. Now you're going to learn that I can put your sorry ass on the mat anytime I choose!"

I made fists, and closed the distance between us. Jim raised his fists. As we got close Jim let go with a right hook. I blocked it with my left forearm and released my right squarely at his chin. I heard his teeth click as his head snapped back and he staggered back a couple of steps. I had hit him firmly, but not nearly as hard as I could.

Jim shook his head and charged in toward me. My right leg released a kick to his stomach. Jim doubled over and fell backwards, hard.

I had hoped Jim would stay down, but he didn't. He got up. There was rage in his eyes. He ran at me. I stood there. I let him get close and start punching. I put my palms flat on his chest and pushed him away, hard. Jim went flying back into the ropes, and then toppled forward. He hit the mat face first.

I waited to see if Jim was alright. He raised his head and slowly got up. I turned, went to the edge, and climbed over the ropes. Jim called out to me, "Hey, Fury! I'm not done!"

"Jim, I've made my point! This fight's over. You can't make me bleed. You can't touch me. And I can throw you around like a rag doll. If Adolf or Ladon tells you to kill me, you can't. It will be your funeral. Now grow a brain! Take the money and run!"

I went to the locker room and Jim followed. I pulled on my street clothes and made a demand of Jim.

"Jim, I want my cell phone."

"No way, Chad. I hang on to it."

"After the beating you just took, you think you can refuse? I'll take my phone, now!"

Jim handed it over silently.

"Thank you, Jim. I'll see you back at my apartment."

"Where are you going?"

"I'm going home. I'm going to run. I'll get there before you do."

I walked past Jim and pushed open the locker room door.

"Fury! I'm supposed to stay with you every second! Get yourself back over here!"

I turned back to look at Jim. "I'll see you at my place. Try to keep up."

On my way out I stopped to thank Frank for keeping the place open. He assured me it was no problem. He turned out the lights as Jim caught up with me at the door.

I went to the street and started walking toward home. Jim yelled at me once, "Fury! Get yourself back here!" I kept walking.

It wasn't long until Jim's car pulled up close, and the window rolled down. Jim called out, "Get in the car. We'll talk."

I stopped and put my head down near the open window, "No, Jim. You've got one more lesson."

I turned and started jogging. Jim pulled the car up close. I increased my speed. Soon I was at a full run.

When we got to the intersection, the lights were against Jim. I didn't care. I ran across the street dodging traffic. I ran on, leaving Jim fighting the traffic.

When I got to the apartment, I let myself in, turned on some lights, and got a beer from the refrigerator.

I sat on the sofa and waited, beer in hand. I didn't actually want the beer, I just wanted to paint a picture. What I was doing was what Vitaly might call pure theater. And to that end, I kicked off my shoes and put my feet up on the sofa.

About ten minutes later, my apartment door opened. Jim Clayton walked in.

"Chad, you're here!" There was true surprise in his voice.

"Yes, Jim. I'm here."

"So, what was that all about? Were you trying to show me that you can run fast?"

"No, Jim. Let me spell it *all* out for you. Here's what you should take away from today's lessons.

One. You have options. I'm willing to give you enough money that you can take your family away. You can walk away from this and start a new life.

Two. If Ladon or Adolf tell you to kill me, you won't stand a chance. I'm not going to let you kill me.

And three, you've only been hanging around me the last couple of days because I let you.

The ball's in your court Jim, what are you going to do?"

I couldn't put a name to the emotion I saw on Jim's face. I don't know if it was frustration, or anger, or just what. He stood there a moment.

"Chad, I'm going for a walk!" Jim turned, exited, and slammed the door behind him.

CHAPTER FIFTY-SEVEN

I woke that Wednesday morning feeling anxious about the day. Today was going to be huge. It would be the day that decided several things. First, I didn't know what Jim Clayton would decide. Also, there was Eddie. Today Crazy Eddie might just lead me to the stone.

I rolled out of bed and plodded into the kitchen for my first cup of coffee. There, standing in the kitchen, scrambling eggs in a skillet, was Jim Clayton.

"Good morning, Jim. I didn't know if I would see you here or not?"

"I've made enough for both of us. The coffee's ready too."

I pulled out a couple of plates from the cabinet and placed them by the stove. I took a mug from near the sink, rinsed it out, and filled it with hot coffee.

I leaned back against the sink. I took a sip of the hot liquid before speaking. "Jim, what are your plans?"

Jim didn't answer. He lifted the pan from the stove and divided the contents into our plates. He picked them up and carried them to the dining room table. I followed carrying a couple of forks and my coffee.

We sat, and I waited for an answer to my question. Jim stared at his plate, and then looked at me.

"Chad, Peggy thinks I'm up north, around Winnemucca. I told her I'm on a manhunt with the local authorities."

"OK. I'm sure you had to tell your family something."

"Of all of the things I've had to do, I've hated lying to my wife as much as I've hated anything.

The first killing...it was because I was forced to. My will was completely taken away from me. I can rationalize that. The other things I've done for Adolf, those, well I can rationalize those too. I told myself either I had to or Adolf would make me.

But, no one ever forced me lie to Peggy. I did that all on my own. Not just once, but over and over again. She's a good woman. She deserves better than me."

"Jim. I can't put myself in your shoes. And, I don't know how you'll explain any of this to Peggy. But I do know that you're a good man. Adolf couldn't take that away. Only a good man would be upset that he's lied to his family.

I don't know how it will sound in Peggy's ears. But, the truth will save her life, and yours. Just say the word, and we'll go to the bank. I'll have a cashier's check cut for you."

Jim looked down at his plate. He picked up a fork and took a bite of his eggs. "It needs salt." That was all he said. We ate in silence.

After breakfast, I showered and dressed. Then I made a phone call to Cameron Freeze. I told him there was a slight change of plans. I told him that he should drive himself and meet us by the entrance to the sewer. I explained that after he gave Eddie the heroine and morphine, that I would take Eddie out, alone.

Cameron disagreed. He said that if Eddie became difficult, he had a better chance of controlling him. I couldn't argue with that. We agreed to meet at the entrance around eleven.

I told Jim about the arrangement. He looked sullen. I asked him what he wanted to do. He told me that he would drive.

Jim drove; I had two stops to make. The first stop was at a thrift store. Eddie looked bad and smelled bad. There wasn't time to make him presentable, but a change of clothes and a pair of tennis shoes couldn't hurt.

The next stop was at a grocery store. I bought several bags of cookies. I made sure they were round.

When Jim and I arrived at the storm sewer entrance, Cameron was already there. He walked up to our car. We got out. I took a bag of cookies and the new clothes with me.

Cameron looked at me, "Chad, tell me again why we're doing this?"

"Cameron, there are some very bad people after the artifact that did this to Eddie. I don't know if I dare believe Eddie knows where the stone is. But, he might be able to lead us to the test site where the accident happened. I'm hoping we can at least find a clue there."

Cameron shifted his weight to his left foot. "Chad, I don't think this is a good idea."

Jim interrupted, "Cameron, if you don't want to be answering a lot of uncomfortable questions about a military project you're not supposed to know anything about..."

"OK, I get it guys. I've got Eddie's opiate cocktail ready. Once I give it to him, he should be good for about six to eight hours."

We made our way quickly down the ladder and through the sewer to where Eddie lived. When we got close, Cameron repeated the routine from the previous day. He called out into the darkness, "Eddie. It's Cameron. I have cookies."

This time the answer came quickly, "Eddie knows."

"Would Eddie like his cookies?"

We heard sobbing and whimpering. Cameron reassured

us, "It's alright. He's a little worse today. Sometimes he's like this."

We continued on and found Eddie sitting on his stack of mattresses, sobbing.

Jim and I stood back while Cameron approached.

"Eddie. It's Cam. I have cookies. Nice, round cookies."

Eddie howled, "No Cookie! Too many die!" He sobbed some more.

Cam spoke softly, "Who's died, Eddie?"

"A star stopped singing. A big noise! Then stopped!" Eddie sobbed, "All dead! So many babies."

"Where Eddie? Where did this happen?"

"Six. Six point one eight five four."

"Miles?" Cameron asked?

"No. Bigger." Eddie wiped tears from his eyes. "Times ten."

"Times ten what?"

"Times ten. Sixteen."

"Six point one times ten to the sixteenth miles?"

Eddie nodded. "Six point one eight five four. Times ten. Sixteen."

Eddie threw himself back on his mattresses and howled. Cameron pulled the needle and rubber tube out of his paper sack. He injected Eddie while he lay there sobbing.

Cameron came and stood by Jim and me. I had to ask, "Cameron, just what was all of that? Is that normal?"

"That was a pretty rare event for Eddie. I've seen him do that a few times. Death seems very upsetting to him."

"But who died? What was he talking about?"

"Eddie seems to know where everything in the universe is. He knows the location of every star, planet, and speck of dust. I think what he was describing was the death of a star, millions of miles away."

"Look, Cameron, I can believe a lot of stuff, but this? That's just too much for even me."

"Sometimes I'm not sure what I believe, Chad. I've

seen him right about too many things. He doesn't age. He doesn't get sick, and he knows things."

Jim replied, "Can we just get this over with? Insanity seems to be contagious, and I don't want to catch it."

About that time Eddie started talking, "Cam! Cam! Eddie is better. Can Eddie have cookies?"

Cameron went back to Eddie, and answered, "Of course, Eddie. I'll give you cookies."

I followed and tried giving the clothes to Eddie. "Eddie," I said, "I brought you something. I have some new clothes for you."

"Eddie knows. Eddie saw Chad. Chad has cookies."

I handed Eddie the clothes and the cookies. He shoved a cookie in his mouth and put on the shoes.

"Eddie," I asked, "will you take me to find the Omega Artifact, the stone?"

"Will Chad keep Eddie safe?"

"Yes I will. I will keep you safe."

Eddie looked at Cameron. "Does Cam want Eddie to take Chad?"

Cameron put his hand on Eddie's shoulder. "Yes, Eddie. I do. I'll be there too."

Eddie stood. "OK. We get things, then we go."

"What things," I asked?

Eddie pointed toward Jim. "From him. Bad men gave him things. Things we need."

I looked over at Jim who was standing, looking confused. Jim walked a little closer and Eddie leaned against Cameron.

"Eddie," Jim asked, "what do you think I have, that you need?"

Eddie pointed at Jim, "Where you keep things. Guns. You have cutters." Eddie made a big scissoring motion with his arms. "And things to make holes. And," Eddie flayed his arms wildly, "things go BOOM!"

I turned to Jim, "Do you know what he's talking about?"

Jim's face was tight, and his lips were pursed. After a moment he relaxed and answered. "Yes. I do. But how he knows..."

"Listen," I said, "forget how. Let's just get the stuff and go."

We left the tunnels with Eddie leading and skipping most of the way. When we got to the surface, Eddie insisted that I drive Jim's car. That caused a little argument on Jim's part, but he conceded.

Jim gave me the address of a self-storage unit. I drove about fifteen miles to get there. When we arrived, Jim bolted out of the car and went to the large, red, overhead door of the storage bay. He pulled out a key and put it in the padlock. He looked back at us and shook his head. He hesitated and finally turned the key.

The aluminum door clattered as Jim raised it. The sunlight poured into the dark cavity to reveal that it was about three-quarters full of boxes and hard-shelled carrying cases.

I walked up to Jim, "What is all of this?"

"It's exactly what Eddie said."

Jim opened one of the hard-shelled cases. Inside were two military rifles sitting in foam padding.

"Why do you have these, Jim?"

"This is Adolf's doing. I keep things for him. And I make a few deliveries."

I shook my head, "Oh my God, Jim. No."

"I'm afraid so."

"Listen, Jim, you..."

"No, Chad, you listen! You think I have choices; well I don't. At least, not that many. I'm making a choice right now. There's another case over there." Jim pointed to the far corner. "Inside are Glocks and magazines already loaded. I suggest you take a couple, and some extra magazines."

"No, Jim. I don't need it."

"Chad, please. You may need it."

"Why, what have you done?"

"Chad, I had to tell Adolf about Eddie...about your plans. Adolf is following us. Once we find the stone, Adolf's men will come and take the stone. It's a trap. I've set you up."

"And you're telling me this now because?"

"Because Eddie was right. You're a good man.

I intend to play out my part until I have a chance to take out Adolf."

"Jim, that's suicide!"

"Chad, my life ended in a cheap motel when Adolf told me to kill Carson Little."

Jim quit talking and grabbed a duffle bag. He put four Glocks and several magazines in the bag. Then he grabbed a pair of bolt cutters and handed them to me.

"Go put these in the trunk, then get Eddie. Let's find out what he thinks we need."

I did as asked, and returned with Eddie.

Jim walked over and stood next to Eddie. "Eddie, you know what's here. You know what we need. Would you please point it out?"

Eddie walked up to a cardboard box and patted it. "Jim needs this. It goes BOOM!"

Jim tuned to me, "Chad, just put the whole box in the trunk."

"What's in it?"

"It's C-4."

I shook my head and picked up the box gently. I knew it was safe, but I couldn't help but treat it gently.

When I returned, one more box had been selected and Jim was putting a cordless drill in the duffle bag. I asked Eddie, "Is that everything?"

Eddie shook his head. "Water. Desert is hot. Eddie needs water and cookies. Round cookies."

CHAPTER FIFTY-EIGHT

We left the storage unit with bolt cutters, shovels, and things that go boom. I drove us to a convenience store where we got sandwiches and bottled water. I filled the car with gas. Cameron had to drag Eddie out of the store because he was taking all of the packages of round cookies off of the shelves and didn't want to leave.

Eddie sat in the front seat as I drove us northward, into the desert. I put my phone in the console cup holder so I could see the map on the screen.

After about twenty minutes, I noticed a change in Eddie. I thought it might be that the landscape was bringing back memories, but I couldn't be sure. I didn't want to ask. I didn't want to hear about round cookies.

I took the turns as Eddie called them out. The roads were rough. In some spots they were little more than packed earth. Then the road ended. I turned to Eddie. Eddie smiled. It was a peaceful smile with dirty yellow teeth. But the smile was sitting on a strangely calm face. Eddie didn't speak. He just pointed to the left.

"You want me to go there?"

Eddie nodded.

I drove the car slowly over the hard-packed earth. There was no road. I was simply heading in the direction Eddie pointed out.

I drove for about ten or fifteen more minutes. It was then that Eddie got very excited. "Almost! Almost!"

"What, Eddie?" I asked.

"Eddie almost there."

I strained to look forward as the car crested a small hill. There in the distance was a cliff face. At the bottom of the cliff was something resembling a set of buildings.

Like so many other things in the desert, they appeared much closer than they actually were. We drove for another forty-five minutes before I pulled up at a chain-link gate and stopped the car.

We had been in the car so long that everyone was eager to get out. I would say that we exploded out of the car, but compared to Eddie, everyone else made a leisurely exit.

While Jim, Cameron, and I stretched our stiff limbs, Eddie was full of motion. He jumped and ran along the fence like a puppy looking for a way through. All the while he yelled out "Eddie coming for you! Eddie coming!"

I began to get worried that bringing Eddie was a mistake. I sincerely hoped that we were not going through all of this only to find a stale package of *round* cookies.

We each fell into our respective roles. Cameron went to Eddie, talked to him and kept him calm. I opened the trunk of the car, and Jim extracted the bolt cutters.

Jim and I stepped up to the old rusty chain-link gate and examined our plan of attack. This one was simple. The gate was secured with a chain and a padlock. Cutting the lock was simple, but opening the gate was another matter.

The gate was made to roll sideways. The wheels that allowed the gate to move were rusted away. Sliding the gate was not going to be simple, at least that's what Jim thought.

Jim cut the shackle on the lock. I bent slightly put my fingers through the chain link, straightened up, and walked sideways with the gate.

We got back in the car and Eddie directed us to what looked like the main building of the compound. I drove and parked at the front door.

My heart sank when I saw the front door. I didn't even have to get out of the car to realize just how hard getting in the building was going to be. The entrance was a double-door, all metal. And the doors were welded shut. Someone had taken an arc welder and welded every crack around the doors.

We got out of the car. Jim and I walked a bit looking at the problem. Every door we could see was welded shut, and the few visible windows were secured with iron bars.

Jim commented, "I guess we could blast the bars off of a window, but that still leaves us with the problem of how to get the stone out of the building."

I agreed, "If it's really there."

Jim nodded.

I heard Cameron calling for us, and we went. He and Eddie had gone around the corner of the building. Eddie was hugging the wall. His cheek was against it, and he was rubbing his palms against the surface. "Jim make BOOM! Jim make BOOM! Here!"

Jim and I went to the section of wall and looked it over. Jim looked at me, "It might just work."

"What might work?"

"We drill some holes, about where Eddie's hands and feet are. We pack the holes with C-4, and blast. It might just crack open a new doorway."

"You seem to be the munitions expert. We might as well try."

Jim went to the trunk and pulled out the duffle bag. I took the box of C-4, detonation cord, and blasting caps.

While Jim was drilling holes with the largest drill bit he had, I was cutting the detonation cord to his specifications and trying to figure out how to wire up the detonator.

Jim drilled about a dozen holes in vertical and

horizontal lines that made a nice rectangle. Then he made a few more holes in the center. Jim attached blasting caps to the detonation cord and put them in the holes. I helped him pack the holes with C-4. We took more C-4 and used it to hold the detonation cord against the wall in the shape of a doorway. It was obvious that this was not the first time Jim had done something like this, but I didn't ask.

The entire process took about ninety minutes. I don't know if that's fast or slow, but in the desert heat, it's an eternity. Eddie was the only one who didn't seem to mind the heat.

Jim called out to Cameron and Eddie to get back behind him. We all moved a safe distance back, and Jim pushed the button. The sound was nearly deafening; it made my ears ring. It made Eddie jump up and down and yell, "BOOM! BOOM! BOOM!"

Fragments and dust had blown out almost all the way to where Jim was standing. There was a light breeze and it cleared the dust cloud quickly.

The hole wasn't anything like you might see in the movies. In the movies it would have been a near perfect rectangle. But, here, it was more jagged; more like a series scooped-out rounded indentations. It was, however adequately sized to walk through. We just had to be careful of the debris on the ground.

Inside was dark, but not totally dark. There were a few windows letting some light filter in, but the light seemed to remain confined to the areas defined by the windows.

We were standing in a hallway. The air was musty and somewhat stale. I found that odd because of the lack of humidity in the desert. But, maybe the odor could be best defined as "old".

Eddie was clearly excited. He started off in a dead run down the hallway. He was muttering something; I couldn't quite understand. If I were to guess I would say it was something about cookies.

Jim and Cameron switched on flashlights. Jim handed

me his and went back for his duffle bag. I heard Eddie calling from down the hall. Cameron waited by the opening and I caught up with Eddie.

When I got close to Eddie, I could tell he looked worried. He whispered to me, "Chad hurry. Bad men come. Bad men hurt."

"I'm not surprised, Eddie. Tell me, how many men are coming?"

"Eddie sees ten. Ten bad men."

"Alright. We'll hurry."

Jim and Cameron came walking up to us.

"Jim, Cameron," I said, "Eddie just told me he sees ten bad men coming this way."

Cameron looked a little nervous, "Chad, what does that mean?"

"It's Ladon's people. I can guarantee you don't want to meet them. I suggest we hurry; get the stone and get out of here."

Cameron looked around, "How do they know where we are?"

I pursed my lips and exhaled, "That's a little hard to explain. Would you like to take that one, Jim?"

Jim didn't hesitate. "Knowing them, they probably put a GPS tracker on my car."

"Oh, this is just great! I cooperate with you so I won't be charged with treason, and now there's a pack of killers on our heels!"

I put a hand on Cameron's shoulder. "Calm down. Nobody's dead, yet. Let's just get the stone and get out of here as fast as we can."

Eddie started off in the darkness. We quickened our pace to keep up. We followed Eddie to a stairwell. Eddie went down into the darkness, unimpeded by the thick blackness.

As the three of us descended, Jim was the only one to comment, "This is great! Going from one dark pit into another. We would have to grope around for this thing in the dark!"

Neither Cameron nor I responded. We continued down the stairs until we were at the bottom. When we stepped out of the stairwell we realized Eddie was nowhere to be found.

Cameron called out, "Eddie? It's Cam. Where are you?"

A voice came back through the blackness, "Eddie is here. You find Eddie!"

Eddie kept yelling, and we followed the sound of his voice down the long empty hall. We turned into an alcove to find Eddie facing a huge steel door.

The door reminded me of something you would find in a bank. It was heavy and made of brushed stainless steel. There was a brass wheel that was meant to be turned to open the door, and three, numbered dials across the center. Eddie was spinning the dials.

"These are round! Eddie likes round!" Eddie spun the dials again.

I put my hand on his shoulder, "Eddie, is the stone on the other side?"

He nodded his head, spun a dial and made whirring sounds, "Whrrr, Whrrr."

"Eddie, we need to get to the stone before the bad men."

"Eddie knows."

"Does Eddie know how to make the door open?"

"Eddie knows. Eddie show you how."

Eddie turned the first dial quickly. He stopped at a number and turned the dial back another direction. He stopped and turned it back the other way.

Eddie repeated this process for the other two dials and then began turning the large brass wheel. When Eddie stopped, he pulled on the wheel. The door started to move. I grabbed the wheel and pulled with Eddie.

The massive door swung slowly open. Jim and Cameron pointed their flashlights into the room. The lights landed on the object in center. It was a sandstone block with two iron rings at each end.

"Chad," Jim called out, "it looks like we've found it."

Cameron moved his light around the room. "Gentlemen, we've found a lot more than that." Cameron's light was showing two skeletons embedded in the wall, as though they were part of the wall itself. There was another skeleton merged with the floor, about half-way between the stone and the wall.

Jim's only comment was, "It might help if we had some light."

Eddie came charging between us, saying "Eddie fix it. Eddie make light."

Eddie trotted to the stone bent over, and put the palms of his hands on the top of it. He laughed. The lights flickered overhead, and then came on fully."

Cameron asked, "Eddie, how did you do that?"

"No time," Eddie replied, still touching the stone. "Bad men here. No more time."

From behind me, I heard the sound of a pistol chambering a bullet. I turned. I was facing Ladon. He had his pistol pointed between my eyes.

Ladon spoke in his very distinctive, cold voice. "Hello, Chad. You are to be...congratulated. You've found it."

One by one, nine other men walked into the room and surrounded us.

Adolf took his place next to Ladon. He asked, "Jim. How...are there...lights...in here?"

Jim volunteered, "It's Eddie. He put his hands on the stone. He seems to be able to control it."

The three of us stood in the center of the room. Eddie was kneeling and smiling with his palms resting on the stone.

I looked around. I saw ten pistols pointed at us from all directions.

Ladon lowered his weapon, slightly. "This is excellent," he smiled, "The stone can be directly interfaced!"

Ladon's eyes focused on the man to his left. "Kahn. Be

a good son. Take everything Eddie knows about the stone."

Kahn was a thin man in his thirties with an unruly shock of black hair and steel gray eyes. He nodded, "Yes, father."

Kahn moved quickly behind Ladon and around the circle of men in what seemed to be an effort not to come into the line of fire of any man and the four of us. He pulled a folding hunting knife from his pocket. The knife clicked when he unfolded it.

Kahn walked up to Eddie. He took Eddie's left wrist in his hand and forced Eddie's arm out where he could access it. He cut the inside of Eddie's arm. Eddie howled. Kahn placed the knife on the stone.

Kahn held Eddie's wrist in his left hand, and put his right hand on the bleeding wound. "Tell me how to control the stone."

Kahn started smiling, then he laughed. Suddenly Eddie put his free hand on top of Kahn's and kept it over the cut. Eddie's face was stern. He spoke clearly, and authoritatively, "Take it! Take it all!"

Kahn screamed. He tried to pull his hand away, but it remained locked on Eddie's arm. Eddie spoke quickly, "Take it, take it, take it, take it all."

Kahn dropped to his knees, and shook. Eddie continued the rapid mantra, "Take it, take it, take it, take it all!"

Kahn fell backwards with his knees bent underneath him. Eddie bent over him. Kahn choked and sputtered. Blood ran from his nose and ears. Kahn was still. Eddie let go of Kahn's hand and his arm fell limply to the floor.

I looked at Ladon. His face showed shock turning to anger. Ladon barked at Adolf, "Do it!"

Adolf walked up to Jim and handed him a knife. He looked Jim in the eyes. "Kill Chad" was all he said and backed away.

Jim looked at the knife, and then he looked at me with

sad eyes. "I don't have a choice, Chad. If I don't they'll just make me do it."

"I know Jim. I'm sorry."

"You're a good man, Chad. I won't do this!"

Jim turned suddenly and threw the knife at Adolf. The blade turned over in the air and sank into Adolf's right shoulder. He yelled in pain.

I heard a single gunshot. It came from Ladon. Jim dropped to his knees and fell face first on the floor.

Before anyone could say anything, the room filled with blinding white light, there was a roar like a jet engine reverberating through the room.

The noise stopped suddenly and the light seemed to coalesce into what can only be described as giant broken shards of a mirror.

The shards moved in a counter-clockwise orbit around the stone. The shards swept up every person standing in the room except for Eddie and myself. Then the shards stopped and hung motionless in the air.

"Eddie! What's happening?"

"It's alright, Chad. I'm in control."

"You seem better, Eddie. Explain!"

"There's not much time. The accident merged my mind with the stone. As we got closer to the stone I got better. I thought it would be best to not let on that I was better."

"You did a good job. Where are Ladon, and the others?"

"I've put Cameron in his car. I'm holding the others in the space between spaces. I can't keep them there long. They'll die if I don't bring them out soon."

"Good! Leave them!"

"No. This is bigger than those ten. If they die there's only a thirty-eight percent chance that Earth survives."

"Then what? What do we do?"

"I'm working on it. In the time we've been talking I've run fourteen scenarios. None of them have better than a thirty-eight percent chance of success. I'll keep working on a solution; a plan to resolve this mess.

Until then, there are four books. You must get them and keep them from the others, the El-yanin."

"I know about the books, Eddie. Where are they?"

"I'll send you to them, but first, you need to know that you can help the woman in the hospital. You can wake her up."

Eddie picked up the knife resting on the top of the stone and folded the blade. He tossed the knife to me.

"You'll need this. The blade's titanium. Do what I did."

"How? What? I don't understand."

"There's no more time. You need these numbers: twenty-four, seventeen, four, thirteen. Repeat them back, Chad."

"Twenty-four, seventeen, four, thirteen."

"Good. One more time."

"Twenty-four, seventeen, four, thirteen."

A giant mirrored shard moved swiftly toward me and I fell into it.

In the next instant I was standing in an office. The lights were very bright. I was next to an old looking gray desk with a manual typewriter. There was an old looking metal fan with large blades sitting on the corner of the desk. To one side was a wall calendar with the date August, 1960 across the top. I turned, and behind were a couple of old filing cabinets. I turned a little further and saw a large safe.

I wasted no time. I went to the safe. I was still holding the knife. I put it in my pocket.

I turned the dial on the safe. I spoke as I worked the dial, "Twenty-four, seventeen, four, thirteen."

I pulled the handle and the door swung open. There, inside were four leather books. They looked very old. I picked up the first one. It looked like what I had seen in my dreams. I held it to my face and sniffed. Even the smell was familiar. I tapped the spine. It was hard. There was something in it. I was sure it had to be a data crystal.

I grabbed the other three books and walked past the desk. The light level changed. I looked up to see a row of spotlights shining back toward the desk and the area behind me.

Ahead was darker, but my eyes adjusted. There was a half-wall just ahead of me. I climbed over. I was standing in a gray carpeted room. I recognized this place. It was the Atomic Museum at the university.

I saw a guard moving quickly my direction. He yelled out. "Stop! Put that down! That's museum property!"

I ran out of the museum and straight for home.

CHAPTER FIFTY-NINE

I stood outside Lisa's hospital room and took a deep breath of antiseptic air. So very much had happened up to this point and for some reason I was finding it difficult to push open the door.

Yet, I felt very fortunate to be here. Uncle Allan had been right. I took care of all of the things I could do, and the rest seemed to take care of themselves.

Sirhan was dead. I was free from Vitaly's debt; he was now in mine.

I may have lost the stone, but I had the four missing books. I even took the precaution of removing the data crystals from the spines and hiding them.

It was also a very happy accident that I never mailed my car keys to Uncle Allan. After catching a flight to Oklahoma City, I had my car back.

Now, all that remained was Lisa. I put my hand up to push the door open; it trembled. "Come on, Chad. Straighten up!" I whispered the words, hoping the encouragement would help. It didn't.

What did help was the knife in my pocket. I thrust my hand inside my pocket and let my fingers touch the knife. I recalled Eddie's words to me, "You can wake her up."

I pushed the door open slowly. Doctor Stenson was pulling his stethoscope out of his ears.

"Mr. Fury. I'm glad you're here. I need to talk to you about your wife."

Doctor Stenson's face was solemn; I could tell he didn't have good news. "We need to start thinking about long-term care."

"What does that mean, doctor?"

"It means there's no change in your wife's condition. The hospital wants her relocated to a nursing facility within the next forty-eight hours."

"Which one?"

"That's actually your choice.

I'm going to leave you alone with Lisa. When you're ready, go to the nurse's station and ask for Vicki. She can help you with the long-term care options."

I thanked the doctor and he left. I waited until the door was totally shut behind me before I approached Lisa's bedside.

I bent down over Lisa. I stroked her long, flowing red hair. I kissed her gently on her forehead. I whispered, "Lisa. I'm going to try something. I don't know if this will work, but I have it on good authority that it might."

I took out the titanium knife from my pocket. I unfolded the blade. It went "click" as the blade locked into place.

I extended my left arm and turned my palm up. I inhaled and gritted my teeth together. I brought the tip of the knife to my forearm and drug it about four inches. It burned and stung, and it bled.

I folded the knife and put it away. I reached over and took Lisa's right hand. I let her palm rest against my bleeding arm. I covered her hand with my right hand. I watched Lisa's face. There was no change.

"OK, Chad. Give her something." I chose to think about Crazy Eddie and finding the stone. I replayed the events in my mind. There was no change. My heart sank and I felt emotion filling my throat.

That's when Uncle Allan's words came back to me, that emotion disrupts thought. Maybe that was it? Maybe I needed to somehow send her strong emotions?

There was only one emotion that I could feel at that very moment, my love for Lisa. I let my mind fully acknowledge that I love her. I closed my eyes and concentrated on just how much I love Lisa.

I felt fire fill my chest and consume my limbs as I thought about Lisa and just how much I didn't want to be without her. I heard myself muttering, "I love you, Lisa. I love you," over and over again.

All at once a feeling like hot lava shot down my left arm. I could feel the heat through my right hand covering Lisa's hand. Tears poured down my cheeks. I could no longer speak as white-hot tears rained on the floor.

Lisa's back arched. She inhaled, deeply. Her eyes fluttered open as her back relaxed. She turned her head toward me and spoke, "Oh, Chad! I love you!"

She started to sit up. I scooped her up in an embrace. I held her tight, and wept.

ABOUT THE AUTHOR

This is Doug Gorden's second attempt at authoring a novel. The first novel was "Chad Fury and the Dragon Song", published in 2014. The novel was a huge success, selling over two copies (not counting the copies he purchased himself).

Doug found the second book to be more difficult than the first. Not only because it is longer, but it is the second in a planned trilogy and as such, needs to be a bridge between books one and three.

If Doug's second book is as successful as the first, he is committed to completing the trilogy. Hopefully, the third book will be ready in 2017.

To all of Doug's fan out there (whoever the person is who bought the two copies…I'm hoping it wasn't his mother…) Doug thanks you from the bottom of his heart for your support and encouragement.

Made in the USA
Charleston, SC
01 June 2016